SECOND ACTS

Teri Emory

Amberjack Publishing
New York, New York

Amberjack Publishing
228 Park Avenue S #89611
New York, NY 10003-1502
http://amberjackpublishing.com

Publisher's Cataloging-in-Publication data

Names: Emory, Teri, author.
Title: Second acts / by Teri Emory.
Description: New York, NY: Amberjack Publishing, 2017.
Identifiers: ISBN 9781944995317 (pbk.) | 9781944995348 (ebook)
| LCCN 2017933489
Subjects: LCSH Female friendship--Fiction. | Middle-aged
women--Fiction. | Interpersonal relations--Fiction. | Love stories. |
BISAC FICTION / Contemporary Women.
Classification: LCC PS3605.M66 S43 2017 | DDC 813-6--dc23

Cover Design: Mimi Bark

For Ken. Thanks for the room of my own and for everything else.

"There are no second acts in American lives."

- F. Scott Fitzgerald

PART I:
PASTS AND PROLOGUES

SARAH: A CHANGE OF PLANS

"Day and night, and day again.
And people come and go away forever."
—Judy Collins

I WAS DREAMING ABOUT Paris.

I resisted the intrusive ring of the phone, wanting to stay in my dream. Ellie and I were strolling through Le Marais, window-shopping.

"Mom," she was saying, "remember the first time we came here, when I was twelve? You bought me a headband with the Mona Lisa painted on it, and I wore it to school every day for a year."

The phone finally nudged me out of sleep. It was Helen, my former sister-in-law. No one else would call so early. As usual, she seemed to be in the middle of a story that began before she dialed my number. I can barely follow Helen's train of thought when I am fully awake. Now, I just let her talk.

I divorced Helen's brother, Martin, almost fifteen years ago, but Helen and I have stayed close. She still calls me several times a month and likes to prattle on about people I hardly remember from years ago when Martin and I lived near her and her husband, Sidney, in Acedia Bay, Florida. She always finds a way to interject an anecdote about Martin in which he is portrayed as sane and likable—even admirable. He's volunteering at a shelter for the homeless, she'll say. He's taken up yoga. He's bought a kayak. He's become a vegetarian.

No matter. I was married to the man for ten long years, and I took notes. Just once, I'd love to tell her that if her spiel about Martin doesn't include some words like "Such a pity! Struck down in the prime of his life!" then I'm not interested in hearing any more. I never say this directly, of course. Instead, I punctuate Helen's unruly sentences with strategic "uh-huhs" that for most people would speak volumes. Helen, however, is sarcasm-challenged—can't recognize it, can't produce it.

"I ran into your friend Violet Bailey last week," she was saying. "She insists you were the best thing that ever happened to Acedia Bay, and her life hasn't been the same since you moved back to New York."

"I miss Violet too," I said agreeably, still half asleep.

"I sent Ellie a plane ticket," Helen said. "She'll definitely be here for Sidney's birthday party." *Oh, right, Sidney's sixtieth.* Helen's called me ten times about it. "I told her I'd pay for Doug to come too, but she says he's swamped with schoolwork." I wasn't sure if Helen knew that Ellie and her boyfriend Doug lived together in Morningside Heights near the Columbia campus. Ellie probably thinks, rightly, that her Aunt Helen would disapprove.

"I still haven't given up on your coming, you know," Helen went on. "You're not worried about Martin being here, are you? All he ever says is what a good job you've done with Ellie. He's probably bringing Pauline with him—you know he's still seeing her, right?—assuming she can find someone to stay with her kids. She's a terrific mother." Helen believes it will strengthen her case with me concerning Martin if I learn that the women in his life are upstanding citizens, and she rarely misses an opportunity to sing the praises of Pauline or the others who preceded her.

"It would mean the world to Sidney to have you at the party. To both of us," Helen said. "Why not stay for a few days? You haven't visited in, what, more than four years? Ever since Kevin moved in with you. Tell him we'd love to see him again, but on our turf this time. I can't believe you've never brought him to Acedia Bay."

"Kevin will still be in Dallas on business. He's visiting his son there," I said. To his credit, Kevin graciously accepts the continued presence of my former in-laws in my life. He even claims to enjoy their company when they visit us in New York.

"So come alone," she said. "Let me buy your plane ticket."

I liked the idea of helping Sidney celebrate his birthday. Besides, even my best jokes about Martin were getting a bit thin; seeing him might inspire some new material.

"I've got frequent flier miles I can use," I finally told Helen. "If it's okay with you, though, I'll ask Violet if I can stay at her house." I figured Martin, and mother-of-the-year Pauline—if she showed up—would surely sleep at Helen and Sidney's.

I MET MARTIN in Manhattan when I was twenty-eight. My apartment was a rent-controlled, third-floor walk-up on the Upper West Side, an easy walk from the Café Luxembourg. I was working as a senior editor at *The Abbott Literary Review*, where I had just landed a plum assignment: a series of critical essays on the Algonquin

Roundtable writers. Apart from my recurring fantasy of moving to Paris one day, I had never considered living anywhere but New York.

I was also teaching a night class in fiction writing at the New School. My students were over-privileged and overwrought young adults recently out of college. Most still lived at home, but they thought of themselves as counter-cultural because they subscribed to *Mother Jones* and went to poetry readings in Hell's Kitchen. Existentialists with trust funds. They dressed entirely in black, chain-smoked during the breaks, and fantasized about the life of the mind. I loved their essays about alienation and ennui. Even when their punctuation and grammar were shoddy, their passion was real.

I was ripe for marriage when Martin came my way. Both my mother and my hormones were sending me persistent messages about making babies, but I had not dated many promising candidates for fatherhood. Among my recent suitors were an ER physician who worked seventy hours a week and fell asleep in restaurants; a struggling sculptor who decided he'd do well to return to his ex-wife, what with her trust fund and all; and a television producer with a rather expansive definition of fidelity.

Martin introduced himself to me while we were waiting in line for tickets to an outdoor performance of *Much Ado About Nothing* in Central Park. He was thirty-two at the time, a public relations director at Chase Manhattan. We talked for an hour as the queue inched along. We exchanged business cards, and he called the next day to ask me out to dinner. I was grateful to spend an evening with a man who could stay awake all the way through dessert, who had no heiress girlfriend waiting in the wings, and who expressed reasonable interest in marriage and children. Six months later, Martin proposed to me during the intermission at a performance of *A*

Chorus Line, and I said yes.

Shortly after we married, family connections led Martin to a lucrative job offer to be vice president of marketing at Fieldstone Public Relations in Acedia Bay, where Helen and Sidney had lived for many years.

"It's near *Jacksonville*," Martin said, as if he were talking about a sophisticated world capital. "The climate is good. This is a great opportunity for me, Sarah. For both of us, really."

To Martin, the decision to leave New York was an easy one. He had no family there, no friends either. Martin's relationships with other men were activity-specific. He was in a monthly poker game with some guys from his office. He played racquetball with one of our neighbors. He went to Yankees games with Al, someone he'd known since high school, but with whom, to my knowledge, he'd never had a conversation about anything but baseball. For Martin's purposes, any males willing to share his interests, for limited segments of time, qualified as friends.

For me, though, it was hard to imagine living a plane ride away from everything and everyone I knew in New York City. My parents were still alive then. I could stop by their place for brunch any Sunday. Beth and Miriam, my best friends since we met in college, both lived near me in the city, and seeing them regularly was fundamental to my routine. I couldn't imagine the editor of a literary journal would find work in Acedia Bay, Florida. What kind of life would await me a thousand miles from the Strand Bookstore and Balducci's?

"We can fly back to visit as often as you like," Martin said. "And won't Acedia Bay be a better place than Manhattan to raise a family?"

And so I agreed to take a detour from the life I had always wanted.

I was already pregnant with Ellie when Martin and I

became Florida residents. We settled into a two-bedroom place in Woodridge Gardens, a flamingo-pink, stucco apartment complex with a swimming pool on the grounds and weekly bingo in the clubhouse. It was July when we moved in. My ankles swelled from the humidity. I learned to run errands in the mornings when it was still reasonably cool. In the afternoons, the air outside was like a wet wool blanket, and I'd sequester myself in our air-conditioned apartment and wait for five o'clock, when violent electrical storms would take over the skies. Thirty minutes later, there would be no sign that it had rained, except the humidity was even worse.

I decorated the baby's room in primary colors. I ordered a layette by phone from a grandmotherly saleswoman at Saks in New York. I baby-proofed every inch of the apartment, though I knew we'd probably move to a house before the baby was mobile. I came to enjoy grocery shopping at the Publix, where well-mannered teenagers loaded groceries into my Honda, refused to accept tips, and called me Ma'am. I used my New School faculty ID to obtain a Visiting Academic card to the Acedia Bay Hospital medical library. I spent hours there perusing obstetrics journals. The most advanced science course I'd ever taken was high school biology, but I didn't let that stand in my way. I'd never known a tricky situation I couldn't read my way out of, and bearing a child would be no exception. I drove my obstetrician crazy, grilling him on his knowledge of obscure childbirth complications. Finally, when I demanded he send a vial of my blood to a lab in Sweden to check for a problem that occurs once in every three trillion pregnancies, he'd had enough.

"With most women, I worry that caffeine or alcohol could have bad effects on their pregnancies," he said wearily. "In your case, Sarah, I'm tempted to burn your library card."

True, I felt healthy and the baby seemed to be developing fine, so I let up on him. But I didn't quit reading the journals.

Our daughter arrived two weeks early, in the middle of a tropical storm during our first steamy September in Florida. Just six pounds with a full head of silky, black curls like Martin's, and almond eyes like mine; she was perfect. I held her in my arms and apologized for having arranged it so that she'd have to go through life with Acedia Bay on her passport. *Remember, you were conceived in Manhattan*, I whispered as I held her. We named her Elinor, for my grandmother. We called her Ellie from the start—most people do, except for our divorce lawyers, to whom she would come to be known as *minor child, female*.

Martin's job in Florida turned out to be the good opportunity he had been promised. We were soon able to afford a large house (later, legally, our *marital domicile*) in a new development down the road from Helen and Sidney. We bought white wicker furniture for the sunroom. I planted gerbera daisies on the front lawn. I perfected recipes for homemade mayonnaise and key lime pie. For Ellie's sake, for the sake of my marriage, for the sake of my sanity, I found ways to derive pleasure from the small routines of domestic life. A forcibly happy stranger in a strange land.

Ellie was just learning to crawl when I landed a job teaching English Composition at Acedia Bay Junior College. Most of my students were the first generation in their families to attend college, and my attempts to expand their literary frame of reference pretty much failed. They found my assignments irrelevant to their vocational plans.

"I'm majoring in occupational therapy (or accounting)," they'd say. "What good will it do me to read 'Bartleby, the Scrivener?'"

I'd tell them that the world was in desperate need of

occupational therapists (and especially accountants) who can deconstruct Melville.

Just like poor Bartleby, they'd answer, "I would prefer not to," missing completely the irony of their response. I yearned for my angst-ridden New School rebels back in Manhattan.

I met my friend Violet Bailey at the college. She taught a course on the ecology of North Florida. She introduced me to other part-time instructors who, like me, were educated young wives and mothers, begrudgingly transplanted to an outpost of their husbands' choosing. My colleagues banded together on weekends with their families to socialize at swap meets and to gorge on all-you-can-eat catfish specials at restaurants on the bay. I could never get Martin to participate in these outings. He'd had "enough of people" at work, he said.

No one event signaled the inevitable death of our marriage. Our relationship disintegrated little by little. First we stopped having sex. Then we stopped touching each other at all. Martin brooded and retreated from me, from everyone except Ellie. I suggested marriage counseling, but Martin declined. I couldn't bring myself to leave him, though. As long as he remained an attentive father to Ellie, I held out hope that he could still be a husband to me.

I had endured eight years in Acedia Bay, when Martin, about to be offered a partnership in his company, announced that he was quitting his job. He said he needed time to Think About Life. I soon found out that the only "life" he needed time to "think about" was his own. He showed no interest in going back to work or in doing much else. Apparently, Thinking About Life (a career, by the way, that pays rather poorly) was all he could handle. We had enough in savings to scrape by, but I persuaded the dean at the college to let me teach a class in conversational French to make a little extra money.

After Martin quit his job, we argued all the time. I'd come home from teaching to find him sipping coffee and reading a book at the kitchen table. I'd ask, "How are you?" and he'd reply that he'd appreciate my not speaking to him in such a disapproving tone. Our voices would get louder, our words more disagreeable, until, at last, I'd cry, at which point Martin would accuse me of being manipulative. He'd retreat to the spare bedroom for the night, and I'd sleep alone in our king-sized bed. After a few months of this routine, the separate sleeping arrangements became permanent, but the arguments stopped. We had run out of things to say to each other.

One day Martin was supposed to pick up Ellie from her ballet class while I was at my office on campus. Ellie's teacher called me to say that the dance school was about to close for the day, and Ellie was crying because no one had come for her. Martin had simply forgotten. That's when I began to Think About Divorce. Finally, I left him.

I stayed in Acedia Bay after we split up, too disheartened and enervated to make any big changes. Too, I thought it would be good for Ellie to see her father as often as he could make time for her. Ironically, Martin left Acedia Bay before I did. A good job in Miami, he'd said.

Martin has moved around quite a bit since then. Twice a year, he sends Ellie a plane ticket so she can fly to wherever he's living and see him for a few days. Ellie keeps the details of these visits to herself. She and I adhere to an agreement tacitly instituted when she was a young child: I never say anything negative to her about her father, and she avoids talking to me about him at all.

Which is why, apart from Helen's updates, I get only sporadic news about Martin's life. I estimate that Martin has had six careers (not including Thinking About Life) and at least a dozen girlfriends since our divorce, but I may have lost count. A few years ago, a friend called to report that she had run into Martin in Atlanta, where he had acquired hair transplants, a business card that said *The Martin H. Roth Group, International Marketing Consultants,* and a very young massage therapist as his live-in girlfriend. Sometime later, Helen let me know that the massage therapist had left Martin for a chiropractor, and Martin was joining a startup computer company in Nashville with plans to move in with a country-western lounge singer named Pauline.

The last time I set eyes on Martin was more than three years ago, at Ellie's high school graduation. I had arrived hours ahead of the ceremony to save a row of seats for our contingent: me, Kevin, Helen, and Sidney. Helen had placed her sweater on the chair next to hers to reserve it, I knew, for Martin, but he arrived late and he sat in the back by himself. When the ceremony ended, he made his way through the crowd and slapped a check in his daughter's hand by way of a present. He wouldn't shake Kevin's outstretched hand. He left without saying a word to me. Ellie took it all in, biting her nails, eyes darting nervously from Martin to me to Martin again. I wanted to kill him.

ON THE SUNDAY before I left for Sidney's birthday party in Florida, I met Beth and Miriam for our monthly brunch, a tradition we started after I moved back to New York. Miriam had made reservations for us at an East Village bistro located in a building that had once been a shoelace factory and was still in the midst of renovation. I had to duck beneath scaffolding to get in the front door.

Miriam waved to me from the back of the restaurant. Her pale green blouse perfectly matched her eyes. Amazing, how many articles of clothing she owns in that color. She had been there for about fifteen minutes, she told me as I sat down, long enough to have learned that our waiter was an aspiring actor awaiting a callback for a deodorant commercial. Miriam, beautiful and outgoing as she was when we met in college, engages strangers and collects details from their lives as if she were preparing to write their biographies.

"Something to drink?" the waiter asked me.

"A mimosa."

"With a little Chambord?"

"Without. I'm a purist," I said earnestly. He nodded his approval.

Beth arrived a few minutes later. She was dressed, as usual, mostly in black, a necessary precaution, she says, lest anyone be able to guess just by looking at her that she lives in Connecticut and not Manhattan. She caught the waiter's eye and mouthed, "Cappuccino."

"Sorry I'm late," she said, glancing at her watch. "Nicole called from school just as I was walking out the door. She's doing a psych paper, and she thought I might have some books that would help. It's hard to believe, for all the tuition we pay, that the campus library wouldn't have everything she needs. Maybe she misses me, just wanted to talk to her mom. Jim, of course, is at work, so he didn't get to talk to her. You know, most of the time she doesn't even say 'Where's Dad?' when she calls. She just assumes he's at the office. Anyway, she sends her love to both of you."

Ellie comes to me from time to time with a question about her schoolwork, but then she rejects my ideas. Last year she was home for spring break working on a paper about the women's movement. I dragged out my souvenirs. Showed her my t-shirt: "A woman without a man is like a fish without a bicycle." She rolled her eyes in that dismissive way she does with me. *Nice male-bashing, Mom.*

"I wouldn't mind if Ellie asked for my advice now and

then," I said. "Miriam, remember when Ellie was in high school? She used to call you to talk about schoolwork and tell you about her crushes on boys. She always took your advice."

"I'm not her mother," said Miriam. "Your daughters may call me Aunt Miriam, but they think of me as Auntie Mame. Not quite like other grownups. No kids of my own, for one thing."

"Oh, yeah, unlike the responsible adult I am?" I said.

"You know what I mean. To Ellie, you are *the* grownup who matters."

"Until, as I've told her repeatedly, I take up residence abroad and live in a manner that will cause no end of embarrassment to her, her future husband, and my grand-children to come," I said brightly.

"Ellie must love when you say that," said Beth. "And Kevin? What does he think about *la vie de bohème* that you're planning?"

The waiter returned, asking us to choose from the menu on the blackboard across the room. We decided on omelets. Miriam ordered a hot crab dip for us to share.

"Did you see the dessert list?" Miriam asked. "*New York* magazine says their truffle cake is the third best choc-olate dessert in the city."

"How is it possible for a middle-aged woman to eat as much as you do and never gain an ounce?" Beth asked.

The old jibes—teasing Miriam about the way she looks (and her sex life), Beth for abandoning Manhattan (and being rich), me for being obsessed with traveling (and preferring books to real life much of the time)—I love them. They remind us of how well we know each other. And for how long.

I told them about Sidney's party in Florida.

"Will Kevin go with you?" Miriam asked.

"No, he won't be back in time. Anyway, I'll bet he's

not entirely sorry to miss being in the same room with Martin."

"Can't say I blame him," said Beth. "I'm sure he still remembers that Martin wouldn't even shake his hand at Ellie's high school graduation. But you'll have a good time, and you can see Violet while you're there. Don't forget to tell her we expect her to be at our fall bash again this year. Fifteenth annual!" Beth and Miriam had visited me so often when I lived in Florida that Violet had become their friend, too.

"Oh, God!" Miriam cried. "The Gillian gala. I'll have to start thinking about a date."

"Why don't you come by yourself?" Beth asked. "Jim is inviting so many new people this year. I'm sure some of them are single."

"No, thanks," said Miriam, holding up her hand like a stop sign.

We finished our meal, including a shared slice of New York City's third best chocolate dessert, and made our way to the street. Beth offered to drive us home.

"I've got some shopping to do," Miriam said. "You can drive Sarah home. I'll just take the Lexington Avenue train uptown."

We watched Miriam disappear down the stairs to the train. Beth slipped her arm through mine as we walked to the lot where she had parked.

"Are you all right about Florida?" she asked. "Being with Martin and everything?"

"I can survive seeing him in a crowd. He'll be polite to me because Ellie will be there."

We got into Beth's car and headed to the West Side Highway.

"I don't know that I'd ever get over being angry at Martin if I were you," she said, looking straight ahead as she drove.

"Well, you know how it is when you are forced to deal with something you can't change," I said. "I just tell myself that Martin was the right father for my child. I was meant to have Ellie. I have finally accepted the fact that Martin has no intention of spending a minute or a dollar on his child that isn't court ordered. I got tired of being sad about how things worked out, and being angry at him just wore me out. So I avoid thinking about him."

"Yes, I know what you mean," Beth said, her eyes on the road.

I suddenly regretted what I said. Of course she knew, better than I, how to cope with helpless sadness and anger. Her world nearly came apart not long ago. I changed the subject.

"How are things at the museum?"

"Being on the board takes more time than you'd think. They've talked me into giving tours this fall. Once a month, I'll dust off my BA in art history and play volunteer docent-for-a-day. Which reminds me, I'm trying to talk Jim into going to Rome to see the Caravaggio exhibit that's opening in the spring. If he won't take the time, would you come with me? It would make up for your never having visited me in Italy when I studied there."

I didn't have the money to visit Beth in Italy thirty years ago, and I'd have to go into debt to travel with her now. Depressing how little progress I've made in some ways. I'll need a windfall, or a miracle, to join her. For as hard as I work, why am I still struggling?

"Sounds great," I said, forcing a smile.

———

ON MY FLIGHT to Florida, the passenger next to me, in an ill-fitting suit and a terrible toupée, looked remarkably like the lawyer I had hired when I divorced Martin.

Barney Palmer was a good ol' boy with a veneer of

Southern gentility and a reputation for getting the wheels of justice, or whatever, to turn reasonably fast when it came to divorces. He warned me that some Florida judges, if they sensed even the slimmest hope of salvation for a marriage about to be torn asunder, were known to order a couple into prolonged marital counseling instead of granting an immediate divorce.

"Don't get sentimental on me now," Barney drawled as we headed for the judge's chambers in the Acedia Bay courthouse. "When His Honor asks if you still have any feelings for Martin, there's no need to be recalling how much you used to love him or that he's the father of your child or any such foolishness. Say that you *detest* the son of a bitch and that you regret you ever met him."

The whole thing took less than twenty minutes. The four of us—Martin, his lawyer, Barney, and I—sat like school children in front of the judge, watching him flip quickly through a pile of folders, listening as he prepared to officially release Mr. and Mrs. Martin Roth from each other's lives. The judge asked us if we thought there was hope of rescuing the marriage. Martin just shook his head. I said, "No, Your Honor," rather energetically. Martin never looked at me, but I snuck a glance at him from time to time. He looked tired, he had gained some weight, and he somehow seemed shorter than he was when I was married to him. When the hearing was over, I went home and wrote a poem I entitled, "Was the S.O.B. Always So Short?" It was clever and funny and only the slightest bit mean, considering how I felt about Martin at the time.

After our divorce, Martin sent child support payments more or less on time but excused himself from being a father in most other ways. The infinite worries that define parenthood were left entirely to me. Does she need an algebra tutor? Does she need braces? Should I raise her allowance? Should I let her go to a rock concert? Is that heat rash, or chickenpox?

Ellie, so demanding of me, was content with whatever little time and attention her father afforded her. I juggled my work schedule to drive carpools, to race to pediatrician visits, to deliver green eggs and ham to Ellie's class for Dr. Seuss Day, to attend teacher conferences and dance recitals. Martin would fly into town for maybe one event out of every dozen in his daughter's life, and Ellie would happily talk for days afterwards about how nice it was for him to have come.

———————————

I EXPECTED TO see Helen when I landed in Jacksonville. Instead, Sidney was at the gate, ashen and jittery.

"There's—um—no party, Sarah," he began. He was fiddling with his car keys. "Martin had a heart attack. We got the call from what's-her-name, the girlfriend, Pauline, early this morning." He paused for a moment, and then he began to race uncomfortably through the rest of his news.

"Martin died en route to the hospital. We're going to have his body flown in from Nashville. You know, Jewish funerals should be the next day after, so we don't want to wait. It's a little complicated because of the distance, but I'm trying to arrange everything for tomorrow. He'll be buried next to his parents in that cemetery on the north side of town."

"Sidney, slow down. What do you mean?"

"I know, it doesn't seem real to any of us. Young guy, always active, seemed healthy."

"And Ellie? My God, how is she?"

"She came in late last night. She was still asleep when we got the call. It was so early this morning, and then I had to—um—go make some arrangements for the—um—and then I came here to get you, so I don't know."

We were moving along with the tide of people

heading for the baggage claim. My mind leapt to the family drama that had ensued when Martin and Helen's parents died. For both funerals, each family member took on a predictable role, as if they were working from a script. Helen was expected to remain dignified and self-effacing in her grief, and she didn't disappoint. Sidney, famous for his allergy to open emotion, was permitted to retreat, and, except for his occasional appearances to provide bulletins about funeral arrangements, we barely saw him. Martin, as usual, remained in charge of being angry. He criticized the rabbi; he snapped at the funeral director; he made snide comments about well-intentioned neighbors who brought casseroles and cakes for us as we sat *shiva* for a week. Practical details fell to me—calling family and friends, making sure there was enough fresh coffee on hand. I wrote eulogies for both of Martin's parents and read them at the funerals. Ellie was so small and so sad, too young for the rituals surrounding death to offer her any comfort. I imagined her now, stunned and silent, trying to figure out her role.

Ignoring the wheels on my suitcase, Sidney picked it up by the handle and walked me to his car. As he drove, I tried to evoke the feeling of being in love with Martin, but all I could recall were the last years of our marriage, when I dreamed frequently of my husband's demise. The widow fantasies I had confided to Violet, and my caustic wit at Martin's expense, now seemed surreal and reckless.

"It's so good that you're here," Sidney said as we pulled into the garage of the yellow stucco house that he and Helen had lived in for more than thirty years. I knew Sidney wouldn't want to deal with Helen's raw grief alone.

I found Helen curled up on a chintz-covered chair at the kitchen table. Her eyes were swollen and red. She stood and put her arms around my neck.

"Helen, I know how awful this is for you," I began, but

she interrupted me.

"I'll be fine, sweetie. Go to Ellie, she's in the guest room."

I let go of Helen and made my way down the hall. I knocked softly on the guest room door.

"Come in."

Ellie was sitting cross-legged on the bed, still in pajamas. She was pale, but she didn't look as if she had been crying. I sat on the bed and put my arm around her.

"Honey, I'm so sorry," I said.

"It doesn't seem real, Mom. I spoke to him yesterday. He told me about a book he was reading on transcendental meditation."

From the front hallway, I heard the doorbell ring and then Sidney's voice greeting the family rabbi.

"Can I get you anything?" I asked Ellie.

"Um, maybe find me an iron, okay? I bought a new dress for Uncle Sidney's party," she said. "It's just a black linen thing, and it got a little creased in my suitcase. I guess I'll wear it to . . ." her voice broke, and then she asked me to leave so she could get dressed.

"If you want to talk . . ."

"Not now, Mom."

I returned to the kitchen. Rabbi Weisgall introduced himself. He had never met Martin, and he asked if we knew who might want to say a few words at the service.

Helen wiped her eyes and stared at me. "Sarah, I remember what you said about Mama and Daddy at their funerals. Would you please?"

The rabbi looked at me expectantly. I thought about the poem that I had written the day I divorced Martin. Not exactly the stuff eulogies are made of.

"Helen, I . . ." I began, and then saw Ellie standing in the doorway to the kitchen. The rabbi told her how sorry he was. She looked away.

Helen pressed on. "Ellie, don't you think your mom should say a few words tomorrow?"

Ellie remained stony-faced. "I don't know," she shrugged.

Rabbi Weisgall looked at Ellie and then at me.

"Sarah, why don't you and I go outside?" he suggested, and so we excused ourselves and walked out the back door.

We sat at the wrought-iron table on the patio. The mid-day Florida heat and the fragrance of orange trees were overpowering and familiar. Years ago, Martin and I had wept with Ellie as we buried her goldfish under the satsumas in our own backyard, only a mile from where I was sitting.

"In some ways, this may be harder for you than for the others," Rabbi Weisgall began. "Death is always harder for those who have unresolved conflicts with the departed."

I shook my head. "Rabbi, I'm sorry that Martin died, but I have no conflicts about him. We had an unhappy marriage and a bitter divorce, and except for Ellie, nothing that passed between us has meaning for me anymore. I loved him a long time ago, but I can't summon up many positive feelings for him, even now. He disappointed Ellie so many times over the years, and I can't forgive him for that. I just want to help her get through this."

"I understand that forgiveness may take some time, but I hope you'll find a way," he said. "You may be surprised how doing the eulogy will help you. And Helen. And especially Ellie. I expect that Helen is asking a great deal of you, but I think you're up to it. She has great respect for you."

"I love Helen. But my relationship with her has nothing to do with Martin anymore."

"I can perform the service without your saying anything, but you may feel different by tomorrow. For your own sake, I hope you do. I can't begin to know what you're experiencing now. But perhaps God is offering you a way to unload a burden you didn't even know you were carrying."

As we walked back in the house, Sidney met us to say that Pauline would be arriving with Martin's body late that night. The funeral was set for the next morning.

Ellie pulled me aside. "Are you going to do it?" she asked.

"Oh, Ellie, I'm not sure I can."

"You should do it, Mom, for Aunt Helen. She can't do it, and Uncle Sidney wouldn't know what to say. Otherwise only the rabbi will speak, and he didn't even know Dad. Really, you knew him best."

"Let me think about it," I said. "Listen, I'm going to stay with Violet tonight. Would you like to stay with me?"

Ellie sighed. "No thanks. Maggie will be here soon, and I want to stick around." Maggie was Helen and Sidney's daughter, a few years older than Ellie. Unlike me, Maggie wouldn't press Ellie to talk or cry.

I borrowed Helen's car to drive to Violet's house, grateful for the solitude of the ride. In my head was a slide show of events I hadn't thought about in years. The yellow roses Martin sent me after our first date. Martin and I happily cooking our first Thanksgiving dinner in our tiny New York apartment, and our last Thanksgiving together in Florida, when I demanded that he pack his clothes and move out. Martin's dark moods and punishing silence during our last years together. Ellie's face when she caught sight of Martin and me in the bleachers at her swim meets. Ellie's face when Martin didn't show up to see her in the school play. The promises Martin and I had made and broken to each other.

"Poor Ellie," was Violet's first reaction. "And you, too."

We sat at Violet's dining room table, where we had spent many evenings commiserating about single motherhood and our unreliable ex-husbands. A dozen years older than I, Violet had been a Savannah debutante who married and started a family before she was twenty and was divorced when her children were still very young.

"Where's Grant?" I asked.

Grant Bailey is Violet's second husband. Violet likes to let people know how thoughtful Grant is. How sensible. How unlike her first husband.

"He's at a partners' meeting at the office," she said. I heard a teakettle whistling. "Something about a new associate. He called to say he wouldn't be home for dinner. You know, after being married to the likes of Brice Auden, it's nice to live with a man who keeps me informed of his whereabouts. And is honest with me. Brice Auden, as I know I've told you many times, would rather tell a lie even when the truth would do as well."

I smiled. It never fails to amuse me when Violet talks about her ex. I love how she always refers to him by his full name.

She retrieved the kettle from the kitchen and poured the boiling water over a strainer of loose tea into a Wedgwood teapot.

"Now, tell me how things are at Sidney and Helen's," she said. She handed me a delicate porcelain cup and saucer.

I told her about Helen's request and my conversation with the rabbi.

"Great idea," she said calmly.

"What?" I thought she was kidding.

Violet poured some tea into my cup. "Well, not many of us get to do this. Think of it as a chance to rid yourself of some residual demons. And to show your daughter that even under terrible conditions, her mother remains on the high road."

"Vi, you know how difficult my life was when I

was married to him. He was so self-indulgent. Chronically depressed and *depressing*. Remember how I used to complain that he had no friends? Here we are, at his *funeral* for God's sake, and the only person who can say a few words about him is . . . *me*? Weren't you the one who said Martin's midlife crisis had gone on long enough to earn a place in the Smithsonian? I've spent years covering for him when he wasn't there for Ellie, and I can't believe—"

"Look," she interrupted, "Martin is—was Ellie's father. You married for love, even if he turned out to be a miserable disappointment as a husband and father. My mother told me that sometimes the best way to win a battle is to kill the competition with kindness. It's too late for you to kill Martin, but you can win this last battle in your war with him. You can bury him with kindness. Ellie will never forget that you did this for her. And who knows? Maybe the rabbi is right about the healing power of forgiveness."

"I don't know what to do," I said slowly. "Violet, do you mind if I try to reach Kevin? I probably should call Beth and Miriam, too."

"There's a phone in the guestroom. Take your tea with you, if you like."

Kevin wasn't in his hotel room, but I left a voicemail telling him about Martin. Answering machines picked up at both Beth's and Miriam's houses, and I hung up without leaving messages. I lay down on the bed and thought about what the rabbi and Violet had said about forgiving Martin. The idea had simply never crossed my mind before. Resenting him or ignoring him just came so easily. Now there didn't seem much point to holding on to my anger. Not if I could help Ellie and Helen by letting go.

I stayed up all night to write the eulogy. I was

surprised at the sweetness of memories that surfaced alongside the old resentments. One of the great mysteries of life is how love holds on. Even when it wounds or scars or fades, so often it doesn't entirely let go.

In the morning, I drove back to Helen and Sidney's house, surprised not to feel the slightest bit tired. Everyone was awake when I walked in the house. The living room furniture had been rearranged to ready the house for Sidney and Helen's friends who were likely to pay their respects during the *shiva* period ahead. Martin didn't have any friends in Acedia Bay, and relatives whose calls he never returned would be unlikely to fly in for the occasion.

A circle of rented folding chairs and boxes of china and table linens filled much of the living room. From the kitchen, I could hear the crew from Kolodney's Katering, Acedia Bay's only kosher food service, clanging pots and pans. Ellie and her cousin Maggie were together on the sofa, which had been moved against the back wall. I kissed them both, and Maggie whispered to me, "Ellie slept pretty well, I think. But she's not saying much."

A petite brunette I figured must be Pauline was sitting nervously on the edge of one of the folding chairs in the corner of the dining room. If I had to guess, I'd say she appeared to be plotting her escape. Under the circumstances, I'm not sure how I would have behaved in her place. I have to admit, I was wondering how Martin had described me to her.

I held out my hand to her. She looked surprised and a little wary, but she offered a limp handshake and a thin smile. She stayed perched on the chair.

"Did you sleep here last night?" I asked, desperate for conversation. Idiotic question, I thought immediately.

"Yes, we—um—the plane got in very late," she said. "This is such a big house and Helen and Sidney didn't seem to mind . . ." Her voice trailed off. My God, I thought, she's practically apologizing for being here. I patted her shoulder and excused myself. She looked relieved to be left alone again.

I heard Sidney's voice coming from his study. He was on the phone, giving someone directions to the cemetery. He motioned for me to come in as he hung up.

"I wrote something to say about Martin," I said.

"I'm glad. We need to go, the car's waiting. It will be a small group, right at the cemetery. Ready?" He ushered me out to the car.

About twenty friends of Helen and Sidney gathered at the graveside. Pauline seemed to be trembling as she slid into the seat next to Helen. Ellie sat next to me, clutching my hand. I saw Violet and Grant in the back row. Rabbi Weisgall said a prayer and then motioned to me to step up in front of the group, next to the coffin. I let go of Ellie's hand and walked to the rabbi's side.

"Some of you will no doubt find it unusual that I am speaking here today," I began. "But Martin was an unusual man."

I looked at Ellie, who was beginning to sob, and I went on.

"Few people know better than I how complicated a person Martin was. But it's also important to remember he was a man of great imagination and intelligence, with an adventurous spirit. I know this is so, because our daughter inherited so much of what was good in her father."

I talked about Ellie's early childhood, when Martin was a loving father, before he became too self-absorbed and depressed to notice us. (Violet often referred to this as Martin's Pre-Blue Period, but I didn't say so.) I told the story of the Halloween when Martin went to Ellie's nursery school and painted pumpkins to look like Sesame

Street characters. And how he had been the only father in the history of Brownie Troop 180 to accompany the girls on a weekend camping trip.

"Family life—relationships of all kinds—were sometimes challenging for him, but he was proud of his daughter, and he loved her," I said. "Like all of us, he did the best he could. It's important to remember that."

The rabbi finished the service, and Helen, Sidney, Ellie, and I each threw a handful of dirt on the coffin. As we walked back to the car, Ellie leaned her head against my arm.

Back at Helen and Sidney's house, I mingled absent-mindedly with the group that had returned from the cemetery with us. Violet and Grant made their way to me through the small crowd.

"We've got to get to work," Violet said. "How long are you staying in town?"

"I think Ellie will want to stay for the week, but I'm not sure what I'm doing. In any case, I think I'll stay here with Ellie. Can I get my suitcase from your house later?"

"I'll leave the back door open for you. Listen, call me when you get back to New York," she said, hugging me. "I assume the Gillians' annual bash is on again? We'll come up if we can."

"Oh, of course. The invites are in the works. I know Beth expects to see you there."

I looked around the room for Ellie. She was politely answering questions about Columbia and her plans for law school, tolerating anecdotes from near-strangers about their memories of her as an adorable, young child. Everyone was trying to be kind, but I could tell Ellie was grateful when I led her away.

"How are you doing?"

"Maybe it will hit me later, Mom, but now it's just kind of strange. I mean, I'm sad, but . . ." She shrugged her shoulders.

"It's normal to be numb at this point. But it will start to feel real, maybe when you least expect it. You know your dad really loved you, don't you?"

"Oh, yes. I do," she said, with a kind of finality that let me know she didn't want to talk anymore.

"I'll stay for the week if you want me to."

"No, you should go back. Maggie will be here. And Uncle Sidney is so nice, he bought a plane ticket so Doug can come tomorrow. I understand if you want to leave. This has got to be really weird for you."

"I'll be fine if I know you are," I said.

"You can go, Mom. Really."

I RETURNED HOME the next day, leaving my daughter to sit *shiva* with her father's family. On the plane, fatigue washed over me. I closed my eyes and almost slept, half-dreaming of Ellie as a small child and me as a young mother. Martin, athletic and youthful as he was when we first met, came in and out of the picture, smiling and holding his arms out toward Ellie and me. I called his name and tried to reach for him, but his hand kept slipping away.

My flight got me back to New York in the late afternoon. I parked my suitcase with the doorman of my building without going upstairs, and I walked to Broadway. Being in Florida had reminded me again how much I had missed the city during my ten-year exile in Acedia Bay. I turned onto 72nd Street, stopped into a new gelateria, and treated myself to a scoop of mango sorbet. By the time I reached Riverside Park, the sun was starting to set, casting streaks of orange on the windows of the high-rise apartments across the river. I sat on a park bench until the sky grew dark, thinking about meeting and marrying Martin in Manhattan, wondering if our life together might have been different if we had never moved to Acedia Bay.

The light was flashing on the answering machine when I got back to my apartment. Two messages. The first was from Kevin, characteristically brief. "Honey, I just spoke to Violet. *Jeez!* I'll try you again around ten, your time."

The second message was from Miriam. Hearing her voice reminded me that she and Beth still didn't know about Martin. "Hi, hope you're home safely and that you had the sense to use your sunscreen in Florida. I want a *full report* on Martin's behavior at Sidney's party. Oh, and here's a sign of the times. Beth has sent email invitations to her party this year. Emily Post be damned! Call me."

I switched on my computer, skipping over emails from the office. I skimmed the first page of the monthly issue of *L'Arrondissement,* an online newsletter for Americans like me who believe that if life were just, they'd have a *pied à terre* on the Rive Gauche. Featured this month: a report on the controversy surrounding the removal of Jim Morrison's remains from Père Lachaise cemetery.

The header on Beth's email invitation contained about fifty addresses. I recognized most of the names from previous gatherings at her house, the usual assortment of family, old friends, some of their Connecticut neighbors, and Jim's business associates and clients.

James Gillian and Dr. Beth Jacobs Gillian
invite you to the Fifteenth Annual Fall Bash
at their home, "Château Crummy Acres,"
in Laurel Falls, Connecticut
RSVP regrets only, please

I tried Miriam's number, then Beth's. Still no one home. I turned my attention to the small pile of mail that had accumulated in my brief absence. Just a few bills. I shuffled through the envelopes, pulling out the ones that looked most alarming.

One of the few good things about my marriage was that I didn't have to worry about paying bills, at least during the years when Martin worked. I could teach part-time and be home with Ellie as much as I wanted. I had even started taking classes at the university in Gainesville to get my doctorate. I still have my notes on the subject I was considering for my doctoral dissertation, "Fatalism and Feminism in the Poetry of Dorothy Parker." When I got divorced, though, I simply couldn't afford to be a part-time teacher anymore. And graduate school just dropped off the agenda.

When I left teaching, I freelanced at first to keep my schedule flexible for Ellie's sake. My early gigs were a hodge-podge of assignments from anyone I could get to hire me. A few associates from the college had me edit their academic work: I revised a textbook on the life of a nineteenth-century mystical rabbi and edited a series of articles on how to maximize soybean production. I wrote speeches for newly promoted executives and local political candidates. I served as sometime restaurant critic and film reviewer for the *Acedia Bay Tribune*. I created easy-to-read brochures on low-cost funerals and pesticide-free lawn care. While writing a pamphlet for a physician ("What Every Woman Should Know About Healthy Bones"), I learned about an opening at her hospital for a marketing director, someone who could write. My physician client put in a good word for me, and the job was mine.

A few years later, when the hospital was sold and my position was eliminated, I returned to New York with Ellie. Since then, I have worked at four different healthcare companies. Three of them have evaporated—victims of mergers, acquisitions, and financial manipulations I'll never understand. The euphemisms for the layoffs (downsizings, re-orgs) hardly camouflage what everyone involved in the caprice understands all too well: a handful of people are going to get rich as a result of all this, and the rest of us may lose our jobs.

For more than two-and-a-half years now, I've been vice president of the editorial department at Tri-Tech Healthcare Marketing. The company puts together conferences for drug companies to help them launch new drugs or pump up the sales of existing ones. When I interviewed for the job, Joey Selber, founder and president of the company, talked about himself nonstop for almost three hours before asking me if I had any questions.

"How did you choose the company name?" I asked. "Tri-Tech" didn't seem to me to have much to do with the company's mission.

"*Very* interesting story," he said. Later, I would come to learn that Joey considers every word that leaves his mouth to be fascinating. "I was looking for a name that sounded, you know, like we were in the Big Leagues, even though I *literally* started the company in my garage. So my wife Lorraine, she says to me, Why not try 'tech' in the name? Like in 'technical'? *Try* tech, get it? Tri-Tech!"

When I think back to this conversation, I am astounded I ever took the job.

Tri-Tech now has about sixty employees, but the office still has the feel of a Mom-and-Pop operation. Joey, of course, is Pop, but there is no Mom, unless you count Lorraine Selber. Her main contribution, apart from having inspired the brilliant company name, is to send holiday cards to the staff in December. The cards look the same every year: A photo of Joey and Lorraine wearing over-sized Santa caps and holding a sign that says:

We are so happy to have you in the Tri-Tech family.
Enjoy the holiday of your choice!

Joey proudly points out that this greeting "covers all the bases: Christmas, Chanukah, that new black people's holiday, Kew-antsa, or whatever."

Most of Tri-Tech's employees are very young, at least compared to me they are. No accident, since Joey, who turned forty-three this year, prefers to be surrounded by people who he believes know less than he does. He tells the young staff how to dress for client meetings (nothing "too designer" is his usual advice to women; a "navy blue, part-polyester jacket that doesn't wrinkle" is his recommendation for men) and monitors their phone calls to make certain they are projecting the proper Tri-Tech image.

Tri-Tech's Operations VP, Lawrence Zimmerman, and I seem to be the only employees who are exempt from Joey's fashion and business etiquette coaching sessions. Lawrence is a fifty-five-year-old black man, a devoutly religious Episcopalian, with a brilliant mind and polished manners that help to offset Joey's crudeness. Lawrence's involvement in his church is a constant source of irritation to Joey. Not that what Lawrence does in his own time interferes in any way with company business—Joey simply feels that devotion to Tri-Tech should pre-empt all other human activity. Lawrence's talent and intelligence notwithstanding, Joey believes that his having taken on a black person as a partner in the company demonstrates how progressive Tri-Tech is. After his third martini during a plane ride we took together last year, Joey confided to me that he misses the good old days, before political correctness and discrimination lawsuits took the fun out of running a company.

I recently went to battle with Joey over a candidate for an assistant editor's position. Joey always gets the final vote on new hires. The best applicant by far was Rebecca Carson, a woman with a journalism degree who had been a healthcare reporter for a small newspaper. Though she was in her thirties, she looked and dressed like a teenager. She was under five feet tall, weighing maybe ninety pounds, with a wild mane of reddish curls streaked platinum blonde at the ends, an oddly asymmetrical face, and pouting crimson lips that looked like a collagen experiment gone wrong. She also had an elaborate tattoo of a peculiar winged creature on her right wrist, which Joey couldn't keep from staring at throughout her interview.

"Are you kidding?" Joey said after Rebecca had left. "She looks bizarre. What's with the black nail polish? And the tattoo? What the hell is that *thing* on her wrist?"

"Joey," I said calmly, "she worked for a newspaper. She's not used to corporate salaries. We can get her for *thousands* under budget."

That did it. Joey acquiesced and I hired Rebecca, though I had to promise Joey that I'd keep her and her tattoo away from clients' eyes.

I spend my days at Tri-Tech supervising Rebecca and four other staff members. Our job is to write whatever Joey needs to keep the company going—new business proposals, speeches, reports, handouts that are distributed at the conferences we choreograph. Never at a loss for a cliché, Joey describes the company's mission as helping our clients "improve the bottom line."

"At the end of the day," he says, "all a drug company wants is to push a pill, move a molecule, make a buck."

In the self-created biography he forces me to include in everything we send out, Joey bills himself as someone with "an impressive background in the healthcare marketplace." In fact, for ten years before he started Tri-Tech, Joey was the Pittsburgh-to-Binghamton regional sales manager for a company that manufactured prosthetic limbs. The company went public and soon was bought by a large corporation. Joey made a small fortune from his stock options, which is how he got the money to open Tri-Tech.

Savant Pharmaceuticals is the source of most of Tri-Tech's business. Richard "Doc" Shortland, PhD, Savant's Senior VP of Marketing, and the product managers who report to him throw about twenty million dollars of business to Tri-Tech every year. Thanks to them, I get to re-invent Joey's singular marketing idea over and over so that Joey can deliver rousing talks to Savant's sales reps. These talks are based on the sales training course Joey developed in his garage. I've recycled the damn thing at least thirty times.

Sometimes Tri-Tech is also asked to recruit doctors from well-known medical schools to speak at the big conferences. I'm the one who actually recruits them. On principle, Joey avoids conversing with anyone in possession of an advanced degree or academic title, unless, like Dr. Shortland, the person is a potential source of business.

Doc and Joey can barely tolerate each other. They play a mine-is-bigger-than-yours game—a childish, testosterone-driven competition—which Doc invariably wins. "I'm going to the corporate headquarters in Geneva again next week," he'll say to Joey. "If your little company continues to do right by us, maybe I'll take you along on one of these trips. Ever been to the Alps, Joey?"

I frequently accompany Joey to the conferences so I can make last-minute changes to his PowerPoint presentations. My academic background can become wasted ammunition in Joey's ego war with Doc Shortland. Whenever we're with Doc, Joey likes to refer to me as "*Professor* Roth" and to intimate that my doctorate is "in process." Doc pretends not to hear him. Joey manages to appear impressed with my achievements (even the

PART I: SARAH

ones he invents), though in private he says that he can't believe I spent "good money" getting a B.A. in French and a master's degree in twentieth-century American literature. He has been even touchier than usual on the topic of higher education ever since his alma mater, Southeast Pennsylvania College of Pharmacy, was forced to close. A *60 Minutes* investigation last year exposed the correspondence school as a diploma mill, and Joey unceremoniously removed his framed diploma ("Honors Graduate, 1978") from his office wall.

Funded by Savant's extravagant budget, Doc Shortland's regional meetings—typically three or four days long—are held at luxurious resorts. The business part takes up about an hour a day. The rest of the time everyone is pretty much on vacation. The doctors sometimes seem a little sheepish accepting Savant's bounty; even as they sip their single-malt Scotch and line up for early tee-times, they vow to remain impartial in their assessment of Savant's products. The Savant sales reps behave as if the meetings were their last days on Earth. They storm the hotel spa for massages before breakfast; they scramble onto helicopters for afternoon sightseeing tours; they demand Courvoisier Napoleon to complement the flavor of their after-dinner Cohiba cigars.

When the meetings are held in Las Vegas, Joey usually brings Lorraine along. She plays video poker and shops in the overpriced hotel boutiques, and then Joey entertains everyone at the cocktail receptions with an accounting of how much of his money she has squandered. When I hear drug companies piously justify the expense of new drugs, I will forever recall a scene I witnessed at a recent conference: Joey and Lorraine, arm in arm with Savant sales reps, embarking on a faux gondola ride along a faux canal at the Las Vegas Venetian hotel. The Selbers, who have never ventured abroad, raved about the new hotel because, as Joey observes, "It's *exactly* like Italy, but you don't have to put up with all those annoying foreigners who don't speak English."

I survive at Tri-Tech because I have no choice; I need the paycheck. My annual bonus pays for most of Ellie's expenses at Columbia. And happily, I can function at this job using only a tiny fraction of my mind. I sustain the hope—dwindling!—that I will one day use the rest of my brain cells on the kind of work I put aside when I married Martin and left my job in literary publishing. Maybe even finish the short stories from decades ago that dwell, half-written, in dusty boxes under my bed.

I can barely remember what it feels like to spend my days doing something I care about. So many years of mind-numbing work, dysfunctional corporate environments, idiotic bosses. But I'm stuck where I am, at least for a while longer. Joey has promised that after I've completed three years at Tri-Tech, he'll make me a partner. I'll get a huge bonus up front and shares of company profits over time. My three-year anniversary is coming up in December. I certainly wouldn't leave before then, and I'm sure I'll have to put in some time—five years? Ten?—before the profit-sharing is actually mine. I'm hitched, for the time being, to Joey Selber's lightless star.

Except for minimal child support payments from Martin, I've had to raise Ellie entirely on the money I earn. Summer camps and dance lessons, contact lenses and orthodontia, the inordinate tabs that teenagers can run up for clothing and entertainment—all of it was on me. Martin's parents left Ellie a small inheritance to be used for college, so Martin never considered contributing further. The inheritance barely covered one semester's tuition. I could have taken Martin back to court to get him to pay more of his share over the years, but the thought of what it would mean to deal with him again—threatening letters, angry phone calls, expensive lawyers—was more than I wanted to take on. Now I just continue as I always have: I provide everything Ellie needs, pay the rest of my bills (sooner or later), and worry, worry, worry about how I will live when I get too old to work. The problem is, my eyes glaze over at the first hint of talk about finances, mine or anyone else's. I don't know what I was doing while everyone else my age was learning how to manage money, but when I hear terms like "IPO" and "limited partnership," I feel as if I'm trying to catch up in algebra class, having missed the lesson on solving quadratic equations. Jim Gillian, Beth's husband, is, of course, a genius at this stuff, and Beth has tactfully suggested several times that I let Jim or someone from his firm help me set out a financial plan for myself. I trust Jim completely, but I would be embarrassed for anyone I know to wade through my pitiful finances right now.

I've had a few small windfalls, and I suppose I should have regarded them as opportunities to change my dreary financial picture. Instead, when a great aunt on my father's side left me a gift of three thousand dollars in her will, I took Ellie to France for her twelfth birthday. With the severance bonus I received from the downsized company where I worked before I started at Tri-Tech, Kevin and I took a Scandinavian cruise. Ever since my first trip to Europe, a college graduation present from my grandmother, I have used days-in-Italy (or Spain, or Greece) as a basic unit of money measurement. When I get my hands on any money not earmarked for basic living, I don't think about buying real estate or shares of stock. I think, instead, What's the weather in London? How long can I stay? Can I manage, finally, a trip to Asia? South America? I have promised Beth that I will call Jim for financial advice as soon I get my hands on my bonus—and before I call a travel agent.

Kevin isn't much better prepared for retirement than I am. He's still recovering from the downfall of the architectural firm he owned and lost long before I knew him. His partner in the business lied to him, misled clients, and swindled their company out of two million dollars. After Kevin tried in vain to recover the money and woo clients back, he had no choice except to declare bankruptcy and look for work. He's now a consultant for a company that builds retirement communities.

Kevin's son Brendan told me most of what I know about this. Kevin doesn't like to talk about his past. He listens to my stories about old friends and lovers, my family, my work, but he reveals little about himself before we met. He insists that he has already told me everything that matters. He says, "I'm here now, aren't I? What else do you want from me?"

I'm mystified that he even has to ask. The answer is all around him. It's the stuff of late-night TV monologues. It's the theme of the movies he's quick to dismiss as chick flicks. It keeps Oprah on the air and pop-psych claptrap on bestseller lists. It sells better than sex on magazine covers. It's the answer to Dr. Freud's famous question, and it's my answer to you, Kevin.

I want you to talk to me.

After four years of living together, darling, would it be asking too much for you to tell me a little something about yourself?

I wish you'd stop treating me like an intruder. I want you to love me so much that you can't help but tell me everything. I want intimacy, not the detachment that is like background noise when we are together, distant and unnerving, too faint to identify, too persistent to ignore. It keeps us apart in a way I can't really describe and which you won't acknowledge.

"Leave it alone, Sarah," you say. So I do.

And things between us are fine, really. I'm fifty-two years old and I live with a kind man who is good to me and is fond of my daughter. I don't want to march off into old age alone. Kevin and I have a peaceful life. It should be enough.

———

It was almost eleven o'clock when the phone rang. Kevin, predictably late.

"You must be in shock," he said.

"It was quite a weekend. Did Violet fill you in?"

"She said things went as well as could be expected. How's Ellie? Did she go back to school?"

"She'll be with Helen and Sidney for the week. I asked her if she wanted me to stay, but she said she'd be okay. Did you hear who gave the eulogy at the funeral?"

"You can be proud of yourself," he said. "Not many people could do that."

"How are things going for you? Did you see Brendan?"

"Work's okay. The building's on schedule. Brendan did manage to squeeze in a fast dinner with me. He got a promotion at work. Still no sign of a girlfriend, at least not one he wants to talk about with his old dad. He seemed a little tense. Betsy was here for a few days last week. You know how Brendan gets when she's around."

I've met Kevin's ex-wife Betsy just once, when Brendan finished his master's degree at MIT and we were all in Boston for his graduation. Nothing that Betsy said or did all weekend seemed to please Brendan, who was impatient and rude with her the whole time. Later, I asked Kevin to help me understand why Brendan had behaved like a petulant teenager with his mother. Kevin was annoyed with me for having asked, as if I were prying, and he never gave me an answer.

"Still coming home on the thirtieth?" I asked.

"As of now. I'll let you know if things change. You going to work tomorrow?"

"Of course. Joey will be back from the conference I missed on Friday, waiting to punish me for not being there to rewrite his speech the last dozen times. It was a men's health conference—you know, urologists, Viagra jokes, a laugh a minute. Before I left for Florida, I assured him: Joey, you'll be fine. I'm leaving you a list of all the euphemisms I can think of for 'impotence.' He was irritated that I asked for the day off, and the irony is that I feel somewhat gypped because of how I wound up having to spend my time. Maybe you can write me a note: Dear Joey, Please give my girlfriend Sarah an extra personal day off from work. She took last Friday off to go to a birthday party in Florida, but she wound up giving the eulogy at her ex-husband's funeral, so it shouldn't really count."

"You're starting to babble. Sorry you had such a rough weekend. But you need to go to sleep. And so do I."

"Kev, do you suppose that I'm now entitled to be called the Widow Roth?"

"That's enough, kiddo. Get some rest."

I climbed into bed, trying to remember how long it had been since Kevin and I had stopped adding, "I love you" when we said goodnight.

MIRIAM:
LEARNING CURVE

"We both know what memories can bring;
They bring diamonds and rust"
—*Joan Baez*

The New York Times
Spring Education Supplement

Reading, Writing, Action!

Jenny Wong is concerned about the current state of the cinema. She expresses dismay at the pervasive stereotypes of women and minorities on screen. She is disappointed that her generation of filmgoers is willing to forgo good story-telling in favor of dazzling special effects. She laments the limited financial resources available to independent filmmakers.

It's certainly not unusual for an aspiring film director to hold such opinions. What is remarkable, though, is that Jenny Wong is in the eighth grade. She is one of twenty-five students in the "Film on Fridays" program at McCollum Middle School on Manhattan's East Side. She and her classmates share a deep appreciation for—and strong opinions about—movies and movie-making. They've developed their ideas in this unique course, which Miriam Kaplan, a reading specialist, and self-described "film freak," debuted at the school last September.

"I wanted to design a program that would help to develop reading, writing, and critical thinking skills," Ms. Kaplan says. "I don't expect that many of these kids will wind up in the film business, but the skills they develop here will serve them well wherever they go."

Ms. Kaplan, who reminds people that she has been teaching at the school "long enough to remember when it was still called Junior High School 67," spent a year getting the program under way. There was no place in the budget for it, nor was there much time in an already crowded school day.

Undaunted, Ms. Kaplan donated a TV and VCR to the school and begged local video stores for contributions of tapes for a film library. She spent evenings and weekends on the phone, garnering support from colleagues, parents, and school administrators, looking for ways to shift schedules so no other subjects would be neglected.

"Film on Fridays, if you'll excuse the expression, is no Mickey Mouse class," she says. "We meet just one afternoon a week on school time, so I expect students to do a great deal of work at home." The curriculum includes writing film reviews as well as papers on acting and directing techniques, even the history and business of movie-making.

Students in Ms. Kaplan's class eagerly anticipate new experiences as they develop into mature filmgoers and critics.

"I'll be thirteen next month, so I'm hoping my

mom lets me go to PG-13 movies from now on," says Jenny Wong. "I think I'll be like totally in college before I can see any R-rated stuff, though."

THE *TIMES* ARTICLE included a photo of me lecturing to students. Behind me is a giant poster for West Side Story, which I first saw when I was Jenny's age. I tell the kids that Lincoln Center now stands on the streets where the movie was filmed. I don't tell them that Kenny Scott, the heartthrob of my eighth grade class, gave me my first French kiss during the chorus of "Officer Krupke."

The article makes me sound like a natural born teacher. Like Miss Jean Brodie, still in her prime, "putting old heads on young shoulders." When my mother read the *Times* piece, she reminded me that in college I had resisted my parents' advice to become a teacher. Mom and Dad thought that college was unnecessary for girls anyway, except as a venue for snaring an educated husband. However, a married woman (of course, they were certain I'd get married) who became a teacher would work only during the same hours when her children (of course, there would be children) were in school. I tormented my parents by changing my major a few times a semester during my first two years at Buffalo. The more obscure the field of study, the more difficult for my parents to understand, the better. I was especially pleased with myself during my sophomore year, when I imagined my mother trying to explain to her Mah Jong group that I was majoring in Ethical Social Systems, which I soon changed to Slavic Literature, and then Medieval Art History.

The summer following that year, I had a job as a counselor at an underprivileged children's camp in the Catskills. In the mornings, the counselors—college students like me—did schoolwork with the campers. Sitting in the camp cafeteria and helping the kids sound out words in their simple books, I instinctively understood how to teach them to read without making them feel ashamed. In the fall, I changed my college major, for good, to reading education.

I used to worry about my image—the spinster school-teacher—but I'm long past that. It seems silly now, but I sometimes felt as if people my age who were aggressively making their mark on the world viewed my career choice as uninspired. "Those who can, do; those who can't, teach"—a saying I loathe. I remember wishing for an impressive job title, or at least a business card to offer when a man handed me his and asked for mine. I don't give a damn anymore about what other people think. One of the few benefits of getting older. Besides, the truth is that I am happier at work than most people I know, including the corporate ladder-climbers who were so quick to judge me years ago.

As to my personal life, these days I run it the way a manager would operate a business: with an appointment calendar and clearly defined job descriptions. Occasionally, I catch a movie with Wayne and Thomas, the couple who live next door. Weather permitting, I pencil in a colleague at work for tennis in Central Park. I frequently take my old friend Cameron with me to social events when I'd rather have a date than go alone.

I called Cameron just yesterday and invited him to the Gillians' party. He's sociable and bright enough to hold his own. I can dress him up and take him anywhere. I can depend on him not to drink too much or flirt with other women. He'll tell me how lovely I look. He'll use the right silverware at dinner. He'll graciously thank the hosts. He knows I'm not likely to fall in love with him, and he doesn't care.

It's as much a surprise to me as to everyone who knows me that I've remained single. In my twenties, I returned several engagement rings to perfectly nice men who were almost right for me. A lawyer. An advertising executive. A history professor. We went through predictable courtship rituals. We met each other's families. We invented private jokes. We planned our wedding and how we'd decorate our home. We made lists of names for the children we'd have.

With each engagement—there were at least six—I described myself as being "in love." As if "love" were a geographical destination, a place on a map. *Have you ever spent time in Miami? In Marrakesh? In Love?* What was missing in each relationship, I could never say. *No, I've never actually been in Love, only visited the suburbs.* I called things off when I realized that sooner or later we'd wind up—the lawyer and I, the ad exec and I, the professor and I—sitting silently across restaurant tables like countless other mindless married couples, barely aware of each other.

My parents, who had reminded me every day of my young life that I was beautiful and smart and therefore destined to marry well, responded to my behavior with a mixture of confusion, frustration, and worry. In the end, they grew resigned to what they saw as my sad fate. My mother attended wedding after wedding of her friends' daughters, bought gifts for other people's grandchildren, and fended off questions about Miriam's "situation." After my father died, twenty years ago, and my brother and his wife moved to Phoenix, Mom stopped asking me about the men in my life. We had a new bond connecting us. We were both women who had to go it alone.

In recent years, I've had a succession of social companions and bed partners who I knew from the outset showed little promise for the long run. I dabbled with the long run just once, when I was convinced that I had met the right man to grow old with. When things ended with him, my life took a definitive turn: people stopped describing me as "Miriam, who is single"; I became "Miriam, who never got married." As if I were beyond the possibility.

———————

TWELVE YEARS AGO, when Sarah still lived in Acedia Bay, Beth and I visited her to celebrate Beth's completion of her internship in psychotherapy and the beginning of my one-year sabbatical from teaching. Sarah's friend Violet insisted on throwing a barbecue in our honor while we were in town. Violet is publicity director of the First Coast Environmental Conservancy, and every nature-loving historian, writer, and photographer in the Southeast was in attendance at the party, drinking mint juleps from Violet's silver-handled cups and speculating on the ingredients in her famous barbecue sauce.

I was talking to Violet's mother, who was already close to ninety at the time, when I heard a male voice behind me.

"Gorgeous as ever," said the voice, making "gorgeous" about four Southern syllables. When I turned to see his face, I saw the man looking down at Violet's mother, seated in her wheelchair.

"Miz Della! Be still, my heart," he said.

"You rascal, stop flirting with me!" said Della, beaming. "Peter, have you met Violet's friend from New York? Miriam Kaplan, this is Peter Robinette. Peter is a photographer. He visits us a few times a year, breaks some hearts, and then disappears home to Savannah."

"And what brings you to Florida, Ms. Kaplan?" he asked, smiling at me. His dusky blue eyes were as cool as a winter sky.

"Do you know Violet's friend, Sarah Roth?" I asked. "I was her college roommate. So was Beth, that tall blonde over there in the black dress. We like to come down and check on Sarah from time to time."

"I do know Sarah. Violet brought her to Savannah once, and we three went to dinner at Elizabeth's."

"Who's Elizabeth?"

"I can tell you've not been to Savannah. Elizabeth on 37th Street is a restaurant, one of my favorites."

We had moved to one of the round tables set for dinner. Peter pulled out a chair for me. He sat in the chair next to mine, continuing to smile and look into my eyes, not leering, exactly, but reminding me of the pivotal moment in *Gone with the Wind* when Rhett gazes up the staircase and sees Scarlett for the first time. He makes her feel, she says, "as if he knows what I look like without my shimmy."

I pointed to the camera dangling from his shoulder. "Are you the house photographer?" I asked.

"I don't usually bring a camera to parties, but I promised Violet I'd get some candids. I'd do anything for her."

I believe we sat at that table and talked for a long time, but I have no idea about what. In the years since, I've tried to remember details of that afternoon in Violet's backyard, as if some elusive scrap of memory could patch my heart and help me make sense of what I felt, and still feel. But what actually happened that day I can't say. Only feelings remain, with excruciating clarity. Being swept away by something out of my control. Spinning through space. I had never thought it possible, not for me, but there I was, almost forty years old, falling in love with a man I had known for less than ten minutes.

Sarah, Beth, and Violet were there, but they never talk about Peter anymore. If I say his name, they look away and change the subject. Violet still blames herself, as if my having met Peter at her house makes her responsible. I know they think they're protecting me by avoiding Peter's name. I wish they would tell me what they recall, but my pride won't let me ask them. I feel foolish enough at still being heartbroken after all this time.

BACK IN NEW York a week after I met Peter, I received a small package from him. Inside was a silver frame with a photograph of Violet, Sarah, Beth, and me that he had taken at Violet's barbecue. Oblivious to the camera, we appear to be sharing a confidence in the shade of the huge magnolia tree in Violet's backyard. A note in Peter's perfect script was taped to the back of the frame. It said, "Lovely! Peter."

When the phone rang that night, I was at my kitchen table, examining swatches of fabric and paint, planning the apartment renovations I was going to undertake during my sabbatical from teaching. When I answered the phone, Peter greeted me the way he would every time he called me from that moment on, "Hi, Sugar." With his Southern accent, it sounded like "Ha, Shugah."

I thanked him for the photo.

"Think of it as an early birthday gift," he said. I imagined that Violet had told him my fortieth birthday was coming up.

"It was very thoughtful of you," I said, rather formally.

"I'm glad you like it. And I understand this is an important birthday. A new decade! I have another idea. May I take you to dinner?"

"Dinner? Are you going to be in New York?" My heart was racing.

"Actually, I wanted to take you to Elizabeth on 37th." I could imagine his handsome face, his mischievous smile, as I struggled to speak.

"In Savannah?" I finally asked.

"Well, that's the only Elizabeth on 37th I know. I thought you might want to see the city. Do you like to sail?"

"Sail?" I realized I was sounding idiotic. "I've never been, but I've always wanted—"

"I hope next Thursday is a good traveling day for you. I was able to get reservations on direct flights both ways. I'll have to send you back on Sunday because I have an out-of-town shoot, but we'll have a long weekend together."

"You already have a plane ticket for me? How did you know I'd say yes?"

He laughed. "Just a hunch. Pack a dress for Elizabeth's and something to wear on the boat. If you don't have what you need, we'll buy it here. It's not New York, but we actually have some shops you might enjoy."

"This is the craziest thing . . ."

"Have a good week. I'll overnight the plane ticket to you. I'll see you at the airport."

After Peter hung up, I stared stupidly at the receiver in my hand.

I called Violet, who confirmed that to the best of her knowledge, Peter was not a homicidal maniac.

I ate half of a frozen chocolate cheesecake without bothering to defrost it.

I called Sarah, who asked if I had noticed Peter's resemblance to Steve McQueen (I had).

I examined my entire wardrobe and selected, then rejected, five possible dresses to wear to Elizabeth on 37th.

I called Beth, who, in her best therapist's manner, made me promise to pack condoms.

I picked up the phone half a dozen times to call Peter and cancel. Each time, I hung up without dialing.

I lay awake all night, trying to catch my breath.

———————

WHEN MY PLANE landed in Savannah, I was gripped

by a wrenching, oh-my-God moment of doubt. *What if he's not here? What if he sees me and decides he's changed his mind? What if I hate him?*

But Peter was at the gate, waving to me, behaving as if we weren't virtual strangers. He kissed me on the cheek and hugged me, saying, "Welcome to Savannah. I'm so glad you're here." He led me to his black convertible, put the top down, and drove me to his house.

I was a little surprised that Peter didn't live in the heart of the city. I had imagined him in a charming, old house overlooking one of the historic squares I had read about. Instead, we arrived at a subdivision on the outskirts of town that looked like any suburb I had ever seen. I don't like suburbs much. Even the fancy ones, like Beth and Jim's gated enclave of manicured lawns and high-columned manors, leave me cold. Peter's neighborhood was far more modest than the Gillians'. At least, I noticed with no small relief, the houses were not identical boxes side by side.

Peter pulled into a cul-de-sac called Stephan Marc Lane.

"Let me guess, a Civil War hero?" I said, pointing to the street sign.

"Not exactly," he said with a laugh. "I think it's the name of the developer who built these houses in the nineteen-fifties."

He parked in the driveway of a dark brown, wood-shingled house. A large magnolia tree, like the one I remembered at Violet's house in Florida, graced the front lawn. He reached across me to unlock the door on my side of the car.

"I'm not trying for an early grab here," he said. "But that lock is tricky sometimes."

I smiled weakly. He jumped out of the car and walked around to my door to offer his hand as I got out. So effortless, his good manners.

Sunshine poured into Peter's living room from a skylight in the cathedral ceiling. Enlarged photographs of mountains, rivers, and city skylines lined the walls. The floors were gleaming strips of oak. Through a large arched doorway was a dining room with a circular glass table and six chairs; beyond it I could see the black and white ceramic tiles of the kitchen floor. Furniture in the living room was spare and dramatic: a black armoire with louvered doors, floor-to-ceiling bookshelves that framed a bay window, two futons—one deep red, one dark purple—near the fireplace, a slab of streaked white marble that served as a coffee table. I could have been standing in a loft in SoHo.

"Peter, it's beautiful!" I said.

"The place was a mess when I bought it. I've been fixing it up for ten years."

I noticed some photos of a young woman on the dining room wall. "That's my daughter, Michelle," he said. "My favorite model. She's in college up north. Come, let me show you my studio. It was the first thing I designed when I bought this house."

He has a grown daughter. And a life I know nothing about. I am hundreds of miles from home, spending the weekend with a stranger. *Have I lost my mind?*

A few feet from the house was a structure that resembled an enclosed gazebo. He held the door open for me and switched on a light. In the middle of the room were two drawing tables covered with cameras and lenses. Against one of the windows, boxes of negatives and film were piled waist-high. At the far end was a door that led to a small darkroom.

"I used to live in the city, in a restored guest cottage. Great neighborhood, but there was no room for anything like this. I was renting studio space, but I needed a studio at home."

"You built this yourself?" I asked.

"Yes. Not that difficult, actually. It's mostly a matter of finding the time."

It was already evening. Peter grilled steaks, which we ate on the back porch. After dinner, we moved indoors to the purple futon, where we sat for hours, sipping wine, exchanging stories about our work, our friends, life in Savannah, life in Manhattan. He didn't say a word about his marriage or about any other women in his life. I didn't mention my string of ex-boyfriends. He never touched me.

Suddenly, I yawned.

"Sorry," I said. "I was up so early this morning." I didn't tell him that anxiety about coming to see him had made it impossible for me to sleep all week.

"You must be tired," he said. "Let's get you to bed."

He hadn't shown me his bedroom earlier, though he had already put my suitcase on a small bench beside his dresser. The room was painted steely gray. Dominating the wall facing the bed was an antique mirror framed by leaded glass in brightly colored geometric shapes.

Peter sat on the bed. "Come here, *Shugah*," he said, holding his arms out to me. "I've wanted to do this ever since I set eyes on you at Violet's house."

Peter talked the whole time he made love to me, narrating each move we made, describing what my body looked like to him, how my touches made him feel. The words he whispered and the expression on his face dissolved every trace of inhibition. It was intoxicating. For all my sexual experience, this was new territory, a new language. I felt happy. I felt safe.

———————

I AWAKENED ON my first morning in Peter's house to the smell of coffee and the sound of dishes rattling in the kitchen.

"Hello?" I called.

"I'll be right there," Peter answered. "I left my old robe for you on the bed."

I looked around the room at the aftermath of our night. Just a sheet covered me. The blankets were in a tangle on the floor at the foot of the bed. On the small night table were the remains of the citrus-scented candle whose glow had cast our flickering shadows on the wall while we made love. Next to it, on its side, was the wine bottle we had emptied.

I slipped Peter's faded blue bathrobe around me, dug my cosmetics case out of my suitcase, and made my way to the bathroom. I thought about showering, but I was reluctant to wash the smell of Peter off my body. I brushed my teeth and splashed water on my face. I ran my fingers through my disheveled hair.

In the bedroom, Peter was on the bed, propped up on his elbow, naked except for a towel wrapped around his waist. Two cups of coffee, a plate of fruit, and a basket of croissants were on a tray in front of him.

"I hope you're hungry," he said.

"I'm starving."

"I can imagine. Well, this should help. I know you have a healthy appetite. Violet told me that your friends are jealous that you can eat anything you want."

"So, you did a background check on me? What else did Violet say?" I asked.

He grinned and leaned forward to kiss me on the cheek. "Enough to know I wanted to invite you here."

"Not fair. I demand the phone number of someone who can give me the lowdown on you."

"I can do better than that. My mother lives on Tybee Island, not far from here. I need to drop off some photos at her house. I know she'd love to meet you."

"You like surprises, don't you? Does she know I'm here? Who will she think I am?"

"I told her a friend from New York was visiting. That satisfied her. We can stop off and say hello to Mom, and then I can show you around town. We don't need to be at the restaurant until nine, which gives us plenty of time for Mom and a walk around Savannah. We probably should get going, though."

I stepped into the shower, letting the warm spray cover me. My arms and thighs ached a little from all the activity in bed. I was leaning over the sink, blow-drying my hair, when from the corner of my eye I saw the bathroom door open. As I lifted my head to the side, there was a sudden flash of light.

"Peter!" I cried. "How could you take a picture now? You could have waited until I finished drying my hair. And until I was wearing something other than your bathrobe."

"For the record," he said, planting a kiss on the back of my neck, "you look lovely wet or dry, and in anything you wear."

I pushed him out of the bathroom. "Let me finish or we'll never get out of here."

"I could think of worse things," he called from the other side of the door.

———

WE FOLLOWED THE highway signs to Tybee Island. "Have you always lived in Savannah?" I asked. Considering the night we had just spent, it felt strange to be asking so elementary a question about Peter's life.

"I was born forty-six years ago in a hospital just a mile up the road," he began, pointing straight ahead. "My mother grew up in Savannah. Her family had been here for generations. Dad was from Texas, but he had distant cousins who lived here. Mom and Dad met at a Lutheran church social one weekend when Dad was in town visiting his family. The story goes that after one dance with Mom—she was a real looker in those days—Dad told his cousin he had just met the woman he was going to marry. And they did marry, just three months later. My sister Agatha was born the next year. I arrived five years later. Mom and Dad were the happiest pair I ever knew. Dad had a heart attack and died three years ago. No warning. Six months later, Agatha died of cancer. Mom has never been the same since that terrible year."

I reached for his hand and squeezed it.

"What else do you want to know?" he asked.

I thought, *I want to know about your marriage, of course. And about every woman who's ever laid claim to your heart.*

But I asked, "Where did you go to college? How did you become a photographer?"

"Mom's brother, my Uncle Jasper, was a camera collector. He had hundreds of strange-looking cameras all over his house. None of his own kids were interested in them, but I was fascinated. He'd tell me tales about them—how the miniature ones were used by spies, how one of them had come from a burlesque theater where they took naughty pictures backstage. One summer when I was in high school, Uncle Jasper taught me how to shoot pictures. It was the only thing besides sports that ever held my attention for more than two minutes when I was a teenager.

"After high school, Uncle Jasper persuaded me to try South Florida College, where a friend of his taught photography. I became the photographer for the campus newspaper, and I managed to earn a degree in photography, with a minor in painting. After college, I got a job with a nature preservation group, kind of like your friend Violet's, but in South Florida. I thought I'd be soaking up the sun in the Keys, shooting pictures of endangered flora and fauna. Instead, I found myself in charge of the fund-raising newsletter, taking headshots of rich people who donated money to the organization.

"Then I entered a photography contest with photos I had taken of manatees playing off the South Florida coast. I won first prize, and someone wrote a story about me that ran in a national magazine, and all kinds of interesting offers came my way. Pretty soon, I was able to leave my regular job and make a living as a nature photographer. That's when I started all the traveling I told you about last night. I was also able to move back to Savannah."

"What happened to Uncle Jasper's camera collection?"

"He left the cameras to Jasper, Jr., his son. Junior, as we call him, has been married and divorced about four times. One of his ex-wives got the cameras when Junior ran out of alimony money."

"How sad for you," I said.

"I just hope those beauties are in the hands of someone who appreciates them. I still have the old Nikon that he taught me to shoot with.

"Well, that brings me to the present. Your turn."

"I was born in Brooklyn, New York, exactly forty years ago tomorrow."

"Oh, is it your birthday?" he asked, feigning surprise.

I grinned. "My parents grew up on the same street. They were high school sweethearts, and they married right after graduation. My dad became a lawyer by going to college and law school at night. It took him twelve years to finish. I hardly saw him when I was a kid. I have a younger brother, Neil, who lives in Phoenix. He's married, two kids, owns a chain of high-priced hotel gift shops. Mom worked for years at Bloomingdale's, in the children's department, which came in handy because she got a discount. We didn't have much money, but we always wore very nice clothes. I went to a public elementary school, the same one my parents had gone to. I even had one of my mom's teachers in the second grade. Everyone in our neighborhood was Jewish or Italian."

"I dated the only Jewish girl in my senior class," said Peter. "Her name was Naomi, and she and her family seemed so exotic to me. We had to stop dating because her mother was always threatening to put her head in the oven if Naomi and I got serious about each other."

"Naomi's mother probably had good reason to be concerned."

"What do you mean? I'm a respectable Southern gentleman."

"So you say."

"Go on," he laughed. "Tell me more about you."

"In high school, I became friends with some girls whose families were rather well off. They introduced me to the idea of going to college away from home. My parents nearly freaked out when I told them what I had in mind. I was the first girl in my family to go to college, and no one ever went away to school. My family was very proud that our relatives were smart enough to get into Brooklyn or City College. 'Jonas Salk went to City College,' my mother said, with lots of hand wringing. 'It's not good enough for you?'"

Peter laughed. "Does your mother have a real New York accent?"

"Oh, yes. And she's always surprised when people guess immediately where she's from. Anyway, I prevailed. I went to the State University at Buffalo, which was as far away as I could get and still pay in-state tuition. It was the best thing I ever did. I met Beth and Sarah there. When we graduated, I stayed on in Buffalo to get a masters degree in education. For a while, I considered moving out west after college. It was the late sixties, after all, and everyone my age thought that California was the center of the cultural universe."

"I remember those days," Peter said. "The Mamas and Papas. California Dreamin'."

"Exactly. When I got my degree, though, there was a shortage of teachers in New York City schools, and I wound up in Manhattan. I love my job, and it's great having summers off. Not to mention the occasional sabbatical, like this year. My dad died right after I graduated from college, so I feel good about living near my mother. She's still in the same apartment in Brooklyn."

We had arrived at Tybee Island, and he was pulling into a parking spot at the marina. "I thought I'd give you a preview of our day on the water tomorrow," he said. About thirty boats were docked at the shore. "Let's take a walk. We can see my boat."

"How long have you known how to sail?"

"My father always kept a sailboat. I've been sailing all my life."

He took my hand, and we walked along, admiring the boats.

"Do you think I could guess which one is yours?" I asked.

"That's her," he said, pointing to a thirty-foot sailboat in front of us. "Named for the love of my life." On the back was painted the name: *Michelle II*.

"Is there a *Michelle I*?" I asked.

"I sold the first *Michelle* and bought this as a present for myself after my first big show at the Telfair Museum. This boat's supposed to sleep six, though it helps if half the sleepers are under the age of twelve. Come, let's go see Mom."

———

EMMA ROBINETTE WAS sitting in a swing on the front

porch of her condo when Peter pulled into the driveway and honked the car horn. Petite, with a knot of wispy silver hair on top of her head, she had the gait and the presence of a woman half her age. She waved and almost ran down the porch steps to greet us as we got out of the car.

"Hi, Darlin'" she sang out. She kissed Peter on the lips. "I'm so glad to see you. You, too, Miriam. How lovely you are, child!"

"So nice to meet you, Mrs. Robinette," I said.

"Oh, please call me Miss Emma, like everyone else does. I understand this is your first trip to Savannah. I'm sure it can't be anything as exciting as New York, but I know Peter is happy to have you visit."

"I'm thrilled to be here. I haven't seen much yet. I did get a look at the *Michelle II*, though."

"Of course, that silly sailboat. It would be like Peter to take you to the marina first thing. Just like his father. Come on inside. I just fixed some sweet tea for y'all."

She led us up the stairs and into her condo. "Did Peter tell you that I had the best time of my life once when I visited New York?"

"When were you there?"

"My late husband and I took a train up to New York City, right to Manhattan, almost twenty-five years ago, for our anniversary. We stayed at the Plaza Hotel and we went to see *Man of La Mancha* in a Broadway the-ay-tah. I still have the dress I wore. We even ate in Chinatown. It was the first time I ever tasted Chinese food. No one could talk me into ridin' on those subway trains, and I've been sorry all these years that I didn't do it. Do you live right there, right in Manhattan?"

"Yes. And I take those subways almost every day. You didn't miss much, trust me."

She handed me a glass of iced tea with a sprig of fresh

mint floating on top. It tasted syrupy and delicious.

"Oh, but you're so lucky to live in such a place," she said. "I regret that I haven't been except that once."

"Whenever you want to come, you just call me," I said. "My apartment is not as grand as the Plaza, but I think you'd be comfortable at my place."

"Aren't you sweet, Miriam! I just may surprise you one day. So what do you children have planned for the weekend?"

"I'm taking Miriam to a birthday dinner tonight, Mom. And tomorrow, we'll go for a sail," said Peter.

"Peter, I hope you'll give Miriam a proper tour of the city," said Emma. "You know, Miriam, all the squares and the parks in Savannah were laid out by James Oglethorpe in the 1700s. My mother was a descendant of one of his cousins. We Southerners are just crazy about family history. Everybody likes to tell about their famous relatives. I hope I'm not boring you."

"It's fascinating," I said. "I can't wait to walk around."

Peter pulled out an envelope from his jacket pocket. "Here are the photos, Mom."

Emma opened the envelope and took out several black and white photos of people dressed in formal attire.

"We had a welcoming party, a formal dinner, if you please, for the new minister of our church last month," Emma explained. "I've given up trying to get Peter to come with me to church, but I managed to persuade him to take pictures at the dinner. I'm so proud to have such a talented son. Thank you, honey," she said, turning to Peter. "I'll give them to Reverend Collins on Sunday."

Emma wanted to know everything about me. She reminded me of Violet's mother, Della, who always made me feel as if there were nothing in the world she'd rather be doing than talking to me. Emma leaned forward in her chair, looked intently into my eyes as she asked one question after another. Wasn't it a challenge teaching in a city school? How did I spend my summers? Did I live near my mother? Did I often go to Broadway *the-ay-tuhs*?

Emma accompanied us to the car to say good-by, slipping her arm through mine as we walked.

"So lovely to meet you, dear. I hope to see you again," she said as she kissed me on the cheek. Peter hugged his mother and we got back into the car.

"What a treasure," I said.

"She's very wise, a good judge of character. She liked you, I could tell."

"You need to bring her to New York some time."

He took his eyes off the road long enough to look at me and wink, mimicking what his mother had said, "I just may surprise you one day."

We spent a most of the afternoon at an outdoor art show at City Market, where Peter introduced me to some of the painters and sculptors he knew who were exhibiting. By late in the day, we had worked our way through cobblestone paths to River Street, sidestepping swarms of tourists descending from mammoth buses. We strolled past souvenir shops, sipping sweet tea from paper cups.

"Nothing like Miss Emma's," I said. "Where's the mint?"

"You've been spoiled," Peter said. "You started with the best."

We passed a store selling nautical gear. "Say," Peter said, "what kind of shoes did you bring to wear on the boat?"

"Sneakers. Will they do?"

He pulled me into the shop. "We need to get you proper sailing gear." He insisted on buying me a pair of green leather deck shoes and a matching windbreaker.

"Green is your color," he said. "With those eyes . . ."

In fact, I had brought a jade green dress to wear to

Elizabeth's. What Peter couldn't have known, and what I didn't know at the time, was that over and again, I would find myself drawn to buying and wearing green. For years to come, when I opened my closet or bureau drawer, I was reconnected with that moment in Savannah. I didn't believe I was consciously choosing to spark those memories. But the past is never where you think you've left it.

We drove back to his house to change for dinner. We faced each other a little self-consciously in his bedroom, slowly removing the clothes we had been in all day. I slid my jeans off and pulled my shirt over my head. He unbuttoned his shirt and I stroked his chest.

"We have a little time," he said. "Let's see if we can work up a good appetite."

As we fell onto the bed, he reached over to the small stereo on the night table and switched on some music, a tape of Ella Fitzgerald singing Cole Porter songs. Peter sang along: *When they begin the beguine/It brings back the sound of music so tender . . .*

"I never thought I'd live to hear Cole Porter with a Southern accent," I said. "But I could get used to it."

We explored each other's bodies in the fading daylight streaming in through the window. After we made love, I slipped into my green dress, feeling contented, peaceful, and happy.

THE HOSTESS AT Elizabeth on 37th was a large woman with a lacquered bouffant hairdo and a bronze complexion that bore the effects of more than six decades of unfiltered sunlight.

"Hi, you sweet thing" she said, kissing Peter on the cheek. "Wherever have you been keepin' yourself?"

"Layla, this is my friend Miriam, from New York."

"Welcome to Elizabeth's, Miriam," she said, guiding

us to a table near a stone fireplace.

"This was built as a mansion for a cotton broker in around 1900," Peter said as we sat down. "The current owners have tried to retain traditional Savannah colors, like the peach and the green you see."

I opened a menu. "I wish I could taste a little of everything they serve."

"From what I heard about your appetite, I figured as much," Peter said. "When I called for reservations, I took the liberty of asking the chef to prepare a sampling of their best dishes for us to share. Hope that's okay with you."

"Okay? It's perfect."

Peter Bruceled at the delight on my face as I tried each distinctive dish: Southern fried grits in red-eye gravy, black-eyed peas and Georgia shrimp, coastal grouper with peanut sauce.

"Ready for dessert?" Peter asked as our waiter cleared away our empty plates.

"Did you take care of ordering that for us, too?"

Peter was looking over my shoulder towards the entrance to the dining room. I turned to see several of the waiters and Layla, the hostess, heading our way. Layla was holding a plate with a slice of pecan pie and a lit candle. When she caught my eye, she began to sing "Happy Birthday." Everyone in the restaurant joined in the singing and applauded when I made a wish and blew out the candle.

"Happy birthday, Miriam," Peter said. "I hope your wish comes true."

In a way, I got my wish. Not a day has passed in the years since I blew out that candle, without my remembering how I sat across from Peter Robinette on my fortieth birthday, at Elizabeth on 37th Street in Savannah, Georgia, certain that I had found the love of my life.

We left Peter's house early the next morning and drove to the marina. I wore my new green deck shoes and windbreaker.

I had never been on a sailboat before. I was nervous that Peter would depend on me to help in some way, to do something I didn't know how to do. As soon as we got on the boat, though, it was apparent that I was in capable hands and Peter wouldn't expect much of me. With one foot on the edge of the sailboat and the other on the pier, Peter helped me step onto the *Michelle II*, and then he handed me the ice chest of sandwiches and drinks we had packed. He began to work at loosening the knots in the ropes that held the boat to shore.

"It looks like it rained last night. Those ropes are going to be hard to untie," I said, as I watched him tug on them.

"If you're going to be my first mate, you'll have to learn proper sailing language. These are lines, not ropes."

"And what exactly are the duties of the first mate?" I asked warily.

The lines were free, and Peter hopped onto the sailboat. He lifted my chin to look at me.

"Just to keep the captain happy," he said.

I moved around the deck awkwardly at first, but after a while I grew accustomed to the boat's sway. We sailed south for hours, past destinations with romantic, prophetic names: Thunderbolt; Isle of Hope. Peter dropped anchor when we reached a quiet inlet. I lay back, knees up, on one of the cushioned seats on the deck, and he sat down and pulled my legs across his lap.

"Does your daughter know how to sail?" I asked.

"Of course. She comes for a month every summer, and we spend most of our time on the water."

"And her mother? Was she a good first mate?"

"Hardly. I should have known better than to marry a woman who was afraid of the water."

"How long were you married?"

"Almost five years."

"How did you meet?"

"Joan's mother has a winter house in Palm Beach. She was on the board of that preservation group I told you about, the one I worked for after college. She introduced me to Joan."

"What is Joan like?"

"Joan grew up in Connecticut, never wanting for anything. I've never cared about being rich, which didn't sit well with Joan or her family. When Michelle was born, the differences between Joan and me became clearer than ever. I dreamed about teaching Michelle to sail and taking her camping with me when I went on nature shoots. Joan and her mother were talking about cotillions and boarding schools. Michelle was still a baby when we got divorced. Joan moved back home right away."

"And Michelle? Is she more like her mother or her father?"

"A little of both. She's twenty now, and she's studying painting at college, which I guess makes her somewhat like me. When we're together, we talk about art and photography and sailing. When she's with her mother, I don't know what goes on. Joan is probably sizing up eligible young men from suitable Darien and Westport families for Michelle to marry.

"Say," he said, moving my legs off his knees, "you haven't had a complete tour of my boat. Why don't we go below for a while?"

We descended to the cramped cabin. Most of the space was taken up with sailing gear and tools. There was hardly room for us to stand.

"How do you sleep here?" I asked.

"I haven't slept on the boat for a while. Give me a few minutes and you won't recognize this place."

In short order, Peter rearranged the gear and expertly reconfigured some of the built-ins, and soon there was a double-sized mattress on a platform in front of us. He pulled me down on it and tore at my clothes. I lay down on my back, and Peter straddled me with his knees, gently massaging my breasts and shoulders.

"Tell me what you're thinking," he said softly. "What can I do for you?"

I told him exactly what to do. I found words for fantasies that had long been only fragmentary images in my mind. *I want to let go completely.* As I talked, he reached for some ropes—lines?—that were hanging nearby. He tied my hands loosely over my head, attaching the lines to a hook on the wall behind me. For what seemed like hours, his hands and mouth slowly, scrupulously, attended to every inch of my body until, at last, he climbed on top of me. He untied my hands so I could reach around him and pull him closer, and as soon as he entered me, we came together in noisy, heaving gasps.

———

"REMIND ME, WHAT time is your flight tomorrow?" Peter said.

"Noon. I can't believe how quickly the weekend passed."

"We'll find some way to see each other soon. I haven't been to New York in years. I'll come visit you."

"Remember my friend Beth? She and her husband have been hosting a fall party for the past few years, usually in October. That's only about a month from now. Will you come up for it?"

"Let me know when it is. Don't worry, we'll make other plans if need be."

I kissed him, hard, on the mouth. "I've made my plans. I'm planning on having you with me at the party."

Part I: Miriam

I called both Sarah and Beth as soon as I got home. We have confided our most intimate moments for as long as we've known each other. When we were younger, especially when we lived together in college, no detail of our romantic and sexual adventures was off limits. We felt entitled to know everything about each other's boyfriends—their sexual talents and techniques, their fantasies, their inhibitions. Over the years, though, the tenor of our discussions about men has changed. Beth, who in college had regaled us with hilarious tales about the limited sexual repertoire of her boyfriend, "the most repressed psychology major on earth," stopped talking about her sex life when she married Jim. Sarah, well known in our dorm for her comprehensive lecture on the fine points of fellatio, has never told me about the role that sex played in her divorce, or how things are in bed with Kevin. Still, I knew I could say anything to them.

"I'm crazy in love with this guy," I said. "I know the geography is impossible, but I've never felt this way before. You need to help me believe this is real, give me hope that it can work."

They both said I had never sounded happier. And they couldn't be happier for me.

PETER CAME NORTH in October, four days before Beth and Jim's party. At Peter's request, I guided him to some of my favorite Manhattan spots. We took a tour of the MOMA and spent an evening listening to Bobby Short sing at the Carlyle. Over drinks at the Plaza, we toasted the memory of his parents' visit to Manhattan. We walked the streets of the West Village, stopping for paella at the Sevilla and cannoli at Ferrara's. We strolled through Central Park, sauntered down Fifth Avenue, rode to the top of the Empire State Building.

"Makes me think of *An Affair to Remember*," I said.

"I guess I should be glad I don't remind you of King Kong," he laughed.

And after each sightseeing foray, we raced back to my apartment and made love. The night of the party, we took the train to Connecticut. At the Gillians' house, their children, Adam and Nicole, greeted us at the front door.

"Hi, Aunt Miriam," Nicole said. "You look so pretty."

I introduced Peter to them.

"Nice to meet you both," Peter said. "You know, I've never been to Connecticut before."

"Where are you from?" Adam asked. "You have an accent, sort of."

"Funny, I was going to say the same thing about you," Peter said. Adam and Nicole giggled.

I looked around the living room for Violet and Sarah. Violet had just started dating Grant, and she had brought him with her from Florida. Sarah had come alone. I spotted the three of them at the bar that had been set up near the grand piano.

"How are the multi-state commutes going?" Violet asked us.

"She's exhausting me," said Peter. "I'm just a country boy. This big-city pace is too much. I can barely keep up with her."

"Don't let him kid you," I said. "He's got more energy than anyone I've ever met."

Beth and Jim were working the room, greeting guests and leading them to food and drinks.

"Everything under control here?" Beth asked as she and Jim approached us.

"More or less," said Sarah. "These two," she pointed at Peter and me, "may need some supervision, though."

"Oh, good," Jim said. "Will you guys do something shocking to liven things up? Take off your clothes and jump into the pool, perhaps?"

I closed my eyes for a moment, imagining about how it would feel to swim naked with Peter in the Gillians' pool.

"Your house is so unusual," Peter said to Jim. "Did you design it yourself?"

"Yes, with help from my college roommate, who's now an architect," Jim said. "Harold designed the original house and all the renovations we've made over the years."

"Gee, I wish I had a college roommate who did something useful," said Sarah. "Mine have chosen the so-called helping professions. Teacher and shrink. And me a writer. Why didn't any of us do something practical with our lives? Plumber, maybe? Divorce lawyer! Now, that would be a great roommate to have!"

"I handle some divorce in my practice," said Grant. "I'm not sure I'm such a good roommate, though."

"No comment," Violet said, winking at him.

We started toward the buffet table. Beth pulled me aside.

"How's it going?" she whispered. "I'd almost forgotten how handsome Peter is."

"Everything is great," I said. "Except he leaves tomorrow."

"Don't think about it now. Enjoy the night."

Peter and I filled our plates and found a quiet table in a corner of the living room. Violet and Grant joined us, and then Sarah made her way to the table, bringing with her a couple who introduced themselves as Mark and Ellen, "country club friends" of the Gillians.

"Our hosts have requested that we do something scandalous and memorable tonight," I said to them. "Do you have any suggestions? We're not from Connecticut, so we don't know what would shock you."

"Let's see," said Mark. "You'll have to go a long way

to beat the scene at the Laurel Falls Club a few weeks ago. In front of about a hundred people in the lounge one night, this guy we know, in his fifties, jumped on the bar, got down on one knee, and loudly proposed marriage to his twenty-three-year-old girlfriend who was sitting on a stool in front of him. All eyes, of course, turned to her. She said, 'Uh, no. I don't think so.' Just like that. Then she marched out. They haven't spoken since, from what I understand. Sure was memorable."

"I'll bet we can do better," Sarah said. "Come on, folks, let's be creative."

"How about this," Peter said. He turned to me. "Miriam, I'd like to invite you to Savannah."

"I've already been to Savannah," I said. "Nothing shocking about that."

"I thought we should try being together for a lot longer than a weekend," he said.

No one said anything for a few moments, and then Sarah broke the silence.

"You win, Peter," she said. "Memorable and, if you look at Miriam's face you'll agree, shocking as well."

"Miriam is not shocked," I said carefully, as if I were talking about someone else, a character in a movie. "But Miriam lives in New York, and Miriam has a job . . ."

"Miriam is on sabbatical, remember?" said Peter.

Mark and Ellen exchanged looks that told me my current life would soon be the topic of discussion at the Laurel Falls Club. Sarah and Violet were watching me expectantly.

"You know," I finally said, "this is the best offer I've had all day."

I don't recall any more about the party. I remember Peter and me on the train back to Manhattan, then lying together in my bed. I curled up in his arms, feeling the easy rhythm of his heartbeat. How could he sleep?

My mind was darting wildly between cosmic thoughts about how the rest of my life would go (Does he love me? Does this mean he wants to get married?) to ridiculous, mundane details of preparing a move to Savannah (Should I sublet my apartment? Will I need my winter coat?).

I got out of bed at sunrise and sat at my kitchen table. I heard the newspaper being delivered at the door. Would I be able to have the *New York Times* delivered to my door in Savannah? I was on my third cup of coffee when Peter appeared in the kitchen.

"You look like a woman with a lot on your mind," he said.

"I've been up all night, trying to decide what to say to you."

"Don't say anything now. Take this week to think. We could have some fun, you know, if you'll say yes."

"How did you know I wouldn't just turn you down flat last night? Or walk out? After the story about that poor guy hopping on the bar at the country club . . ."

"That man didn't know his woman very well. I wouldn't have asked if I thought there was a prayer of your walking out on the spot. Of course, I was secretly hoping you'd say yes right then."

"Just give me a little time. Listen, you'd better get dressed. You don't want to miss your flight."

"I understand I missed the highlight of my own party," Beth said on the phone.

"You wanted something memorable? Your friends Mark and Ellen will be talking about the evening for some time to come."

"Tell me everything. I want to hear it from you."

"He wants us to try living together. It's all so crazy

69

right now, I can't think straight. I love him, Beth, but he hasn't said he loves me."

"You know how men are. Maybe he thinks that he's showing you he loves you by how he behaves."

"I can't just walk away from this, but I need something more from him before I give up my life here. I can't go without some kind of commitment."

"You don't have to give up your life. Why don't you go to Savannah with the idea that this is a rehearsal? Give yourself through, say, New Year's, to see how it works. What do you have to lose?"

"On one hand, it seems so right, but maybe I'm just letting great sex—and I do mean great sex—and the romance of it all guide me, but . . ."

Beth laughed. "You are seeing yourself as a character in a movie, the romantic movie you've wanted to star in all your life. Look, if it turns out that there's nothing lasting here, you'll know by New Year's. I don't want to encourage you to do something dangerous, but I think you'll regret it if you don't give this a try."

"I feel like I'm jumping off a cliff."

"Of course, you must. But we'll all be here to catch you if need be. Don't you think it's incredible that you happen to be on your sabbatical right now and you're free to go? Maybe it's a sign from the heavens that this was meant to be."

"How comforting. The New York City public school gods are smiling on my love life."

I packed a few cartons of my things and shipped them to Peter's house. I left my ficus tree and the contents of my freezer with Thomas and Wayne next door. I filled out the Post Office form for forwarding my mail to Savannah, hesitating when I had to indicate if this change of address was "temporary" or "permanent." I checked "temporary," and on the line that said, "Until what date?" I wrote

Part I: Miriam

January 1, which was exactly two months away.

It's funny how memory works, how some events are preserved forever in your mind, while others dissolve. Physical pain, for example, is an experience that can be remembered only second-hand. You'll pass out before agony devours you. The same is true of emotional trauma. Mother Nature eliminates the stinging sensations from your memory bank. You can talk about having been hurt, but you can't re-create the pain. Selective memory protects you, doctors say.

On the other hand, I remember almost every student I've taught. More than twenty years of young faces, smiling or sullen, and I can put a name to most of them. But much of the time I spent in Savannah, desperately hopeful and in love, is a blur of shapes and sounds that stubbornly remain out of my mind's reach. Like a narrator in my own life, I can recount a version of tender and happy moments with Peter, but I can't re-create the exact feelings. Like a patient who recovers from a gunshot wound, I can talk about how I felt when the pain relented a little. The details are mostly lost, the fine print barely legible. Yet a pervasive sorrow and jagged feelings, like shards of glass, still linger in my heart. What does that say about Mother Nature? And more, what does it say about me? Selective memory, I should like to tell the doctors, is sometimes not selective enough.

Peter and I settled quickly into a comfortable routine living together in Savannah. He spent most mornings in his studio or at the college. I read, rented movies, took his car for drives into town to learn my way around. Some days, his talkative neighbor Winnie stopped by for a visit, often bringing samples of her baking. Once a week, Miss Emma had us to lunch. Peter took me sailing every weekend. I met his colleagues and friends. With rare exception, though, I can no longer distinguish one day from another.

I do remember the first time Peter told me he loved me. It was the only time he ever said so during a moment when we weren't actually making love. We were on his sailboat, watching a glorious sunset. He stood behind me with his hands around my waist. "I love you, Miriam," he murmured. I turned around to see his face, but he was looking straight ahead, focused on the deepening purple sky.

A few weeks after I arrived in Savannah, Peter had to leave town for an assignment in Montana. He said he'd be gone for five days.

"I'd invite you along, but I don't think the accommodations will be too comfortable," he said. "Do you mind being here alone?"

"I'll be pining away for you the whole time! I'll just read some trashy novels, get my nails done, and dream up something enticing for when you return."

"Mmmm. Best cure for jet lag I can think of."

ONE MORNING WHILE Peter was away, Winnie rapped at the back door.

"Right from the oven," she said, handing me a warm covered plate. "You should eat these before they get cold."

Winnie joined me at the glass table in the dining room.

"I'm putting together a weekend package to the Keys," Winnie said. She was a semi-retired travel agent who worked from an office in her house. "Peter loves Key West. You should talk him into signing both of you up."

"Winnie, these are delicious," I said, biting into one of her buttermilk biscuits. "When is the trip?"

"In early February. But knowing Peter, he'll wait until the last minute. I've booked most of his travel for years, and he drives me crazy. Because of him, I've become Savannah's expert on getting last-minute reservations."

"Peter does like to be spontaneous."

"My late husband Bert was a psychologist. He once called Peter an excitement junkie. Peter took it as a compliment, but I'm not sure it was meant as one. When Peter delays making plans for his trips, I think about what my Bert said about him: it's as if he can't commit to anything because something more exciting could turn up."

Winnie must have seen the dark look on my face.

"Oh, Honey, don't take this wrong. I love Peter. And I'm sure you will be happy together. I can see the way he looks at you. Was there ever a more romantic man?"

When Winnie left, I grabbed the keys to Peter's car and drove myself to a nearby mall. I bought a lavender lace teddy and some new perfume. *That should take care of his jet lag.*

I rented a copy of *It's a Wonderful Life* and watched it that night, alone in Peter's bed. I replayed, again and again, the scene when Jimmy Stewart and Donna Reed fall in love as they share a phone receiver. The look on Jimmy Stewart's face as he catches the scent of her hair filled me with longing for something indescribable that I knew was missing from my life.

"Michelle will be here for the holidays," Peter said when he returned. He had spoken to his daughter on the phone. "She's flying in on Christmas day."

Christmas, I thought, then New Year's. So soon. January first, the date that I had told the U.S. Postal Service would be the last day of my temporary change of address.

"Something wrong?" he asked.

I realized I was frowning. "Not about Michelle's coming. I'm dying to meet her. It's just that talking about the holidays reminds me that time is passing, and I need to decide . . ."

"Aren't you happy here?"

"I'm happy with you, Peter. But it all still feels like a fairy tale. I haven't given any thought to making a real life here. I don't even know if I can. We haven't talked about the future, and I can't give up the life I have in New York without knowing more about . . ."

I started to cry. Peter put his arms around me and pulled me close.

"What's wrong with a fairy tale?" He paused. "Look, let's make an agreement that we'll put off talking about this until the weekend before Christmas. We can just look forward to Michelle's visit and enjoy all the Christmas parties we'll go to this month. Let's not spoil our fun. Promise me?"

I promised.

It felt odd to be spending the holidays in a place where no one even mentioned Chanukah. For the first time since I had come to Savannah, I missed New York. I longed for a look at Lord & Taylor's Christmas windows, the giant menorah at the synagogue on Park Avenue, the ice-skaters in Central Park.

How many holiday parties did I go to in Savannah? Whom did I meet? What did I wear? Selective memory again. I remember only one December event clearly, the small dinner party we went to at his friends Travis and Betsy's house on the Saturday before Christmas. I had pushed to the back of my mind the nagging thought that before the weekend ended, Peter and I were going to discuss what would happen after New Year's.

"Travis is about five years older than I am," Peter told

me as we made the short drive to the party. "He went to school with my sister. He was married for about ten years, and then his wife left him for a woman. It took him a long time to recover, as you can imagine. But then, just a few years ago, he and Betsy got together."

"Who else will be there?"

"Their neighbors, Louanne and Peyton . . ." Peter began.

"Love those Southern names."

"Well, not all of us are as lucky as you, to be named for Old Testament heroines," Peter laughed. "Louanne and Peyton are retired, getting ready to move out West, I think. You'll be the youngest person at the table tonight. And, of course, the most beautiful."

The evening at Travis and Betsy's began with a tour of their antebellum house. Near the front door was a glass case that displayed Betsy's collection of Civil War photographs. Portraits of their ancestors lined the walls leading up the stairway to the second floor. Some of the ornaments on their Christmas tree, Travis explained, had been in his family for more than a hundred years. Betsy's great-grandfather had hand-carved the massive dining room table and ten matching chairs.

Talk at dinner centered on pensions and retirement. The topic seemed remote to me. Though I faithfully contributed to my retirement plan at school, I had never given much thought to how I wanted to live when I stopped working.

"It's hard to believe this will be our last Christmas in Savannah," Peyton said. "But ever since our son and daughter-in-law moved to Arizona, we've sort of known we'd head west eventually. I think Louanne started packing the day our grandson was born out there."

"We'll just stay in town when we stop working," said Travis. "I can't imagine living anywhere else. And we have the condo in Hilton Head to use on weekends. Now that I've got Betsy hooked on golf . . ."

Travis turned to Peter. "And you, sir? Will you just sail off to exciting ports?"

Peter talked about an artists' retirement colony in Mexico that he had visited years earlier. "There's a marina right on the property, so I could keep my sailboat, assuming my health stays good enough so I can still hoist the sails. Of course, I'd have to submit a portfolio of my work to get accepted. If I absolutely have to grow old, this is the spot . . ."

Peter had actually told me about the place once before. He had shown me pictures of the colony. And sitting at Betsy's heirloom table, with his friends smiling and listening intently, Peter probably used the same language as he talked again about the pristine beaches on the Gulf of Mexico, the charming white stucco cottages, and the list of accomplished artists in residence. But when he described it this time, I caught something that I had missed before.

There wasn't a single "we" in his story. "*My* sailboat . . . *my* health . . . *my* retirement . . ." And suddenly I saw what should have been visible all along: Peter, so expert at grand romance and heart-stopping passion, was incapable of, or just plain bored by, whatever it is that holds couples together over time. He was happy to have me at his side for as long as I wanted to stay, and as long as a romantic whirlwind engulfed us. But he couldn't bring himself to ask me to stay for good. He couldn't risk commitment to anything without a guarantee that the heady feelings would last. Which they never can. Winnie's husband had it right: an excitement junkie.

I also recalled a French word I had learned from Sarah: *lagniappe*, meaning a bonus, a pleasant surprise. It was the perfect word to describe how Peter saw me: extra, unexpected, a gift. Which is not the same thing at all as a partner for life.

When we got back to Peter's house, I asked him to stay with me in the living room. He knew at once that something was wrong. We usually headed straight to bed as soon as we returned from a long evening out. This was a conversation I wanted to have sitting upright, fully clothed.

"I can't do this anymore," I said.

"What is it?" he asked, but in a way that told me he already knew what I was going to say.

"I feel as if the role I can play in your life was set before you met me. I'm forty years old, Peter. Do you think I'll stay here for ten years and then wave from the shore as you sail off to Mexico? You haven't said you want me with you. It hasn't occurred to you to ask if I even like Mexico."

"I just don't think in terms of marriage anymore. I'm sorry if that disappoints you."

"You're missing the point, Peter. It's not necessarily marriage I want. I want you to think about me automatically when you make important plans for your future."

I thought I saw his eyes get teary.

"I'm sorry, Miriam. I never meant to deceive you."

"You didn't deceive me, Peter. You told me exactly who you were, in a thousand ways. I just wasn't listening."

I ASKED WINNIE to find me a seat on a flight back to New York.

"I'm sorry you're leaving, dear," she said. "Don't worry, I'm the last-minute specialist, remember?"

Winnie came through with a plane ticket for Christmas morning. Over the next days, I packed all my things in the same boxes I had used when I first came to Savannah. Peter had carefully saved them in the garage. I left hanging on the bedroom wall the enlarged photo of me in my green dress, the one he had taken the night of my birthday.

Peter made himself scarce at the house while I packed to leave, claiming he had Christmas shopping to do. It was probably true. Last minute for everything.

I called Miss Emma to say goodbye. "Your invitation to New York still stands," I told her.

"I do hope I see you again, Miriam. Please keep in touch with me. My son doesn't have much sense sometimes, but that doesn't mean you and I can't be friends."

On the morning I left Savannah, I put Peter's Christmas present—a new bathrobe—under his tree, along with a scarf I had bought for his mother.

I refused his offer to drive me to the airport.

"You'll have a long wait at the airport for Michelle's flight. She won't be in until this afternoon. I'll just call a taxi."

When my ride arrived, we stood in the doorway and watched the driver put my suitcases in the trunk of the car. Peter reached in his pocket and pulled out a small, flat package loosely covered with several sheets of red and green tissue paper.

"I didn't have time to wrap it properly," he said. "I hope you'll forgive me."

Inside the tissue paper was a delicate ceramic tile, intricately painted with a scene of a familiar Savannah street corner. A tiny sign on one of the buildings said "Elizabeth on 37th."

"I know the artist who makes these," he said. "He did this one especially for me to give to you. We had some fun that night, didn't we?"

"Yes, Peter," I said. "We had some fun."

I held Peter's present in my lap for the whole ride to the airport. I don't recall anything about the flight home, or landing at LaGuardia, which must have been frenzied with holiday travelers. I do remember high snowdrifts on the sidewalks and the first biting breath of winter air as I stepped outside the terminal. And I know I was back in the city for the last few days of Chanukah and in time to see the tree at Rockefeller Center and the shop windows on Fifth Avenue, still decorated for the holidays.

BETH:
SLEIGHT-OF-MIND

"Yesterday,
All my troubles seemed so far away
Now it looks as though they're here to stay."
—Paul McCartney

INSOMNIA IS A WAY of life for me lately, a perverse menopausal dividend. I'm awake before sunrise every day. No hope of falling back to sleep. I don't even try anymore. I lie still in my bed, tuning out the soft rattle of my husband's breathing, ignoring the impending daylight trickling in through window shutters.

A familiar mental ritual fills the minutes between this premature awakening and the rest of my day. I traipse through my memories like a tourist without a roadmap, lingering in neighborhoods that appear safe, avoiding war zones. Trying to fathom how I got here.

Despite my training as an analyst, I give my childhood short shrift in these pre-dawn exercises. I'm sure that what I'm after is linked to grownup things. Psychoanalysis shed light on my life's beginnings. It's my adulthood that remains in shadow.

My thoughts travel easily to the early days with Jim,

before we were married, when he was in graduate school at Cornell. We lived on Prospect Street in Ithaca for two years, in a crummy, furnished apartment where there was never enough heat and the roof leaked. We had a two-burner stove and a copy of *Macrobiotic Kitchen Magic* from which we concocted endless and largely tasteless variations on overcooked vegetables and brown rice. We had to sell Jim's books at the end of each semester to afford groceries.

Thirty years ago. Before our two children were born. Before I was a therapist. Before we were voted Laurel Falls Citizens of the Year. Before we were on a first-name basis with our mayor, two Senators, and an army of lawyers and financial wizards who help us manage the fortune Jim has earned. Before Jim's company bought the apartment for him in Lower Manhattan so that he can catch a nap and return to his office for the opening of the London and Tokyo markets.

Before our son Adam died.

Once my mind travels to Adam, scenes from his life unfold before me like a film in slow motion that I can't help but watch to the end.

He's four years old, pleading to delay bedtime for one more reading of *Alexander and the Terrible, Horrible, No Good, Very Bad Day.*

He's seven, dressed for soccer practice in the uniform that is two sizes too large, calling to me from the garage, "Hurry, Mom! Coach doesn't like it when we're late!"

He's eleven, laughing at one of his own silly jokes, with a grin that reveals neon orange rubber bands coiled around his braces.

He's fifteen, sitting on the old blue sofa in the family room, holding hands with his first girlfriend, Sheila, and watching his favorite movie, *ET*, for the hundredth time.

He's nineteen, a freshman at college, and he's calling

to say his roommate is too weird, college is too hard, he's coming home for the weekend. The conversation that was the beginning of the end of his life.

He's twenty-two, and he and Jim and I are sitting together in a therapy session with several other families. It's Adam's fourth stay at his fourth drug rehab center in two years. He is too thin and his affect is blunted from medication. With robotic delivery, he tells the group that he is ready to move beyond addiction to recovery. I want to believe him.

He's twenty-three. It's his birthday and he's opening presents. He thanks Jim and me for the leather jacket, his sister Nicole for the Beatles CD, his grandmother for the bicycle helmet.

He's twenty-three and five days, and a funeral director is suggesting that, in light of the circumstances of Adam's death, the casket would be better left closed at the service.

Three years have passed since Jim and I buried our son. Jim doesn't talk on his own about Adam. If someone else mentions Adam's name, Jim clenches his jaw and responds in few words. Our daughter Nicole now says she's thinking about becoming a drug counselor when she graduates from college, but I'm not sure how much of that is real, how much is Adam. Hearing her talk about it makes me frantic. Will any of us—Jim, Nicole, me—ever be all right again?

After Adam died, I took six months off from my psychotherapy practice. I couldn't imagine guiding patients through their twisted lives without my own feelings getting in the way.

I dealt with my grief in frequent counseling sessions with Dr. Dominick Moros, who had supervised me in my analytic training and is the best therapist I know. Dr. Moros (we have become colleagues, but I cannot bring myself to call him by his first name) respected my refusal to take antidepressants. I needed to talk, talk, talk my way through heartache; I didn't want my mood chemically elevated. He helped me to put my lingering guilt in perspective and to focus on the people in my life who loved me and depended on me to love them.

Throughout those terrible months, Sarah and Miriam put their own lives on hold, spending every possible minute with me in Connecticut. Jim's way was to grieve in solitude, but I needed my friends. Sarah was between jobs; instead of looking for work, she took the train up from the city every Monday morning and stayed until Friday, when Miriam took over for the weekend. They let me talk, sleep, rage, be silent as I needed to.

Eventually, I pieced myself together well enough so that I now present to the world an uncanny, lifelike replica of my old self. I wake up every morning. I shower, I dress. I see friends. I laugh. I treat patients. I volunteer at the museum. I give thoughtful advice to my daughter. I make love with my husband. Time, the sages say, is a great healer.

Ah, but I have fooled the sages. Time brings no relief. I have outlived my first-born. Nothing, nothing, *nothing* can be the same for me since Adam left this life.

MY FIRST APPOINTMENT of the day is a new patient. Madeline Foster, a middle-aged woman. My age, in fact. A woman with a good job and a nice family and close friends, who says that most mornings it's an effort for her to get out of bed.

Madeline describes herself as someone who has always done what was expected of her. Women like Madeline and me, we were taught to follow the rules. There was a time when we may have talked defiantly, flirted with the bohemian, but ultimately, we wound up rebelling only against our own longings. Madeline says she thought that being a grownup meant she had to trade excitement for security. We all thought like that.

Madeline and I are alike in one fundamental way, members of the first generation of women to feel entitled to interesting lives. And so, as disappointments accrue and our spirits fail, we take high-powered jobs and gourmet cooking classes and, only as a last resort, lovers. We raise funds to fight breast cancer and save endangered animals and put more books on school library shelves. We indulge in New Age rites to get in touch with our spirituality. We enter therapy (or become therapists) to get in touch with our emotions. We have devoted ourselves to meeting the needs of husbands and children, yet we speculate from time to time about what life might have held in store had we married different men, or not had children, or not married at all.

In the middle of our lives, we wonder if it is too late to renew ourselves. We wonder why we are sad so much of the time.

Following the rules, we've discovered, is painful and costly.

Madeline says she has become invisible to her husband. He works eighty hours a week. When he's home, he reads or sleeps. The last time they made love was on a vacation in Bermuda, almost two years ago. They have two sons, teenagers Madeline describes as "a handful, you know, like all kids these days." Madeline is a legal secretary, having sacrificed a promising career years ago as a creative director at Saatchi & Saatchi.

"Why did you leave advertising?" I ask.

"Bill was away so much on business. I couldn't keep a job where I had to work long hours or where they asked me to travel. One of us had to be available for the children. Becoming a legal secretary made things convenient.

For everyone."

"Do you like the work?"

"I'm pretty good at my job, so my bosses always say nice things about me.

"Why do you think you're depressed?"

"I know the signs. I've read a lot about it, and some of my friends have told me I seem quieter than usual."

"Quieter?"

"Subdued, really. I'm usually a talker, at least with people I know, but I don't feel like saying much these days."

"Why do you think that is?"

"I don't have anything interesting to say. I feel old and tired and boring. Boring!"

At this, she begins to sniffle. I hand her a box of Kleenex.

"Dr. Gillian," she says, "can you give me some medication? I know you're not a medical doctor, but I think I should be on Prozac or something."

"Let's hold off on that for now, Madeline. I can have you evaluated at some point by a psychiatrist who will prescribe something for you if needed. But I'd like us to talk some more first." I see the familiar flicker of disappointment in her eyes. I know what that look means: She was hoping for a shortcut to happiness.

She's probably ventured into one of the dozens of Internet chatrooms devoted to depression for a dose of "reliable" medical updates and testimonials from the Prozac/Paxil/Zoloft-faithful.

I've spent time in the chatrooms myself, of course, to get a handle on the research my patients tell me they conduct. I've read the comfortably anonymous exchanges of information and advice. I'm convinced that drug companies and health plans pay shills to proselytize in cyberspace.

"Don't waste your time talking to some shrink who just takes your money week after week. Get on the fast track," writes BlueNoMoreinOhio in the blackcloud.com chatroom. I've seen the online newsletters, touting the advantages of "pharmacological intervention" (meaning, antidepressants, which are relatively cheap) over "long-term counseling" (the kind I do, which the health plans find too expensive). I'm lucky that I have a practice in a place like Laurel Falls, where most people can afford psychotherapy without worrying about being reimbursed by their insurance companies.

No use in my trying to balance Madeline's ideas with talk of the side effects of antidepressants. She's so tired of being sad, she'd willingly tolerate a little drowsiness, diminished sex drive, anesthetized feelings—for just a quick jolt of happiness. She wants the fast track.

"See you next time, Dr. Gillian," she says, with only the faintest dismay in her voice. Women like us, we do as we're told.

I end office hours early so I can drive to New Haven. Dr. Moros has asked me to present a case study to one of his classes for first-year students.

The small lecture hall is already full when I arrive. Dr. Moros greets me with a warm hug. I take a seat at the desk behind him on the stage and listen to his introductory remarks on today's topic: "Finding the Main Idea in the Depressed Patient's Psychosocial History." I scan the faces in the room as he speaks. They're so young, these therapists-to-be.

"Your challenge," he begins, "is to figure out from what your patients tell you about themselves whether they are experiencing a situational depression or something more pervasive."

On the blackboard, Dr. Moros writes: "Text and Subtext."

"The text is what the patient tells you about his or her life," he says. "The subtext is the deeper psychosocial picture—childhood, family, work, medical history, previous emotional bouts. The patient may present with an isolated, seemingly anomalous episode—a phobic reaction, a panic attack, some other sudden behavioral change that has brought on a depressive state, or, in fact, is itself activated by an undiagnosed, low-level depression. Maybe an overwhelming event—death, divorce, family crisis—has engendered neurotic symptoms. The patient may be functional in most ways—able to work, take care of children, et cetera. The text, that's merely the beginning of the story. 'I'm fine,' the patient says, 'except for the occasional migraine I get whenever my mother calls.'"

The students laugh at this. Dr. Moros doesn't smile, waits for the laughter to subside.

"Or, the text is, 'My dog died and I can't stop crying,' and then you find out that Fido's death isn't the issue at all, that it's a repressed childhood trauma or kinky sex dreams that have brought on anxiety or depression. Fido may turn out to be just the trigger. The therapist must then go in search of the subtext: the main idea, the patterns of behavior, the recurring themes, the fantasies. Many people miss the main idea of their own lives—dependence, loss, shame, disappointment, fear, work, friendship. And, of course, love in all its forms. Love! The big main idea of most people's lives. And the most complicated."

He introduces me as a gifted therapist, says it's an honor to have me present one of my cases to the class, etc. He jokes that I am a survivor, a former student of his. I begin my presentation on Angela, a forty-year-old woman, a stay-at-home wife and mother (we don't say housewife anymore), in a marriage she characterizes as "having the usual ups and downs."

PART I: BETH

Angela was referred to me by her internist because she had begun to have panic attacks in public places. Her nineteen-year-old daughter was about to be married. Angela had been married at about the same age. In the months before she came to me, Angela had grown increasingly agoraphobic, paralyzed at the thought of going to movie theaters, grocery stores, and, especially, shopping malls. This meant she had not been able to shop for a dress or do much else to prepare for her daughter's wedding. And Angela was petrified at the thought of walking down the aisle in the church. All of this I learn from what she tells me—her text.

I ask the class: Where do you begin to find the recurring themes? The subtext? Why panic attacks, and not some other behavior? None of the students' responses goes in the right direction—to Angela's conflicted feelings about her own early marriage, which she has transferred to her daughter. A pattern, a theme. Maybe the main idea of her life.

I review Angela's three months of treatment, how she came to realize that she was depressed. I point out her neurotic identification with her daughter. I suggest that she somaticized her anger and disappointment at her own life into panic attacks, whose physical symptoms gave her permission to avoid participating in her daughter's wedding. The people in Angela's life were more likely to be sympathetic to episodes of shortness of breath and heart palpitations than to vague, depressive complaints.

I ask if the class has any questions.

"Did she go to the wedding?" asks a budding therapist in the first row. "Did she get over the attacks?"

I knew Angela wasn't going to be a quick fix, I say. We worked out a plan with her family and her priest for Angela to be seated in a front pew of the church before the wedding ceremony began, so she wouldn't have to walk down the aisle. Her internist prescribed Ativan to get her through the day. Angela continued to see me for several months. The panic attacks subsided. And then, as our sessions increasingly focused on the problems in her marriage, she stopped coming to therapy. This happens sometimes when you get too close. Some people discover that the main idea of their lives is something they don't want to face. Examining the subtext seems risky, or uncomfortable, or just too much work.

The young student looks crushed.

I lean forward from the lectern. "Nothing is perfect," I tell him.

IT'S RAINING HARD as I leave the building. I have no umbrella. I pull my blazer up to cover my head, and I run to my car. I turn on the car radio to catch the weather and traffic report. It's a quick-moving storm, says the chipper voice. Should be out of the area in the next half hour. I decide to stay where I am until the storm passes. I leave the ignition key turned so I can listen to the radio without running the engine. I can almost hear Jim's impatient rebuke: You'll kill the battery, Beth.

The oldies station is paying tribute to "sixties chicks." The DJ promises Janis Joplin, Joni Mitchell, Mary Wells. "Up first, Linda Ronstadt and the Stone Ponies. Make sure your mom is tuning in," the DJ yells. "I'll bet she remembers where she was the first time she heard this one . . ." *You and I travel to the beat of a different drum . . .*

He's right, this DJ with the earsplitting voice. I remember where I was. In the dorm, Goodyear Hall, at Buffalo, living with Sarah and Miriam. Our cramped room—the only triple on the floor—was redolent with the mingled scents of three perfumes (Sarah's L'Air du Temps, Miriam's Shalimar, my Réplique). Faint traces of marijuana and the incense we burned to mask the smell were in the air, too. Music was loud and constant. The songs we played—from record albums lined up on a makeshift bricks-and-boards bookcase—reflected both the turbulent times we were living in and our aching desire to find true love.

The Vietnam War and growing social movements colored everything about our college years. Sarah, Miriam, and I were often distracted by the frenetic energy of campus events. We accepted as gospel that just about any sit-in or teach-in (anti-war or pro-liberation of any group) was a far more valuable use of our time than, say, calculus class.

We righteously chose our priorities. We skimped on study hours to gather signatures in support of anti-war groups. We cut classes to accompany our boyfriends to a barber who would make them "Clean for Gene" McCarthy when they canvassed voters. We begged for extensions and pulled all-nighters to finish term papers after long days of organizing teach-ins. We emptied our meager checking accounts for train tickets so we could march on Washington.

We were so sure of everything we were sure of.

There were endless late-night discussions in the dorm, which usually began high-minded (politics of the day, poetry of the ages) but ended up, sooner or later, at sex. All three of us had come to college as virgins, though Sarah and Miriam claimed vast experience at the "everything but" game that was the way of all flesh in the era before the Pill. French kissing was as far as I had gone.

We guessed that Miriam would be the first to lose her virginity. Sex was already the big main idea of her life. Men were drawn—still are—to her easy charm, her perfect little body, her gorgeous face. Later in our lives, one of the men she almost married would describe her appeal: "Miriam communicates only one message, no matter the words that come out of her mouth: 'Imagine me in bed.' And so, we do."

Early in the first semester of freshman year, it was Miriam who found the name of Dr. Sanford, the gynecologist near campus who dispensed birth control without undue lecturing. Miriam went on the Pill after meeting Alex Van Buren, a political science major, at an anti-war demonstration in late September. By homecoming weekend in October, she had succumbed to Alex's crusade to get her into bed. The morning after she slept with him for the first time, Miriam described the night to Sarah and me in such detail that I actually remember her first sexual experience as vividly as my own.

Sarah was the next of us to visit Dr. Sanford, after successfully capturing the attention of Claude Lequesne, the teaching assistant in her Survey of French Literature course. Claude was an older man—twenty-four, as I remember—who talked at length about an ex-wife and young son he had left at home in Marseilles. Sarah happily imagined herself on regular visits to the south of France, stepmother to a *petit garçon*. Even after she learned that Claude's wife was not exactly ex, and he returned to France, Sarah credited her first lover with great tenderness and impressive technique in bed. I think his speaking French to her during sex allowed her to overlook his shortcomings.

My turn came when I was nineteen, during my sophomore year, in Bradley Garrison's creaky bed on the top floor of a rambling wood-frame house near the campus. Bradley shared the house with four roommates, who were downstairs at the time, smoking hashish and blasting a Jefferson Airplane album. The thumping bass of "White Rabbit" shook the walls as Bradley unbuttoned my pale blue Army/Navy-store workshirt and kissed my neck. He worked his mouth down my body to breasts, stomach. I moaned convincingly, though I was mostly thinking, as he tugged at the zipper of my bell-bottom jeans, that I should try the Stillman Diet that I'd heard could knock off ten pounds in a week. It was over for Bradley in thirty seconds. "Did you . . . uh . . . um . . .?" he asked. "Oh, yes," I lied. Eventually, I managed to train Bradley in the mechanics of foreplay (knowledge of which I had acquired from late-night catechisms in the dorm), and I began to enjoy orgasms on a regular basis. Bradley and I broke up when we realized, after some months, that we had little in common when we weren't horizontal. At least we were honest with each other—we never even pretended to be in love.

The following semester I took up with David Thierry, a psychology graduate student. After several tedious episodes in bed, I tried reading erotic love poems to him— Pablo Neruda, e.e. cummings. David yawned. I splurged on a push-up bra and black lace underpants. He blushed. Finally, shyly, I suggested oral sex, remembering, as I made my request, Bradley Garrison's generosity and finesse in that department.

"If you really want to, babe," David said, leaning back against his mirrored headboard, "go right ahead."

Incredibly, I did.

In spite of David's limitations, I continued to see him until the end of that year, when he graduated and moved to Michigan to pursue a doctorate. I hardly thought about him for a long while after that, except for the times when Sarah and Miriam could persuade me to tell the "Go Right Ahead" story about David to new women friends who hadn't heard the tale. Then, a few years ago, I was under the dryer at the hairdresser's when one of those advice columns in a women's magazine caught my eye. A reader had written to ask about overcoming her husband's inhibitions in bed. The advice offered was replete with seduction techniques guaranteed to unleash the husband's libido. "Read provocative books, wear enticing outfits to bed, tell him exactly how to please you," urged the columnist, described by the magazine as the noted clinical psychologist and sex therapist, David Thierry, Ph.D.

I've wondered what goes on in late-night colloquies in women's dorms these days. I'm sure that my daughter has been to bed with a boyfriend or two, but from what I can tell, her generation has more in common, sexually, with their grandmothers than with their mothers. Caution and monogamy rule again. No surprise. By the time Nicole was old enough for us to have the Talk—where babies come from and all that—it was the AIDS era, and I felt obliged to frame the information I gave her within rules I had once thought archaic. My generation took the Pill and worshipped the *Kama Sutra*. No blood tests, no condoms, no inhibitions. Sex was life affirming, not fatal. Long before AIDS existed, of course, our generation learned that sex is one of life's most complicated ventures, but for a while there, the people we most admired blithely advocated something they called free love. They were no less sanctimonious than today's teen idols, who appear in public service announcements, solemnly reminding their peers that free love has given way to safe sex. Neither generation has it right, though. Nothing that happens between lovers is ever truly free. Or safe.

The rain lets up, and I make my way onto the highway and home to Laurel Falls. As I pull into the garage, the DJ is leading into ". . . one of the best covers ever of a Beatles tune. Judy Collins, 'In My Life.'" Our song, Jim's and mine; he sang it to me at our wedding. *There are places I remember / All my life, though some have changed . . .*

I turn off the engine, step out of the car, enter the code to disarm the security system. Our code is 1776. Adam chose it when he was in the third grade, the year he played Thomas Jefferson in his class play. *Some are dead and some are living / In my life, I love you more.*

Jim is not home yet. He's having dinner at Le Cirque with new partners from his London office. They'll be here for the party. In the old days, just our close friends came to our fall party, often with their young children. Everyone wore jeans. I did all the cooking. Jim sang and played the piano. Adam and Nicole helped us clean up the mess the next day.

Now that Jim invites business associates, it's a different kind of party. We hire caterers and bartenders and parking valets and a cleanup crew, and Gillian Investments foots the bill. The men will be in coats and ties, the women in designer cocktail dresses. No one will think of bringing children. All I do is send invitations, approve the menu, and direct the staff we hire. Our house is different now, too. With the additions we've built—master bedroom suite, remodeled kitchen, enclosed patio, pool and cabana—our living space is twice what it was when we first moved in.

Another Lean Cuisine for me tonight. Still hoping the clingy creation that Miriam persuaded me to buy for the party will hang the right way on my middle-aged hips. While the scant portion of frozen chicken piccata (270 calories, 7 grams of fat) gets irradiated in the microwave, I check the answering machine for messages. The caterer for the party has an unusual South African Cabernet she would like to discuss with me. The pianist needs directions to our house. The Laurel Falls Museum of Fine Arts wants to know when I'll be available to discuss this year's fundraiser. Two hang-ups without messages. The Caller ID screen says the calls came from the Carnegie Grand Hotel in Manhattan. Wrong number, no doubt.

Next to the phone is a note from Carmen, our housekeeper. "Nicole she call. She is okay. No thing importante." Carmen has worked for us since the week we moved into this house. It's a cliché, I know, for rich people to describe their household staff as family, but I can't imagine life in Connecticut without Carmen. Of course, we could have hired someone willing to live in, but having anyone but Carmen take care of the house (and all of us) is unthinkable. She was a godsend through our many renovations, translating my wishes into Spanish for the construction crews, choreographing the moves of tradespeople all over the house. When I was in graduate school, Carmen would come to work early and stay as late as I needed her to drive carpools or fix dinner for Adam and Nicole. The kids loved her. Those were the years when Jim had just started to build Gillian Investments, and the routine of his being at work all the time, turning into a ghost at home, had just begun. Carmen was my friend and confidante, sympathetic and reliable.

I turn on the TV above the counter to give myself company as I eat dinner at the kitchen table. I catch the end of a *Law & Order* rerun: Sam Waterston and Jerry Ohrbach are exchanging cynical remarks on the outcome of a white-collar corruption trial. *Dateline* is next, featuring a report on recent art forgeries in Italy. A ten-second teaser for the story shows a sweeping aerial view of Rome. The voiceover, in Italian-accented English, insinuates government complicity "at the highest levels." I smile, wondering if students at the Rome Academy of the Arts, where I spent the second semester of my junior year, are today gathering in sidewalk *caffès* to gossip about this latest scandal.

The phone rings. I mute the sound on the TV, but my eyes don't stray from Stone Phillips's chiseled face on the screen. He's doing the lead-in to the piece about the fake masterpieces. It's Jim calling. Dinner is running late, he'll stay in the city tonight. No, I don't mind, I tell him. He asks about my lecture in New Haven, but I can tell he's not really listening to my response; he's covering the mouthpiece of his cell phone and talking to a waiter. Laughter in the background. I'm watching the camera shots of the Vatican Museum as I remind Jim that I'll need his help to get ready for the party. "I'll be home early tomorrow," he says. "Sleep well."

By the time I hang up, the *Dateline* story about Italy is over. I decline Jane Pauley's invitation to stay tuned for a warning about unnecessary cosmetic surgery, and I wend my way upstairs to the bedroom.

———————

IN MY JUNIOR year at Buffalo, shortly after I applied to the study abroad program, I received a threatening letter from the dean, informing me that I had to declare an actual major before I left for spring semester in Rome. I had already taken some art history classes, so I figured I could major in art history and still graduate on time. I didn't exactly know what I would do with my degree, though I had a vague notion that I could be happy working in a museum, looking all day at beautiful things.

The Rome Academy of the Arts—*L'Accademia delle Arti*—draws students from all over the United States and Europe, serious young musicians, artists, and scholars. The art history program, led by renowned Renaissance experts, was meant for students far more serious and accomplished than I. And yet, over the semester I developed a deep appreciation for masterpieces of the *quattrocento*, participated in lively discussions about the Church's patronage of the arts, took countless curators' tours of obscure galleries and churches, and made weekend expeditions to the Uffizi in Florence. But I was distracted from a true commitment to scholarship by one of my own life's big main ideas, or rather, by one of the main characters in the drama of my life. In Rome, I fell in love for the first time.

He was a grad student from Vermont, in Italy to study music composition at the Academy. We met at a reception for new students. According to the notes about him in the orientation booklet, he had been awarded a scholarship to the Academy based on a sixteen-minute chamber piece he had composed, "Trio for Piano, Cello, and Violin in G Major: La Chamade." I noticed him at the bar, wearing a brown suede jacket rubbed shiny at the elbows. He was chatting comfortably in Italian with the bartender.

"Hi, I'm Beth Jacobs, art history," I said.

"*Molto piacere*, Beth. *Io sono* Andrew Carino. Music composition."

"Not the famous composer of La Chamade?"

"That's me."

"What does *la chamade* mean, anyway?"

"It's French, for a wild beating of the heart."

Two hours later we were making love in his dorm room, across the piazza from the Academy's women's residence where I lived. Afterwards, Andrew and I lay in each other's arms, drinking cheap wine—the kind that the *vino-olio* stores poured from spigots into empty mineral water bottles and sold for a few hundred *lire*, less than a dollar.

"When did you know that you were musical?" I asked him.

"Always, I think. My kindergarten teacher said that I didn't pay attention in class. When my parents asked me why I wasn't listening to my teacher, I told them, 'I want to listen to her, but instead, I hear the music that's always in my head, and I can't stop hearing it.'"

"Are you hearing me, or is there music in your head?"

"Both," he said. "Your music is inside me now."

There must have been rainy days, cold temperatures,

difficult moments in Rome, but I remember only warmth and sunshine and joy. People who saw us together knew at once how happy we were. Giovanna, the owner of our favorite coffee bar on Viale Trastevere, greeted me excitedly every morning as I took my seat under an umbrella at an outdoor table: *Un cappuccino per la bella signorina americana?* I can still see Andrew sitting across from me, his head buried in a copy of the *Rome Daily American*. His blond hair, several shades lighter than mine, drew attention from every Italian we met. Giovanna would tease him, *Buon giorno, Robert Red-a-ford! Un caffè macchiato?* I pronounced Andrew's name the way the Italians did: *An-DRAY-a*. Beth has no equivalent in Italian; Andrew called me *Bella*. Beautiful.

Over the semester, I dragged Andrew through art galleries and Renaissance churches all over Rome and nearby towns. He escorted me to weekly concerts given by students at the Academy, and to Milan for a performance of *La Bohème* (my first opera) at La Scala. We said, "I love you" to each other a hundred times a day.

By all rights, we should have returned to the States when classes at the Academy ended in June. Both of us needed to get summer jobs. Our families were expecting us. But fate intervened, in the person of Tito Fabrizzi, Andrew's friend and mentor at the Academy. Like most upper-class Romans, Dr. Fabrizzi and his wife Marilena escaped to their country house to avoid the heat of Rome in July and August. Would we accept a small compensation, he asked, to mind the Fabrizzi *palazzo* in the Flaminio area of Rome until the family returned from their summer in Gallipoli? He apologized that he couldn't pay us more than a half-million *lire* a month—a little over two hundred dollars—but the house was *molto bella* and he'd leave us his ancient Fiat 500 for outings *alla campagna*—to the countryside. It would be a comfort to him and his wife to know that reliable people were keeping an eye on their home. Would we mind watering the plants and feeding the family cats, Mimi and Rodolfo, as well? "My sister in Gallipoli is allergic," he said. "Alas, we must take our *vacanze* without the cats."

Andrew and I moved into Dr. Fabrizzi's home right after classes ended. The palazzo, three stories high, was built in the 1850s and sat on a bluff overlooking the Tevere. Like so much else in Italy, the house was dazzling, and full of maddening impracticalities. The exquisite marble floors throughout the place were cold and slippery, except where they were covered by Persian rugs so beautiful that Andrew and I hesitated to step on them. In each of the three bathrooms was a claw-footed bathtub with ornate brass fittings, but no shower. The kitchen countertops were inlaid with magnificent cerulean tiles, yet the refrigerator held little more than one day's provisions for the two of us. The freezer was barely large enough for one ice-cube tray and a can or two of the frozen blood-orange juice concentrate we liked to buy at the Standa, the only supermarket for miles.

Shopkeepers welcomed us to the neighborhood, proud to introduce us to specialties from their own regions of Italy: Try this ricotta, made the same way my grandmother did in Sicilia. This is how we cook steak in Firenze. Let me give you a recipe for the best osso buco, the Milanese way. Have you heard the legend about this Frascati wine?

Nowhere else existed for us. We didn't talk about the future; there was only our borrowed *palazzo*—on borrowed time—and exhilarating adventure every time we walked out the door. We used our student IDs to get free concert tickets and cheap train fares. We hardly drove Dr. Fabrizzi's Fiat—gasoline was more expensive than train tickets—though one afternoon Andrew did insist on taking the car out to quiet roads near Castel Gandolfo so he could teach me to drive a stick shift. Every car I've owned since then has had a manual transmission.

As often as we could, we splurged on excursions out of town. We slept on lumpy mattresses and shared bathrooms with other travelers in cheap *pensiones* from Venice to Positano. We traipsed through palaces and ancient ruins, museums and vineyards. We toured artisans' studios where sparkling Murano glass and delicate cameos and exquisite leather boots were still crafted by hand. Inside the Grotto Azzurro, Andrew nearly capsized our tiny rowboat when he leaned over the side to retrieve a bracelet that had slid off my wrist into the phosphorescent water. On a narrow street in Naples, a small boy belted out *O Sole Mio* from the second-floor window above his father's bakery and bowed to our applause with a sweep of his arm. "*Bravissimo!*" Andrew called to him. "*Che bella voce!*"

Che piacere . . . How happy we were. And how I yearn for that life, my old life, when I believed the world was full of possibilities. What I wouldn't give to feel joyful and hopeful again! To feel for one hour the way I felt every day I spent with Andrew.

Andrew, fluent in Italian and French, who sang arias to me in bed. Andrew, who three times hitchhiked from Burlington to Buffalo to visit me at school and meet my friends after we returned from Italy. Andrew, who in the end said he loved me but just didn't ever want to be married. Andrew, who married someone else, just as I did, not long after we parted. Andrew, who still owns a piece of my heart.

The last time I heard news about him was ten years ago. Sarah ran into him at O'Hare while traveling home from a business trip. He was a music professor at a small college in California, passing through Chicago on his way to judge a young composers competition. He showed Sarah a photo of his two sons, though not his wife. Andrew looked the same, Sarah said, handsome and boyish. Sarah gave him an update on me. "Two kids? A Ph.D.?" he said with admiration. "Well, tell Dr. Jacobs— no, I guess she's Dr. Gillian now—that I said *ciao*."

MY SENIOR YEAR was coming to a close when things ended with Andrew. Friends were busily pursuing graduate schools and auspicious job offers, but I was too dispirited to plan my next move. In a half-hearted attempt to find work, I mailed my résumé to a handful of museums in the northeast. I can't even recall what I wrote I was qualified to do. Two museums sent back form-letter rejections. The rest didn't bother to respond. Among the entities that ignored me: the Laurel Falls Museum of Fine Arts, where I now sit on the board.

My advisor suggested I look into a summer school program that might keep me occupied until I could summon the energy to begin job-hunting again. I wound up at Ithaca College in a graduate seminar on nineteenth-century European painting. Influential curators from major museums were lined up as guest lecturers. I arranged for a student loan to pay for tuition and the dorm room. I figured I could get a waitressing job to cover my living expenses for the summer.

The day after graduation, I drove from Buffalo to Ithaca College in the used, bright yellow Volkswagen Beetle that my parents had given me as a graduation present. The sign at the entrance to the Ithaca campus said, "Welcome to IC. Last day for summer registration. Follow signs to gymnasium."

At the gym I was told that there was no record of my loan.

"I'm sure it's a mistake," I said to the dour woman who

was handling "Last Names, A-J" from behind a folding table. "The loan was approved."

"Go to the bursar and work it out with them. Job Hall, second floor," she said impatiently. "Next in line, please."

Walking across campus to the bursar's office, I considered my alternatives if things didn't work out at IC. Go back to Mom and Dad's house in Riverdale, take up residence in my old bedroom with the flowered drapes and the canopy bed. Get my old summer job back, waiting tables at the Blue Windmill Steak House in Yonkers. Maybe register with a temp agency, look forward to a few months of typing, filing, answering phones. I imagined the voice of my brother Bruce, who was spending his summer studying for the New York Bar exam: *A degree in art history! What do you expect?*

"You look like you're having a bad day," said the good-looking guy working behind the counter at the bursar's office. He was dressed like a student, though something about him made him appear a little older. His hair, I realized. His sideburns were sandy brown, but the rest was almost all gray. "Maybe I can help."

"Sorry, do I look upset?"

"You look just fine to me," he said with a grin. "I'm Jim Gillian. What can I do for you?"

I told him about my experience in the gym.

"Let me check on something," he said. "Do you know your student number? Write it down for me—your name, too. Where do you go to school during the year?"

"I just graduated from Buffalo."

"What's your degree in?"

"Art history."

"Oh, I'll bet you're here for the European Painting seminar."

I nodded. "If I can manage to register."

"Wait right here," he said.

He disappeared into a back office and resurfaced a few minutes later, carrying a blue folder with my name on it.

"Well, Beth Jacobs, I have some good news for you. They've put you in Eastman Hall, much better than the Towers, where most summer school students have to live. And you're right, the loan was approved, but the money is not being sent directly to IC. This is the kind of loan that's paid directly to students. You should have your check in about a week."

"I have to pay tuition today or I can't register," I sighed.

Jim motioned for me to lean in towards him.

"Here's the strategy," he whispered. "Just write a check for the tuition. Your check will have to get processed in the world-class bureaucracy here at the bursar's office. That's sure to take a week at least, and your loan check will probably arrive in time to cover it. Worse comes to worse, trust me, it will take weeks before anyone at this place will be able to figure out what to do about a check that's been returned from your bank. They'll eventually redeposit it, by which time your loan check will definitely be in your account. Meanwhile, you'll be well into Delacroix—maybe even an Impressionist or two—before anything happens."

"Are you in the art history seminar, too?"

"Nope. I just graduated from IC, starting an MBA at Cornell in September. I'm working here for the summer."

"But you seem to know something about art."

"Oh, yes. My dear mother wouldn't let me get a bachelor's degree in business. She had this idea that I'd regret it for the rest of my life if I didn't pursue liberal arts in college. So I majored in humanities, minored in business administration."

"A wise woman," I said.

"Yes, she was. Um, she died two years ago. My parents were in a car accident. Both of them . . ."

"So sorry. What will you do when you finish school?"

"Go to Manhattan, figure out how economics works outside of textbooks, and make a great deal of money. The usual business student's agenda."

The people in line behind me were getting restless. "I guess I'd better be going. Meanwhile, it's nice of you to try to help, but I'm not sure your plan will work."

"Believe me, lots of people survive this way. Myself included. You went to a big school, you should know that beating the bureaucracy is a major college sport. Besides, what other options do you have?"

I shrugged.

"You know where to find me if you run into anymore trouble," he said. "But this should work."

He was right. It did.

My classes ended at noon every day. I took to spending afternoons at a diner in town where the owners didn't mind that I sat and read at one of their booths for hours every day, enjoying free refills of coffee. Finding a waitressing job turned out to be near impossible. Business is down in a college town during the summers. No one was hiring. I was at my usual table at the diner one day, scanning the local want ads, when a pile of textbooks landed without warning in front of me.

"You never came back to tell me what happened," said a familiar voice. "I was afraid the banking police had locked you up for check kiting."

"Hi, um, Jim, is it?"

"Yes, it is," he said, sitting down. "I'm disappointed, Beth Jacobs, that you barely remember my name. How's it going?"

I filled him in on my latest crisis.

"Some professors, especially in the social sciences, do research during the summer and need assistants. Why don't you check out the bulletin boards at that other school in town, you know, Cornell? It's just up the hill," he said, pointing with his thumb.

"Thanks, wiseguy. How are things at the bursar's office?"

"Stupefyingly boring. I can't wait until classes start in the fall. I'm getting a head start on some reading," he said, pointing to his books. "Tell me, what do you do for fun these days, Beth?"

"Fun? Oh, yes, I remember fun. I once had fun in my life. Now all I do is go to class, get rejected for jobs, and obsess about money."

"That's no good. Tell you what, why don't you come over and let me cook dinner for you tonight? I make the best spaghetti sauce in the Finger Lakes."

"Is this a pity date?"

"It's not pity, and it's hardly a date. You can meet my roommate, Harold Rosenblatt. We've known each other since kindergarten. Harold's finishing his architecture degree at Cornell this summer. You can also meet his girlfriend Sharon Greta, just back from the Eternal Peace commune in Berkeley. She's thinking of changing her name to Sunshine or Moonbeam, I forget which, and trying to talk Harold into adopting a less establishment name for himself. He can't decide if Solar or Harmony goes better with Rosenblatt. If you come, maybe they'll let you vote."

"I'll be there," I said. He stood up to leave, and I noticed for the first time what a nice body he had.

I wandered down the hall of the psych department at Cornell until I found an occupied office. "Sonya Needham, Associate Professor" said the handwritten sign pasted to the open door. A young woman with straight auburn hair almost to the hem of her mini-skirt was standing over the desk, examining papers. She jumped when I rapped on the door.

"Sorry," I said. "Is there anyone I could speak to about a summer job?"

"Are you a psych major?"

I shook my head. "I just graduated from Buffalo. I took a few psych courses there. Intro, child psych. And a class on 'The Psychology of Twentieth Century Art,' if that counts."

She smiled. "Of course it counts. Do you know anything about Cayuga House?"

I shook my head. "I'm new in town."

"Cayuga House is a women's counseling center, just off the Commons in town. This work I'm doing is part of a grant that funds the operation. We have to interview some of the women who have been receiving services. I need someone to conduct the interviews and proofread the report as I write it. I can pay you minimum wage, up to twenty hours a week. Do you think you could start tomorrow?"

———

I WOULD BE married for more than a decade and the mother of two children before I went back to graduate school for a doctorate in psychology, but I consider that summer the start of my career as a therapist. I got caught up in the mission of Cayuga House, which seemed more meaningful than anything I was learning in the painting seminar that had brought me to Ithaca. By chance, I said at the time, I discovered that art history was not meant to be my life's work. Years later, in my own therapy, I came to see that meeting Sonya may have been a stroke of luck, but leaving art history behind was not entirely a matter of chance. Thinking about art meant thinking about Italy, which meant thinking about Andrew. In a way, I gave up on art so I could give up on him.

Like many of my generation of therapists, I'm skeptical of Freudian concepts, especially about women. But the older I get, the more deeply one of his ideas resonates within me. After all that has happened, I do believe, as Freud did, that the world is full of accidents, but the mind is not.

JIM AND I were married on a warm June afternoon the same week he finished graduate school. Sonya insisted that we hold our wedding in the backyard of her house in Cayuga Heights. Jim's friend Harold, later the architect who would help us design and expand our home in Laurel Falls, was his best man. Both Sarah and Miriam were my maids of honor. I wore an ankle-length white satin dress with diamond-shaped fishnet inserts at the midriff, a crown of daisies around my head, and no shoes. Jim was in a second-hand tuxedo he had picked up at a thrift store in Binghamton, a Day-Glo-orange bow tie with matching suspenders, and Earth Shoes he had coated with black shoe polish. His hair was almost to his shoulders; mine reached to my waist. Before we spoke our marriage vows, the Unitarian minister who performed the ceremony delivered a sermon about the ecological impact of gas-guzzling American cars, the urgency of zero population growth, and the immorality of the Vietnam War. We promised to love and honor, though not necessarily obey, each other. I suppose we've done better than many at keeping our word.

Close to a hundred friends and family members were there, applauding when Jim kissed me after the minister pronounced us married. My mother, raised by Methodist parents in a small Iowa town, sat primly through the ceremony, her lips frozen in a polite smile, too baffled by what she saw to say much. My father, Jewish and from New York, liked to think of himself as a sophisticated man of the world, though the world he knew was pretty much limited to Riverdale and the upholstery business he ran with his brother Norman. Dad posed what he thought was a clever question to everyone at our wedding, including the minister: What's the matter—a hippie rabbi they couldn't find?

Three friends of Jim's, recent graduates from the music department at Ithaca College, played acoustic guitars and sang sweet and dignified versions of Beatles, Motown, and protest music throughout the afternoon. Sarah likes to say that I was the only bride in history to walk down the aisle to "Draft Dodger Rag."

The day after our wedding, we loaded our many cartons of books and a few shabby suitcases of clothes into a small trailer that we hitched to the back of Jim's Datsun, and we drove to Manhattan to begin married life. Jim had been hired into a management training program at a small brokerage company with offices on lower Broadway. Before I left Ithaca, Sonya recommended me to the director of a community counseling center on the Lower East Side, who promised a job would be waiting for me when I got to the city.

We carted our meager belongings up four flights of stairs to our new apartment, a tiny one-bedroom on First Avenue near 87th Street. We had rented it sight unseen from an ad in the *Times*, making arrangements over the phone while we were still in Ithaca. The landlord mailed us a lease; we signed it and sold my yellow VW so we could send him a check for the first month's rent and security deposit. We spent our inaugural nights in Manhattan in sleeping bags on the floor of our bedroom.

With Jim's first paycheck, we bought a waterbed—absurdly large for the room and expressly forbidden in our lease. In those days, "waterbed" was code for frequent and unconventional sexual activity. I don't recollect anything particularly unconventional, but we did make love at all hours and with the freedom possible only before there are children sleeping in the next room (*we might wake them*), or phones that must be answered in the middle of lovemaking (*it could be the office*), or exhausting daytime schedules that keep nighttime passions at bay (*maybe over the weekend, okay?*).

Friday morning, the day before the party. A crystal-clear memory unravels as I start to awaken. I'm a new mother, being wheeled out of Lenox Hill Hospital with Adam in my arms. A kind nurse—I would have described her as "older" in those days, but she was probably no older than I am now—is giving me advice.

"Okay, New Mom, don't be starvin' yourself to try to fit into your old clothes. You're nursing that baby; you need your strength. Eat when you're hungry, sleep when the baby sleeps, and for the next six weeks, don't pick up anything heavier than a fryin' pan, except for the baby. You've got a big, strong husband, and no one's delivered a baby out of his body lately, so let him do the heavy lifting."

The clock radio clicks on and my reverie dissolves like sugar on the tongue. I'm no longer at Lenox Hill, no longer a new mother. Back to the future. I open my eyes, remembering that Jim stayed in the city last night. NPR's *Morning Edition* bulletins connect me to the world outside my bedroom. It's Luciano Pavarotti's birthday. The Paul-McCartney-is-dead craze began on this day in 1969. Yesterday, a judge awarded a Tampa couple joint custody of Fred and Ginger, their trained sea lions. Unseasonably warm temperatures are expected in the Metro area for the weekend.

I sit over a cup of coffee with Carmen, who thanks me again for hiring her son Javier to help set up the house for the party. He's twenty-two, finishing an associate's degree in computers at a community college. Javier had a brief wild period when he drank too much and drove too fast, but one DUI arrest was enough to scare him into saving his own life. People say he's a good kid—smart, nice-looking, wants to make something of himself. People used to say things like that about Adam.

No patients scheduled until next Tuesday. Over the years I've learned it's best for me not to plan on being at work on the Friday and Monday around our fall party. I gave my office manager a long weekend, but I need to spend an hour or so on patient charts at the office today. I figure I can be back at the house by late morning, when deliveries for the party will be starting.

My office is a ten-minute drive from home, in a nine-ty-year-old, three-story building whose past tenants have included a savings bank, a messenger service, and a detective agency. A primary care group now owns the building and occupies the entire first floor. On the second floor are the offices of Leonard and Roberta Oberman, both speech therapists. Their daughter Emily was a high school class-mate of Adam's. The Obermans came to Adam's funeral and sent a generous donation to the Laurel Falls High School library in Adam's memory. But when I run into them in our parking lot or at the sandwich shop across the street, they can't get away from me fast enough. They don't know how to answer my friendly questions about Emily. It's awkward making chitchat with a mother who has lost her son. I've stopped trying to engage them; I smile and wave, and I let them escape.

The top floor of the building, less than half the size of the two lower floors, is all mine: waiting room with a partitioned-off area for Caryn, my office manager; a large alcove for me where I can do paperwork; a therapy room; a former broom closet I turned into a kitchen. I've rented this space since I opened my practice, even though Jim has always thought it would make more financial sense to buy something. But I'm used to this place, and, in a contrary way, I like being responsible for the one small aspect of my life with Jim that makes no financial sense.

Caryn has left a neat pile of patient charts on my desk. I am halfway through them when the phone rings. I pick it up, forgetting to let the call ring through to the answering service.

"Dr. Gillian," I say, still making notes in one of the charts.

"Beth Gillian? Beth Jacobs Gillian?" A male voice.

"Yes, this is she. Who's calling, please?"

Silence. I put my pen down. "Hello?" I hear him inhale.

"*Ciao, Bella. Stai bene?*"

"My God. Andrew?"

"Did I catch you in the middle of a miracle cure?"

"I'm alone here today. How are you? Where are you?"

"I'm in New York."

"In the city?"

"Yes, at a conference. I'm staying at the Carnegie Grand."

"Did you call my house yesterday?"

"Twice. I hung up when I got your machine."

"Welcome to the modern age. We have Caller ID. I saw the name of your hotel."

"Sorry I didn't leave a message. I chickened out. Then I called again a little while ago. Your housekeeper said you were at your office. I took a chance . . . "

A chance.

"Beth, do you think I could see you?"

"What do you mean?"

"I mean see you, meet you in the city. God, I know how insane this must sound to you, but I need to see you."

Need. "Can you tell me why?"

Silence.

"Andrew?"

"I'm having a bit of a crisis . . ."

"What kind of crisis?"

Pause, and then, "It's hard, over the phone . . . I know I'm asking a lot. You can't imagine how long I've thought about whether I should call you."

"I guess I don't understand, why me? After all this time?"

"Because I need to talk to someone who knows me but won't judge me. And you, *Bella*, are the least judgmental person I have ever known."

Something primal in his voice makes me ask, "How long are you in town?"

"I fly back to California on Wednesday."

"We have something—something important happening at our house this weekend. Can I call you back?"

"Could I see you on Monday? Oh, you're probably working . . ."

"As it turns out I'm off on Monday. But Andrew, I have to think about this."

"If you can't see me, I'll understand, really I will, but I don't want to talk about it on the phone anymore. Don't call me, just come if you can. I'll be in the lobby of my hotel at ten on Monday morning. Look for me at the coffee bar near the reception desk. I'll have a cappuccino waiting for you."

"I hope you understand, I can't just say yes right now."

"It helps just hearing your voice. But come if you can."

"Take care, Andrew."

"*Ci vediamo, Bella.*"

As soon as I hang up the phone, I relocate everything I know about Andrew to my emotional waiting room, the part of my brain that is disconnected from my feelings.

I concentrate on finishing the work on my desk. I make a list of the stops I have to make on the way home: Pick up Jim's jacket from the tailor. Drop off overdue videos. Gas up the car. I won't think about Andrew, won't let my heart say his name again until after the party.

I'm expert at this . . . compartmentalizing. It's how I manage my memories of Adam. Put them in the waiting room, call out to them one at a time, as I can bear to face them. It's a game I play well, a sort of sleight-of-mind. Now you think it, now you don't.

It's how I survive.

PART II:
CHANCES AND CHOICES

SARAH:
BETWEEN THE LINES

"There's something happening here.
What it is ain't exactly clear."
—Stephen Stills

As if Mondays weren't bad enough, facing five new, excruciating days at Tri-Tech, Joey has decided we now need mandatory 8:00 a.m. meetings to start the week. He got the idea from listening to an audiotape course called *Finding Your Inner CEO*, from which he has already learned the importance of generating (or having his assistant generate) elaborate agendas, tortuous spreadsheets, and four-color Gantt charts to accompany his every move.

This past Monday, Joey and his assistant, Sally, were whispering nose-to-nose when the rest of us filed into the conference room. We dutifully took our places: Lawrence and I—Tri-Tech's only vice presidents—as well as the company's ten directors and senior directors, sank into the high-backed leather chairs around the table. Everyone else crowded into the two rows of molded plastic chairs that lined the edge of the room. Sally surveyed the group with a knowing air, tapping her fingers on her color-coded folders, whose contents were a secret to everyone except her and Joey. Sally has worked for Joey since the birth of the company in his garage, and she understands that in a small company like Tri-Tech, knowledge is power.

Raymond Albano rushed to grab the seat on Joey's left, the chair facing Sally. Raymond came to work for us fresh from the PharmD—pharmacy doctorate program—at Rutgers. Joey hired him when Tri-Tech's main competitor, The Edward Saylish Health Marketing Group, put a full-time medical director on staff. In his days as a prosthetic limb salesman, Joey shared his territory with Ed Saylish. Though the two haven't seen each other for years, the feral rivalry born in their Pittsburgh-to-Binghamton days flourishes to this day. Joey went berserk when he heard that his arch enemy had hired an employee who could be introduced to clients as *Doctor* Somebody. Tri-Tech can't afford a physician. We got Raymond Albano, PharmD, instead.

Raymond and Joey are perfectly matched. Raymond can hardly believe his good fortune at having landed a position with such an impressive title right out of graduate school, and he admires, respects, and reveres Joey. Joey can hardly believe his good fortune at having persuaded a PharmD to join Tri-Tech for the price of a senior director's title and a piddling salary, and he considers himself fully entitled to Raymond's admiration, respect, and reverence.

I watched as Raymond uncapped his fountain pen, turned to a fresh sheet on his legal pad, and looked expectantly towards Joey. Sally circled the room, handing out copies, from her blue folder, of the two-page agenda she had prepared for what would probably be a five-minute meeting.

"Savant Pharmaceuticals has a new CEO," Joey began. "The whole New Jersey operation is about to be restructured. Doc Shortland has been promoted and is moving to Switzerland. The official announcement will probably be made next week, but Shortland called me over the weekend. He wanted me to hear the news directly from him."

I could imagine the conversation: Shortland's torturing Joey with false modesty about the promotion, Joey's pretending to be happy for him. In front of Tri-Tech staff, however, Joey positioned himself as an insider, a peer in the highest echelon of corporate power.

"Shortland told me in confidence that Savant made him an offer he can't refuse—he's gonna head up Savant's European territory," Joey continued. He was twirling a rubberband through his fingers, his creepy Captain Queeg-like habit. "I'm meeting with him tomorrow to strategize about the changes at Savant. I'll let you know if there are any take-aways from that meeting. Questions?"

No one said anything. Raymond was scribbling furiously. I did have a couple of questions, which I kept to myself: Is "strategize" a real word? Who invented the use of "take-aways" as a noun? Who in this room would appreciate Dorothy Parker's famous observation about Switzerland? ("The Swiss are a neat and industrious people, none of whom is under seventy-five years of age. They make cheeses, milk chocolate, and watches, all of which, when you come right down to it, are pretty fairly unnecessary.")

Red folder in hand, Sally took her position in the doorway to distribute the handouts as the crowd dispersed.

"Sarah, stay for a minute, will ya?" Joey called to me.

"What's up?"

"You used to teach French, right?"

"Uh, yes," I said cautiously.

"I thought so. Shortland was telling me he has to learn French in a hurry. I guess he's going to need it in the new job. I think he already speaks Swiss, but not French."

"You mean German?"

"Whatever. Shortland remembered talking to you about Europe at the meeting in Palm Springs last year. He had a cast on his arm, couldn't play golf, so you were stuck babysitting him for the afternoon."

"He's smart, and he's not bad company when you get him away from Savant." Or away from you, Joey, I wanted to add.

"I can put up with anyone who gives us so much business. Whaddaya think, can you teach him to speak French in a month?"

"What?"

"He can't go to classes, like at a school or anything. He needs lessons at times that are convenient for him. Can you do it?"

"I'll need to talk to him first. It's not like teaching someone to drive a car. Learning a language is—"

Joey interrupted me. "Make yourself available to him," he said.

"I'm a little concerned about my workload as it is. If I have to be at Savant so often . . ."

"It's only for a limited time. And I'll see to it that your bonus this year reflects the time and effort you're putting in on this." He checked his watch. "You should probably get to Shortland right away."

"CONGRATULATIONS, DOC," I said to Shortland on the phone. "I know you and your wife must be excited about this move."

"Edna's already got our house on the market. Joey told you about my need to learn French in a hurry?"

"Indeed he has. I understand you already speak German, right?"

"I studied in Munich for a year, a thousand years ago

when I was in college."

"We've got about a month, right? I probably can teach you enough so that you'll be able to make simple conversation, and maybe you'll get a feeling for the language. That's if we meet for a few hours every day."

"I'll leave my mornings free for you. Tell Joey to lease you a car so you can get out here from the city."

"I'm going to insist that you do homework, you know."

"I guess I'm in for it. I hope Joey's giving you combat pay for this, Sarah. Tough duty."

"My pleasure, Doc. I'll gather some books and tapes for you, and we'll get started. Maybe even before the week is out."

"I have meetings all day tomorrow. Let's shoot for Wednesday."

Twenty-four hours after my conversation with Doc, Joey's brother-in-law, Alvin, who owns a Ford dealership in Queens, delivered a hideous, metallic purple Explorer to me at the garage in our office building. He parked the car next to Joey's prized silver BMW. Joey leaned against his own car, watching with a paternal air as Alvin ran through all of the Ford's features for me, emphasizing the vehicle's macho virtues: ruggedness, power, off-road capabilities. As if I were likely to need four-wheel drive in my commute to Parsippany, New Jersey. Had I been consulted beforehand, I would have requested something other than an SUV, which is way too high off the ground and a royal pain to climb in and out of in high heels and a skirt.

The next day I drove to Savant's corporate headquarters to begin French 101 with Doc Shortland. I spent the morning with him, and by the end of our session, he had learned a few essentials: how to introduce himself, how to ask for directions to the men's room, how to order—and send back, if necessary—a bottle of *vin rouge*.

By the time I returned to Manhattan and parked the car, it was close to lunchtime. I picked up a sandwich from the coffee shop in the lobby of the building, planning to eat in my office while I caught up on messages. I knew a pile of Post-It notes would await me, strewn all over my chair like oversized confetti. Joey can't figure out how to send email or be bothered organizing his thoughts into memos; he prefers to scrawl his ideas, one at a time, on sticky blue and yellow squares.

My staff are more likely to send emails with their urgent grammar queries or pleas for help in persuading Joey that his prose needs editing. "Of Orientate, Parametize, and Securify" read the subject line of a recent email sent to me by Dana Greene, the senior copy editor I hired shortly after I arrived at Tri-Tech. Dana and I see eye-to-eye on Joey and Tri-Tech.

> The above words, as you know, do not exist, except in Joey's mind. Will you PLEASE break the news to him? I'm still recovering from last week's skirmish over his obsessive use of "quality," especially as an adjective (as in "Tri-Tech is a quality company" and, my favorite, "Our best quality is our quality staff").
>
> With thanks, from your quality copy editor,
> Dana.

I ran into Lawrence in the lobby of the building. He greeted me as he always does, as if I were exactly the person he was hoping to meet.

"Have you talked to Rebecca yet?" he said, as we waited for the elevator. I shook my head. "She had a go-around with Joey this morning. She's helping you to recruit speakers for Savant's epilepsy conference in Palm Springs, right? One of the neurologists on our list, named McBride, lives in Brooklyn. Turns out that he's a neighbor of Joey's. Apparently, Dr. McBride is an aging hippie type—ponytail, earring, never wears a tie. He also happens to be a renowned expert in the field. Rebecca finally nailed him this morning to chair the panel discussion at the meeting. Joey immediately vetoed the idea, insisting that Dr. McBride looks unprofessional, and we can't have Savant thinking that we don't know how to recruit the right sort of people for their conferences. Joey made Rebecca call Dr. McBride and rescind the invitation. I don't know what story she made up, but she was fit to be tied. She came to me after she had already uninvited the doctor, or I would have intervened with Joey."

"Is he just nuts?"

"I think he's worse than usual this week because of all the changes at Savant.

"Should we be nervous about Savant? I mean, is Joey just over-reacting, the way he usually does?"

"No way of knowing. I tend to be optimistic, but all that matters for us is how Joey reacts."

The elevator doors opened onto the fifteenth floor, home to Tri-Tech's offices.

"See if you can calm Rebecca down," Lawrence said. "I've got to talk to Joey about another issue. Apparently, he stayed here late last night and did some unsolicited redecorating. Raymond Albano came in today to find his beloved Mets poster taken down and his office furniture totally rearranged."

"Why?"

"You know, one of Joey's screwy notions about corporate image. Raymond didn't say a word. He doesn't even object when Joey insists on dressing him—I'm sure you remember the time Joey took Raymond shopping for new socks and ties before he let him appear at the Savant conference in Tampa. Raymond's certainly not going to put up a fuss about how his office looks. Good luck with

Rebecca."

Understandably, it was hard for some people to figure out how Joey and Lawrence came to be business partners in the first place.

"Timing," was Lawrence's explanation, which he had provided to me over lunch one afternoon shortly after I was hired. I had been witness to one of Joey's temper tantrums that day—something to do with a junior staff member who had called in to say she wouldn't be at work because her baby was sick—and Lawrence had asked me to lunch to persuade me not to quit.

"I met Joey at a healthcare conference almost six years ago," Lawrence told me. "It was just before Meridian Health Plans, where I had worked for ten years, announced that they were moving their corporate head-quarters to *Louisville*, for goodness sake. I declined their offer to transfer me, which meant I got a paltry severance in spite of all the years I had put in. So, I thought, maybe the time is right for me to start my own consulting firm. I began to look into it, talked to people who might want to join me.

"And then, the same week that Lucy and I were about to celebrate our silver anniversary—twenty-five years of marriage!—she was diagnosed with multiple scle-rosis. We had two daughters in college. It wasn't the right time for me to take financial risks. I needed a dependable income and good health benefits. I had to drop the idea of starting my own business. Joey happened to call around that time—he had heard about Meridian's move to Louis-ville, and he guessed that I would be looking for a new job. Tri-Tech was getting ready for a leap—Savant had just become a client—and Joey's accountant was saying that the company needed a more sophisticated business plan, and someone to administer it. Joey offered me a piece of the business and the salary and benefits I was looking for.

So, here I am."

"And here I am, too," I said ruefully. "I'm trying to put my daughter through Columbia, and I need a reliable income and health insurance benefits. Like you, I have had jobs disappear out from under me. Tri-Tech seems to be growing, but I'm not sure I can work with Joey. Does he often act up the way he did this morning?"

Lawrence sighed. "Joey is moody and impatient, and he has the manners of a farm animal. But he's canny and shrewd—and committed to being successful. A born salesman. He's been smart enough to hire a few people with the background he lacks—you and me, for example—but mostly, he likes a young staff that he can control. One day he may decide he doesn't need either one of us. You and I are both smarter than Joey, but he has a killer instinct for business that you and I lack. You should stick around long enough to get that partnership and the big three-year bonus. I built that bonus into the business plan so we could attract talented people like you. I'd love to have you as a partner. And in the interim, working here will pay your bills."

It's been almost three years since Lawrence gave me that advice. In that time, his daughters have finished school, and the ravages of MS have sentenced his wife Lucy to a wheelchair. Though I've been tempted numerous times to leave, I've remembered Lawrence's words and have remained where I am, paying Ellie's college tuition, and holding out for Joey to make good on his promise.

———————

I COULD HEAR Rebecca's voice in the hallway as I approached her office. She was finishing a phone conversation with her boyfriend. "We need you at this rally, Craig," she was saying. Rebecca and Craig fell in love last year at a PETA protest in front of the Waldorf Astoria, while hurling pellets of red paint at mink-clad guests leaving the hotel. Craig is a drummer in an alternative rock band called Hollow Men, but just in case a record deal doesn't come through in the near future, he's holding on to his current job at Starbuck's.

Rebecca works in a small, windowless cubicle. She complains about it at every opportunity, even makes pointed comments about "how nice it must be to have a view of the Hudson River" whenever she comes down the hall to visit me. She'd love a change of venue, but Dana Greene is in a more senior position and has been at Tri-Tech longer than Rebecca, which makes Dana next up for a move out of the "slums," as Rebecca calls the interior offices.

Rebecca hung up as I eased into a chair next to her desk.

"Trouble in paradise?" I said lightly.

"Men!" she said. "The *most important* demonstrations of the year—the ones that coincide with the start of the holiday shopping season—are this weekend, and Craig's backing out to play a gig in Hackensack. Which reminds me, you won't mind if I leave early on Friday, will you? I'm one of the organizers, and I have to be in front of Macy's in time for rush-hour shoppers."

"Not a problem," I said. Animal rights activism is Rebecca's religion; she's as pious as any zealot. As long as she does her work at the office, I don't mind giving her leeway now and then so she can observe the rites of her canon. Joey would be splenetic if he got wind of how I accommodate Rebecca. Still, with every request, Rebecca approaches me in an antagonistic way, as if I were likely to say no. I get the feeling sometimes that she's just itching for an opportunity to argue with me, the way Ellie did during the worst days of her moody adolescence.

"How's the recruitment going?" I said. I listened for

the next few minutes as she ranted, telling me what I already knew about her encounter with Joey. "I'm sorry he made you do that," I said when she finished. "I know how difficult Joey can be. Just treat everything that Joey says as raw, unedited copy. Most people have a filtering system; they're socialized enough to edit themselves. Joey doesn't operate that way, so you have to be his editor. Force yourself to find the valuable idea—and there usually is one hidden in his murky prose—*before* you react to what he's saying. I'll let him know he's out of line. He's not used to working with women as peers. I'm still training him. Remember, you report to me. Let me run interference for you."

"You're a vice president, Sarah. You have more say here, you have a great office, you get to go on trips to terrific places. I just have to put up with him and sit in my crummy office and edit his lousy stuff. For what?"

Yes, I wanted to say, *I have an expense account and a big office with a view. I'm almost twice your age, and I've paid dues I hope you won't have to pay.* "Tell you what, Rebecca. You're putting in a lot of hours on this epilepsy meeting, so I think I can justify taking you to Palm Springs with us. The conference is part of a new-product launch for Savant. That means we'll have a big budget to work with."

Rebecca's eyes widened. "I could go to Palm Springs? I hear it's beautiful."

"Not my kind of place, really. All those fake lawns and fake lakes. And streets named for dubious cultural heroes—Monty Hall Drive, Gene Autry Trail. But we'll stay in a great resort for four days, and you'll have some free time to enjoy the place."

"Thanks. Do you think I could bring Craig with me, if he buys his own plane ticket?"

I sighed. For as smart as she is about some things, Rebecca is slow to catch on to the unwritten behavioral code at Tri-Tech. I could just about hear Joey's response: *She wants to bring her dopey boyfriend? The drummer from Starbucks, the one she's not even married to? To a Savant product meeting?*

"No, Rebecca," I said firmly. "If you'll notice, Lorraine Selber is the only non-Tri-Tech person allowed to come to these meetings. Don't even bring it up."

"Just thought I'd ask. Meanwhile, did you hear about Joey's redecorating binge? Raymond is such a wimp; he didn't even say he minded. Do you think the editorial department is next on Joey's list?"

"Not a chance," I said, standing to leave. "He'd be starting up with the wrong woman."

I spent the rest of the day with the door to my office closed, a signal to my staff that I was writing and didn't want to be disturbed. Joey has put me on a project that's a departure from what Tri-Tech normally does for its clients. I'm designing, and will be leading, several focus group sessions for Pushpa Rao, one of Doc Shortland's product managers. A rising star in the company, Pushpa recognizes that few women—especially young women—get to lead the launch of a new product, and she's grateful for the opportunity that Doc has given her. Joey has turned the project completely over to me. I know why: He is uncomfortable and out of his league with Pushpa, who's from India and has a doctorate in chemistry. If you count the fact that Pushpa is a woman, that makes three strikes against her in Joey's book. He doesn't mind so much that women have advanced to executive positions, but he doesn't think it's fair that he has to adapt his behavior to a new social order.

"It's just not the same anymore, traveling for business, now that you have to take women into account," he says wistfully. "I mean, with men, no matter what city you're in, you can always find a sports bar or a strip club, something fun to do when the conference is over. In the old days, when I was on the road all the time, I knew the best places in every town in upstate New York. The whole picture has changed, with women running the show more and more. Not that I'm sexist—you know I'm not sexist, Sarah, just look at the salary I pay you, haha—I just think it all used to be easier. And anyway, now that Lawrence is my partner, with his religious morals and all, I'd never get away with putting a big night on the town on the company Amex."

The drug that Pushpa is trying to launch is a sleep medication called Repoze. Savant plans to spend a bundle on it, targeting much of its marketing to elderly patients and the people who care for them. For over a month, I've been doing preliminary research for a questionnaire that will help us recruit doctors and nurses for the Repoze focus groups. I've also spent considerable time studying the drug itself—dosages, side effects, interactions with other drugs—in preparation for leading the focus groups. Joey has told Pushpa that I'm an "experienced facilitator," which is probably how his *Finding Your Inner CEO* tape has advised him to describe ex-teachers like me.

I spent several hours organizing more than fifteen pages of the handwritten notes I had made over the last month and entering them into my computer. I refined my ideas for both the recruitment questionnaire and the focus group sessions. My years of teaching and writing lesson plans were serving me well for this project. I named the file "Repoze-Focus Group" and saved it in the "New Projects" folder on my hard drive.

"You still here, Sarah?" The whiny voice of Fawn (née Frances) Mardiss, Tri-Tech's travel director, was coming through the speakerphone on my desk.

This was one of Fawn's rare days in town. Joey keeps her flying all over the country to survey hotels and conference centers for client meetings, and to be on site when the meetings take place. Off the top of her head, Fawn knows which Four Seasons Hotel has the best caterer, which Hyatt the most challenging golf course, which Ritz Carlton the most agreeable concierge. She can recite how many minutes and dollars are required for a limo to every luxury hotel within fifty miles of every airport in the country. A day or two in advance of each conference, Fawn checks into the hotel she's contracted with and terrorizes its staff into submission. Menus are scrutinized: are there the right number of low-salt, vegan, and kosher alternatives? Room assignments are checked: Have Joey and our client (usually Doc Shortland) been assigned equally splendid suites? Do all the invited speakers have the appropriate "amenities" (fruit baskets, wine, souvenirs) awaiting them in their rooms? Recreation options are reviewed: Have enough horses been reserved at the stables for afternoon rides along the beach at Amelia Island? Enough seats for Barry Manilow's show at the Mirage in Las Vegas? Private-tour tickets to the Matisse exhibit at the Chicago Art Institute?

Back home at Tri-Tech, Fawn focuses most of her energy—with laser-like intensity—on Joey. If Sally is Joey's lieutenant, Fawn is his handmaiden. Office gossip has it that Joey and Fawn have been fooling around for years, a logical assumption based on Fawn's apparent obsession with pleasing him. I try not to think about what they might be up to. I don't particularly want the image of Joey and Fawn naked to enter my consciousness.

"Yes, Fawn," I said into the speaker.

"I need to talk to you about your travel for the next few meetings. Can I see you for a minute? I want to wrap this up as quickly as possible." Making travel arrangements for all of us is part of Fawn's job, but she considers it an annoyance to work on behalf of anyone except Joey.

"Okay, but I . . ."

Fawn was in my office before I could finish my thought. She looked dramatically different from when I'd last seen her, ten days earlier, before she left on a whirlwind trip through the Midwest. She was still a redhead then. One of the perks of Fawn's job is that Joey lets her charge hotel beauty salon appointments to the company. In the last year alone, Tri-Tech has subsidized three perms, at least eight radical haircuts, and coast-to-coast tinting, streaking, and highlighting of her tresses, with mixed results. Fawn is in her late thirties, with a pear-shaped figure and leathery skin that add a good ten years to her appearance. Her hair color du jour, meant to be platinum blonde, I guess, made her look prematurely gray rather than glamorous. Her current perm (an unfortunate memento from a layover at the Sheraton in Cleveland) had fried the ends of her locks into brittle wisps.

"Thanks for staying late to see me," she began—obviously implying that I customarily left work before she did, proof that I was less committed than she to Tri-Tech's success. Joey promotes the idea that employees who log in the most hours at the office are somehow more valuable to Tri-Tech. He rewards those who routinely spend ridiculously long days at work—even if there is no evidence that they are accomplishing anything of value by doing so. Joey treats them to expensive lunches, makes a point of complimenting them publicly.

"It's not too late," I said. It was ten after five. "What can I do for you?"

"I'm trying to get reasonable airfares for the meetings coming up. Joey was saying, and I agree, that if we put you on a red-eye back from Palm Springs, we'll save a bundle."

"Not a good idea, Fawn. It will take me a week to recover. I don't mind leaving here very early in the morning, or getting back late at night. But I'm too old to handle all-nighters." I forced a smile.

"Funny, Lawrence said the same thing."

"Lawrence is going to these meetings?"

"Maybe the one in Palm Springs. Someone Lawrence knows from Harvard is now a big shot at Savant and will be at the meeting. Joey thought it might do us some good if Lawrence was there."

"Lawrence doesn't want to fly all night either? Imagine that."

"Just like you, he said he's too old."

"What about the meeting in DC?"

"I'll book your plane tickets this week."

"Flying to DC from New York is ridiculous. I live in Manhattan, remember? It's crazy for me to go all the way to the airport, when I can get on a train at Penn Station, which is ten minutes from my house. I won't save any time by flying, and Tri-Tech won't save any money . . ."

"Joey feels, and I'm with him on this, that as a vice president, you should be flying down. The directors—Raymond and the others—are taking the train."

"Tell Joey I'll swear not to tell anyone at the meeting in DC how I got there. Then book me, please, on the Metroliner."

Fawn pursed her lips. "I'll have to run this by Joey. Have a good evening."

———

KEVIN WAS ON the phone with his son Brendan when I got home from work. I heard Kevin promising to leave a key with our doorman. "See you tomorrow, son," he said. He hung up and leaned over to peck me on the cheek.

"Brendan's coming?" I said.

"Yeah, a college friend of his is getting married in Brooklyn on Sunday. And there's an old pal he wants to spend time with while he's here. Lilly, I think. She's going to the wedding with him. I told him we'd take them out to a nice restaurant on Saturday night. Maybe that Thai place on . . ."

I interrupted him. "The Gillians' party is Saturday night."

"Oh, right. Brendan and Lilly can just come along. There's lots of room in that monster SUV you're driving these days."

"Violet and Grant will be here from Florida, and I promised we'd put them up in Ellie's room for the weekend and drive them to the party with us." I felt my jaw tighten, heard my voice starting to rise.

"Then Brendan will just sleep on the sofa in the living room. He and Lilly can take the train to Connecticut."

"Brendan is six foot three. Our sofa is too small for him. I suppose I can ask Miriam if Violet and Grant can stay with her. But we can't just show up at the party with two extra guests."

"You know Beth and Jim won't mind. What's the big deal?"

I shook my head in exasperation.

"Why are you upset, Sarah?" he said. "This is a very small thing, really. What's your problem?"

"My problem? My problem is that you O'Neal boys—you and Brendan—don't mind leaving things until the last minute, and you don't think how your lack of planning affects anyone else. Brendan must have known about this wedding for some time. Why didn't he give us more notice?"

"My son doesn't need a formal invitation to visit me. Elinor drops in whenever she feels like it."

"This is Ellie's home. And she's a college kid, not a thirty-three-year-old adult. Besides, I wouldn't let her impose unreasonable demands on my schedule."

"Is it unreasonable for my son to want to visit me?"

"You know that's not what I'm saying. But every time he comes, we don't know his plans until the last minute, or his plans change without notice. His visits are never easy, they're chaotic and disruptive."

"What are you talking about? Brendan asks very little of us."

"Except, perhaps, when he wants to see a concert. Tina Turner, maybe?"

My trump card. When Brendan was in graduate school, he once asked me to pick up tickets for him and a friend for a Tina Turner concert at Madison Square Garden. Kevin and I were both out of town on business the day of the concert, but we left a key for them so they could use our apartment while they were in town. When I got home from my trip, the key was still with the doorman, and the hundred-dollar concert tickets I had stood in line for hours to buy were still on the dining room table. There was a phone message from Brendan: He had suddenly realized, in the hours just before he was to board the train to New York, that he was behind on his dissertation, and he needed to stay in Boston to work at the library.

Kevin turned his eyes away. He didn't want to have this conversation. "Why are you still carrying on about that? Can't you drop it? I paid you back for the damn tickets."

"The money is the least of it. Maybe I would have let this go if Brendan had ever apologized. Or if his father had reprimanded him for his bad manners."

"He's an adult, Sarah. I don't reprimand my son anymore."

"Adults try to be considerate of other people's feelings. And their schedules."

An icy silence set in.

"Do you want me to tell Brendan to find another place

to stay for the weekend?" Kevin finally said.

"No, don't be ridiculous. Just do me a favor, call him back and make sure he's actually coming. Then I'll see if Beth is all right with two more guests at the party. I'll ask Miriam if she can have Violet and Grant stay at her place. If she can, I'll have to call Violet and Grant, too, to let them know to take a cab take directly to Miriam's from the airport."

"I'm sure it'll all work out," Kevin said.

Yes, I thought as I walked to our bedroom and shut the door. It will all work out, as soon as I make ten phone calls and upend everyone's plans for Brendan's sake.

I heard the beeps of the telephone buttons from the other room; Kevin was calling Brendan. A few minutes later, Kevin yelled from the kitchen, "It's definite, Sarah. Brendan will be here on Friday afternoon."

"Fine," I said, from my side of the closed door. I pushed the automatic dial button for Beth's phone number.

"You sound pissed," Beth said when I told her about Brendan and Lilly. "Really, you know it's no problem on our end. We'd love to have them. What's going on there, Sarah?"

"I can't talk now," I said.

I called Miriam next; she was delighted to offer her place to Violet and Grant and to accompany them to the party. She, too, heard the tension in my voice.

"Let me call Violet," Miriam said. "Sounds like you have a lot going on at your house tonight. Anything you want to talk about?"

"No, but thanks. I'll see you Saturday."

"Have you checked the mail?" Kevin called from the kitchen. "There's something from Sidney Greenberg for you."

"From Sidney, not Helen?" On the rare occasions

when my in-laws communicated by mail, it was Helen who wrote. She occasionally sent clippings from the local papers in Acedia Bay, mostly social announcements or obituaries. I couldn't remember ever receiving a letter from Sidney.

"Yes, in an envelope from some hotel."

The letter was handwritten on stationery from the Doubletree in Nashville.

Sarah,

I'm in Nashville, meeting with Martin's lawyers and gathering his personal effects. I'm the executor of Martin's estate. Martin left a sizeable inheritance to Ellie, which I'm sure is no surprise to you. He invested the money his parents left him, and his investments did well. I know Ellie is an adult now, but before the money is disbursed, you should make sure she has reliable financial advice. As soon as things are settled I will let Ellie know what's going on. You may want to talk to her before I do.

Martin's girlfriend Pauline found a key to a safe deposit box in Atlanta, and a letter, undated, in which Martin makes reference to another lawyer. I think the letter was written years ago, when Martin wasn't at his best. It's a little confusing, but I'm trying to sort it all out. I'm going to Atlanta when I finish here.

The good news is that there seems to be at least half a million dollars, maybe more, for Ellie. But it may take a while before we know what's what. I'll be in touch.

Love, Sidney.

I hadn't even considered the possibility that Martin had money to leave Ellie. So much money, too. Enough for law school, for whatever she needs to start her life.

Ellie would be at her moot court class tonight. I called her apartment anyway, left a message with Doug. "Tell her to call me tonight, no matter how late," I told him. "I have great news for her." I made a mental note to talk to Jim Gillian, get the name of a financial advisor. But to Kevin, I didn't intend to say a word. For the first time since we've been together, I found myself deliberately hiding something important from him. And I was thinking, *You're not the only one who knows how to hold things back, Kevin.*

———

DOC INTERRUPTED OUR French lesson to tell me that Savant had chosen his replacement and would reveal the name soon, probably after the weekend.

"This is going to be a surprise to Joey," Doc said.

"A pleasant surprise?"

"That's a good question. I'm sworn to secrecy, but I can tell you this much: Joey wouldn't have picked this person."

I wasn't sure what else to say on the topic. I knew that Joey would want me to press for more information, but I had no desire to play Twenty Questions with Doc Shortland.

"Let's just get back to our lesson, shall we?" I said. "We were at the train station, buying tickets for a trip through the Alps. *Alors, à quelle heure voudriez-vous partir, monsieur?*"

———

I ASKED SALLY to schedule a few minutes for me with Joey.

"What's the subject of the meeting?" she asked, flipping through Joey's appointment book, which she keeps open on her desk.

"Shortland's replacement."

"I can give you fifteen minutes at four-thirty." The

palace guard, protecting the king.

"I think he'll want to know about this before then. I only need about five minutes."

"I'll check with him and let you know. He's tied up with Lawrence now and can't be disturbed until late in the afternoon."

Tied up with Lawrence for hours? I've never known the two of them to spend so much time together without a referee.

"You know where to find me," I said.

On my desk were itineraries for the meetings coming up and a note from Fawn: "I've got the travel agent holding these flights for you. Please initial each page if you approve." She had spelled "approve" with one *p*. As if we had never spoken, Fawn had booked me on the red-eye for my return flight from the Palm Springs meeting, which would get me back to New York around dawn. I was also scheduled to fly to Washington.

I dialed Fawn's extension.

"Fawn, about my itineraries . . .?" I began.

"Um, Joey wants me to get the best prices on airfares."

"If he's so concerned about costs, why is he insisting that I fly to DC?"

"I'm just following his orders. He's the boss. Oh, and Rebecca is scheduled on the same flights as you for the Palm Springs meeting."

"Did Joey tell you to book Rebecca's flight?" I asked, surprised.

"I never do anything without Joey's permission, Sarah."

I dialed Sally's extension.

"Sally, as it turns out, I will need fifteen or twenty minutes with Joey after all."

"He's still in conference with Lawrence Zimmerman," she said. As if I wouldn't know which Lawrence she meant. Sally is especially irritating when she gets formal and officious, which she's been doing with more frequency lately.

"Let me know when he's free. I need to speak to him today."

Raymond appeared as I was reaching for the phone to call home. I wanted to check on whether Brendan was in yet.

"Should I come back later, Sarah?"

"No problem. Have a seat."

"Joey says you're working on some project with Pushpa Rao at Savant."

"Yes, a focus group connected to the Repoze launch."

"Joey thought you might need some help, what with having to be away from work so much to give those French lessons."

Something struck me as odd. It sounded as if Raymond had rehearsed what he was saying.

"Those French lessons *are* work. And so far, I'm not having any trouble staying on deadline with my other projects." I realized I sounded defensive. Why defend myself to him?

"Yeah, I know. Maybe Joey just wanted to make sure you have the necessary support for this Repoze thing. I mean, my pharmacy expertise may come in handy. If you like, I can take a look at what you've put together so far and orientate you to some of the pharmacy issues with this class of drugs."

Orientate? Now I was sure that Joey had coached him.

"Thanks *so much* for offering," I gushed. "I'll let you know if I need help."

I reached for my phone to signal him that our meeting was over. Raymond slithered out of the room.

A familiar wave of anxiety swept over me. I've been a casualty of corporate shakeups often enough to know the signs. Lawrence could be wrong; perhaps the Savant restructuring didn't bode well for Tri-Tech after all. I thought about all that had been amiss lately, or was just different somehow, trying to figure out how the pieces connected. Shortland's French lessons—a way to keep me out of the office for a few hours every day? But, why? Joey and Lawrence sequestered all afternoon today. Fawn's absurd travel arrangements for me. Rebecca scheduled to go to Palm Springs without my knowledge. And Raymond: Why the hell did Joey send him around?

It occurred to me that, except for the Repoze program and Shortland's French lessons, all projects in my department were team activities. I prefer it that way. Writing is a lonely business, and I think corporate writers do better by working cooperatively. My three junior editors research and fact-check all our manuscripts. Rebecca creates new copy and collaborates with Raymond to make certain the scientific information is accurate. Dana fine-tunes every paragraph—scrutinizing content and layout, ferreting out inconsistencies and errors in punctuation and grammar. The last edit is mine. I sign off on every piece—proposals for new business, Joey's presentations, handouts for the conferences. Of course, I supervise at every stage, though I don't hover. I trust everyone who works for me to do a good job. Without me, Joey could pull my staff together and get a clear picture of where each project stands.

Not everyone likes the group editing process I've set up. Rebecca, especially, is sensitive about Dana's changes to her writing. Dana and Rebecca don't like each other much, anyway. Dana's polish and confidence—bred into the bone of high-achieving families like hers, and nurtured at Dalton and Yale—don't mix well with Rebecca's raw ambition and bachelor's degree from Fairleigh Dickinson, the college famously known in the Northeast as Fairly Ridiculous. And Dana appreciates the friendship of other women. She and I see each other from time to time outside of work, and I know she's made overtures to Rebecca, asking her out to lunch and such, though not lately.

Rebecca operates more the way I've seen men behave at their jobs: reflexively defensive, competitive, and territorial. Dana has lately described Rebecca as someone who would shoot her own grandmother if Granny stood in Rebecca's path to the corner office. Nonetheless, old-fashioned feminist that I am, I had consistently lobbied on Rebecca's behalf, kept her insulated from Joey. Was she trying to unseat me? Didn't she understand that women can't survive in the workplace—certainly not in a place like Tri-Tech—without loyalty to each other?

It seemed that Joey wanted me gone, but I couldn't tell if he was about to fire me or if he intended to marginalize me so I'd leave on my own. Was anyone else about to get the ax? I wanted to think that my presence would be missed—I'd come to the company with more writing experience than anyone else, after all, and I had managed my department and the company's clients pretty well. And I thought I was managing Joey better than most. But I've been laid off, and watched others get laid off, too many times not to understand the primary operating principle of corporate life: No one is indispensable.

I figured I was safe, maybe, for at least a month. Joey wouldn't get rid of me until Shortland left for Switzerland and the French lessons were over. Joey didn't want Shortland—or any client—ever to get the impression that things at Tri-Tech were unstable. That would bring me close to the end of the year, and my three-year bonus, the one that was tied to the partnership Joey had teased me with from my first day at Tri-Tech. Nothing was in writing, though. All I had was Joey's word.

At least I could count on the usual end-of-year bonus

that was based on the formula in the employee handbook. Joey had completed my annual review in August, a few months early. He described my performance as "superb," giving me a rating of 9.6 out of a possible 10. According to the Tri-Tech's human resources policy, this excellent annual review assured me of at least a fifteen percent year-end bonus (not counting what Joey had promised me for my having agreed to schlep to New Jersey to give Shortland his French lessons), plus a ten percent raise in salary. The raise was supposed to begin at the time of the review, but Joey asked if he could defer the increase until the end of the year, and include it retroactively in my bonus check. "It will make our cash flow a little easier for now," he had said. "I'm sure you understand—after all, you'll be a partner soon, and you need to start thinking in terms of what's good for Tri-Tech." Of course I didn't mind, I had told him.

What a team player I'd been. What a good sport. What a damn fool.

I pulled up the New Projects folder on my computer and opened my "Repoze—Focus Group" file. This was one project no one else could easily complete on time. I was the only one with the right background, the only one who had been in frequent contact with the client, the only one familiar with the product. Raymond? He knows pharmacy, but he has no idea how to design or run a focus group, though he wouldn't let that stand in his way. Like Rebecca, he coveted the trappings of my job—the big office, the title, the travel. And he'd do Joey's bidding without hesitation.

Maybe I'm being paranoid, I thought. *God, I hope so; the last thing I need is to be unemployed. Again!* But, as Beth says, even paranoiacs have real enemies. I needed to talk to Lawrence, the only person at Tri-Tech I could trust. If he knew what was going on, he'd tell me.

PART II: SARAH

Lawrence was slumped over his desk, head in his hands. My knock startled him.

"You okay?" I said.

"I guess so. Come on in," he whispered, motioning me to close his door. "I think Joey has left, but I'm not sure who else is around."

"Lawrence, what's going on?"

He didn't answer for several moments.

"Have a seat, Sarah. I do have something to tell you." He took a deep breath. "I'm leaving the company."

"What? Why?"

"Joey is about to make some major changes here. And it doesn't seem as if I fit in to his new plans."

"He fired you?"

"It's not that simple. I'm a partner. But, yes, in effect, he's fired me."

"When are you leaving?"

"Joey wants me to clean out my office over the weekend. He'll probably have one of his critical announcement meetings next week to tell the staff about me. With all the appropriate four-color handouts, I'm sure."

"What will you do? Do you have another job?"

"I've been in this business for a long time. I have contacts."

"Remind me, how long have you been with Tri-Tech?"

He hesitated for a second, and then said pointedly, "Four years and seven months. Just five months short of being vested in the retirement plan."

"Unbelievable. Is there nothing you can do?"

Lawrence sighed. "The terms of the separation agreement Joey is trying to work out with me are pretty specific about my not revealing some things to other employees."

"I'm so sorry, Lawrence. Sorry for you, and for me, too. I can't imagine working here without you."

A worried look came over his face. "Sarah . . ." he

began.

"Is there something more?"

"I think you can guess."

"Am I next?"

He leaned forward and spoke deliberately. "Smart executives always keep their résumés current."

"Thanks, Lawrence. You've just confirmed what I've been suspecting. Joey wants to cut costs, and he can get younger, less experienced people to work here for half our salaries. Am I getting warm?"

He nodded slowly. I knew he had already told me as much as he could.

"Hey," I said, "can I help you pack your stuff or anything?"

"No, thanks anyway. I'll do it tomorrow."

I stood up and walked to his side of the desk.

"Give me a hug," I said. "You'll be fine, you know. Some great company will know they'll be lucky to have you. Promise you'll keep me posted on what's happening with you?"

"Of course I will. Lucy and I will have you and Kevin over for dinner sometime soon. And Sarah, you'll be fine, too. No matter what happens here."

The Repoze file was still on the screen when I went back to my office. I transferred it to a floppy disk and deleted the file from my hard drive. I slipped the disk and my copy of the *Tri-Tech Employee Handbook* into my brief-case, turned off the light on my desk, and made my way out the door.

I was halfway home, bobbing and weaving on the Broadway uptown local, when I realized that Joey had left the office for the day without speaking to me. Not even Shortland's replacement, which I had told Sally was the topic I wanted to discuss with him, had piqued his interest enough to make him want to see me.

Part II: Sarah

***

Brendan O'Neal had already set himself up in Ellie's room by the time I got home. I found him lying on Ellie's bed, watching CNN, idly flipping through an *L.L. Bean* catalogue. I tried to ignore the mud-caked hiking boots that he rested nonchalantly atop the white duvet. He stood to greet me, tentative as usual, awkwardly wrapping his long, bony arms around my shoulders. Brendan is skinny and pale, with dark, curly hair that has seldom been privilege to a decent haircut. His eyeglasses, hopelessly large and too rounded for current fashion, give him a goofy, bookish mien. He still looks like a grad student, though he finished at MIT a few years ago and now works for a computer software company.

Brendan looks nothing like his father, nor has he acquired any of Kevin's social grace. Kevin is so affable, so easy with people. Stocky and athletic, with a ruddy complexion and thin, reddish hair, Kevin always looks as if he's smiling, even when his face is in repose. He is an impeccable dresser—one of the first things I noticed about him was the way he was dressed the night we met at a mutual friend's birthday party. Most of the men were in khakis and open-necked shirts. Kevin wore gray slacks, a black cashmere turtleneck, and a silk tweed blazer. In contrast, Brendan's clothes rarely match, and he always looks as if he's slept in them.

I steered Brendan into the kitchen and poured some wine for both of us.

"Where's the wedding on Sunday?" I asked.

"Park Slope, wherever that is. I assume I can get there by subway?"

"Easily. Your dad said you were also planning to see an old friend while you're here. Do you know if she'll be coming with us to Connecticut tomorrow night?"

"Connecticut?" he said blankly.

"Didn't your dad mention my friends' party?"

"I'm not sure. I don't think so, though."

Damn it, Kevin. "Major soirée at my friend Beth's house," I said. "She and her husband have this huge party every fall. Guaranteed great food. Gorgeous house."

"I'll have to ask Lilly. It may be a little weird for her. Are you sure we can just show up?"

"The hosts are already expecting you. I assumed your father would have thought to mention it," I said. My sarcastic tone was lost on Brendan.

I heard Kevin's key in the door.

"Sushi delivery!" Kevin called from the foyer. "Futomaki, California rolls, green tea ice cream for one and all."

I grabbed the bags of food from Kevin's hand and we exchanged a perfunctory peck on the cheek. Kevin and Brendan embraced. Lots of backslapping, mock punches, no kissing.

"You look great, son," Kevin beamed. "Sarah, doesn't Brendan look great?"

In truth, Brendan appeared to me as he always did: listless, disheveled, and slightly uncomfortable.

"He looks terrific," I said. "Listen, guys, I'm not very hungry. Maybe I'll just leave you two alone for some male bonding."

"Are you all right?" said Kevin.

"Tough day. I'm a little tired. And I think that glass of wine got to me."

"What's going on, Sarah?"

I said, "Brendan, could I speak to your dad privately for a minute? I'll see you in the morning."

Kevin followed me to our bedroom. I sat on our bed. Kevin remained standing, leaned his elbow on the dresser.

"Here's the summary of my day," I said. "Lawrence is leaving the company—Joey fired him, or did whatever you have to do to get rid of a partner. I think I'm next, though I probably have a month before anything happens to me. I've worn myself out just thinking about this all day today, and I don't really want to talk about it anymore just now."

Kevin put his arms around my shoulders. "That bastard Joey!" he said. "What can I do for you?"

"I'm not sure what anyone can do. But for now, for this weekend, I would love to just enjoy Beth's party and not think about my stupid job until I need to go back to it on Monday. okay?"

"Whatever you want," Kevin said.

"And Kev," I said pointedly, "for some reason, Brendan is clueless about the party. Can you please see to it that, if he is joining us, that he has something decent to wear, and that his friend, if she's joining us, knows what time we're leaving the city? You can tell them I plan to be on the road to Connecticut by six-thirty tomorrow evening, and anyone who isn't ready can't come with me. You might also mention that the hosts are expecting us . . ."

"Okay, Sarah. Please calm down," Kevin said. He doesn't care much for arguing. He grew up with an alcoholic father, and though I don't have a complete picture of Kevin's upbringing, I can surmise that he had his fill of confrontation at home. As a result, he does his best to keep disagreements from escalating. When I think kindly of him, I ascribe this trait to his good nature and his success at having overcome a dysfunctional childhood. When I am irritated with him, I view his reluctance to get angry as further evidence of his emotional distance from me. Sometimes I think a strong, fair fight would do our relationship some good. The closest we come is an occasional volley of peevish remarks, followed by a couple of days of silence, and then amnesia.

"I'll talk to Brendan," he said. No explanation for why he hadn't talked to Brendan about the party before tonight.

I was almost asleep when Kevin crawled into bed next to me. I was on my side, turned away from him. He put his arm around me and bent his knees so he could slide his legs close, parallel to mine.

"Sarah?" he said.

"Mm?"

"I realize you don't want to talk about what's going on at the office, but I thought of something . . ."

"What?"

"You need to protect yourself."

"No kidding."

"Get a lawyer. Get some advice."

"I don't have money for a lawyer. And I don't have a case, at least not yet."

"What about Bruce Jacobs? You can talk to him at the party tomorrow night."

"Beth's brother? He handles copyrights and patents."

"But he works in a huge firm. A good one. He'll know an employment lawyer."

I shifted around to see Kevin's face. "I'll think about it. But not now. I'm exhausted."

"I just want you to play this *smart*. You've put up with Joey for three years. You should have that bonus and a share of the company. It's what he promised you, after all. But you may need a lawyer to help you get it."

In a crisis, no one is more reliable than Kevin. He knows how to comfort me without managing me, knows when I need to be held, or helped, or simply left alone. When my parents died—both of them of heart attacks shortly after Kevin and I met—Kevin was unfailingly dependable and loving. I've lost my job twice since we've been together—both times due to factors beyond my control—and Kevin kept me from letting my anger paralyze me. He helped me to mobilize the confidence and energy I needed to find work again. Now he was already at full battle alert, preparing to take up arms against Joey on my behalf.

So what if things weren't perfect between us? What did it matter, really, that he tended to hold things back from me? That sometimes, even in bed, he seemed detached, walled off? If Kevin was somewhat secretive and removed by nature, I could also point to plenty of times when he was on my side, by my side. As if we were a real couple.

As I drifted to sleep, feeling the warmth of Kevin's body nestled against mine, the flaws in our relationship seemed trivial. The last thought on my mind before I nodded off was, *Things could be worse.*

Late Saturday morning, I was awakened by the sound of our cappuccino-maker whipping milk into foam. Kevin had left a note taped to the bathroom mirror:

> *Brendan and I have gone in search of suitable duds for the party tonight.*
> *His friend Lilly, and fresh bagels, await you in the kitchen.*
> *K.*

I smiled at his message, then saw my face in the glass. *You look awfully happy for someone who is about to be unemployed*, I thought.

Lilly had the *Times* spread out on the dining room table and was about to bite into a heavily buttered pumpernickel raisin bagel when I padded into the room.

"Hi. I hope you're Lilly," I said. "Otherwise, I'm going to have to insist that you leave that bagel right where it is!"

"And you must be Sarah," she answered, smiling.

"Did you bring these bagels? Thanks," I said, starting to make a cappuccino for myself. "What time did the boys leave?"

"Around ten, I think. Brendan told me to come early, for breakfast, but he forgot to mention that he had to go shopping for something to wear to this party tonight. Typical! He told me to wait here for him, said it shouldn't be long. I hope you don't mind."

"Happy to have you," I said. I guessed Lilly to be in her mid-twenties—not much older than Ellie—though I never would have taken her for a college student. Exceptionally pretty, Lilly had the sophisticated look that some women easily acquire as soon as they enter the work force. Her dark hair was blunt cut and styled, not just chopped, to shoulder length. Her nails were freshly manicured. She wore taupe suede pants and a beige silk turtleneck; her outfit was especially flattering to her tall, slim body. I couldn't help wondering what attracted her to Brendan.

"Tell me about yourself," I said. "How do you and Brendan know each other?"

"I met Brendan in Boston. One of his roommates dated one of mine."

"I had the impression that you two were—um—involved at one point."

"No, no," she said emphatically. "Brendan and I are not even that close, really, but we like the same kind of music and stuff. He sometimes calls me when he's in New York. We both know the guy who's getting married tomorrow, so we'll go to the wedding together."

"You went to MIT?"

"Not me. I went to art school. I'm a fabric designer now."

"How interesting."

"Well, it isn't really. I know I'm lucky to be doing anything even remotely related to art, but most of the stuff I design is for cheap fabrics—the kind that wind up as sheets and curtains you'd never want in your house," she said, her eyes wandering appreciatively over our furniture. She shrugged, as if to indicate that she was resigned to her disappointing job.

From where I sat, I could see a small tapestry suitcase on the floor near the living room sofa. "Is that yours?" I asked.

"I hope you don't mind," she said. "Brendan thought it would be a good idea for me to bring my clothes for the party and just change here. I live in the Village, and I wasn't sure I'd have time to get back there before we left for Connecticut."

"That's fine," I said. So, Kevin had taken me seriously when I warned him I wanted to leave for the party on time. "I think you'll enjoy the party. Beth and Jim, the hosts, are old friends of mine. Beth was an art history major. Wait until you see her art collection."

"Is that your daughter?" Lilly asked, pointing to Ellie's high school graduation photograph, which sat in a leather frame on one of the bookshelves in the living room.

"Yes. She's a senior in college now, but she hasn't changed much since that picture was taken."

"She doesn't really look like you," Lilly said, studying my face.

From birth, Ellie has resembled her father's family. Like all the Roth women, Ellie is a beauty, just over five feet tall and small-boned, with dark skin that tans easily; large, expressive, dark brown eyes; and wavy, almost-black hair. I'm taller than average, with auburn hair and blue eyes, and, like the women in my family, moderately attractive in an ordinary sort of way. From time to time, people say that Ellie shares my smile, and though I'd like to believe that some part of her body resembles mine, I don't see it.

"I know. Lucky her, I guess, not to look like her old mom."

"No, you're very pretty," said Lilly, as if she were expressing a simple statement of fact. "And you look so young for your age. Oops, I didn't mean that the way it came out."

I laughed. "I'll take it as a compliment. I was fortunate to be born into a family where no one gets gray hair. And my mother had lovely skin. This stuff is all in the genes, don't you think?"

"Mostly, yes. I look very much like my mother. How about personality? Likes, dislikes, talents, that sort of thing? Do you suppose that's all inherited, too?"

"I'm not sure. My daughter is quite different from me. She's good at things I could never do—math, for example. She has a lovely singing voice; I can barely carry a tune. And look at Kevin and Brendan! They look nothing alike, and they couldn't be more different—in temperament, I mean. Kevin is so outgoing, Brendan is so quiet . . . "

Lilly interrupted me, looking puzzled. "You're kidding, right?"

"Why do you ask?"

"About Kevin and Brendan. I mean, being adopted and all, Brendan wouldn't necessarily . . ."

Lilly locked her gaze on my stunned face.

"You didn't know, Sarah, did you?" she said quietly. I shook my head. "Oh, my God. I don't know what to say. Brendan told me years ago. Betsy, his mother, became pregnant with Brendan when she was in college, but the father didn't want to marry her. She's Catholic, you know, so she'd never consider an abortion. Were they even legal then? Anyway, Kevin was at college with Betsy, and he wound up marrying her shortly after Brendan was born. Kevin is the only father Brendan knows or wants to know."

I said, "And Kevin considers himself Brendan's father. Maybe that's all that matters." I tried to sound convincing about this.

Lilly was speaking very quickly. "This all came up when one of our friends in Boston went on a mission to find her biological parents. Brendan said he had no interest in contacting his own biological father, didn't want to make Kevin feel bad. And then, the week before Brandon graduated from his master's program at MIT, his mother decided to tell him who his real father was. She sent Brendan a letter, with pictures of the guy from thirty years ago and a current phone number for him somewhere in the Midwest. The letter said that she had been in touch with the man all these years and that Kevin was aware of all of this. Brendan just went crazy. I mean, her timing was bizarre—right before graduation and everything. Brendan says he had always told her that he didn't want to know anything about the man, but she sort of forced him to deal with all of this. Brendan was so open with me, and we don't even know each other very well. I just assumed you'd know."

Yes, you would assume, as any normal person would, that Kevin would have thought to mention to the woman he's lived with for four years that his son was adopted. Especially since his son shares the information even with mere acquaintances.

"Lilly, stop apologizing. Let's just forget it happened. And do me a favor, will you? Don't mention to Kevin or Brendan that you and I have talked about this. No need to make it a bigger deal than it is." Lilly looked relieved.

I, too, was relieved. A woman I had known for thirty minutes had just helped me see a truth about Kevin that had eluded me for years. The information was strangely liberating, as if I'd suddenly lifted a translucent shield from in front of my face—a filmy barrier that had permitted light to enter my eyes but which kept my brain from identifying the real shape and color of things.

"Scratch a lover," said Dorothy Parker, "and find a foe."

MIRIAM:
TOUCH AND GO

"And her heart is full and hollow
Like a cactus tree"
—Joni Mitchell

I STAYED IN TOUCH with Miss Emma for a few years after I left Savannah. From time to time, she sent cheery missives on her pale blue monogrammed stationery: *I hope you are happy, dear, and that we'll see each other again soon.*

I replied on picture postcards with seasonal bulletins from New York. *My school has been closed for three days because of a snowstorm. The tulips are already blooming in Central Park. They say we're in for a hot summer.*

Now and then, Winnie and I exchanged letters, too. *I'm cashing in on the local tour business,* she wrote. *That scandalous book,* Midnight in the Garden of Good and Evil, *has made Savannah THE place! Everyone wants to come here, to see Johnny Mercer's house and meet Miss Chablis. I'm bringing in tourists by the bus and plane load, filling up hotel rooms, even giving walking tours myself. Looks like the Good Lord never intended for me to retire after all!*

I often wondered how and when I'd manage to see Miss Emma and Winnie again. Then, after a long spell of silence, a letter from Winnie:

> *Dear Miriam,*
>
> *I am sorry to be the one to tell you this. I wasn't even sure I should write, but I thought you would want to know.*
>
> *Miss Emma died last Monday. She had a bad fall a while back. It was downhill after that, you know how things go with older people. Anyway, she was not herself. She moved in with Peter, and she was at home with him when she passed. It was a beautiful funeral. All her church friends were there. Miss Emma was 88 years old. She had a good life.*
>
> *I hope all is fine with you. Again, I am so sorry to write with sad news.*
>
> *Love, Winnie*

I wanted permission to call Peter.

I tried to convince myself that it was simply a matter of good manners to call an old friend who had just lost his mother.

Winnie would probably let Peter know that she had written to me about his mother. He would, naturally, wonder why I didn't call. After all, I'd been so fond of Miss Emma.

I could keep the conversation brief, chatty, superficial. *Yes, I'm still teaching at the same school, still living in the same place.*

I'd resist the temptation to ask what I really wanted to know. Have you fallen in love with someone else? Have you taken her to Elizabeth's? Where do you keep the picture of me in my green dress? Do you look the same? Do you still sail? Does it clutch at your heart to think of me?

But I didn't call. Instead, I sent a donation to have a

tree planted in Miss Emma's memory in an Israeli forest close to Bethlehem. Jewish people do this all the time when someone dies, but I didn't think anyone at Prince of Peace Lutheran Church in Savannah would honor Miss Emma quite the same way. I knew she would have loved the idea. I gave Peter's address as the place where the certificate documenting the location of her tree was to be sent.

A thank-you arrived weeks later, a folded white card—the kind you order right from the funeral home—with a line drawing of prayerful hands, and pre-printed sentiment in raised black letters: *The family of Emma Robinette is grateful for your kind expression of sympathy at her passing.* Below this, handwritten in deep blue ink: *How nice of you to plant the tree for Mom. I hope you are well. Peter.*

I MET CAMERON Murphy, my date for the Gillians' party, years ago, when he sold me the co-op apartment I still live in. My down payment came from money Dad left me when he died. Mom objected to the idea—buying my own home instead of waiting for a husband to provide one further deflated her dwindling hopes for me.

After the closing on my place, I didn't see or hear from Cameron again until we ran into each other one morning years later, while shopping on the Lower East Side. I noticed him eyeing me as we perused the selection at A. Altman Luggage on Orchard Street.

"Miriam, isn't it? Miriam Kaplan?"

"Yes?"

"Cameron Murphy. I sold you a co-op uptown many years ago."

"Cameron. Of course. You know, I'm still at the same place."

"I assume you got rid of the bathroom wallpaper."

"I can't believe you remember that. Awful, wasn't it?"

"And hard to forget. Black background, hundreds of lime green peace symbols that actually glowed in the dark."

Cameron had aged well. The gray at his temples and the soft wrinkles around his eyes added interest to what had once been a rather undistinguished youthful face.

"I ripped down that paper right after the closing," I laughed. "I actually saved a scrap of it, in case I ever had to prove I once had the most bizarre bathroom walls in Manhattan."

The little I once knew about Cameron Murphy was slowly coming back to me. Murphy Realty was a family business. He worked with his father and a sister. He had been married when I knew him years earlier, but I saw no wedding ring now. Wife had some political job, maybe? They had kids, twin boys.

"Do you still teach?" he was asking.

"Still at it. I'm flattered that you remember."

"I remember you, all right. You're quite—um—memorable. And you still look the same."

He's flirting. Need to find out about the wife.

"Why, thank you. I seem to recall you had twin boys. They must be—what?—close to thirty now?"

"Now *I'm* flattered! My boys are thirty-two, both married. The older one works in the business with me. He and his wife have given me a granddaughter. The brightest, prettiest, most willful four-year-old alive. Has me wrapped around her finger."

"And your wife? Didn't she have some sort of community service job—in the mayor's office, maybe?"

"Right again. She worked in the mayor's cultural affairs office."

"Not any longer?"

He took a breath. "She passed away five years ago."

"Cameron, I'm sorry. I didn't mean to . . ."

"I don't mind talking about it. Charlotte had cancer. She was in and out of Sloan-Kettering for years before she went. It was a tough time for us all, but well, you know what they say, life goes on."

"Are you buying luggage for a trip to someplace exciting?" I asked, eager to veer from the topic at hand.

"This set is for the kids—the whole family's going on a Disney cruise. And you?"

"The school year just started, so I don't have plans to travel any time soon. But I wanted to treat myself to some new luggage." I tapped the retractable handle of a bright red suitcase.

"Are you planning on taking that with you?"

"I was just going to wheel it to the subway."

"Before you do, can I buy you a cup of coffee?"

Over onion rolls and a platter of smoked white fish at Ratner's, Cameron showed me pictures of his children and his perfect granddaughter, and, though I didn't ask, offered up painstaking details about the late Charlotte's hard-to-diagnose disease, the suffering she endured, the treatment she tolerated, the bravery she exhibited, the void she left in his life.

He asked what just about everyone asks me, or wants to: How come you never got married? And I gave the answer I always give: Just lucky, I guess, (smile), no really, I came close a few times, but things just didn't work out. I don't discuss the Savannah episode; I don't go into details at all. I haven't met a man in ages who has thought to ask for further information on the subject.

Which explains, to a certain degree, why Cameron and I are now several years into a relationship that's no deeper or more complex than it was when we had that breakfast together at Ratner's. We've been to bed a few times, though not very recently, and the experience was pleasant, but not the stuff that gives rise to lingering desire. We have enough in common so that we can thoroughly enjoy an occasional evening out without yearning for even one extra minute together. He'll never appreciate my addiction to movies, and I'll never understand his devotion to golf, but none of it matters since nothing between us . . . matters. As my students say these days, it is what it is.

———————

VIOLET AND GRANT, up from Florida for the Gillians' bash, stayed at my place for the weekend. Cameron came by early Saturday afternoon to watch a football game with Grant before we left for Connecticut. It was an Indian summer day, perfect weather for the party.

Violet had brought me a gift of *Goldfinger* on DVD.

"I understand this movie has special meaning for you," Violet said. "I must have seen it years ago, but I don't remember for sure. All the Bond movies kind of blend in my mind."

"Oh, but this one is unforgettable," I said. "Especially the first few minutes. Sean Connery emerges from murky waters onto the shore of some banana republic, probably meant to be Cuba—the movie was made during that era when we worried every minute about the Russians attacking us from Havana. Anyway, he sneaks from the water into a fortress and sets a timer on a bomb. Then he unzips his wetsuit, sticks a red flower in the lapel of the white dinner jacket he's been wearing all along, and strolls into a nearby cantina, where he cavalierly lights a cigarette and listens as the bomb goes off in the distance."

"How can you possibly remember all those details?" Violet laughed.

"Because this is the movie that catapulted me into adolescence. I've never been the same since the first time

I saw it. I fantasized endlessly about meeting a man like Connery. It was one of the first videos I ever bought, and I've run it so often that the sound is scratchy."

"It's hard for me to understand how you can stand to see movies over and over," Cameron said. "I don't have the patience to sit through most of them even once."

"Everyone has patience for something, Cameron. You just save yours for the golf course."

It's a good thing that now and then Cameron and I gently call attention to the differences between us. Just in case, in a moment of temporary insanity, we ever considered taking each other seriously.

THE GILLIANS' HOUSE is a marvel of space and light, and remarkably cozy, considering the size of the place. It's also a testament to how successfully Beth and Jim have blended their different notions of how the house should look. Beth's art collection—mostly nudes sketched in sepia or charcoal—is neighbor to an eclectic assortment of international pop culture posters that Jim has amassed on his business travels. In their entry foyer, a delicate sketch of a reclining female from eighteenth-century Provence shares wall space with a poster, in Hebrew, for the movie *Fargo*. On the dining room wall, an etching of two playful Italian Renaissance cherubs hangs next to a colorful, Mondrian-like street map of downtown Tokyo.

The four of us—Violet and Grant, Cameron and I— were barely in the front door when I heard someone call my name, then Violet's. It was Sarah, maneuvering her way through the crowded living room, with Kevin in tow. She was wearing a midnight blue, tuxedo-style pantsuit, the kind of outfit only willowy women like Sarah can carry off.

"Wow!" I said. "Very Diane Keaton."

"Diane Keaton should be so lucky," Kevin said.

As if Kevin weren't there, Sarah threw her arms around Violet and Grant and led them towards the bar that was set up near the kitchen. My attention went to Kevin, who was shaking hands to greet Cameron but following Sarah with his eyes.

"Haven't seen you for a while. How are things in the world of real estate?" Kevin asked Cameron. "And you, darling Miriam, you look spectacular, as always. Great dress."

I'd found the dress in a vintage clothing store in the Village. It was 1930s-style cream-colored satin, ankle length, cut low in the back.

"Thanks, Kev. You look pretty spectacular yourself. Where's your son? I heard he was coming."

"Brendan and his friend Lilly are on a tour of the house with Jim. Have you seen the new Jacuzzi in the master bedroom? Twelve people could fit in it."

"What does the sign outside mean, Château Crummy Acres?" Cameron said.

"It's an old joke," I said. "From Beth and Jim's impoverished student days in Ithaca. Their landlord was a pompous twit who taught in the philosophy department at Cornell. He bought a vineyard on one of the Finger Lakes, gave it a snooty French-sounding name—*Maison du Lac*, I think—and proceeded to bottle wines under his own pretentious label. Beth and Jim swore that if they ever had the chance to christen a piece of property, they would choose the most incongruous, ridiculous name they could. Hence, Château Crummy Acres."

Kevin and Cameron laughed. "I love the whole idea," said Kevin. "Aren't Beth and Jim the least ostentatious rich people you've ever met?"

"Yes, and to think I knew them before they lived like this," I said. "I assume we'll all be sitting together tonight.

Where did Beth put us?"

Kevin nodded. "We're out back, on the glassed-in patio. Sarah and I checked out the place cards. Except for someone named Gabe something, it's the usual crowd at our table, plus Beth's brother Bruce and his new wife—what's her name?"

"We just call her Number Four," I said. "I think her name is Kimberlee, spelled l-e-e, which distinguishes her from Number Three, spelled l-y. The current Mrs. Jacobs is twenty-four, an aerobics instructor. The original Mrs.—Number One—was a chemist around Bruce's age. He seems to lower the age requirement and occupational standards with each succeeding wife."

Kevin laughed. "I'll try to forget you said that when I meet Number Four. See you two later. I'm going to catch up with Sarah."

Cameron and I moved toward the bar, passing the tuxedoed young man with Beethoven hair who was playing an ornamental rendition of "Wind Beneath My Wings" on the grand piano.

"*Beaches*," I said automatically.

"Excuse me?" Cameron asked.

"The movie this song is from. Bette Midler, Barbara Hershey. The ultimate chick flick."

"Another one I haven't seen, and probably never will," he said, handing me a glass of Cabernet. The pianist had moved on to the theme from *Out of Africa*.

"How about this one?" I tried. "Gorgeous scenery, Meryl Streep and Robert Redford."

Cameron shrugged.

"*Out of Africa*," I said.

"'When the gods want to punish us, they answer our prayers,'" said a male voice behind me, practically in my ear. "It's what Streep says to Redford when he disappoints her."

Turning to see who was speaking, I inadvertently spilled a few drops of my drink on the man's jacket.

"Oh, sorry!" I said. "Let me get some club soda . . ."

"Not to worry," he smiled. "I'm Gabe Bryant." Cameron and I introduced ourselves.

"I think you're at our table tonight," I said.

Gabe looked intently at me. "I apologize for staring, but I'm trying to place you. Do you work at Gillian Investments? I could swear I've seen you before."

"No wheeling and dealing for me. I'm a reading teacher. Cameron is in real estate."

"How do you folks know the Gillians?"

Before I could answer, Beth and Jim appeared.

"Everything looks gorgeous," I said to Beth. "Including you."

"I'm glad you talked me into getting this dress, even though I can barely breathe in it. Have you seen Sarah in her tuxedo?"

"She's a knockout."

"And you! How many women could get away with a clingy number like that?" Beth said.

"Jean Harlow, maybe?" said Gabe. "Myrna Loy? I know, Kim Basinger in *LA Confidential*. Brunette version, of course."

"Overrated movie, but thanks for the compliment," I said.

"Don't you like *film noir*?"

"The real thing, yes. But that one? More like *film latte*."

Gabe smiled. "I thought they did a great job. I'd love to hear some more of your ideas."

Jim shook Cameron's hand. "Welcome," he said. "I'm glad we finally got you up here."

"Thank Miriam for finally inviting me. What are the chances of my getting a tour of the place?"

"How about now? All right with you if I steal him for

a few minutes, Miriam?"

The two men headed towards the stairway to the second floor. One of the reasons I like Cameron's company at parties is that he doesn't expect me to take care of him. He likes to work the crowd himself, look for openings to talk about golf and real estate, distribute his business card.

I turned to Beth. "I've somehow missed the hors d'oeuvres. Where is that woman I saw earlier with the tray of puffed pastry goodies?"

Gabe Bryant's voice was in my ear again. "I just remembered where I saw you before."

"Really, where?"

"A *Times* article, maybe last spring? You're the teacher who started a film program in one of the middle schools in the city."

"You remember that piece after all this time?"

"Apart from the lovely picture of you, I had good reason to remember. I have the article pinned to a bulletin board in my office."

"Whatever for?"

"Long story. Let's just say I was interested in what you were doing."

Beth said, "I'm glad we decided to seat you two at the same table. Looks like you'll have a lot to talk about. Will you excuse me? The caterer seems to be flagging me down."

Out of habit, I checked Gabe's left hand. No wedding band.

I asked him, "Do you live around here?"

"No, in the city. I'm remodeling a brownstone in Yorkville. I feel like I've been living in a construction site for five years."

"I live in Yorkville, too. East End Avenue. You know the white high-rise with the circular driveway in front? I've been there for twenty years."

"I'm surprised we haven't run into each other at Grist-edes."

Something like a tiny electrical current passed between us. A flash—light, heat, danger ahead. I took a deep breath. Standing near Gabe made me feel shaky, in a distantly familiar way. A sexual frisson? No, more like an old wound starting to throb, the way my Uncle Fred's bad shoulder does when a storm is approaching.

"Will you excuse me? I need to—to—um—" I stammered.

"I'm sure we'll have a chance to talk at dinner," he said.

I meandered through the crowd, eavesdropping on snippets of arcane chatter, racking my brain to remember names and stories of people I see once a year, at this event. I gave my annual wave and wink from afar to Mark and Ellen Whatever-Their-Names-Are, who bore witness, years ago in this house, to Peter's invitation for me to join him in Savannah. At every Gillian party since, they've studiously avoided anything resembling real conversation with me, for which I am grateful. I managed to slink unnoticed past a woman who was vehemently advocating that people like her, with lactose intolerance, be covered by the Americans with Disabilities Act. One of Jim's London partners was expounding on the future of e-commerce. ("The Asians still find the idea most seductive.") A woman who had just published a children's book about lesbian mothers was describing her experience on a promotional tour. ("And then in Salt Lake, no radio show would book me.") I caught scraps of local gossip about celebrities who reside in Connecticut; now I know where David Letterman boards his pets and why Meryl Streep recently switch dry cleaners.

A menu in gold calligraphy was propped up on a small easel in front of the chafing dishes at the buffet. *Vitello tonnato, pommodoro a riso, carciofi alla giudia, tagliatelli ai funghi porcini*. Italian, of course, Beth's favorite. The guests were beginning to fill their plates and take their seats at round tables that were set up all over the first floor of the house. Our table on the patio gave us a commanding view of the pool and hot tub as well as a floodlit weeping willow on the far end of the Gillians' property.

Sarah seemed keen to sit next to Beth's brother Bruce. From what I could overhear, Bruce was urging Sarah to call him at his office on Monday. "I'm sure I can get you the right person," he was saying. Kevin listened intently, nodding in agreement with Bruce. Sarah realized that I was tuning in on their conversation. I flashed her a "What's up?" look; she responded with a "Not right now" shake of her finger. Number Four, the toned and talkative Kimberlee Jacobs, engaged Cameron in a lengthy discussion about the merits of dietary supplements for weekend athletes. Grant gave me an update on his grandson's dyslexia. Brendan and Lilly, absorbed in gossip about their Boston cronies, were oblivious to the rest of us. Gabe Bryant sat directly across the table from me. Every time I looked his way, his eyes were on me. Great, soulful eyes, sparkling above what my mother would call a million-dollar smile.

I heard Violet ask Gabe if he might be related to a Jessie Bryant she knew in Atlanta.

"Afraid not," he said. "The only female Bryant I know is my mother. There used to be another Ms. Bryant, the one I was married to for eighteen years. She and I created a junior Bryant, another male. After we divorced, she dropped the Bryant from her name."

"And the junior Bryant?" Violet asked.

"He's married, lives in North Carolina, works in his father-in-law's car rental business. His wife has kept her own name, so she's not exactly a Bryant, even if she is part of our family."

The opening bars of "As Time Goes By" reached us from the living room.

"Did everyone see the little sign on the piano that says the pianist's name?" Lilly said. "It's Sam Humphrey. No kidding. I wonder how often people ask him to 'play it again, Sam.' Do you suppose that Humphrey is really his last name? Or did he just make it up to capitalize on the Bogart connection?"

"I recognize a lot of the lines from Casablanca, but I've never seen the whole thing," Cameron said.

"You know, no one in Casablanca ever actually says 'Play it again, Sam,'" Gabe said.

"You seem to know a lot about movies for someone who works for an investment company," I said to Gabe. "What do you do for Gillian Investments, anyway?"

"It's not so much what I do for them, but what they do for me. I don't work there," he said.

"When you said you thought you had seen me at the office, I assumed . . ."

"I can see why you might get the wrong idea. I do visit Jim's office from time to time, but I'm not in the investment business."

"What do you do, then? Let me guess: Fix computers? Cater lunches? Deliver office supplies?"

The others at the table had drifted off into their own conversations. Random phrases flew through the air . . . *laptop in the taxi . . . holistic soybean diet . . . time-share condo . . . plane tickets online . . .*

"Gillian Investments is a major supporter of the organization I work for," Gabe said. "I'm with one of those not-for-profit cultural groups that survive at the mercy of corporate sponsors. Gillian sort of pays my salary, but I don't exactly work for them, if you see what I mean."

He reached into his wallet and pulled out a business card, handing it to me across the table. "The New York

Independent Film Institute," it said across the middle of the card, "Gabriel B. Bryant, Executive Director."

Cameron and I said our goodbyes to Beth and Jim. Cameron went in search of the teenaged parking valet who had the keys to his Lexus.

Gabe Bryant found me in the foyer. "Just tell me if I'm out of line, and I'll go away. But I'd really like to see you again sometime soon, and not only because you are incredibly pretty. I think we'd enjoy spending time together. And while Cameron seems like a very nice guy, I'm afraid he's not for you."

"Is that so? How do you know I'm not crazy about him?"

"I can see that you like him well enough. But I'm betting you could never be crazy about a man who can't sit all the way through *Casablanca*."

I said nothing.

Gabe smiled. "Look, no pressure here. You know I'm interested in you. You have my card. Call me if you'd like to meet for a cup of overpriced coffee in our neighborhood sometime, argue about *film noir*. Whatever."

Cameron, jiggling his car keys, reappeared.

"Take care, Gabe," he said.

"You, too," said Gabe. "Nice to meet you. Both of you."

VIOLET AND GRANT went to bed as soon as we got back to my apartment. Cameron stayed for a brandy.

"It's been a long time since I saw that happen," Cameron said. "That guy Gabe. You swept him off his feet."

"Cameron, it was only . . ."

"Don't think I'm not jealous. Not that you and I have ever considered making what we have anything more than it is. What I envy is the way that Gabe looked at you.

I'm used to men eyeing you, but this was the damnedest thing . . .

"I hope you'll understand this, Miriam. I'm crazy about you—what man in his right mind wouldn't be? But I'll never feel about anyone the way I felt about Charlotte. I don't know everything about your past, but I know you've never been married. I'm sure you've been in love, but I guess it wasn't the kind that lasts."

"It's ridiculous to be talking this way about someone I just met. We're not teenagers."

"I know what I saw. Listen, you know I'm not going anywhere. You can call me any time; I'll always be glad to see you. But, as comfortable as it is when we're together, why should you settle for comfortable? For me it's different—I lost the love of my life, and I'm not looking for anything more than . . . than what you and I have had, whatever you want to call it. You could have something more. Could be that you recognized that tonight, for the first time in a while. And you should have whatever you want in this life. Invite me to the wedding, will you?" Cameron said, planting a peck on my forehead before he left.

"I WASTED DECADES, doing what I thought I *should* do," Gabe said.

It was Saturday morning, a week after Beth and Jim's party. We were digging into mounds of French toast at the Green Kitchen diner. I had asked him to breakfast. He was telling me the story of his life.

"You can't imagine how I envy people like you who have always worked at something they love. I have a master's and a Ph.D. in history, but I spent more than twenty years managing my family's plumbing business. No, I'm not a plumber, but I ran the company. All that grueling academic work, to wind up scheduling home repairs. My brothers left town for college and never thought about returning to work with Dad. They still find it amusing to call me Dr. Drainpipe. I was the dutiful son. After graduate school, I came back home. Dad's health was starting to fai,l and he needed me. Besides, working in the business gave me a pretty good income, and I had a wife and son, so . . . It was supposed to be a temporary arrangement. Turned out to be twenty years."

"What did your wife do?"

"Trudy started going to school to train in a number of fields, never finished anything. Most of her jobs were entry level receptionist gigs, that sort of thing. Not a whole lot of ambition there."

"Where is she now?"

"I'm not sure."

"Excuse me?"

Dark cloud over his face. "She's an alcoholic. Been in and out of treatment for years. Has spells of sobriety and then falls off the wagon. Last I heard she was living with one of her sisters in Virginia. Our son Oliver wants nothing to do with her. After he got married, he decided that he didn't want to see her anymore. She was, let's say, badly behaved at his wedding. When he and his wife Moira have children, he may have a change of heart. I haven't spoken to my ex-wife since Oliver and Moira's wedding."

"Tell me about your work now."

"I've been crazy about films since I was a kid. Jim Gillian and I went to high school together. He was always a film lover, too. When he was in a position to put some serious money into a cultural project, film was his first choice. He rescued the New York Independent Film Institute from bankruptcy, helped turn it into a training ground for young filmmakers and an archive on filmmaking. My father had died, and I was selling the family business and looking for a new line of work, maybe teaching. You can imagine how surprised I was when Jim called me to talk about the Institute. We hadn't even seen too much of each other over the years. No one but Jim would have hired me even to scrub the floors at a place like the Institute, but Jim figured that I had acquired some business sense during my years at Bryant Plumbing. He trusted me to handle the money he was putting into the place. And he knew that I loved movies. These days, we get donations from a number of sources, but Gillian Investments is still our primary supporter. My income is less than half of what it was when I was selling appliances, but I've never been happier."

"It occurs to me that you and I may have met before, at Beth and Jim's wedding. Or maybe at their son's funeral."

"I was on a flight to the Cannes Film Festival the day Adam died. By the time word reached me, I had missed the funeral. I spent some time with Jim when I got home, but I don't know how much good I did him. He didn't talk much about Adam. Still doesn't. And I missed Beth and Jim's wedding day. I was in graduate school, in the hospital with appendicitis. But my parents were there."

"Your parents were close to Jim?"

"During college, after his parents died, my family sort of took him in. He'd spend holidays with us—Thanksgiving, Christmas and Chanukah."

"Chanukah? With a name like Bryant? And those Nordic good looks?"

"Mom's family name was Bernstein. My middle name. Dad was Dutch and Irish. We had a Christmas tree and we lit Chanukah candles. We went to the Good Shepherd Church on Easter Sunday and to Grandma Ida's house for Passover seders. I don't think I was ever christened, but I know I was *bar mitzvah*-ed. I have pictures of myself in a ruffled tuxedo shirt, dancing the *hora* to prove it."

"And now?"

"I'm comfortable in most churches and synagogues, except for the really fanatical, dogmatic ones. But I don't go to either very often. You?"

"Secular Jewish. No strong pull to follow any rituals. Most of the time I believe in God, I think." I took a sip of coffee. "Can you tell me now why you kept that *Times* article about me?"

"I was out of town when the piece ran. My assistant clipped it out for me. She tacked it to my bulletin board, where it still hangs. She thought maybe we could do something for your kids, possibly give them a tour of the Film Institute. And, as an afterthought, she mentioned how pretty you were. She used to work for a matchmaking service—can't help herself."

"But you never called."

"Meant to. Then it was summer, and I figured you'd be off from teaching and I'd just wait until September. And then, truthfully, I forgot. If I'd known you were friends with the Gillians, I could have tried you over the summer. Hey, I've been doing all the talking. Tell me the story of *your* life."

"What can I tell you? You already know about my work, and you met my closest friends at Jim and Beth's party. What's left?"

"I'll bet everyone who meets you wants to know why you never got married."

"Wow . . . ready to start with the big questions, huh? Not my favorite topic."

"Tell me the reason."

"I can ask you the same question. Why haven't you remarried?"

"I've had one serious relationship since my divorce. We

lived together for six years. I wanted to get married, she didn't. When she left, rather than staying in the apartment we had shared, I bought the dilapidated brownstone I keep trying to make habitable. I started at the Film Institute around that time, too. Since then I haven't had much of a social life. The women I meet through work are generally too young for me. So, if you'll pardon the somewhat crude summary, I've simply learned to do without. Okay, now it's your turn."

I shook my head.

"Hey," he said. "I've already told you about my dismal professional history, my alcoholic ex-wife, the girlfriend who dumped me, my son's dysfunctional relationship with his mother, and my meager salary. All I know about you is what I read in the *Times*, plus a few biographical tidbits I picked up at the party."

My cell phone rang. Saved by the bell. I explained that I was waiting to hear from my mother, letting me know she'd landed safely in Florida. She spends from November through March in Boca Raton with her sister Sylvia.

The caller ID screen said "Florida," with no phone number.

"Miriam, it's Aunt Sylvia."

"Where are you calling from? Is Mom there yet?"

"She's here. I'm at the hospital with her. She wasn't feeling so good on the plane, and we went in the cab right from the airport to my doctor's office. He sent us over to the emergency room at the hospital. In an ambulance!"

"What's wrong with her?"

"She sort of fainted, and then the left side of her body went numb. It may be a stroke. Miriam, can you come? I don't know what questions to ask, and she'll want you here."

"Of course. Has she been admitted?"

"What do you mean?"

"Are they keeping her in the hospital? Is she still in the emergency room?"

"I'm not sure where she is. They won't let me see her. They keep telling me to stay in the waiting room."

"Has a doctor seen her yet? Which hospital are you in?"

"Palmetto Community. You remember, it's the one where you came to see me when I had my bypass. A doctor is with her now. I think he's a neurologist. He gave me his card. Wait a minute, here it is. Donald Capper, M.D."

"Give me his number. I'll be there as soon as I can."

Gabe walked back to my apartment with me.

"I'll take you to the airport whenever you need to go," he said.

"You keep a car in the city?"

"The Film Institute leases it for me. I seldom drive it. I keep it in a garage right around the corner from my house. I even have the keys with me. Whenever you're ready, I'll drive it over and pick you up."

I left a message with Dr. Capper's answering service. Couldn't get any further information from the ER. My mother was being examined, I should try again later.

I called my brother Neil in Phoenix. I didn't expect him or his wife Kathy to offer to come East. I was right.

"You have no idea how busy things are at the stores right now," Neil said. "The California expansion is a killer. I'm breaking in a manager at a spa hotel in Long Beach, and I've got a prima donna foreman renovating the West-wood store. But Miriam, please give us an update when it's convenient. Kathy and I will be at the kids' lacrosse finals all weekend. You can catch me on my cell."

———

For a mere fortune—the airlines are ridiculous about

last-minute reservations—I got a seat on a late afternoon flight from Newark to West Palm Beach. Gabe insisted on staying with me while I got ready to go.

"I won't get in your way," he said. "Point me to your TV."

I left word on answering machines at Sarah's and Beth's, told them I'd call again from Florida. My principal wasn't home either. I left her a rambling message.

I threw some lightweight clothes, enough for a few days, into a small carry-on suitcase. I grabbed a sweater, too, remembering how frigidly air-conditioned they keep hospital rooms in Florida.

I spent the ride to the airport in Gabe's car on my cell phone, hoping to speak to the doctor, get some information from the ER. No luck.

Gabe pulled up in front of the airline terminal.

"Are you sure you don't want me to park the car and wait with you inside?"

"I'll be fine. I can't thank you enough for everything."

"For what? Do me a favor, write down your cell phone number for me. You have my business card with you? Good. It has all my numbers."

"You've done so much already."

He leaned over, squeezed my hand, and lightly kissed my cheek. "I hope your mother is all right. Let me know what's going on."

———————

I PICKED UP a rental car at the West Palm airport and drove directly to Palmetto Community Hospital. During Aunt Sylvia's stay there years ago, the small building had looked old and dreary, with peeling paint and gloomy corridors. Since then, they've had a facelift and a public relations overhaul. On the drive over to Palmetto, I saw their highway billboards and heard their radio ads asking,

PART II: MIRIAM

"When it comes to your health, why go to strangers?" The implication is that Palmetto Community is the sort of neighborly place where, say, Marcus Welby would have sent his own family for medical treatment.

One change is immediately obvious: Everyone who works at Palmetto except the doctors now wears what look like designer pajamas in shades of soft green and coral that match the new carpets and wallpaper. The result is that you can't tell the janitor from the head nurse. I had to ask six people before I found someone who could lead me to Aunt Sylvia. I finally found her, dazed and nervous, in a lounge near the ER. She cried when she saw me.

"Where is Mom?" I said. "Have they admitted her?"

"They won't tell me anything."

I approached the green-and-coral-pajama crew at the circular work station in the middle of the ER. No one knew anything about Mom. I asked for Dr. Capper.

"He'll be back down in a minute. Please take a seat in the visitors' lounge."

An hour later, Dr. Capper finally appeared. He was about my age, with a tan too deep for someone who should know better than to bake in the sun.

"Your mother has had a TIA, a transient ischemic attack. Do you know what that is?" he began, in a condescending tone that I wouldn't take even with my slowest seventh grader.

"A kind of mini-stroke, right?"

"Very good. Yes, it's affected her speech and her movement on the left side of her body. Sometimes the effects are temporary. It's too soon to say much more."

"You're admitting her, I assume."

"As soon as we have a bed for her."

"Where is she now?"

"In one of the examining rooms here in the ER."

"She's been here for eight hours. Is anyone with her?"

Dr. Capper stifled a yawn, glanced at his watch. "These are questions you'll have to ask one of the nurses."

"But I'm asking you. My mother is seventy-eight years old, she's probably scared out of her mind, and no one has thought to let her eighty-year-old sister see her. You're lucky my aunt didn't have a coronary in the waiting room. When is my mother likely to get a bed?"

"Again, you'll have to ask the nurses."

"And again, I'm asking you. If you don't have a bed for her, I'd like you to find another hospital that does. And I want to see her right now."

"Miss Kaplan, I realize how emotional a time this must be for you, but we have to follow procedures here. I can take you to your mother. I'll see her when I make rounds over the weekend."

By the time I'd finished talking with Dr. Capper—or, rather, when he was finished with me—Mom had been moved to a bed on the Intensive Care Unit. She was dozing when Aunt Sylvia and I walked into her room.

"Mom," I whispered. Her lashes fluttered, eyes opened, though her left eye and that side of her face were drooping. I held her limp left hand in mine. She moved her mouth slightly as if trying to speak, but no sound came out.

"I just wanted you to know I was here," I said. "Go back to sleep. Can I get you anything before I go?"

She moved her head slightly. Then she dozed off again.

The next day, neither Dr. Capper nor any doctor covering for him came to see Mom. No tests had been ordered. No one on duty could tell me anything about her condition.

Mom was not yet permitted a phone in her room, and my cell didn't work inside the hospital. I asked one of the nurses on the floor to call Dr. Capper's service and leave an urgent message for him to call me back there, at the

ICU. And when he did, an hour later, I fired him over the phone while I was standing at the nurse's station in the center of the unit. I was within earshot of a half-dozen nurses and aides. Some of them, hearing my end of the conversation, gave me a thumbs-up.

"I don't advise you to change physicians at this point," he said. "Maybe you don't realize how complicated this situation is, especially since she really doesn't have her own doctor here. After she's stabilized, she can go back to her internist in Brooklyn. But until then, she came in through our ER, I took her case, and I'll be happy to see it through. Now if you'll excuse me . . ."

I found a pay phone and called Sarah. She's worked in a hospital and she understands healthcare. She usually has creative ideas on how to outsmart the system.

"Make your case to the chief administrator of the hospital," she advised. "If you get nowhere, threaten to make this the lead story on tomorrow's local news. TV stations in South Florida love features about heartless bureaucrats trying to take advantage of old people. And stories about arrogant doctors are always a hit."

At my first hint of media involvement, Ted Jaffa, Palmetto's CEO, expressed his burning desire to do whatever was best for Mom. He led me down the hall and introduced me to Dr. Amanda Ling, who agreed to take over Mom's care. She immediately ordered CAT scans and blood work, called in a range of specialists, patiently answered all my questions (without making me feel like an idiot for asking them), comforted Mom, calmed Aunt Sylvia.

"In two or three days, we should have a handle on things," she told me.

I called my brother.

"I can't stop thinking about Mom," he said. "Kathy is concerned, too. We haven't told the kids, no need to upset them until we know more, right? Kathy thinks they're a little young to understand." Neil and Kathy's boys are teenagers.

"I think their grandmother would like to hear from them. From you, too."

"You know, I meant to call over the weekend, but with the time difference and all it was too late when we got home from lacrosse. By the way, both your nephews won trophies. I hope you sent our love to Mom."

"I'm thrilled beyond words that lacrosse is going so well for you, Neil. Shall I tell you what I was doing while you were enjoying yourselves? I was firing an incompetent doctor, monitoring overworked nurses to make sure they didn't make any critical mistakes with Mom's medication, keeping Mom's spirits up, trying to figure out how we will manage if she needs ongoing care, and preventing Aunt Sylvia from having panic attacks in the hospital corridors."

"Everyone handles stress differently, Miriam. For me, it helps to be with my children to get my mind off Mom. You know you can call me any time."

"I may not be able to do this alone, Neil. You've been away for twenty-five years. I've never asked you for help with Mom before."

"I'm not in the mood for lectures, if you don't mind. I have a family to take care of and ten stores to run. Just tell me what you need."

He has a family and important work to do. A life that matters, unlike mine. "Do you suppose that you and your family can manage to call her today? Your sons are old enough to comprehend that their grandmother is sick. She would feel better if she heard from them."

MOM WAS ABLE to stay awake only for short intervals. She wasn't in pain, but she was scared by what had happened to her and frustrated by her inability to move without help or to speak clearly. What she was able to articulate sounded like gibberish. During her long naps, when it wasn't too hot outside, Aunt Sylvia and I took walks in the park behind the hospital. Over and again, Aunt Sylvia told me how hard it was to lose the people you loved as you got older. "You don't get used to it. I've already buried a sister and brother, a husband, and these days, I go to funerals all the time. So many friends—gone! It never gets easier."

Neil called the unit once, from his car phone, when Mom was asleep. I took the call at the nurse's station, but it sounded as if he were talking from inside a tunnel and I could only understand about every other word he said. He and Kathy sent Mom a showy floral arrangement studded with birds-of-paradise and gold Mylar bows. Flowers aren't allowed in patient rooms on the ICU. I instructed the nurses to find a home for my brother's gift on another wing of the hospital.

The prognosis for a speedy recovery was not good. Dr. Ling was concerned about the care Mom would need when we got back to New York. Physical therapy, speech therapy, monitored medication, around-the-clock nursing care.

"I'll get someone here to look into skilled nursing facilities and assisted living centers near your home in New York," Dr. Ling said.

"That would be just a short-term thing, right? Her speech seems improved, even if she's still mixing up some words. And the paralysis is almost gone. She does pretty well with a walker."

"Too early to say how much more we can expect her to improve. She was in good health before the TIA, and that will help her. But her age is a significant factor. A one-hundred-percent recovery is unlikely. She will probably regain most of her mobility. The speech may take more time. However, for a while—and I can't tell you exactly how long—she can't realistically expect to go back to her home, or even to yours. You should also know that your mother is a candidate for another TIA—even with the blood thinners and everything else we're doing for her."

"When will she be discharged?"

"We need to make sure she has somewhere to go, a facility that can give her the treatment she needs. I assume you want her back in the New York area, but I'd like to watch her here for a few more days."

Dr. Ling put her hand on my arm. "Do you have anyone to help you through this?"

I wondered if she meant, "This would be easier if you were married? Or is that my own voice I think I hear? Or my mother's?

"I'll be fine," I said.

Back at Aunt Sylvia's I checked messages on my cell phone for the first time in days. Sarah and Beth sent love, wanted me to call when I could. Violet, who had heard about Mom from Sarah, offered to drive down from Acedia Bay—three hundred miles away—if she could be of any help to us. My principal left word that she had found a substitute to take over my classes. Film on Fridays, though, would most likely be a study hall until I returned. No one else was prepared to teach it.

Gabe had called. Twice. He left his first message on the day after he'd driven me to the airport: "I hope all is going as well as could be expected down there. Call me when you can."

The second message was just an hour old: "I called the Gillians tonight, and Beth says no one has heard from you since you spoke to Sarah a few days ago. We're all hoping that your mother, and you, are doing all right. I had an idea that maybe I could send a speaker to your film class this week. Let me know and I'll call your school."

———

"Gabe, it's Miriam."

"So glad to hear your voice. How are you? How is she?"

I told him, as succinctly as I could manage, what was happening.

"You may feel overwhelmed, but it really does sound as if you have things under control," he said.

"If only . . ."

"What?"

"I was going to say that I'm exhausted, and the hardest part may still be ahead of me. Making arrangements for getting her back to New York and in the right environment. Not to mention facing the fact that my mother will never be the same again. And I hate doing this by myself. My brother is no help."

"Anything I can do?"

"You already did. Do you really think you can find a speaker for my film class?"

"I'm not promising Spike Lee, but I think I can get someone to entertain the kids."

"They'll never forget it, I'm sure. Thanks."

"And Miriam, let Beth or Sarah know how you're doing. Why don't you keep your cell phone turned on?"

"Doesn't work in the hospital. You can leave messages, but you'll have to wait for me to call you back."

"Yeah, well, don't play too hard to get, will you?"

The next day my principal called again to let me know that a young film director who had won an award for his documentary about Kurt Cobain was coming to address my Film on Fridays class. The kids were ecstatic. That nice man from the Film Institute had set it all up.

LEANING ON A walker and with help from a nurse, Mom was finally able to totter down the full length of the hallway. There was talk of moving her out of the ICU and to a regular bed over the weekend. Her speech remained slurred and she sometimes had trouble finding the right words for what she wanted to say. She requested make-up, instead of milk, for her coffee, and she asked for an extra blanket because the room was too "short." She occasionally called me Gladys, the name of her sister who's been dead for twenty years.

Still, we reminisced about my childhood in Brooklyn and I told her funny stories about some of my students. I brought her some of her own clothing to wear. I found a manicurist from a nearby beauty shop who was willing to come to the hospital to do her nails. The less Mom looked like a patient, the more her spirit seemed to emerge.

A social worker was assigned to help arrange for Mom's care back in New York. She gave me lists of toll-free numbers for advice and information, and stacks of brochures with glossy photos of smiling, silver-haired people in wheelchairs, being fed and read to by empathetic caregivers in "modern, home-like" facilities. I stashed the materials in a pile on Aunt Sylvia's dining room table, vowing to give them some attention over the weekend.

The idea that Mom might never be able to go home, never live in her own apartment again, terrified me, but in her presence I treated the prospect of her stay at a facility as good news, just a temporary, necessary step on her road back to herself. A hundred times, Aunt Sylvia asked when Mom would be able to get "back to normal." A hundred times, I evaded the question. Keeping Mom's spirits high and Aunt Sylvia's anxiety low took all of my energy.

On Friday morning, I persuaded Aunt Sylvia to keep her regular hairdresser appointment and to join her weekly canasta game instead of going to the hospital with me, assuring her that new developments with Mom were unlikely. Anyway, apart from emergencies, things slow down in hospitals as weekends approach. Nurses are staffed to the minimum, doctors make only necessary rounds, no lab tests or special procedures are ordered. Dr. Ling's partner, a young neurosurgeon from Dublin, charmed Mom with his brogue and friendly smile late Friday afternoon, explaining that Dr. Ling would be off for the weekend but that he would stop by each day. The social worker, too, was off until Monday. It was going to be a long two days. Mom was still sleeping most of the time. Awake, she felt just well enough to be bored by staying in bed but not well enough to leave her room except for brief jaunts down the hall.

"You don't have to stay here all weekend just to watch me sleep," Mom said. "Go take a walk on the beach, do some shopping. Please, dear, for me."

Her words were still a bit garbled, but I was heartened. She was sounding like a slightly inebriated version of her old self. "You win, Mom. I'll find something to do in the morning and come see you in the afternoon."

The sky was still light when I left the hospital on Friday evening. A late-afternoon thunderstorm had cooled the air and filled the potholes around the parking lot. I stood under the flamingo pink stucco overhang at the front entrance, trying to remember where I had parked. A taxi pulled up to the circular driveway, splashing water from one of the puddles onto my legs. Through the window, I caught the driver's eye; he mouthed an apology. The back door of the taxi swung open.

"Sorry," the passenger called to me. I was bent over, brushing drops of water off my sandals. "This is not the entrance I had in mind."

Gabe, dressed in jeans, a tropical print shirt, and a Yankees cap, stepped out of the taxi. Before I could speak, his arms were around me.

"You shouldn't have to do this alone," he said.

AUNT SYLVIA INVITED Gabe to sleep on the couch at her place, but he had already reserved a room at a small hotel nearby. She insisted on cooking dinner for the three of us before he left for the night.

"Is he your boyfriend?" she whispered when he was out of earshot.

"Not exactly."

"He came so far, and he's not your boyfriend?"

"Really, I hardly know him."

"He looks at you like he's your boyfriend," she said. "If a handsome man like him looked at me that way, I'd be happy to be his girl."

In the morning, I met Gabe for breakfast at the Miramar Cuban Bakery and Café, adjacent to his hotel. The full measure of his being in Florida with me was just starting to register.

"When things calm down, I imagine I'll be able to process the fact that you came all this way for me. A gutsy move, arriving unannounced."

"Well, no guts, no glory."

"And the expense. A last-minute ticket like this . . ."

"I'll confess: I had a frequent flyer ticket I had to use before the end of the year. Meanwhile, fill me in on what's happening with your mother. I'd love to meet her, if you think it would be all right."

Out of ICU now, Mom was permitted to have visitors beyond immediate family members. I expected Gabe's presence might confuse her, but when I introduced him, Mom behaved as if it were completely natural that he had shown up. She called him Neil a few times, and once she asked him why he hadn't brought her grandchildren to see her, but for the most part she made sense of what was happening around her. On occasion she was adorably flirtatious with Gabe, insisting, with fluttering eyelashes, that he call her Celeste instead of Mrs. Kaplan.

"It makes me feel younger, hearing you call me by my first name," Mom insisted.

At times, though, what came out of her mouth was stream-of-consciousness—sometimes hallucinatory, sometimes painfully candid.

"My beautiful daughter," she said out of the blue, pointing to me but looking at Gabe. "Why she never got married, I can't understand."

"Celeste!" Aunt Sylvia said. "Please, it's not the right time for *all that*."

"Mom, are you scheduled for physical therapy today?" I said, clumsily trying to change the topic.

Mom showed no sign that she had heard me. She continued talking directly to Gabe, in a conspiratorial stage whisper. "She came so close, and with handsome young men, like you. Rich ones, too. Of course, I never met that Southerner—what was his name again? A humdinger, that one. She was never the same."

I avoided looking in Gabe's direction. Aunt Sylvia's eyes, wide with surprise, caught mine. I turned away.

Mercifully, a nurse appeared with a thermometer and a blood pressure cuff and asked us to step outside while she examined Mom. In the hallway, Gabe broke the painful silence.

"Ladies, where can I take you two to dinner tonight?"

I breathed deeply for the first time since Mom had begun her discourse about my love life.

"Not me," Aunt Sylvia said. "Three's a crowd. You two go, try one of those nice restaurants at the beach."

Gabe repeated his invitation to Aunt Sylvia, but she held firm.

"Enjoy yourselves. You deserve a little fun, Miriam darling."

Gabe and I sat at an outdoor table at a seafood restaurant on the water. We avoided talking about Mom's outburst, though the temptation—for him to ask more, for me to attempt some explanation—clung to the air between us.

"What happens when you get Celeste back to New York?" Gabe said.

"I've got a stack of brochures about places in the city. My homework for the weekend was going to be reading them and coming to some kind of decision. That was before you showed up."

"I came to help, Miriam. Maybe I can do your homework with you."

"Tomorrow, then. For tonight, I'd like to enjoy the beautiful weather, and your company, and some Florida shrimp, and conversation that isn't sad or worrisome. Do you think it's terrible of me to want to escape from all of it for a few hours? I've had no one but Aunt Sylvia to talk to all week, and I worry that she's going to keel over any minute."

Gabe reached across the table and laced his fingers with mine. "Your aunt is probably asleep, your mother is in good hands, and there's nothing we can do for either of them until tomorrow. Maybe it will help you to think more clearly if you unwind a little tonight. We can make like we're on a date, even see if there's a movie to catch somewhere before it gets too late. And then in the morning, it's back to reality. Sound reasonable?"

It did.

We wound up at Gabe's hotel, having rented *Adam's Rib* to watch on the VCR in his room. We kicked off our shoes, climbed onto the king-sized bed and leaned back against the huge pillows. He clicked the remote, and as the video started he reached for my hand. What pleasure to watch a movie with a kindred spirit. From time to time, one of us would reach for the remote, pause the film, and offer commentary. Gabe said, and I agreed, that this film was the best of the Hepburn-Tracy series. I said, and he concurred, that Judy Holliday was never better than in this role. Like me, Gabe kept his eyes on the screen and didn't budge until the last film credits rolled.

He clicked off the TV and moved his face close to mine. "Tired?"

"A little. I probably should get back to my aunt's place."

He rubbed his fingers along my neck. "I can imagine what this week has been like for you," he said. "I don't want to complicate matters. But Miriam, I'm dying to get close to you. Not just physically, though I can't count how many times I have thought about making love to you. Something happened to me when we met at Beth and Jim's. Bolt of lightning! My mother's family—the Jewish relatives—they use a word, *bashert*. Have you heard it?"

"It means something that's meant to be. My family uses the word all the time, too."

"My mother believes in *bashert* relationships between men and women. Divinely inspired, and all that. I've been asking myself since I saw you and haven't been able to get you out of my mind, whether this is what Mom has been talking about. You are gorgeous—no, please don't give me any false modesty, you know you are—and at first I thought this was all about chemistry. But when I felt as if I had to get on that plane and be here with you, I knew there was something else going on. With the situation here, I certainly didn't come with the idea of getting you into bed. Not that I would fight you off, mind you. I just felt as if I wanted to be with you, to help you, to . . . Oh, God, my timing is probably just terrible."

"Gabe," I said, "I *am* attracted to you, and your coming

here has touched me in a way I'll probably never be able to describe to you. But you should know this: I stopped believing in *bashert* a long time ago."

Gabe moved his body around and pulled me to him, kissing me long and hard and passionately. It made my heart flip, the way it hadn't since . . .

"I know you must think I'm crazy," he whispered in my ear, "and I don't want to rush you . . ."

"I need some time," I whispered back. "Please, not tonight, not here . . . "

"I know," he said. "Miriam, I want more than just your beautiful body. You still haven't told me your story—who you are, where you've been. I need to understand why you gave up on *bashert*."

"You may be disappointed," I said. "My story may not be so interesting after all." *He's thinking about what Mom said in the hospital.*

"Try me."

"Where should I begin? My first kiss? The boy who gave me his ID bracelet in junior high school? Getting lavaliered in college? Getting engaged? Getting engaged again? And again?"

"I want to hear it all. But speaking of sleep, both of us could probably use some. I think I need to walk you back to your Aunt Sylvia's place—before I wind up ripping your clothes off and driving you so wild with desire that you'll insist on spending the night, and my reputation with your Aunt Sylvia will be ruined."

"Aunt Sylvia has already had a few words to say about you."

"Like what?"

"She noticed the way you looked at me. She found it endearing."

"Endearing? That was lust, my darling."

PART II: MIRIAM

THE NEXT MORNING I tucked Aunt Sylvia into a taxi headed to the hospital, and Gabe and I set ourselves up at the dining room table at her condo. We plowed through pamphlets and booklets—even a video or two—which the social worker had given me from at least a dozen facilities in the New York area. In a couple of hours, we had narrowed the choices to three, all within a reasonable distance from my apartment as well as Mom's neighborhood. I figured some of her friends would visit her if they didn't have to travel too far.

"Your friend Sarah, the one in healthcare, think it would be a good idea to call her?" Gabe suggested. "She may know how we should check these places out."

We! He was in this with me. "I think I can catch her at home now. This time of the morning, she's probably still in her bathrobe, doing the Sunday crossword puzzle," I said.

Sarah recognized the names of all the nursing facilities on our short list and knew them to be reputable. She offered to do additional research online. "I can find out if there have been any recent problems with them—licensure issues, that kind of thing," she said. "I'll also call around to see who has vacancies."

"You're the best, kiddo," I told her. "Call me back if you find out anything I need to know. I'm on my way to the hospital. Leave a message on my cell. Meanwhile, how the hell how are you, Sarah? I haven't talked to you since the party. I saw you huddling with Bruce Jacobs. Everything all right?"

"Just ducky, except I'm going to lose my job any minute, and there's something, um, complicated going on with Kevin. Too much to go into over the phone. I'll fill you in at brunch."

"I'm so sorry. I can't wait until we can talk in person. I hope to leave here before the weekend. We're overdue for brunch—you know how we usually like to do a postmortem on the Gillian soiree."

"Couldn't be helped, with your being away. And, Miriam? I'd love to know what's going on with Gabe. Beth told me that he called Jim to ask for advice about joining you in Florida. Wouldn't you love to have been a fly on the wall for that exchange? I'm guessing it's hard for you to talk now, right?"

"Oh, yes. Absolutely," I said, with an exaggerated lilt to let her know that Gabe was nearby.

"The vote up here is unanimous. Gabe's been elected Mensch of the Year."

"I agree."

"Oh, and one more thing. I have some advice from Beth. She's known Gabe for a long time, and she has one of her profound, therapeutic insights for you."

"I can't wait. Out with it."

"She says, please do your best not to fuck things up with him."

Gabe took a flight back to New York at dawn on Monday morning. Driving him to the airport felt sweetly domestic, as if we had long been in the habit of performing mundane kindnesses for each other.

"I'll call you tonight," he said.

"Gabe, no matter what happens, I'll never forget . . ."

"Stop right there. I'm happy I came. You take care, and tell Celeste to behave herself. I'll see both of you when you get home."

BETH:
LOST AND FOUND

*"Well, then, what's to be the reason
for becoming man and wife?"*
—*Noel Paul Stookey*

SIX-THIRTY. THE MORNING AFTER the party. I've slept fitfully and not long enough. With effort, I raise my head; there are streaks of mascara on the pillowcase because I fell asleep before I washed off my makeup. Jim has already left for the office. His new partners will need him night and day until they return to London. He'll sleep in the city all week.

"Call you later," I heard him whisper as he tiptoed out.

The party was a grand success. Everybody said so. There were no marital brawls or unruly political squabbles or regrettable drunken incidents. (We've had all three at previous gatherings.) The parking valets neither lost anyone's keys nor damaged a single car. MaryJo's Catering managed to find ripe blood-oranges for the salad and *ventresca di tonno*, the rich tuna in olive oil that makes a perfect sauce for cold veal. In spite of his hesitation about an evening of theme music, Sam Humphrey did a masterful job playing the movie scores I requested. I knew the music would be just right, not too intrusive or too stuffy. The kind that stirs up nice feelings.

The cleaning crew is due at nine. Carmen is coming to supervise them. Nothing urgent for me to do, nowhere I have to be today. Half asleep still, I tilt my head to scan the framed pictures on the dresser. A Sears Studios Portrait of Adam, age four, and Nicole, less than a year old, smiling as they sit in the doorway of a façade meant to look like a playhouse. A black-and-white of Jim's parents strolling on the boardwalk in Atlantic City, wheeling Jim in a fancy pram. Sarah, Miriam, and I amid a sea of bodies in front of the Washington Memorial, holding aloft a banner that reads, "Give Peace a Chance." A shot of me at the *Bocca della Verità* in Rome. I am pretending, *Roman Holiday*/Audrey Hepburn-style, to be frightened as I tentatively reach towards the gaping Mouth of Truth.

"Put your hand in, and tell me I'm the best lover in the world!" Andrew had called to me as he snapped the picture.

My eyes come to rest on a Polaroid of Jim and me, tanned and gleeful, festooned with leis at a luau in Maui. There's no hint in our smiling faces of the knotty truce that led to our being in Hawaii, or the restive months that preceded the trip. It was the vacation we took, Jim says, instead of getting a divorce.

————————————

CARMEN WAS AT the house with me six years ago when I found out about Jim's affair. Jim and I had celebrated Valentine's Day a few days early, the night before he left on a business trip to Tokyo. The work on enlarging our pool and putting in a new cabana had just begun, and Jim's gift to me was a white hooded terry cloth beach robe and a pair of iridescent flip-flops in the same shade of blue as the designer logo on the pocket of the robe. I gave him a silk tie splashed with bright cartoon icons of stock market ticker tapes, the World Trade Center towers, the *Wall Street Journal* banner—meant to represent the financial world he had already conquered. I made arrangements for the kids to sleep at friends' houses for the night, and, by candlelight in the dining room, I served him his favorite dish, lasagna with sweet sausage. After his second glass of Chianti, Jim yawned and said he'd better be turning in early; he had a long flight ahead of him the next day. When he fell asleep in our bed without a kiss or a word, I truly forgave him. He had been working so hard lately.

My practice was already flourishing by then, but I cancelled all my appointments for Valentine's Day so I could be at home. With Jim in Tokyo, I had to make myself available to the crew from All-Green Landscaping. They arrived early in the morning to survey our property, to draw up plans that would accommodate the pool and cabana. By noon, they were still wandering around the backyard, but they said they wouldn't need me for a while.

I went up to my bedroom to pay some bills. There was a charge on our American Express bill, dated February 1, from Le Boudoir. It made me smile. Le Boudoir is a fancy lingerie shop on Madison Avenue, not far from the tiny Manhattan apartment where we lived when we were first married. That shop was one of many in our neighborhood whose prices were way beyond our modest income at the time. When Jim got his first promotion and bonus, he bought me a silk nightgown at Le Boudoir, and we spent an entire weekend celebrating on our waterbed.

For a moment, I was touched that Jim would travel all the way uptown from his office on Wall Street to buy my Valentine's Day present in a store that had sentimental meaning to us. And then I remembered: My beach robe and flip-flops had come in a box from Bloomingdale's.

It didn't take me long to find the sales slip from Le Boudoir amid the crumpled receipts that Jim routinely tossed from his billfold onto a leather tray he kept on his dresser. I pulled the tray onto my bed and rummaged through the heap of papers, finally extracting a credit card receipt with a pale yellow sheet stapled behind it. "Le Boudoir, Lingerie and Finery for the Discerning Woman," the paper said across the top. Only one purchase was listed: Silk peignoir; color—hot pink; style—"Temptress"; size—small. Price—$198.00. Plus tax.

Maybe it's for me. A surprise for another occasion. But I had just passed my birthday, and our anniversary was months away. Besides, even on my best days, I'm a size medium. I knew, I *knew* there was someone else. Someone better suited than I to a hot pink negligee. Apparently, I was more the terry cloth robe and flip-flops type.

Carmen heard me cry out. She came running up the stairs with a mop raised in the air as if she expected to have to use it as a weapon. Her eyes darted around and then fixed on me, sitting on the bed, surrounded by small mounds of crumpled paper.

"Miss Beth, you okay?" she said, still holding the mop aloft, her eyes continuing to search the room.

"It's fine, Carmen. Except . . . except, I just found out something, um, about my husband."

"Mr. Jim? Is he all right?"

"He's fine," I said sharply. "Just fine."

Carmen dropped the mop. "Miss Beth," she sighed sadly, "I'm so sorry. I can do something for you?"

"Thank you, Carmen, but there's nothing you can do. I never should have screamed. I'm sorry I frightened you. You can go back downstairs. I promise, I'm all right."

Carmen left, closing the door behind her. I walked to the window and saw the men from All-Green huddling over their clipboards, shuffling papers, condemning the shrubbery to doom. *Let them take out every bush, every tree, every damn blade of grass. They can tear down the house, for all I care.*

I sat down at the writing table, the one Jim referred to as the New Hope table—we had bought it in that small town in Pennsylvania . . . when? Five years before? Seven? A terse laugh escaped from my throat.

"New Hope," I said aloud.

I pulled a legal pad and a pen from the drawer. I rolled the pen around in my hand. It was blue, with gold lettering on the cap: *Gillian Investments.* I unscrewed the cap of the pen and scrawled across the top of a sheet of lined yellow paper, "THERE MUST BE FIFTY WAYS TO LEAVE YOUR LOVER" and underlined it three times. I stared at what I had written and recited the lyrics in my head: *Just walk out the back, Jack. Make a new plan, Stan. No need to be coy, Roy. Just set yourself free.* A man's list. Not right for me.

I couldn't think straight enough to write anything that made sense. I moved the pen aimlessly across the sheet of paper, scribbling meaningless doodles on the page. My head was pounding. My breath was coming in short, shallow gasps. Random thoughts, irrational and angry, raced through my brain. Sell the house and everything in it before Jim returned to the states. Get Dr. Moros's help in farming out my patients to other therapists. Empty bank accounts. Buy a co-op in Manhattan. Or take off for Italy. Call the American School in Rome to ask about immediate vacancies for Adam and Nicole. Call Sarah and Miriam, they'll come to stay with me if I ask. Call my brother Bruce for the name of the vicious divorce attorney in his firm, the one they called "Jaws." Hire a private detective; find out who Jim has been screwing and since when. Does he love her? Is this his first affair? Who else knows about this—his friend Harold? Other friends? His partners? Call them; demand to know what they know. Call Jim, remind him, *You have two children. What about them?*

I quickly calculated the time difference between Laurel Falls, Connecticut, and Tokyo, Japan. Fourteen hours. Perfect. Jim hates to be awakened by a ringing telephone.

"Hello?" His sleepy voice.

"Good morning, my love."

"Beth! Is something wrong?"

"Why, no, Jim. Why do you ask?"

"What time is it? *Jesus!* It's four in the morning here."

"Really," I said flatly.

"Beth, are you okay? The kids?"

"Everything's just fine here. The landscapers are milling around the backyard, and I'm just lounging in our bedroom, yours and mine, thinking of you . . ."

"Beth! What the hell is going on?"

"Well, there is one tiny issue. I know how *busy* you are and how *important* this trip is to your business, but I did have one little question to ask. First of all, sweetheart, are you alone?"

"Of course I'm alone. It's the middle of the night."

"Just checking. You see, I was paying some bills, and I ran across a receipt for what I'm sure was a beautiful love-gift, except that it must have slipped your mind that I don't wear a size small. And I look lousy in hot pink."

Silence.

"You bastard. Who is she?"

Silence.

"Oh, maybe you can't remember which one she is? Important man like you, it must be difficult to keep all your women straight."

"I'm coming home, Beth. We need to talk in person."

"You are in no position to tell me what *we need* to do. That's what divorce attorneys are for. I'm hanging up now, Jim."

Jim was back in Connecticut the next evening. I had spent most of the hours since our phone call in bed, crying, sleeping, hatching imaginary, vindictive plots for revenge. Carmen took care of the kids, told them I was coming down with a virus. I was just out of the shower when Jim's taxi pulled into the driveway. I heard Nicole greet him. "Did you bring me a silk kimono, Daddy?"

"Where's Mom?" Jim asked.

"Probably sleeping," Adam said. "She has the flu or something."

Or something.

"WHO IS SHE?" I spoke softly. The kids were asleep in their rooms down the hall.

"She's . . . she was . . . um . . . there's nothing anymore. It's over."

I stared at him.

"Who was she?"

"Someone who worked with one of my clients. She left last week, went back to London. God, this is hard, Beth."

"Hard for whom?"

"I hate myself for hurting you. It just happened once. I swear, it was the only time. She's not coming back."

"I see. And you bought her a two-hundred-dollar nightgown to say *bon voyage*? How thoughtful."

Silence.

"What I can't figure out is why you left clues for me to follow. I mean, charging her present to our American Express card? You know I write the checks to pay household bills. You're not a stupid man—you deliberately let me find out *this way*. For maximum effect."

"You give me too much credit, Beth. I was weak and stupid, but, honestly, I didn't want to hurt you. I love you . . ."

"Don't you dare say that to me!" I said through clenched teeth. "I can't trust you. I don't believe anything you say. Don't bother to unpack your bags. Stay in the city. Stay anywhere you like, for that matter, so long as you leave. I can't stand to look at you."

———

JIM SPENT THE rest of the week in the city. He called home every night. He spoke to the kids, but I didn't get on the phone. Nicole, at the height of her adolescent self-absorption, didn't take notice that anything was amiss. Adam was always our family's emotional barometer, hypersensitive to changes in the atmosphere.

"How come Dad is sleeping in town so much?" he asked in a worried tone. "He'll be home this weekend, right?"

I called Miriam and Sarah every day. Sarah said, "I'm divorced—what advice can I give you? Jim is a good guy. You can't keep avoiding him. You know he really loves you, even if he's behaved like a complete shit. What is it with these middle-aged men? I want to tell them all: Go buy a red sports car, get your love handles liposuctioned, but leave that restless little thing of yours in your pants. Beth, you must know every shrink in Connecticut—surely you can find a great marriage counselor?"

And Miriam said, "I've never been married, what advice can I give you? Except this—you have to at least try to work things out with Jim. He's usually a sweetheart, and I love him, but right now I'd like to slap him. Maybe a marriage counselor can talk some sense into him."

At the end of the week, I called Jim at the office. "I'm

ready to talk to you. The kids have a lot going on this weekend; they'll be out of the house most of the time. We'll have privacy."

Jim came home that night. I was in bed, re-reading the notes I had taken at a recent lecture on depression. "Unexpressed anger is often at the root of neurosis," I had written. "Depression equals anger turned inward."

"It's good to be home," Jim said, sitting on the edge of the bed. "I'd like to stay."

"I have a few conditions. First, you've got to get tested for AIDS. Don't look so surprised, and don't say a single word. I'd rather not have to think about whether or not you wore a condom while you were screwing someone else. Just get the damn test. And then, we need to go to a marriage counselor. I'll find us someone. You have to make time to go to the counseling sessions. I'll set up appointments for early in the morning or in the evenings if possible, but you have to be there. Every time, without fail. I don't want to hear that anything going on at your office is more important than showing up for marriage counseling. Agreed?"

"I'll do anything you want, Beth. You can't imagine how I feel. You know how much my family means to me."

"I thought I did."

"We'll survive this, Beth."

"That's your goal, Jim? Survival? I'm looking for something more," I said, as I took off my glasses and reached to turn off the reading lamp. "I won't last in this marriage if the best we can do is survive it."

Jim started to unbutton his shirt.

"I'd appreciate it if you'd sleep in the guest room tonight," I said. I pulled the comforter around me and turned away from him. I heard the sounds of his undressing, and then his footsteps as he headed out of the room.

"Beth?" he called softly from the doorway.

"Mmm?"

"You know, you're the only woman I've ever loved."

I stayed where I was, not responding, and in minutes I was asleep.

INGRID ROSS, PH.D., had once been a guest lecturer in a Marriage and Family Counseling class I took in grad school. She was in her early sixties, married for close to forty years, with grown children and grandchildren. She and her husband were both psychologists in practice together. Ingrid rolled her eyes and shook her head when she told this to the class, as if to evoke our sympathy. I remembered that look on her face—just the right combination of wisdom, humor, and experience—when I called her to make an appointment for Jim and me.

We met with her twice a week for almost six months. It took at least a month of sessions for her to get us beyond our cultivated facades. I'm a therapist, so I know this is not unusual, but I had to abandon my self-appointed role as co-shrink before I could yield to her counseling. Jim had to forsake his reliance on intellect, humor, and social grace before he could talk about what really mattered; he (who is uncomfortable being new at anything) had to learn, from scratch, an emotional vocabulary.

In Ingrid's office, I discovered, first of all, the facts of Jim's affair. Her name was Patricia Remlin. She was single, twenty-seven years old, a consultant brought to New York from London for a brief assignment at one of Jim's client companies. They put her up at corporate housing in Battery Park City, where several people involved in the project would go after hours to have a drink and then work late into the evening. One night, she and Jim were alone in her apartment (I imagined the place, all brass-and-glass furnishings, a terrace facing the Statue of Liberty, cheaply framed *New Yorker* posters on the walls), and they "fell into bed." It was, Jim admitted rather sheepishly, Patricia's idea, though he accepted full responsibility for what happened. He confessed that he was flattered by the attention of a young woman. (A *thin* young woman, he neglected to say. I could hardly forget that the nightgown was a size small.) The reason he bought her the negligee was, he said, that she had joked about having brought only "utilitarian" sleepwear to New York because she assumed she'd be sleeping alone. He "honestly wasn't thinking" when he paid for the nightgown with our joint American Express card. Nicole, Adam, and I were the world to him. He didn't know what had possessed him.

As time went on, Ingrid helped us understand the truth, as opposed to the facts, about what had happened. Jim's company had taken a major leap that year—opening branch offices in six countries; with a smile, Jim said he had imagined the prestige and obligations connected to Gillian Investments might finally turn him into a grownup. (Hearing him say this made me furious. Marrying me and having children didn't make him a grownup?) The latest business deals had made Jim influential and prosperous, but with prestige and wealth came solemn responsibilities to an international coterie of associates, employees, and stockholders. Patricia, young and unmarried, represented youth and insouciance, Ingrid said. ("Not to mention, thighs that don't jiggle," I added.) All in all, Jim had a rather conventional case of midlife crisis. And though Ingrid agreed with me that Jim's sleeping with another woman was a blatantly hostile act, she believed Jim's assertion that anger at me wasn't the force that drove him to infidelity.

However, Ingrid didn't buy the it-was-an-accident

explanation for charging the damn nightgown to our credit card. "Jim, you wanted Beth to find out," she said. "You felt guilty, and you wanted Mother to punish you. You lost your own mother at a young age and married Beth soon after. In some ways, you depend on Beth to mother you."

"He's the one who rescued me when we met," I insisted. "He helped me register for my classes even though I couldn't pay for them. He led me to the job at the counseling center in Ithaca. And though I work, let's face it, we live mostly on his money. If anyone's a parent in this marriage, it's Jim."

"That depends on what you need a parent for," Ingrid said. "Ask Jim. Ask him what you mean to him."

Jim's answer surprised me. "You make everyone around you feel loved and secure," he said. "You're the most natural nurturer I've ever known. Everyone in your sphere—me, the kids, Sarah and Miriam, Carmen—we all know that we can tell you anything, and that you'll listen and understand. Maybe, on some level I've turned that into a 'mother' thing, but I don't want you to take the place of my mother. I want a wife."

"If I mean so much to you, how could you do this to me?" I said bitterly. "And how do I know you won't need to go in search of your adolescence again any time soon? I'm capable of many things, Jim, but I can't turn myself into a teenager."

Jim's voice rose. "How many ways can I say I'm sorry? That I was stupid and callous? That I don't want anything to happen to our family? And just for the record, she wasn't a teenager!"

I took a deep breath, about to explode. Before I made a sound, Ingrid caught my eye. "Tell him exactly how angry you are at him," she said. "Don't hold back. Tell him, so you can let go of the pain and move on."

We spent the last of our sessions developing what Ingrid called a marriage renewal plan. "Like urban renewal, after a hurricane," she said. "You've both been hurt but not ruined by this, the way a storm can rock the foundation of a building without actually causing it to collapse. Still, the windows are shattered, some shingles were blown off the roof, and you've got water damage. And, though we're hoping another storm doesn't hit, it wouldn't be a bad idea to get some insurance that will protect you, just in case."

Ingrid made us agree to take a romantic vacation, for at least a week, to somewhere neither of us had ever been. We were just getting back to civil conversation with each other; romance was still a distant notion. She set out clear guidelines for the trip. Jim had to promise to remind me repeatedly that I was his top priority; while we were away, for example, he was to call his office no more than once a day, and speak for no more than fifteen minutes. I was to avoid my penchant for sarcasm as a way of expressing anger. Ingrid asked me to describe to her a time when I thought my heart "would burst with love for Jim." I answered immediately, "When I told him I was pregnant. Both times."

"Good," Ingrid said. "Now, whenever you feel yourself thinking resentfully about him, I want you to force yourself to remember those moments." And she charged us both to begin each day of our trip by asking ourselves, "What can I do to make him (her) happy today?"

Of course, it sounds superficial and silly; embarrassing, the way everything that goes on in therapy of any kind seems when you talk about it *outside* of therapy. I do this for a living, and still, talking about the *modus operandi* sometimes makes me cringe. Nevertheless, it worked for Jim and me. From the start, the trip was different from any we had ever taken. Jim didn't simply ask his secretary to make arrangements through the company's travel agency, the way he usually did when we traveled. Instead, he brought home brochures for us to examine together. We decided on Maui. The hotel where we stayed for ten days was exorbitant and private—a hideout for celebrities escaping paparazzi and secretly recovering from plastic surgery. We took hula lessons beside a noted media mogul, an aging soap opera diva, and a young man reputed to be the Crown Prince of Somewhere. Who else could afford the place? We drank champagne at every meal, bathed together in the heart-shaped marble tub, and pretended we didn't notice the stubborn hesitancy in our lovemaking. We were still wounded and worried, although occasional flashes of a familiar intimacy gave us hope. We sent Ingrid a crate of pineapples and macadamias, with a note that said, "Aloha! Marriage renewal under way. So far, so good."

THE PHONE STARTLES me. As I reach to answer it, I hear the front door close, then a car door slam. Carmen's leaving. The cleaning crew must be finished.

"You sound sleepy. Too early to call, Mom?"

"That's fine, sweetheart. I should get up anyway."

"How was the party? Sorry I didn't make it this year. Please tell me I didn't miss anything exciting. You know, like some scandal."

"Afraid not. This was a very boring, well-behaved group."

"How did your dress look?"

"Not as good as it would look on you. You still want it for that party?"

"Are you sure I can take it? I'll have to get it altered."

"It's all yours. I'll mail it to you. Find a dressmaker who can turn it into a size six."

"Thanks, Mom. How did Aunt Miriam look? Great

like always, I bet."

"She looked like a 1930's movie star. I haven't spoken to her yet today, but—here's some gossip for you—I think there were sparks between her and Dad's friend, Gabe Bryant."

"He's a really cool guy. They never met before?"

"I know, it seems strange. They've both been to the house so often, but never at the same time."

"Now that I think about him, he's perfect for her. They can spend the rest of their lives watching movies together."

"I'll be sure to tell them you said so."

"I got an email from Ellie Roth this morning. Did you know about the money from her father?"

"I did hear something. Sarah has spoken to Dad about getting investment advice. I haven't had a chance to speak to Sarah. What did Ellie say?"

"She was funny as always. She's coming up to Boston for the Dave Matthews Band concert. She was planning to fly instead of taking the train, she said, since she's now an heiress."

"She said that? How much . . .?"

"*Mom!* Don't let's get tacky. I'm not about to ask her how much money her father left her. I was brought up better than that."

I smile. "You must have wonderful parents. Are we going to see you any time soon, Nicole?"

"Probably not. Crazy busy until Thanksgiving. And the answers to your next two questions are: I still haven't declared an official major, and no one special at the moment but I'll keep you posted."

SUNDAY NIGHT, JUST out of the shower. I catch a blurred vision of myself in the steamy full-length mirror. The image of my moderately Rubenesque body seldom fails to disappoint me. With my fingertips I trace the two hairline scars on my right breast, reminders of lumpectomies that, thankfully, revealed nothing malignant inside me. As to the faded stretch marks on my hips, I'm not certain if I acquired them during pregnancy or as a result of a lifetime of failed attempts at losing weight. Right now, I'm in one of my thinner periods, though no one would likely describe me as thin. No amount of dieting, Jazzercize, jogging, speed walking, or time on the treadmill has enabled me to shed for good the last, stubborn twenty pounds I've toted since adolescence.

"You're so nice and tall, dear," my mother used to say. "You can carry it."

Indeed, I can and I have.

I reach for a tiny, swan-shaped crystal jar on my vanity. From a thin silk ribbon around the swan's neck dangles a booklet describing in a hilariously mangled translation the history of the product in the jar. "Crème Kyoto derives from a cryptic recipe that bestowed the transcendental aura of eternal youth upon a dynasty of Japanese empresses in centuries past." I've been using the stuff since Jim brought it to me from Tokyo two months ago; so far, no transcendental aura. Nonetheless, I gently pat small dots of the emulsion from my neck to my forehead. The wrinkles around my eyes—not "laugh lines" certainly; no laughter could have etched such deep furrows in my face—are no worse than I've seen on twenty-somethings who've overdone their tanning salon sessions. I've brightened my hair with blonde streaks that camouflage the gray and give an overall effect of sun-bleached rather than faded. Jim often says, "Not bad for an old broad." To which I reply, "What do you know? You can't see two inches in front of your nose without bifocals." The comedy patter of long-time marrieds.

Here I am, a middle-aged therapist, with a self-image

still ruled by shallow self-criticism. I'd love to face getting older with defiance and dignity, but the truth is I yearn to be thinner, prettier, and (lately) younger. How pathetic: I've weathered the tempests of a thirty-year marriage, raised two children and buried one; I've earned a doctoral degree and the respect of my patients and colleagues; I'm well traveled and well read, bilingual and cultured—and yet there's only one compliment guaranteed to lift my spirits: *Why, you don't look your age!*

MONDAY MORNING, BEFORE dawn. Predictably, I dreamt about Rome, which usually makes me happy, but I awoke feeling anxious. In the dream I was running up the Spanish Steps, nervous because I was late for . . . for what? I never found out; I was yanked into consciousness by a racket behind the house. Raccoons in the garbage pails again.

My eyes open, my head starts to clear, and I think, a few hours from now, Andrew will be waiting for me at his hotel. Then I think, *Jim!* Have I already cheated on my husband by not telling him about my conversation with my former lover? Is it a betrayal if I see Andrew and just don't tell Jim? Even if I don't sleep with Andrew? On the phone, Andrew sounded to be in search of therapy, not sex. Or is that what I chose to hear? I haven't slept with anyone else since the day I met Jim. I've had exquisite fantasies and minor flirtations, but never for a moment have I seriously considered getting intimate with another man.

And though, in a way, Andrew has never left my heart or mind, the truth is that I have no explicit memory of the sexual act with him. I remember that our lovemaking was always accompanied by music and wine and food. I recall that we made love on the overnight train to Milan, and in tourist-class hotels in a dozen Italian cities, and in every room in Dr. Fabrizzi's palazzo—but how? What did it feel like when he kissed me? How did he like to be touched? Were there words we spoke in whispers to signal arousal? On the outskirts of my memory, only a tangle of sensations endures. The smell of the air on warm Roman nights. The sight of Andrew's seductive smile. The sound of the Italian singer Mina's voice crooning *Che senso ha?* (What sense does it make?), the disconsolate song we played endlessly on a tinny record player we picked up at the flea market. The taste of our favorite after-sex meal, *pizza quattro stagione* from the Trattoría da Paolo. But I've long forgotten what was singular about the actual execution of our lovemaking—how he moved his hands, where our mouths and fingers would go, our propensities, our rhythms.

In these intervening years, between the last time Andrew touched me and right this minute, every sexual circumstance of my life has belonged to Jim. I can't pretend that my sex life with Jim has been unsatisfying in any way. And if there can be no surprises in bed between lovers of thirty years, nonetheless I have no complaints. Jim has always been tender and capable, an unselfish and playful lover. He seems to be in the mood for sex about as often as I am, which is still quite frequently. He can make me laugh one minute and usher me to orgasm the next. He's habitually talkative in bed, spinning erotic tales in my ear. During my pregnancies, he was rapturous about my body, caressing my swollen belly and breasts like fragile, sacred objects, swearing he'd never seen anything more beautiful.

I know that the decision about whether to see Andrew has little to do with Jim. It has to do with me alone, because the thought of seeing Andrew again is irresistible. And maybe I'm feeling entitled to an adventurous, unpredictable moment or two even if (or perhaps, because) I am fifty-three, and menopausal, and still grieving for Adam, and beyond believing that life is ever fair or felicitous for very long. It's simply this: Being with Andrew might bring me a little happiness for a little while. I'll see him. I won't sleep with him. I'll figure out later how to explain things to Jim.

I OPEN THE double doors to my walk-in closet, which is roughly the size of the bedroom Jim and I slept in when we lived in Manhattan. What to wear, I wonder, for a rendezvous, even an innocent one, with the first man I ever loved? Absurdly, I attach what I think is important, symbolic meaning to every article of clothing I select: Black silk pants suit (because it's from an Italian designer); a silk blouse in deep yellow (Andrew once said my hair was the color of honey); gold Paloma Picasso "love and kisses" earrings (for obvious reasons). I decide on my bangle watch, the one I bought from a street vendor on 57th Street, instead of the Cartier from Jim. My wedding band, which in thirty years I've removed only during brief hospital stays, will be reminder enough that I have a husband who loves me.

"*Que linda!*" says Carmen as she watches me gather my purse, keys, a bottle of Evian for the car ride. "You meet Mr. Jim in the city?"

"No, not today," I say breezily. "I'm having coffee with an old friend."

I could swear, there's a look on Carmen's face—not disapproving, but knowing. "Have a nice time," she says.

"You have a good day, too," I say, avoiding her eyes. "*Hasta mañana.*"

THE BURNISHED METAL and smoky glass of the Carnegie Grand Hotel in the far West Fifties of Manhattan rises to thirty floors on the same spot where stood, until recently, a cluster of louche four-story row houses.

Years ago, I took some artwork to be framed at a ground-floor shop in one of those buildings. A young Vietnamese couple owned the store. The wife was also a pastry chef who worked part-time in a small bakery nearby. They lived above the framing shop with their two young children. Economic and political exigencies have led city leaders on a mission to sanitize many of these streets that surround the theater district; formerly apprehensive out-of-towners can now disembark fearlessly from their tour buses and march off to matinees of *The Phantom of the Opera* and shopping sprees at the Disney store. Hookers and drug dealers have left the neighborhood, but so have the residents who were running storefront businesses and living in the rent-controlled tenement apartments that gave way to smart hotels and co-ops and shops they couldn't afford. I wonder, as I pull into the garage adjacent to the Carnegie Grand, whatever happened to the framer and the pastry chef?

"Will you be here overnight, ma'am?" asks the parking attendant.

"Just visiting a guest at the hotel."

"Here you go then," he says, tearing off and handing me half of a perforated ticket that says: ONE DAY ONLY. "Just leave the keys in the car. And enjoy your stay."

I'm early; he said ten, didn't he? There's the coffee bar he mentioned. I'll just . . .

"Bella! Beth . . . you came! My God, you came."

He's grown a beard since I last saw him. Like his hair, it's more silvery-grey than blond. His blue shirt is the same color as his eyes. And he is as gorgeous as he ever was.

"Let me look at you," he says after we hug. He grabs both of my hands and steps back, taking me in. "Unbelievable, you haven't changed since Italy. Still beautiful!" I can't seem to speak.

A waiter is trying to wave us to a tiny bistro table in the center of the room. "Do you have something quieter?" Andrew asks him.

"Of course, sir. How about the booth in the corner?" Andrew and I are led past groups of youngish tourists chattering in German, French, Australian English.

"This hotel came highly recommended by one of my students," Andrew says as he sits next to me in the booth. "He said lots of Italians stay here. So far, I've heard every language spoken in this lobby, except for Italian. At the Salinas College of Music, where I teach, I'm quite famous for being obsessed with Italy. My students make fun of me for the way I behave whenever the subject of anything Italian comes up. Someone mentions *Tosca*, and before long I'm holding forth on the incomparable experience of hearing opera at La Scala, and then I find myself telling them where to eat in Rome and where to buy cameos in Naples, and my students are yawning. Oh, Bella, I'm rambling now; please stop me. You haven't said a word." He reaches for my hand, holds it gently. We stare into each other's faces.

"You promised me a cappuccino," I finally say. "Let me get some caffeine in me, and I'll tell you how my life has turned out. And then you can let me know just why we are here, together in this place, after all this time."

I start with Ithaca. I say nothing about being so despondent when Andrew abandoned me that I was unable to make real plans for myself. I tell him about meeting and marrying Jim, moving to New York and then Connecticut. Becoming a mother. Sonya Needham,

Cayuga House, graduate school. Being in practice as a psychotherapist. Andrew breaks in a few times to ask questions. "How are your friends Sarah and Miriam?" he wants to know. And, "You're married to *that* Gillian? *Jeez*! Even I've heard of him, the Wall Street *wunderkind.*" I blush, feeling a pang of guilt at hearing Jim's name on Andrew's lips.

Andrew brings up having run into Sarah in Chicago. "I nearly called you after that," he says. "But I lost my nerve."

"Why?"

"Stupid male pride. Afraid of making a fool of myself. Seems ridiculous now."

Refills of cappuccino keep coming. I realize I've been going on for over an hour; the hotel staff is setting up for lunch. To appease our waiter, we order sandwiches. I show Andrew my children's high school graduation pictures. "They're beautiful," he says. "Both blond, too. Your son seems to resemble you more than your daughter does. What are their names?" My voice breaks when I say Adam's name.

It takes another half hour to tell Andrew about Adam's life and death. From time to time, tears well in Andrew's eyes, and he shakes his head in sympathy and sorrow. I look away but keep talking. I end my story on an upbeat note—how well Nicole is doing at school, how close we are.

"Did you ever imagine, when we were young, that life could turn out to be so difficult?" he asks.

"Of course not," I say. "And we wouldn't have believed anyone who tried to tell us. At least we had a chance to be carefree for a while. I hear stories all day long from patients who have regrets about missed opportunities."

"Don't you miss it, that carefree feeling?"

I am remembering—and not with forgiveness—how

Andrew's love of freedom had once meant more to him than loving me.

"I think it's your turn to talk," I say, trying not to sound like too much of a therapist. He pulls out photos of two handsome teenaged boys. The older one—Andrew tells me his name is Ian and he's eighteen—has curly brown hair and a serious look in his eyes.

"He's the picture of Marcie, my wife," Andrew says. "And he's like her in every way, which is both a blessing and a curse. He just started college at San Francisco State, where his mother went to school, of course." The younger boy, Benjamin, is all Andrew—straight platinum hair in need of a trim, toothy smile, piercing sky-blue eyes.

"Ben is thirteen," Andrew says. "And autistic. We knew before he was even a year old that something was wrong. He never responded to things the way Ian had, the way healthy babies do. Once we heard the diagnosis, our lives changed forever. This is one of the few pictures I have of him smiling.

"Around the time Ben was diagnosed, I was offered a job at Curtis, in Philadelphia, with a tie-in to the symphony. The big break, the kind of thing young composers dream about. But I turned it down because of Ben. I figured if I stayed where I was, in a small school in Salinas, California, I'd have a reasonable schedule that would allow me to give Ben the attention he needed. Marcie is a sales rep for a textbook publisher. She travels all over the West, and she's never been sorry that her job keeps her on the road. I don't mean to make her sound like a bad mother—she loves the kids—but with Ben, she never took on the project of raising him. And it's a project, I can tell you."

I say, "When I first realized that Adam was not well, that he needed care around the clock if he was going to get better, I remember thinking what a blessing it was that both my children had been healthy up until then. Raising a healthy child is enough of a challenge. But a kid with special needs . . ." I shake my head.

"It's indescribable, what it does to a family, to a marriage," Andrew says. "About a year ago, Marcie got involved with someone else—a doctor. I didn't know about him until she filed for divorce. He has grown, *healthy* kids and a booming medical practice in Washington state. He's what Marcie considers successful. I think she was just holding things together with me until Ian left for school. With him gone, there's no reason to pretend we're a happy family anymore. She's already moved her things to her new love's big house outside Seattle."

Andrew, in a loveless marriage all these years?

"What about Ben?" I say.

"That's the complicated part. At first, it didn't occur to me that Marcie would want to take him with her. I've been his primary caregiver. And I've managed to make a life for Ben that suits him. I have faith in the doctors who treat him, and Ben does pretty well at the special school he goes to. Marcie wants him at a residential place for kids with autism—somewhere near where she'll be living. It's not that she wants to take care of him herself, but she's concerned that people will think she abandoned her son if she leaves him with me. Might not look good to her new crowd of friends. Ben's needs have nothing to do with any of this. But she's willing to spend as much of the anesthesiologist's money as necessary to take Ben from me."

"What does your lawyer say?"

"I don't actually have a real divorce lawyer yet. So far, there's been nothing much to do—just some routine paperwork—so I've been letting an attorney I know handle things for now. He's a friend who wrote my will and checked over the contract when I bought my house years ago."

PART II: BETH

"Not a good idea, Andrew. You need someone good, and tough, to represent you. My brother works for a hotshot New York firm with offices all over the country. Should I ask him to find you someone?"

"Outstanding, Bella. See, you're helping me already."

"Andrew, surely you didn't call me just to get a referral to an attorney."

"No, *cara*, of course not. There's another piece to all of this . . ."

"Yes?"

"When we had the big blowup—when Marcie dropped the bomb about wanting to take Ben with her— she said some brutal things about me."

"People leaving their marriages aren't known for kind departure speeches," I say.

"In this case, her words were cruel, but I'm afraid they also may be true."

"Like what?"

"As you can imagine, the conversation about Ben led to other things. I knew that Marcie never cared for life in a small college town—hence the job that took her away so much. In addition to threatening to take Ben away, she went on a tear about the time I turned down the offer at Curtis. 'It was our ticket out of here, and you blew it,' she said. 'You claimed it was for Ben's sake, but the truth is, you know you're a second-rate musician and you were scared to death of a place like Philadelphia. A backwater is much more your speed.'"

I cringe on Andrew's behalf. "Why is she so angry with you?"

"When she married me, I was on the road to what might have been a very successful, even glamorous, career. She assumed that Salinas was a temporary detour, that eventually we'd be somewhere more exciting, that I would *make it*. She had hopes of raising the kids, especially Ian, in a city."

"How do you get along with Ian?"

"My decision to stay in Salinas meant sacrifices for him. We get along—we can do the father and son bit, go to ball games and such—but I think he's glad to be away. His last few years at home, ours was not a happy household. And he thinks, because of what his mother says, that it's all my fault."

"Does he have any interest in music?"

"He took violin lessons when he was very young, but he didn't stay with it. I have no idea if he has talent. He knows a fair amount about serious music, but he listens to the stuff his friends listen to. His father is a second-rate musician, and he's embarrassed to be the son of a loser."

I wave my hand. "Teenagers always think their parents are losers. Normal for the age."

Andrew shakes his head. "I hope you're right, but ours is not a normal family situation. With Ben, I mean. I guess Ian has always been jealous of all the attention I give to Ben. But it can't be helped. Ben, limited though he is in many ways, depends on me, only me. In a sense, I'm his only connection to the world. If Marcie takes him away, he'll never be the same. And neither will I."

"It's not over yet. For yourself, as well as for Ben, you've got to put up a good fight."

He nods. I glance at my watch. The afternoon is almost gone.

"Andrew," I say, "why did you call me?"

"I've been so caught up in this fight with Marcie, and what she said about me being a failure. It's like a tape I can't turn off; it plays in my mind, night and day."

I was right; he is depressed. "I remember when you told me that music played all the time in your head," I say.

"There's still music, but not much lately . . . You asked why I called you. I was nothing short of desperate to spend time with someone—a woman—who has never looked at me with disappointment in her eyes. When I think about you, all I remember is how sweet everything was. Did we ever have even a bad moment when we were together?"

"Not until you said goodbye."

He squeezes my hand. "I don't know what I was thinking. I was so young and self-absorbed. You wanted us to start thinking about a future together, and all I could think of was my own future. Marriage, kids, didn't seem to fit with my plans."

"But you married Marcie. And you had children."

"After you, I didn't get involved with anyone for a while. I thought that footloose suited me fine. And then, I got lonely. My friends were starting to settle down, and I was thinking, maybe they've got the right idea. I considered getting in touch with you, but, oh, I don't know why I didn't. And then I met Marcie at a concert I gave in Palo Alto just after I finished graduate school. I had just accepted a teaching job at Salinas, and she came to live with me. I guess we were in love, but these days I can barely remember when we were even polite to each other. I can't tell you how many times I've wondered if you were happy and if I would ever see you again. I'd think about Italy . . . It was a magical time."

"It was. That's part of the reason it was hard for me to get over you."

"You're over me, then?" he asks. "Have you forgiven me?"

A bit wearily, I say, "It's been a long time, Andrew."

"You haven't said much about your husband. I hope he's worthy of you."

"He's a wonderful man. A good husband and father."

"And very successful. Rich. Probably handsome, too. I'm sure I'd hate him."

"He's worked hard for everything he has. Not the handsome part; that's a matter of good genes. When I married him, he was a poverty-stricken grad student."

"It must have been terrible for him, too, when your son died."

"His heart was broken. He still finds it hard to talk about Adam, even with me. It's one of the uncomfortable issues between us. Being a therapist, I always want people to talk about things. Jim's outgoing and talkative, but not always about the things that really matter to him. He's got a great relationship with Nicole, and we have . . . a life together, a past that means something to both of us. Even when things are rocky or boring or infuriating, we don't doubt that we belong together."

"So you've never strayed?"

"Never." *Not even today.*

"I'm glad for you, Bella. I know you probably have to be going, but would you come with me for a minute? I have something I want to give you."

He takes my hand and we walk to the elevator. "I accidentally left it in my room. Oh, hell, it wasn't accidental. It was part of a fabulous seduction scene I plotted for this afternoon. Get you here, invent an innocent reason to lure you to my hotel room, and then, *pounce!* Pretty smooth, huh?"

"Debonair as always," I laugh.

"I must have lost my touch over the years," he whispers as the elevator doors open to his floor. "The night we met, I had you naked and moaning in, what, fifteen minutes?"

"It was more like several hours, *signore,* and who had whom naked?"

The red light is flashing on the phone in his room. "Do you want to check your messages?" I ask.

"Not now. I don't want to talk to anyone except you."

He searches in one of his bags, pulls out a CD. "For you." he says.

It has no label. "What's on it?"

"I'm sorry I don't have a CD player here. I'd love to see the look on your face when you listen to it. There are three cuts. The first is a short piano duet I composed last year. It's called *Una Bella Figura*, and your spirit was with me every minute I worked on it. That's me and a colleague from Salinas playing it at a competition in Miami, where we actually won a prize. On the second cut, I'm playing the piano at home—it won't sound like a studio recording—and I'm singing, if you can bear it. It's a John Denver tune; I love the lyrics. And the third cut—it was a real coup to get this—is a song I think you'll remember, from another era."

"Thank you, Andrew. As always, you bring music into my life."

He takes me in his arms, holds me tightly. "I'd give the world for you to stay," he says. "Part of me was fantasizing, when I called you, that you would say you were waiting for me, hoping I would rescue you from some dreary existence, and we could now be together forever. Don't say anything, I know it's crazy. I'll never forget that you came when I needed you, Bella."

"I'm glad I came, too. I entertained a few fantasies myself after you called me. Don't look at me that way; I'm not about to tell you what they were. But I do need to go now. I'll get my brother to recommend an attorney. Promise me you'll call when I give you the name? You'll feel better if you're doing something, rather than being passive. And speaking of doing something, you may want to consider some therapy."

"Ah, the shrink gives advice."

"Indeed. And it comes not just from any shrink, but from one who once gave you her heart. Listen to me: In addition to being untrue, those messages from Marcie that keep playing in your head are unproductive. They're depressing your fighting spirit and paralyzing you. A shrink can help you erase those tapes."

"I promise, I'll call someone as soon as I get home."

"Andrew, please stay in touch with me. I want to know how things are with you; I don't want to lose you again. Who knows? Maybe we can hope to see each other again. I'd love to meet Ben."

"And, *cara mía*, at the risk of sounding like the jilted suitor in a really awful movie, I'd actually like to meet Jim sometime."

"Know what? I think you'd actually like each other."

I PULL OUT of the hotel garage, looking for a spot on the street. I park alongside a hydrant and slide Andrew's CD into the player. Before the music starts, Andrew speaks.

"Bella, if you are listening to this, it means that you have found it in your heart to visit me in New York. This music is for you, my dear, and I send it your way with a love that was born on a spring night in Rome many years ago and which lives in me still. *Ciao.*"

Before the piano duet, Andrew and the other pianist are introduced. The announcer then says, "The title of this piece is Una Bella Figura. The composer says he was inspired by a beautiful woman who once graced his life." Applause follows, and the music begins, soft and sad, in a minor key. I try to imagine Andrew in formal attire, consumed by the notes he plays. I close my eyes, lose myself in the melancholy tune. I wipe the tears from my face.

"You okay, lady?" A meter maid is knocking on my car door. I pause the CD and roll down the window.

"I'm fine, thank you."

"You're next to a hydrant, ya know. Ya gotta move or I'll hafta ticket you."

"No problem," I say. I circle the block and find a metered spot. I put in two quarters to give me thirty minutes. I'll be driving home at the height of evening rush hour, but no matter. I don't trust myself to listen to Andrew's CD and drive at the same time.

The second cut also begins with a few words from Andrew. "I heard this song years ago. The final verse, especially, always brings you to my mind."

It's called "Perhaps Love"; I've never heard it before. *And some say love is holding on / And some say letting go / And some say love is everything / And some say they don't know.* The last lines take my breath away: *If I should live forever / And all my dreams come true / My memory of love will be of you.*

The third cut has no introduction. The first few seconds sound scratchy, as if Andrew had made the copy from an old vinyl album. The music begins, and I laugh aloud. It's Mina's throaty voice, pleading for someone to tell her, *Che senso ha?* I'd love to know myself, Mina, what sense does anything make?

Five-thirty. If I leave now, I won't be home for hours. I reach for my cell phone and dial Jim's private line at the office.

"Hi, sailor. You alone?"

"Just came out of a meeting, have another in fifteen minutes. What's up?"

"Got any plans for tonight?"

"Oh, yeah. Big doin's. The Brits are going pub crawling, but, as you know, I'm way too old for that. So I thought I'd get Chinese takeout, bring it back to the apartment, maybe check out Larry King."

"Gee, you moguls have all the fun."

"What are you up to? You calling from your cell phone?"

"Yes, I'm in the city."

"Oh that's right, you gave yourself a post-party holiday. What are you doing in town?"

"Long story. Listen, I don't have any patients until ten tomorrow morning, so I could stay in the apartment with you tonight. I think I still have clothes and a toothbrush there."

"What a nice surprise. So, what's your pleasure? Hot and sour or egg drop soup?"

"Noooo, no, no," I say. "I have a different menu and a different agenda in mind. I'm not schlepping downtown for mundane Chinese food."

"What are you thinking?"

"First, I'll swing up to Zabar's and pick up whatever they're selling that's obscenely expensive. Russian caviar! French champagne! I've got a very rich husband; he can afford it. Then I might stop off in the Village on my way to you, see if one of those interesting lingerie stores has something trashy but tasteful in black lace."

I can hear other voices in the background at Jim's office. "That sounds like a great plan," Jim says earnestly. "I should be available by around eight. Anything I can do to prepare for this, um, conference?"

"How about renting a really dirty movie? I'm not in the mood for Larry King."

"No problem. Listen, I'd *love* to continue this line of discussion, except I've got a meeting about to begin. But my mind is already working on some creative options for tonight."

"I'll hold that thought."

I start up the engine and head north on Tenth Avenue towards the Upper West Side. I feel simultaneously ener-gized and composed. I've spent the day with a man who has held part of my heart captive for my entire adult life, who inhabited my dreams, who represented incomparable excitement and joy that I couldn't hope to feel again. It turns out that he has held me in his heart, too, and fantasized about me during all the ragged moments of his life. The man who once left me in despair now wanted me—physically, emotionally, in every way. He saw me not as a middle-aged woman worn at the edges, but as the object of desire I once was to him. God knows, it did me good to see that look in his eyes. But though I love the chapter we once created together, my life's story wound up taking an irreversible turn away from him. Sitting with him today, sensing his passion for me, I understood for the first time that my feelings for Andrew are no longer romantic or sexual, but deliciously nostalgic.

I hope there will be a way for us to stay in touch. I always want to know how he is faring, that he is well. Perhaps, from time to time, we can meet for lunch and hold hands and remind each other how lucky we were to have met when and where we did.

Tonight I have a date with my husband. Stopped at a light, I adjust the rear view mirror and catch a glimpse of my face. I'm surprised that my makeup still looks fresh and my hair has held up, and I'm thinking, *Not bad for an old broad.* And wondering just what I will tell Jim about my day.

PART III:
LOGIC OF THE HEART

SARAH: COMINGS AND GOINGS

"Hey, that's no way to say goodbye."
—*Leonard Cohen*

PRIOR TO THE GILLIANS' party, I'd been drunk—liquored up enough to induce a good stupor, I mean—only once in my life. It was sophomore year in college, just after intercession break. My erstwhile boyfriend, the clandestinely married Claude Lequesne, had returned from a conjugal visit to Marseilles with a case of Beaujolais nouveau and a notion that we have a go at re-enacting a few vignettes from *The Story of O*. I was relieved that we both imbibed enough to pass out before actually getting around to the handcuffs and masks, though I remain indebted to Claude for teaching me French slang for an extended spectrum of erogenous zones and lascivious acts.

I hardly drink at all anymore, but at the party I was trying to get at least tipsy enough to forget, a little, the nerve-racking last few days. Maybe I was hoping I'd get talky-drunk and, with impunity, make a scene that would acutely embarrass Kevin. I imagined the kind of drama that might prompt my genteel friend Violet Bailey to excuse me in her uniquely Southern way: "She didn't realize what she was saying, poor dear. Obviously, she'd been over-served."

I did my damnedest to get myself over-served at the Gillians'. I stayed with champagne cocktails, one after another, quaffing my third one before the waiters had even finished passing the hors d'oeuvres. I was sufficiently agitated from the events of the week that the tension didn't leave my neck and shoulders and I didn't even start to feel woozy until we were well into the main course. By then I had cornered Bruce Jacobs for advice about my wretched situation at work and completely lost sight of my wretched situation at home.

I pretty much ignored Kevin. He probably interpreted my demeanor as fallout from the contretemps at my office, which Bruce kept referring to as my "case." I think I told Bruce he was reminding me of something my mother used to say when I argued for something she'd already vetoed: Sarah, you've got a good lawyer, but a weak case. I don't remember if he thought this was funny or not, but he stuck one of his business cards in my hand and told me to call his law firm—Jacobs, Howard, and Mercado—and ask for Kristin Traynor, the attorney in his firm who was the world's living expert on New York employment law.

Despite my chill towards him, Kevin was solicitous all evening—trying to hold my hand (though I rebuffed him several times), bringing me food, making sure my water goblet was full, asking interested questions of Bruce Jacobs on my behalf. Brendan's friend Lilly threw me occasional apologetic smiles from across the dinner table. She knew that she had spilled some pretty important beans, and though I had made it clear that I held her blameless I could tell she was feeling culpable, and a little sad for me.

I dozed on and off on the drive back to the city. I awoke with a start when we dropped Lilly off in front of the brownstone where she lived on Bleecker Street. Lilly leaned forward to tell me that she hoped we'd see each other again.

"I'm sure we will," I apparently replied in cheery, tipsy singsong. "Any friend of Kevin's stepson is a friend of mine."

I followed this intriguing opening, I'm told, with a succinct summary of the circumstances of Brendan's birth, followed by my imagined account of Betsy and Kevin's quasi-shotgun wedding, during which I apparently raised the question of whether "shotgun" is the proper term for nuptials that take place after an unwed mother gives birth and when she marries someone other than the father of her illegitimate child. Not that I actually remember anything I said. I vaguely recall that a cool gust of air blew into the car when Lilly opened her door and left us.

The next thing I knew it was Sunday morning. By the time I awoke, Kevin had already put Brendan in a taxi to the airport and was sitting on the living room sofa, his eyes glued to *Meet the Press*. He ignored me as I shuffled past him on my way to the kitchen.

"Aspirin," I croaked by way of explanation as I haphazardly searched drawers and cabinets. "I thought we had a bottle somewhere . . ." No answer. "Ah, here it is." Silence. "What was I thinking? I'm way out of practice. Drinking, I mean. Like twenty-five years. Maybe more. There must be a Dorothy Parker line for a moment like this. Oh, of course: One more drink and I would have been under the host. Did she say that at a party at Scott and Zelda's house, or . . .?"

"Enough, Sarah."

"Enough what?"

"You have no idea how you hurt me last night. And my son."

I washed down three aspirin with a swig of coffee and settled in for what I could tell was going to be a long sermon. My parting words to Lilly couldn't have comprised more than a few simple sentences, but after Kevin was finished parsing them, you would have thought that each morpheme was a marking on the Rosetta Stone. Hearing him call me snide, vengeful, and heartless, I found myself recalling the times when I had longed for a passionate face-off with Kevin, and I made a mental note to be more careful in the future about what I wished for.

In spite of my hangover, I managed a few stinging ripostes. I didn't want to talk about what I had said; I wanted to talk about everything that Kevin had failed to say. "What else are you hiding from me?" I demanded. "Were you once in the circus? The CIA? Are you a defrocked priest? The second gunman on the grassy knoll? Did you used to be a woman? A young Republican?"

"Knock it off! I don't know what you are angry about. You're carrying on as if I've committed some kind of crime against you. Why should Brendan's DNA matter to you? You should have heard how you sounded. So ugly, to behave like that, Sarah. Hateful. What did you think, that if you were drunk enough I would forgive you? That it would embarrass Brendan less if you could say you were drunk and couldn't control what you were saying?"

"Why in the world would Brendan be embarrassed?" I asked matter-of-factly. "He had already told Lilly, who's just an acquaintance, really, that he wasn't your biological son. What's wrong with saying something that everyone knows is true?"

"It was just so inappropriate."

"You're worried about appropriateness? I see. I suppose there hasn't been an appropriate moment in the last four years for you to tell me about Brendan."

"How could it possibly matter? I couldn't love Brendan more than I do."

I shook my head. "Not the point, how much you love him."

"Whatever you think the point is, this is the sort of thing that families like to keep private."

"Families, private," I said, mulling the words. "So this is an O'Neal family thing?"

"Exactly."

"And I'm not part of your family. Now I get it."

"You know what I mean."

"No, I'm afraid I don't. Why did you lie to me?"

"What are you talking about? Respecting Brendan's privacy is lying?"

"From what Lilly told me, it sounds as if you were a prince—marrying Betsy, raising Brendan. Why the hell would you hide it from me? This is a significant piece of biographical information, Kev. Come to think of it, I gave you a perfect opening. Remember the way Brendan behaved towards his mother at his graduation? I specifically asked you then what was going on, and you blew me off. You could have told me then that Brendan wasn't your son."

"He is my son," Kevin said. "I protect Brendan's feelings exactly the way you protect Ellie's. What you did last night was just plain mean. And you know what I think? That you've never really liked Brendan."

"I like Brendan just fine. This is between you and me, Kev. It's a couples thing. The most important part is that I want you to want to tell me everything about yourself. It's how couples behave. When they love each other, anyway. I'm now thinking about all the other things I half-know about you. How your business went under—the whole story. Were you sleeping with your ex-partner? It wouldn't matter to me if you were; it's ancient history. But it's your history, and I should know the truth about it. You make it sound like it was just a business deal gone bad, but why did you never sue her for the money you say she stole from the company? I've always thought the story had 'woman scorned' written all over it." Kevin just glowered at me. "I don't even know the names of your old girlfriends."

This got him talking. Suddenly, he was Prince Valiant, all chivalry and discretion, defending the honor of the damsels in his past. "I refuse to be blackmailed into talking about intimate moments I've shared with other women. It's vulgar of you even to ask. Some things, Sarah, are just none of your fucking business."

"You can spare me the sordid details, but some names would be nice, anything to give me an inkling of who they were and what they meant to you," I said. "Speaking of which, how about letting loose with some sexual clues to who you are? For years I've begged you to tell me what turns you on, what you think about when you're making love to me. You make me feel like I'm snooping. Like I should be embarrassed to ask. Did all those years in Catholic school permanently inhibit your libido? Do you think what we do in bed is sinful? Is that why you can't talk about sex?"

"I'm sorry to be such a disappointment in the sack," he said with a sneer. "Maybe you should give one of your Jewish boyfriends a call."

And so on, nasty and hurtful, back and forth, all afternoon. Kevin paced the living room, alternately muttering and yelling accusations. I stayed on the sofa, holding my throbbing head and tossing *bons mots* his way every chance I got. We exchanged our last salvo as he was throwing his clothes into a suitcase.

"You don't have a clue about intimacy! You were meant to live alone," I yelled.

"Being alone is a whole lot better than living with someone so vindictive," he answered. "Not that you'll give a shit, but I have a business trip to Seattle on Wednesday, and I'll be there for a week. I'll find a place to stay in town until I leave. You can tell anyone who calls me here to leave messages on my voicemail at the office."

"I'm not your damn secretary," I hissed through clenched teeth as Kevin tramped out the door and slammed it behind him.

―――――――

THINGS AT THE office were peculiar the first days after Lawrence left. For one thing, Joey was gone. He had Sally send around an email saying that he had decided to attend the annual National Pharmacy Alliance meeting in Minneapolis. We were to communicate with him through Sally, who'd be speaking to him every day. She added her own postscript to the email: "You know what this means, everyone. Feel free to wear jeans to the office this week, but no tee-shirts with writing on them, PLEASE!" Joey's definition of business casual dress precludes jeans, but Sally, like a benevolent babysitter, allows us children to bend the strict house rules when Daddy's away. It's cute, the way she even pretends that Joey doesn't know what's going on.

The door to Lawrence's office stayed closed, and no one, at least in my presence, mentioned his name. Late one afternoon when I couldn't find my copy of the *AMA Manual of Style*, I automatically went to Lawrence's office to use his, but when I tried the handle the door was locked and then I remembered, he's gone.

"Is Lawrence around?" I asked Sally, pretending I knew nothing. I could tell I had unnerved her.

"What do you need?" she said with forced geniality.

"I don't want to bother you. Just give me the key to his office and I'll get it myself."

I let her fidget for a few minutes. I watched her pretend to search her desk for the keys. She was scrambling for a way to hold on to what she knew about Lawrence, and especially, to keep me from seeing his vacant office, and I was delighted to see her squirm. I finally let her off the hook, saying I could probably get a copy of the book I needed from Dana or Rebecca. "Thanks anyway. What do you hear from Joey?" I said, smiling.

Lieutenant Sally was back, staunch and unruffled. "The conference is going well. He's making some important contacts for Tri-Tech," she said crisply.

Construction on Route 80 delayed my trip to Savant. I called Doc Shortland from my cell phone to let him know I was running late.

"*Ça va,* Sarah," he assured me. "We've got a company-wide video conference first thing today anyway. You know," he lowered his voice, "the announcement."

"Oh, right, Doc. Your replacement. Not that anyone could ever really replace you, but you know what I mean."

"Just don't worry, any time you get here will be fine. See you soon. How do you say that in French again?"

"*A bientôt,* Doc."

A RECEPTIONIST AT the Savant security desk handed me a visitor's badge, actually a peel-off sticker, with my name and Doc Shortland's printed above the Savant logo. I walked through metal detectors to the atrium of the building, where the morning's video conference was being re-run on a huge monitor. A crawl across the bottom of the screen displayed Savant's stock price and news bulletins about company events around the world.

A man identified as Heinrich Pfeiffer, Savant Worldwide Information Officer, Geneva, Switzerland, was standing behind a podium, smiling, reading from a stack of yellow index cards. "This restructuring will allow Savant Worldwide to continue in its role as a recognized healthcare leader. Savant has long set the industry standard in pharmaceutical research, development, distribution, and professional education. As always, our continued success depends on the talents and energy of our people.

"We are delighted that Dr. Richard Shortland has accepted the position of International Senior Vice President of Marketing, European Division. Doc Shortland, as he is known throughout the company, has had a long and distinguished career with Savant, and we are confident that the best is yet to come."

Pfeiffer's assistant, a young woman in a serious navy blue suit and heavy tortoise-framed eyeglasses, whispered something in his ear. He nodded to her, shuffled his index cards, and spoke again, above the whispers and rustling papers in the room.

"Ursula has just reminded me, I should like to say something about the person who will be taking over Doc Shortland's responsibilities in our Parsippany, New Jersey, USA headquarters. Though relatively new to the Savant family, she has already demonstrated outstanding knowledge, leadership, and commitment. It gives me great pleasure to announce that, effective January one, the Senior Vice President for Marketing in New Jersey will be Pushpa Rao."

When I finished Doc's French lesson for the day, I wandered over to Pushpa's office to congratulate her, but she wasn't around. I noticed book cartons stacked flat against the side of her desk. Preparation, no doubt, for the move down the hall and her takeover of Doc's spacious corner of the twenty-second floor of the building.

The news that Pushpa was replacing Doc gave me a fleeting moment of optimism about my own prospects. I was the only one at Tri-Tech who had even worked with Pushpa. But things at Tri-Tech were too cockeyed for my optimism to last. Surely, Joey knew—probably last week—who would take over for Doc. Normally he would have shared the news with me, asked for my ideas, but he hadn't spoken to me in almost a week.

Joey's absence from Tri-Tech kept the office pretty quiet, but Lawrence's departure and my undependable future at Tri-Tech made me jumpy. I updated my résumé and flipped through my Rolodex, but I couldn't mine the energy to begin a serious job search. Most of the people I would call have had to change jobs as many times as I, but still, I knew I'd be demoralized by their empathy. *That's right, laid off again. I knew you'd understand. Me, too, I prefer the British expression, being made 'redundant' instead of getting fired. You don't know of anything right now? Might I email you my current résumé? Yeah, haha, I'm leaving the dates off mine these days, too. Nice to catch up with you, too. You'll keep me in mind if you hear of anything?*

I'm getting too old for this. People my age are already cutting back on work, retiring early. I'm still surviving from one paycheck to the next. I can't afford to be out of work even for a few weeks.

I DON'T USUALLY feel lonely for Kevin when he is away because I know most days will end with a friendly call from him. But there had been no word from him all week, just an uneasy silence that underscored the precarious state of things between us. I woke up thinking about him and I left a message on his voicemail at the office, wishing him a safe trip. "See you when you get back," I said, with as much affection as I could mobilize.

Helen called as I was getting ready for work. I put her on the speaker so I could dress while we talked.

It sounded as if she was on speaker phone as well. Helen, even for Helen, was unusually chipper.

"Isn't it exciting that Martin left Ellie all that money?" she said. "I spoke to her over the weekend. She said you were going to have that guy Gillian, your friend Beth's husband—what's his first name again?—set things up for her."

"Jim's already working on it. Ellie's coming into the city next week to meet with someone from Gillian Investments. God knows her mother can't give her any financial advice. Helen, can I call you back tonight? I've got to dash off to New Jersey. Anything important going on?" I squirmed into my pantyhose.

"Good morning, Sarah." It was Sidney's voice. "I think you'll want to stay on the phone for a few more minutes. Sorry to get you so early in the morning, but we couldn't wait. I got back from Atlanta late last night."

"Sidney, hi. I sure could use some good news," I said, slipping a black chemise over my head.

"Remember what I wrote you about Martin, that he said something about a lawyer in Atlanta? Martin left a letter with him."

"A letter?" I called from inside my closet, where I was looking for my gray skirt. To spite Sally—and because going to Savant meant I had to dress like a grownup—I wouldn't be wearing jeans to the office.

"Yes. You remember, of course, that Martin went to Atlanta to work for a bank—Southern Federated, I think they were called. They've been out of business for a good five years. He was only with them for a short time, and then he started his own consulting business. Anyway, Southern Federated gave Martin a chance to buy life insurance at a good rate, and he kept it in force until—um, until the end."

"For Ellie? That's great." Where did I put that black cashmere sweater set? I reached to the top shelf of the closet. My satin pants suit—the one I wore to the party— fell to the floor. I tossed it on my bed so I'd remember to take it to be dry-cleaned. Two pieces of paper fluttered out of the jacket pocket—a crumpled cocktail napkin and

Bruce Jacobs' business card. I stuck the card in my jewelry box and pulled out pearl-and-silver earrings and a chunky silver choker.

"First, about the letter Martin left. It's addressed to you," Sidney said. "I just spent two days with Max Bauer, Martin's lawyer in Atlanta. Martin left instructions with Max to give me the letter, which I was then to deliver to you. It's right here, I haven't opened it. Do you want me to FedEx it to you?"

I slid into a pair of black suede heels. "You can read it to me now, Sidney. I don't . . ."

Helen, still on the extension, broke in. "Sarah, maybe you should read it in private. Poor Martin was very troubled over the years. Oh, who am I talking to? Of course you know. Whatever he said in the letter, maybe you should remember that he wasn't always a well man."

"That's fine," I said, daubing eyeliner on my lower lids. I was actually imagining a last, vituperative stab from Martin from beyond the grave. One final criticism, an insult he'd neglected to bestow before he ran out of breath. "I can handle it. Read it to me and then you can send it overnight. How long is it? Honestly, I'm in a rush."

"About two pages." I heard Sidney tear open the envelope. "It's handwritten. Here goes," he said. "The envelope says, 'To my former wife, Sarah Jane Gordon Roth.' It's dated eight, no, nine years ago, May eighteenth."

"My birthday," I said, rattled at the thought. I sat on my bed and picked up the phone. Hearing Martin's words amplified throughout my bedroom was too unnerving. "Go ahead, Sidney."

"'Dear Sarah: A letter like this is one of those ridiculous, melodramatic ideas that come to people who are depressed, full of themselves, crazy, or a combination of all of the above. It's your birthday today, and for some damn reason it's made me sentimental. I probably let you down on a number of special occasions, but maybe what I say here will make it up to you in a way. If you are reading this—and there must be some old joke with this punchline—it means that I'm dead and you're not. My most recent job provided me with a hefty life insurance policy, and though the job has vanished, I intend to pay off the policy and keep it for you. Not for Elinor, though I will leave something for her too, of course. Besides, anything I bequeath to you will eventually be Ellie's anyway. And then there's this stock portfolio I've been building. As of now, anyway, it looks like I may die a rich man. I can imagine how puzzling this will be to you. I will try to explain what prompted me to write a letter like this, not to mention what possessed me to leave my ex-wife a wealthy woman upon my death.'"

"What? Martin left me money?"

"Oh, yes. A great deal of money. I don't have a final number yet, but it'll be several million—"

Helen's voice, teary, interrupted. "Sarah, he loved you. In the end, he wanted to do the right thing."

Sidney speaking again. "Sarah, are you all right, honey? Is Kevin there? I mean, maybe it wasn't such a good idea to read this to you if you're alone."

"I'm fine, Sidney. Is there more?"

"Yes. That was just the first page. Here's page two. 'I don't know if Ellie ever mentioned Cassandra, a woman I dated a while back. When she left me, as every woman since you (and including you) has chosen to do, she had a few words to say about why things between us didn't work out. I'm not going to tell you here everything she said, but I thought you'd appreciate knowing this: Her parting address, a tirade really, sounded as if it could have been written by you. And it made me think, once I stopped trying to blame everything on her, that in the end I wasn't particularly fair or kind to you, and that my only ex-wife and my only child might always see me as a failure unless I could do something to make up for how I treated them.'

"'So here, Sarah, are what may turn out to be my two last gifts to you. The first is an apology and an admission: I wasn't the world's best husband, and I won't make Father of the Year, but I'm admitting that you were completely right about me. You're not the easiest person to live with, but you tried to make things work. When we were married, I mean. The second part, which I suspect you will enjoy almost as much as the first, is that I'm leaving you a great deal of money. Unless, of course, I outlive you. Who can say? Maybe we'll both live to see grandchildren and to make each other furious again. But the money is yours, no matter what. After all, you're the mother of my child. And a great mother at that. Happy birthday and love, Martin.'"

WHEN I HUNG up, I lay down on my bed and closed my eyes. I could almost see Martin's crooked smile, hear the Brooklyn accent I used to tease him about. After all that had passed between us, I never could have guessed that our final chapter would end the way it began, as a love story.

I left messages for Doc Shortland and Sally, claiming a personal emergency that would keep me out of the office for a day or two. Then I called Beth.

"Can you talk fast?" she said. "I've got an early appointment."

I gave her the highlights of my day so far.

"My God, Sarah. What happens now?" she said.

"I assume there will be lots of paperwork, but Sidney seems to think everything will be settled for both Ellie's inheritance and my—my whatever, in the next few weeks."

"Amazing, how one phone call can change your life. Tell me, what did Kevin say?"

"Kevin?" He hadn't even crossed my mind since Sidney and Helen's call.

"Yes, you remember him—good-looking guy, snappy dresser. Sleeps in your bed."

"He's in Seattle on business."

"Normally, I'd say it was too early to call out there, but this is news I think he'd be happy to wake up to."

"Maybe later," I said. I didn't tell her that I didn't even know where Kevin was staying in Seattle. I could call his secretary and ask, although . . .

"Do you want to come up here to be with us until Kevin returns? Jim and I specialize in emotional roller coasters and money management, you know. Kevin can join us whenever he gets back."

I hesitated just long enough for Beth to pick up on something about my frame of mind.

"Sarah, what's wrong?"

"Can't even begin now. Too much for the phone. Thanks for the invite, but I'll pass on Connecticut for now. Let's just stick to our plans for brunch this Sunday. Come to think of it, I'm rich! Let's take a suite overnight at the Plaza."

"We should do that one weekend. But not this one. Jim and I have plans."

"We need to do our review of your party, too. I had quite a bit to drink, as you may remember, so I'll be happy to hear from you and Miriam what I may have missed."

"I've got quite a bit to tell you two myself. I think it's my turn to pick a restaurant for brunch. By the way, did you get a chance to talk to Gabe Bryant at the party?"

"The guy with the great smile who was drooling over Miriam?"

"Miriam's having breakfast with him on Saturday. He lives near her. From what I hear, he's good and smitten."

"That was fast. And she? I haven't spoken to her this

week."

"Intrigued. Flattered. Cautious. The usual Miriam."

"Think he's a possibility?"

"No way to tell with her. But if she'd allow herself to fall in love again, I'd wish Gabe on her."

"Quite an endorsement."

"Sarah, I'm looking at the time. I do have to go. Why don't you give Jim a call and get the name of someone at his company who can walk you through what lies ahead."

"I'll do it. I'm a little dazed . . ."

"You've been a little dazed since I've known you. But now you're dazed and rich. How nice for you, to have some security. Finally."

Financial security, yes. But with Kevin . . .?

"Let me know when and where we are meeting on Sunday," I said.

"Hi, Kevin. I'm getting tired of leaving voicemails, but I'm too embarrassed to ask your assistant for the name of your hotel in Seattle. There's no reason for her to know that you didn't tell me where you were staying. I need to talk to you."

————————

"MOM? YOU ALL right?"

"Fine, darling. Why?"

"It's just unusual for you to call me in the middle of the day. It's lucky you caught me at home. I'm working on my law school applications. You're not at work?"

"Nope, I'm home. Just decided to take the day off. How are you and Doug doing?"

"Fine. He's finished his grad school apps. We're trying not to think about what happens if we don't get accepted at schools in the same city."

"I bet you'll both get in everywhere. NYU still your first choice?"

"Mondays and Wednesdays. Tuesday through Thursday, it's Columbia. That's Doug's first choice for business school. And the rest of the time I think about living on a kibbutz for a year or joining the Peace Corps."

"Not a bad choice on that list. Honey, when is your appointment at Gillian Investments?"

"Let me see, I put it in my Palm—you know, I have to admit it's a pain sometimes to depend on an electronic appointment book. Here, I found it, next Thursday. I'm supposed to have lunch with someone named Allison Tanaka. I guess that means she's paying, right?"

"You're her client. She'll be happy to treat you. She's making money because you're letting her manage your portfolio. Can you have dinner with me? There's something I want to talk about. I'll take you anywhere you want to go."

"How about a few drinks in one of those leather bars in the meatpacking district? We can pretend we're in a mother-daughter episode of *Sex and the City*."

"Perfect. Who do I get to be, Samantha or Carrie?"

"Ugh, Mom. I can't believe you actually watch the show. I'm sorry I started this," she giggled.

"Serves you right. You'll have to go a long way to scandalize me. Do you think your generation invented shocking behavior?"

"I know, I know. Make love, not war and all that. I'm changing the subject now. About next Thursday, let's do dinner."

"I can't wait to see you."

"You sure everything's all right, Mom?"

"Better than it's been in a long time."

I COULD HAVE just quit my job at Tri-Tech, which would have made things simple for Joey as well as for me.

However, it was the end of the year, and though I no

longer was desperate for the bonus or the partnership package, I had put up with Joey and earned my claim to that money. Sidney had said I had about a month until Martin's money would really be mine. Until then, I'd be like one of those stunned lottery jackpot winners, an instant millionaire who continues to show up for work on the assembly line at the tool-and-dye factory until she can come up with a better plan.

"Sarah, I have Joey on line two for you. From Minneapolis."

"Put him through."

I had returned to the office after just one day at home. Doc Shortland was suddenly called to Geneva. No French lessons for the rest of the week.

"Sarah? You remember that PowerPoint presentation we did last year on Dravitin, the allergy medicine for kids? It was a proposal for a continuing ed program for pediatricians, but the FDA held up approval and Savant dropped the whole idea."

Not a word of greeting to me. "I remember, Joey," I said. I had written the entire presentation without any help from him.

"We may have another shot. Looks like the FDA came through and the drug will be out next year. I heard that Saylish has been asked to make a pitch to the Dravitin team at Savant this week. I was able to get to the Dravitin team leader. He says we have a shot at competing with Saylish if we can meet with the Dravitin team this Friday. Can you do that presentation without me?"

Teams and team leaders. Like everyone's at summer camp. "No problem," I said.

"Just get Sally to help you gather anything you need. And take Raymond along with you."

Raymond again.

"Joey, I'm supposed to be in DC next week. That

meeting's still on, isn't it? Fawn hasn't given me my final itinerary."

Hesitation. "Yeah, well, don't worry about that now. Just do the Dravitin thing."

"Everything all right out there?"

"Yeah. I'll talk to you tomorrow. Can you put me through to Rebecca?"

"Rebecca?" He usually goes through me when he needs something from her.

"Uh, yeah, I have a quick question for her."

"WENDY, IT'S SARAH Roth."

"Looking for Kevin?"

"Just wondering what the best way is to get hold of him."

"You mean now? He should be free in about thirty minutes."

"How can I get word to him to call me this afternoon?"

"I'll tell him," she said stiffly. "Or I'll leave him a note like I usually do. I always give him your messages, Sarah."

Leave him a note? Kevin's in the office? "Of course you do, Wendy. Sorry, I wasn't implying that you didn't."

"That's all right. I'm a little bummed out today. It's just that I thought I'd have an easy week, with everyone away. Then when they canceled the Seattle trip, things got nuts here. I'm sure Kevin has told you how busy this place can get."

"He talks about the office all the time, Wendy." Except when he doesn't, like when he neglects to say he's in New York, not Seattle, for the week.

"Is this, like, an emergency? I'll break into the meeting if you need him right away."

"Not necessary. Just leave him a note and tell him he

can get me at home tonight. He has the number."

Wendy laughed. "I'm sure he does."

"Do me a favor. Write that down as part of the message for him. I mean, 'Sarah called. She'll be at home tonight. You've got the number.'"

"Oh, I get it, a joke, right?"

"Yes, Wendy. Hilarious, isn't it?"

THE MEETING WITH the Dravitin team was scheduled for early afternoon on Friday. Raymond and I drove to Savant in his car, an old Taurus station wagon ("a hand-me-down from Ma and Pa Albano," he explained) with an actual mother-of-plastic Madonna velcroed to the dashboard and squeaky springs jutting through vinyl seats. Raymond had gone to the trouble of installing a state-of-the-art stereo system, so we were able to enjoy the musical stylings of Limp Bizkit coming at us from six speakers all the way from Manhattan to Parsippany.

My PowerPoint presentation went well. Raymond, who didn't have much of a role at the meeting, nonetheless made certain that everyone in the room had one of his business cards. When someone wandered in after I'd begun my talk, Raymond almost knocked over a water pitcher on the conference table as he leapt from his chair to press his card into the surprised latecomer's hand. After the last slide, the Dravitin team leader asked if Raymond and I would wait outside the room for a few minutes.

"What's going on?" Raymond whispered in the hallway.

"It's a good sign," I said.

When we were invited to return to the room, we were told that our presentation was "superior" to the competition's, and the team wanted a written proposal from us for a series of continuing education programs—conferences

around the country, video and audiotapes, patient education materials, articles for medical journals. I'd just landed
an easy five million dollars of business for a company
about to fire me.

It was after four when we pulled into the garage in
our office building. Raymond parked his Taurus right near
the purple Explorer. I pointed to a familiar silver BMW.

"Raymond, isn't that Joey's car?"

"Oh, is it?"

"Look, there's the sticker from his kid's school. 'Proud
Soccer Parent, S. Agnew Middle School, Brooklyn, NY.'"

"Then I guess he's here." Raymond avoided my gaze
and shifted his weight from foot to foot as we rode up in
the elevator. He didn't exactly seem surprised at the possibility that Joey was no longer in Minneapolis.

Grace, the part-time receptionist was already gone
for the day. Sally is Joey's assistant exclusively; the rest
of us have to share Grace's services or rely on voicemail
for messages. Grace had left me a stack of pink While
You Were Out slips with messages written in her flowery
Palmer-method script. Dr. "Bess" Gillian (Grace always
gets Beth's name wrong) wants me to try her at home in
the evening. Doc Shortland's office called on Mrs. Shortland's behalf: Could I recommend an intermediate French
conversation tape for her to listen to in her car? Allison
Tanaka from Gillian Investments would like me to join
her and my daughter for lunch.

A few emails, none crucial. Dana was asking if we
were to consider "website" one word or two, capitalized
or not, hyphenated or not. The Dravitin team leader had
already written to thank me for my presentation and
to remind me that they'd need our written proposal by
Tuesday. Pushpa Rao had copied me on her official accep-
tance of Shortland's job.

Still no itinerary on my desk for the conference in

DC. But there was a copy of Gloria Steinem's biography, the one by Carolyn Heilbrun, with a scribbled note from Rebecca clipped to the front cover: "Thanks, Sarah. RNC." I had lent the book to Rebecca ages ago, in the days when I still believed that she and I could be friends. We used to go to lunch together and talk about books, movies, men. I found it strange that Rebecca had suddenly thought to return the book to me after so many months.

At a few minutes before five, Sally buzzed me. I was determined to leave reasonably early. No need for over-achieving at this point.

"Yes, Sally?"

"Joey's here and he'd like to see you before you leave."

"Back from Minneapolis, is he? I hope it won't take too long, Sally. I've got plans tonight," I lied.

"He just asked me to call you. I can't say how long it will take," she said.

I knew immediately that something was up. Joey was dressed in unusually casual clothes—a knit Henley shirt and corduroy pants—not his customary Italian-knock-off pinstriped suit. He was seated at the small round table in his office, his back to me as I stood in the doorway. Facing me in the seat across from him was Sally Ackroyd, tightly embracing a few of her trademark colored file folders.

"How was Minneapolis?" I said, helping myself to the one vacant seat left at the table.

"Actually, I've spent the week in central Jersey," Joey said. First Kevin, now you. How come none of the men in my life seems to be where he says he is?

"Interesting choice. This time of year, most people opt for the Caribbean."

No hint of a grin from Joey, who has no sense of humor, which is perhaps the trait I find most irritating in him. That, and the Queeg-rubberband thing, which he was going at with alarming speed. No smile from Sally, either. She takes her cues from Joey.

"I imagine you want to know how things went today?" I said. Joey looked confused. "The Dravitin presentation?"

"I've spoken to Raymond already. He says the two of you did all right."

"The two of us. How, exactly, did he describe his contribution to the presentation?"

"Sarah, I've got a lot to say, and I know you want to get home, after all it's the start of the weekend, so why don't you let me say what I have to."

"And Sally?" I said, not bothering to look her way. "What's she doing here?"

"You'll understand as I explain. I've spent the week with my accountants, trying to figure out what my next move is. Business has been slow, and then with Shortland leaving, I got good and worried. But the real bullet came over the weekend. You know Lawrence is gone, right? I figured he would tell you."

"I know that you fired him."

"He was a partner, you don't just fire a partner. Dissolving a partnership is a complex and costly process. My liability is enormous."

"Sounds like you've been talking to some attorneys, in addition to your accountants. You've got that lawyer-speak down just right."

"I'm not sure what you're getting at, Sarah. But the bottom line here—and you know I'm a bottom line kinda guy—is that it wasn't personal with Lawrence, and it isn't personal with you."

"So you're firing me."

"I have no choice. I had to let Lawrence go because his salary was a killer. An experienced guy like him, well, you know, I couldn't pay him peanuts. And he had a nice share of profits every year. Now he's demanding that I give him a lump-sum payout, which makes our cash flow situation dicey going into the new year. Between you and me, Lawrence is playing hardball—I didn't think he had it in him—and the result is that I had to rethink the whole company structure."

"Which brings you to me. Next to Lawrence's, my salary is the highest."

"Yeah, again, it's the same thing like I said about Lawrence. You're a seasoned pro yourself, and you add a lot to Tri-Tech in terms of writing know-how and the kind of classy image I think is very important, but I've got to cut down on overhead, period. And remember, it's because of Lawrence that the cash flow problem is so serious now. His payout is costing me a fortune, and he won't even consider letting me spread the payments out over time. I've had to readjust the entire business plan my accountants have been mapping out for months."

"Months? You've been at this for months?"

"I knew at the end of the second quarter of this year that we had to cut costs or we were headed for trouble."

"I see. But you chose not to share this information with me? A company vice president?"

"This company is my baby, Sarah. I'm sure you understand: I'd do whatever it takes to keep it going. As I said, this is not personal. You're a nice girl, really."

"Joey," I said calmly, though I wanted to deck him, "I'm ten years older than you are. I would appreciate it if you didn't refer to me as a girl, nice or otherwise."

"What is it, then, lady? No, woman. Yeah, right. Anyway, what this all comes down to is that the numbers boys—they call the shots—are saying I need less expensive employees on the payroll, even if they're not, you know, as high level as you and Lawrence. Listen, when I started this company, I did everything myself. There isn't any job here I can't do on my own, so I'll make do with employees I can afford, and I'll fill in the gaps. These young kids, like

Raymond, for instance, they have a lot to learn."

"Let me see if I've got this. Letting me go is really Lawrence's fault, because he unreasonably demanded that you pay him what he's owed."

"The part that's unreasonable is that he won't allow us to pay him out over time."

"And your business plan is now to keep only young people on staff because you can pay them less than you pay people with experience."

"These are the hard facts of business these days. Besides the cost of keeping people your age and Lawrence's on the payroll, I've got another factor to consider. With Shortland leaving, you can bet the girl— uh, woman who's taking over for him is going to fill the place up with young people like herself. You look great for your age, Sarah, I'm not saying you don't, but no one would take you for twenty-six."

"But my advanced age didn't prevent you from sending me to do the Dravitin presentation. And, by the way, I landed the contract."

"Why do you think I asked you to do it? You were the only one who could step up to the plate on this one at a moment's notice. In the long run, though, I need someone who's gonna fit in with the new culture at Savant. Hey, I'm no kid either. But I'm the president of this company, and that gives me—whaddaya call it?—kind of a stature, if that's the word. In general, I think the kids at Savant want to hang out with their peers. Besides, there's the matter of what an older employee costs a small company like Tri-Tech."

"You've lost me."

"Fawn was telling me how you've refused to take the redeye back from California. You said, and I quote, 'I'm too old to fly all night.'"

"It was a joke."

"It's the kind of thing younger people would never say to a boss. You tell them what to do, they do it."

"I didn't say it to my boss. I said it to Fawn. And besides," I smiled widely, leaned forward, and whispered, "the business about being too old—it was a fucking joke."

Joey was speechless. He was accustomed to my using words he couldn't understand, but I'm sure he never expected to live long enough to hear me talk that way. I took advantage of his silence to wrest control of the discussion.

"You still haven't explained to me what she's doing here," I said, pointing to, but still not looking at, Sally. "Unless, of course, you need a witness. You need a witness, Joey?"

Joey noisily cleared his throat. "For one thing, she's been my right hand since I ran Tri-Tech from my garage. Next to Lorraine, I trust Sally more than anyone else. And second, as part of the company re-org—"

"Re-org, Joey? Ooh, I love it when you talk corporate."

"Yes, it's a common corporate term. Oh, I get it; you were trying to be funny, right? What I started to say is that Sally has a new position here. I'm rolling out the new organizational chart on Monday. Sally's now vice president of human resources."

"You can call her Marie of Rumania, but it won't make her royalty," I said.

Joey and Sally exchanged a brief, confused look. "You sound a little mad, Sarah," Joey said.

"What did you think I'd say? Thanks for firing me?"

"You're a very savvy woman. I thought you'd understand that I've got to do what I can to save my business. Meanwhile, we have a letter for you to sign. It's a separation agreement, just keeps everything above board and legal."

In my career, I've signed half a dozen such letters.

I've cut good deals on severance packages for myself—continued salary, health benefits, assurances of good references and letters of recommendation—that kept me afloat until I landed the next (terrible) job. What freedom, knowing that I wasn't dependent on Joey's money or a testimonial from him to get another job.

Sally opened her green folder and pulled out a letter typed on Tri-Tech's letterhead, with its artless pink-and-blue design. Lorraine Selber's sister had created the Tri-Tech logo as a project for her Graphics 101 class at Hackensack Community College.

Apart from a dangling participle and a couple of comma splices, the separation agreement letter wasn't too badly written, especially considering that Joey was the author, with some input, I guessed, from some of the numbers boys. My dismissal from Tri-Tech was effective immediately. Tri-Tech was sorry that financial considerations had forced the Company (how much did his lawyer charge to advise him to capitalize Company?) to release a talented employee like me. As founder and president of Tri-Tech, Joey Selber wanted to "personally" thank me for my many valuable contributions to the Company and wish me well in all my future endeavors. If I promised not to sue Tri-Tech for discrimination against me or for any other reason, and never to say anything disparaging about the company or its employees, I could walk away with two whole weeks' pay and health benefits for an additional thirty days.

I took notice of the date on the letter. We were a few weeks away from Thanksgiving, heading into the holiday season, the worst time of year to look for a job. (At another job years ago, I had negotiated several months' additional severance pay using this argument when the company downsized.) I responded to Joey's offer exactly as I would have if several million dollars were not enroute to me.

"Was there ever really a partnership in the works for me, Joey?"

"You mean the three-year thing? Lawrence's idea, mostly. I went along because it seemed to motivate you, and I like to motivate my employees. Obviously, the company is not in a position to offer partnerships at the moment."

"What about the retroactive pay raise going back to August, when I had my review? Not to mention the additional bonus I was promised for schlepping to New Jersey to teach Richard Shortland how to speak French. Now that I think to ask, why did you sign me up for those French lessons, anyway?"

"I don't recall anything about a retroactive pay raise. As for your work with Shortland, that falls under your normal duties, managing a client. And why did I talk Shortland into the idea? Frankly, it made Tri-Tech look good. Do you think Saylish has anyone on his payroll who could teach someone to speak French? With you out of the office every morning for a few weeks, I also got a chance to do some things with your staff, get to know them, so I could figure out how to utilize them when I re-organized the company. By the way, Shortland's leaving for Geneva sooner than expected. He was gonna call you on Monday to tell you the French lessons are over."

"In any case, after the fabulous annual review you gave me, my year-end bonus should be fifteen percent of my salary."

"You need to read the Employee Manual. An employee has to remain with the company through at least December fifteenth in order to qualify for the bonus."

"That's just a few weeks away. You think it's ethical to fire someone in early December and then disqualify her for the year-end bonus?"

"Ethical, that's a matter of opinion. But legal, it is."

Joey nodded at Sally, who opened her second folder—yellow—and pulled out a certified check. She tried to hand it to me, but I didn't make a move to take it from her. Joey motioned for her to put it down on the table, in front of me.

"That's a certified check, Sarah; three weeks' salary—one for the week ending today, and two weeks' severance. Considering the financial situation that Tri-Tech is in, I think it's a very, very fair offer. Sign the letter, take the check, and we'll part friends."

I smiled sweetly. "Friends, Joey? In your dreams."

In a way, I was tempted to sign, grab the check, and split, just to put my life at Tri-Tech behind me and never have to think about Joey Selber again. But that's what I had done in my divorce from Martin. To make things easy in the short run, to minimize what my lawyer had called "face time" with my ex-husband, I had walked away instead of fighting for money that should have been mine and my daughter's. The result: years of having to contend with the likes of Joey Selber in order to make a living.

"It's the holiday season, Joey. No one finds a new job in December. And you're offering two weeks' severance?"

"I'm not required to give you any severance pay at all."

"Your lawyers have obviously advised you on this letter, which means I'm at a disadvantage unless someone representing me looks it over."

"When will you get back to me? I'd like to wrap this up quickly."

"Oh, would you?" I said as I left the room.

By the time Joey and I finished our confab, the office had completely cleared out. One of the building's security guards—an elderly Russian man in a threadbare uniform—was posted at my office door to watch me pack. (Did Joey think I was going to steal something? Trash the office? Did he believe this poor old guy could prevent me from doing either?) The guard wheeled a dolly and some empty cartons to my door, offering, in broken English, to help me get my belongings downstairs and into a taxi.

There was more to pack than I would have guessed. Photos of Elinor, Kevin, and me. My college and graduate school diplomas (displaying them was Joey's idea). A giant poster of the Arc de Triomphe at sunrise that hung on the wall facing my desk so that I could look up from the computer screen from time to time and be reminded that there was life beyond Tri-Tech. Coffee mugs: I packed the one I had bought at the Musée d'Orsay and left behind a dozen with names of drugs and the companies that make them. Three shelves of books—writing guides (which I packed), healthcare and corporate directories (which I didn't). A few novels, the sort I read on the occasional warm-weather lunch hour when I could escape to a nearby park. And, of course, the book that Rebecca had so thoughtfully returned, because she knew before I did that this would be my last day at Tri-Tech.

I left voicemail messages of farewell to my staff and a few others who might care that I was gone. I assured Dana Greene that I'd call her soon. I saved Rebecca until last. I'd always been protective of her, hoping that she'd eventually comprehend that something bigger than her own ambition was on the line at Tri-Tech. Did anything I said get through to her? Probably not. Like Joey, like Raymond, Rebecca was so self-focused that she had few allies at Tri-Tech. I bore no grudge against her. In a way, I felt sorry for her. After all, if Joey had sworn her to secrecy about his plan to fire me, what could she have done? She couldn't afford to jeopardize her job. I also knew that sooner or later, her inability to connect to other women would cost her.

I understood at the first syllable of Rebecca's voicemail

greeting that she had recently changed it. I was expecting the same outgoing message she'd always had: "Hi, it's me, Rebecca; I'm not around right now . . ." I had always thought it a bit too informal for the office, but I had let it ride. Her new message revealed that I had no cause for concern about Rebecca's prospects: "Hello, you've reached Rebecca Carson, vice president of the editorial department at Tri-Tech Healthcare. Sorry to be unavailable . . ."

———

"KEVIN, IT'S SARAH. I'm leaving this message late Friday night. This is ridiculous. Where are you? You'll probably think I'm exaggerating, but my entire life has changed this week. No kidding. For starters, I don't work at Tri-Tech anymore. But that's not even the really big news. Will you just call me, please? Enough!"

I called Beth.

"Did Miriam reach you before she left for Florida? I missed her call. Do you know what's happening with her mother?"

"I was out when she called, too, but I spoke to Gabe Bryant. He was with Miriam when she got word from Florida. Celeste appears to have had a stroke."

"Where is Miriam staying?"

"Her aunt's condo. Gabe says Miriam has her cell phone with her."

"Do you think Miriam's brother Neil will show up?"

"Sometimes I forget she has a brother. Hard to say."

"I guess we'll put off brunch until she gets back. Too bad. I've got so much to tell you both. In keeping with the extraordinary week I seem to be having, I've had yet another life-altering experience."

"I've got a major report to give, too, but I promised myself I wouldn't talk about it until I had both of you with me. Can you give me a hint of what's happening with you?"

"How's this: I lost my job."

"He did fire you! You were right all along. At least you don't have to worry about how you're going to feed yourself. You know what? It was a job worth losing. Good riddance."

"Yes, yes, yes, and . . . not so fast about the good riddance part. I'm thinking of suing the bastard."

"Oh, God, we do have to get together and talk. Is there more?"

"Kevin and I had a momentous fight after your party. We still haven't made up."

"What are you doing, slamming cupboard doors and growling at each other?"

"Not exactly. He stormed out. We haven't spoken since. I thought he was going on a business trip to Seattle this week, and I figured the distance would help cool things down. But the trip was cancelled, except he didn't tell me. I found out from his secretary. He's been in town all week, I don't know where, and he's not responding to my voicemail messages. He doesn't even know about the money from Martin."

"I wasn't aware that you had blowups like this . . ."

"We don't argue much. But we don't talk much, either. Not about things that really matter. This was one of the recurring themes in the fight, which lasted most of last Sunday."

"You want me to come into town tomorrow?"

"I'd love to see you, but you said that you and Jim have plans this weekend anyway."

"We do, and that's connected to my big news. Jim and I are working through some things, too. I promised I'd spend as much time as possible with him this weekend. Saturdays, he's always at the office."

"As he should be. I mean, if Ellie and I are going to

put our fortunes in his hands, I want to know that he's making us richer every minute of every day."

"I'd better warn him what a pain-in-the-neck client you're going to be."

"I was a pain in the neck when I was broke, and I've promised myself I won't let having money change me."

"Thank goodness. Let me know if you hear from Miriam. And give Kevin's voicemail another shot. Don't leave an angry message, and don't try to be funny. Be conciliatory. Make it easy for him to call you back. Nothing good can happen until you talk with each other."

"KEVIN, IT'S SARAH again. Saturday night, around eight. Just calling to say I really wish you were here, and I hope—make that I know—we can work things out, but we have to talk to each other. I miss you, Kev."

Lawrence called to offer congratulations. "You're well out of there," he said.

"In Joey's bizarre version of events, it's your fault he had to fire me," I said. "If you hadn't been so unreasonable, demanding that Tri-Tech pay you what you're owed, then Joey could have kept me on the payroll. Even if I am a feeble old woman of fifty-two."

"I used to think that Joey had a certain kind of smarts—not a refined intelligence, but a caginess," Lawrence said. "After seeing how hung up he is on appearances and how impulsive he is, I'm not sure he'll survive. I knew my best move was to get all of my money up front. He wanted me to take a payout over two years. As soon as I threatened to get a lawyer involved, he caved. You may not have noticed, Sarah, but I'm actually a black person, and I needed to use the word 'discrimination' in Joey's presence only one time. He's probably still having nightmares about the lawsuit I might have filed."

"We can only hope it's keeping him up at night. Meanwhile, he's rolling out his new org chart this week. From what I can tell, everyone left at the company has been promoted to a vice president. Babes in Tri-Tech Land. Tell me about you. How are the job prospects?"

"Excellent. I've got half a dozen lunches lined up in January. Nothing happens in the job market between now and then."

"I tried to make the point about how impossible it is to find a job this time of year when Joey offered me two weeks' severance."

"What are you planning to do?"

"As I told you, my financial status is about to change dramatically, so the only question is how far I'm willing to take things with Joey for the principle. It's no small amount of money we're talking about, but I'm now in the position of not really needing it. I'd love to get what's coming to me, but I don't relish the thought of having him in my life, so to speak, for several years while we pay lawyers to parry with each other."

"Joey won't let this get to court."

"You mean he'll settle? How can you be sure?"

"You know the guy. He's driven by keeping up what he imagines is the respected image of his little empire. Joey worries about losing business if someone from Tri-Tech wears the wrong color socks to a meeting. It's going to be awkward enough for Joey to have to explain to clients why you and I have suddenly vanished. He'd be apoplectic if he thought that Savant was abuzz with talk about a messy discrimination law suit at Tri-Tech."

"So you think I should stand my ground with Joey?"

"I think you should get yourself a very good lawyer."

"Hi, Sarah. It's Raymond. Raymond Albano. This

is the second message I'm leaving for you. I hope you're doin' okay. I know this is a little strange, but I was calling to ask a favor. I hope you don't mind. Remember the Repoze stuff you were working on? I looked in your files and on your computer and I can't seem to find any notes. The thing is, the guy who took over for Pushpa when she got promoted wants to meet with me this week. He's not a pharmacist, just a marketing guy, and he's gonna want to see what kind of focal groups, I mean focus groups, we were planning. Well, heh-heh, you know the number here. Call me as soon as you can, okay?"

TO: sarahjaneroth@home.com
FROM: Dana_Greene@nyc.net
RE: Crazier than ever

Think we'll ever actually get to talk instead of leaving messages? I'm writing this from home. I don't trust that emails at the office are confidential anymore.

Thanks for the recommendation letter. I have a second interview at the Abbott Literary Review next week. I can't bear having Rebecca as my boss. I'm just sticking around the place long enough to get my year-end bonus and then, new job or not, I'm outta here.

You probably don't give a damn about anything at Tri-Tech, but I thought you'd be happy to hear that Rebecca doesn't have a clue how to run things. She's not a bad writer, but she's a disaster as a manager. She spends all day on the phone telling everyone she knows that she's now a VP. She's letting Joey have his way with editorial, even though he made her get rid of the "Beef: It's what's rotting in your colon" bumper sticker on her bulletin board. Raymond pulled an all-nighter in his office recently, cruising the Internet to learn about focus groups. He follows Joey around like a puppy waiting for instructions to roll over.

Sally Ackroyd has taken to sending emails on the hour about new personnel forms we should be worried about—Joey's got her taking some personnel manager's correspondence course (HR for Idiots?)—but everyone, except for Raymond, pretty much ignores her. The evil Fawn Mardiss is a brunette again.

Dana

"Hi, Wendy. Kevin around?"

"You just missed him. He's left for Philly."

"Any way to reach him today?"

"Not until he gets to the hotel tonight."

"Where's he staying? I know I wrote it down somewhere, but I can't lay my hands on it right now."

"The Omni, all week."

Kristin Traynor, the employment law maven at Bruce Jacobs's law firm, was not immediately encouraging about the prospect of suing Tri-Tech.

"It certainly sounds as if Joey Selber is not a very nice person, and he treated you badly, but that's not necessarily enough for a law suit. Thanks for supplying the history of what happened to you. I'll read it carefully and let you know what I think. You're aware, aren't you, that it could be several years before this case, if you have a case, actually gets to court. We could very well lose, and you'll wind up having to pay my fees, which will be considerable."

I smiled. "I've waited all my life to be able to say this: Money is no object."

"You're a rich woman now, Sarah. You don't need Joey Selber's money. If we get as far as a jury, they may not be sympathetic to a wealthy woman. Why are you pursuing this?"

"I endured that lousy job, did everything I was asked to do, and took his word that I'd be appropriately compensated. To be fired was insulting enough, but to be let go because I don't look young enough, and at the worst time of the year for job-hunting, just makes me livid. What if I really needed the money, as most people do? As I assumed I did? I'd like him to think twice before he treats anyone else this way."

"Again, bad behavior, but not necessarily illegal. Though it's true that juries don't generally approve of Scrooge-like, Christmas-eve firings, and your situation is pretty close. But juries are also unpredictable. Have you thought about what you'd accept as a settlement offer?"

"Not yet." I told Kristin what Lawrence had said. "He feels that if Joey thought there were even a chance of word getting out around Savant that Tri-Tech was being sued for employment discrimination, he would be livid. And very nervous."

"We'll probably have to depose some Savant people. Here's what I'll need from you. First, the employee manual from Tri-Tech. Then, do you have a current list of Tri-Tech employees?" I nodded. "Get me a copy, and tell me the ages of all the full-time employees. Next, start thinking of all the clients you had contact with, especially at Savant. Have you been in touch with Tri-Tech or Savant people since you were let go?"

"One editor at Tri-Tech—Dana—has called and emailed a few times. I sent a letter to Doc Shortland wishing him good luck in Switzerland."

"Make sure I have copies of that correspondence. From now on, you are to communicate with no one, except for me, on the subject of Tri-Tech."

Not having Kevin around was starting to feel

normal. Naturally I missed him, but seeing his bottle of aftershave on the bathroom vanity or his Nikes on the closet floor didn't exactly send me into paroxysms of tears. Instead, I found myself mentally listing his traits (smart, interesting, sociable, reasonably nice-looking, generous, etc.) and beginning to wonder whether I liked the idea of Kevin better than Kevin himself. I decided to try his cell once more. This time, he answered.

"Hi, Kev. It's Sarah."

"Yes, Sarah." His voice was flat.

"How are you?"

"A little tired, otherwise fine." Long pause. "Hey, I'm sorry to hear about the job. You're better off out of there, though."

So he got the message I left, but he didn't call. "I'm okay about it, really I am. There's more to the story than you may think. I was calling to ask if I can expect you home any time soon."

"I should be back in New York early next week."

"Will you be coming home? I mean, to our apartment?"

"I guess you want to talk."

"Don't you?"

"I don't know. Didn't we say enough to each other after the party?"

"We were both very angry, but I'd like to think we have more to say to each other." Silence. "Kevin?"

"Yeah, I'm here. Sarah, let's face it. It's not working."

"What?"

"Us. Our relationship. It's not what either of us wants."

"People say spiteful things when they're angry. It doesn't have to mean the end of the world. In a way, arguing isn't all bad. It could actually be helpful, bring things to light."

"I'm not up to any more arguing."

"What are you saying?"

"I think we probably said everything we had to on Sunday. I haven't changed my mind about anything I said. You have *no right* to expect me to divulge confidential information about my family to you." His voice was getting louder.

"Aren't we supposed to be family to each other?" I asked.

"That's part of your problem, Sarah. You don't respect boundaries."

"*My* problem? You are pathologically secretive about essential aspects of your life, and it's *my* problem? And then, after all this time together, you want to end things between us over the phone?"

"Every relationship has limits. You don't seem to understand that. Sometimes, with you, I feel like I can't breathe. Just because you and Beth and Miriam think nothing should go unsaid doesn't mean everyone needs to talk about everything. I don't want to live with someone who insists on knowing every last thing about me."

"Do you still not understand why I was hurt when I found out about Brendan?" My voice was getting louder now, too.

"Everybody has secrets. Some things need to stay private," he said. It sounded as if he were speaking through clenched teeth.

"Is that why you've been so elusive? Not returning phone calls? To protect your privacy? What the hell, Kevin?"

"I really intended to see you sometime after I got back into town."

"But since I called, you figured you'd just give me the news now?"

"See what I mean? You still want to fight."

"I just wanted to talk. Face to face."

"I've got to go. I'll give you a call when I get back," he said.

I almost believed him.

I wandered from room to room, taking inventory. The apartment and all the furniture in it was mine long before Kevin and I lived together. He had been renting a furnished studio when we met. When we were first dating, he claimed to have some furniture and personal effects in storage at a cousin's house, but he never spoke about them again once I told him it was fine with me if he moved into my place. He didn't keep pictures or mementos around, nothing that spoke of the life he had before he lived with me.

He had clothes, books, some kitchen gadgets. Little enough that he could clear out his belongings in a morning. The only household items we owned jointly were the silver wine goblets we had picked out together in Copenhagen when we went on the cruise to Scandinavia. The trip I funded with severance pay from one of my many disappearing jobs.

And I thought, standing in the middle of the living room in the apartment that had both our names on the front door (though mine alone was on the lease): nothing much will change if he moves out. He never entirely moved in.

KRISTIN TRAYNOR FILED my suit against Tri-Tech. The suit asked for all the bonus money and retroactive salary due me, plus unspecified damages.

"We'd be in somewhat better shape if you actually needed the job," she said. "With that money you're about to get from your late ex-husband, you aren't going to break any jury's heart."

"What does it matter how much money I have? I'm

going after what I was promised. What I'm entitled to."

"And it's a good sum, but you're less appealing to a jury, for purposes of a damage award, if you don't actually have to work for a living. Of course, we've got some nice evidence of a pattern of age discrimination. You and Lawrence Zimmerman were the oldest employees, and he fired both of you. According to the list you gave me, sixty percent of the remaining employees are in their twenties; only Selber, and his part-time receptionist are over forty. In any event, we may be getting a settlement offer from Tri-Tech. Selber's attorney let it slip that his client doesn't relish the idea of our deposing those Savant people. You know, of course, we have to have a reason to depose them, something more substantive than simply causing embarrassment to Joey Selber. I'm scheduled to speak to his lawyer this afternoon. I'll let you know if they make an offer."

TO: sarahjaneroth@home.com
FROM: Dana_Greene@nyc.net
RE: Just desserts

I knew you'd want the dirt on Tri-Tech holiday festivities. The usual Selber greeting went out to us all. Joey and Lorraine, once again in their ridiculous Santa getups, remain thrilled to have us in the Tri-Tech family. Citing "somewhat uncertain times in the pharmaceutical industry," the Selbers dispensed with the usual holiday dinner party and instead had us all to their house in Brooklyn for coffee and dessert. A Saturday-night schlep on the subway for a slice of Junior's cheesecake and a cup of hazelnut decaf.

Back at the office, Joey and Rebecca had a knock-down-drag-out when she showed up at work with a spiky crew cut and several new earring holes pierced in just her left ear. Now she's banished for good from face-to-face client encounters. And just when Joey finally had her trained to wear long sleeves to hide the spotted owl tattoo! (Poor thing; all this unpleasantness at work the very same week her Starbucks beau dumped her for a model/personal trainer he met over a latte grande.) Raymond will take Rebecca's place at client meetings, but only after Joey does a wardrobe check on him. By the way, Raymond seems to have blown the Repoze contract. Savant has thrown the project to Saylish.

Bonuses should be in our hands before the week is out. I'm counting the hours. I start my new job at Abbott right after the new year. Hope to see you over the holidays.

Dana

Once Joey got a look at the list of people on our deposition list—every Tri-Tech employee and anyone I could think of at Savant—he was willing to negotiate. Though I'd had delightful visions of Joey strapped to his desk, being forced at gunpoint to sign a fat check made out to me, it turns out that businesses have insurance policies these days that cover them for discrimination suits. Joey's insurance company will pay most of the settlement. I'll get every cent of all the bonus money and salary I was owed, plus my lawyer's fees, and a hefty sum for "damages" that Kristin says is probably less than I might get if we went before a jury, but I feel as if I won. I'm not allowed to breathe a word about the settlement to anyone, and both Joey and I are enjoined from disparaging each other, etc. My rote response to anyone who inquires about my history with Tri-Tech is a deadpan, "I used to work there. Now I don't." And then a grin.

Ellie spent Christmas and New Year's in Rhode Island with Doug's family and then joined me for a few days at a spa in the Berkshires before she went back to school.

Part III: Sarah

While I was out of town Kevin removed his clothes and books—but not the Danish wine goblets—from our apartment. He left a note saying he was staying with friends for now and would let me know when he had a new address and phone number. I took his name off the front door and changed the locks.

I'm waiting for the cold weather to pass before I make a trip to meet with Paris realtors. I figure I should be able to set myself up there soon after Ellie's graduation. I'll keep the apartment in New York, too—the building's going co-op and I plan to buy the place. Ellie and Doug are hinting about marriage after they graduate. The apartment would make a lovely wedding gift from me if they wind up living in New York. Who's to say they can't be happy here?

MIRIAM:
SOMETHING OLD, SOMETHING NEW

"Don't you want somebody to love?"
—*Jefferson Airplane*

GABE WAS AT LA Guardia when Mom and I landed. He drove us directly to Glenwilde Senior Care, a nursing home just a short walk from Mom's house, in the neighborhood where I spent my childhood. Each week of her stay, I spent a few nights and at least one weekend day visiting her. I gleaned slender hope from the guarded optimism of the doctors and nurses. I cheered every subtle change in Mom's condition. Her coloring looks better today. Her appetite seems improved. She's getting the hang of that walker.

Gabe joined me at Glenwilde on weekends. We fell into the routine of his picking me up in his car early in the morning and driving to Brooklyn. He was playful and patient with Mom. She was girlish and vampy with him, the way she had behaved at the hospital in Florida. "Gabe, darling, do you like my perfume?" she'd ask, holding her wrist towards him. "Very sexy, Celeste," he'd respond. "I think you're trying to flirt with me."

We usually left Glenwilde late on those weekend

evenings, stopping for a quick meal on the way back to Manhattan. After a warm-but-not-passionate kiss, we'd go home—separately. The idea of sex seemed absurd to me in light of current events, and I couldn't imagine the right circumstances for intimacy any time soon. A new experience for me, sexual apathy. So this is middle age, I thought.

On the third weekend of this drill, after a particularly strenuous session with the physical therapist, Mom was fast asleep by mid-afternoon Saturday.

"She's probably out for the night," her nurse said. "You can see her tomorrow. Why don't you try to get home before the snow gets too bad? They're saying we're in for a few inches."

Gabe and I drove across the Williamsburg Bridge as the storm was picking up. By the time we reached Yorkville, our neighbors were already salting the front steps of their brownstones.

"Are you up for some bistro food?" Gabe asked. "I've been wanting to try that new French place on First Avenue."

"Let's call and have them deliver to my house. What would you like?"

"Anything that goes with pinot noir. I'll let you off, get the car into the garage, and meet you back at your place with some wine and a movie. Old or new flick?"

"Something old, please. With great scenery and costumes and bona fide movie stars."

"Sounds like a *Lawrence of Arabia* night to me."

"That's an awfully long movie."

"I'm not going anywhere. Are you?"

———

WE WERE CURLED up, platonically, on my bed, finished with our frisée salad and steak frites and most of the pinot noir. I was transfixed by the sight of Peter O'Toole, as T.E. Lawrence, trekking across the desert. Gabe grabbed our empty plates and headed for the kitchen. "I'll just put these in the dishwasher," he said over his shoulder. "Be right back." I gave him a small wave without taking my eyes away from the movie. My favorite moment was beginning.

Without flinching, Lawrence steadily holds his hand above a candle flame. A companion tries to do the same thing but immediately pulls his hand away, cringing in pain. "Doesn't that hurt you?" he asks Lawrence.

"Of course it hurts."

"Then what is the trick?"

"The trick," Lawrence replies evenly, "is not to mind."

I sighed loudly and turned away from the TV to see Gabe staring at me from the doorway.

"Why don't you pause the movie for a minute," he said.

I pressed the pause button. "Why?"

"You didn't even notice me watching you. The look on your face was . . . You seemed so far away. I thought you were about to cry."

"It's a powerful scene."

"Can't you tell me what it is?"

"What?"

"The thing you're trying so hard not to mind, even though it hurts like hell."

"Gabe, please . . ."

"What will make you trust me? What else can I do to show you how I feel about you?"

"I know how you feel about me. I'm just numb. Chronically tired and frantic about Mom. Thinking that I'll be old soon, too, and I don't have a daughter who will look after me. My life seems hard and sad at the moment, and I don't have the energy for . . . "

"For what? For love? For sex? For me?"

"I don't mean that it's hard work to be with you, but a new relationship takes energy to get going. I'm worn out right now. Empty. Even after things with my mother are, um, resolved, let's say, a part of me is thinking that it's too late for me to get involved with someone the way I think you'd like to be. Then again . . ."

"Yes?"

"Then I think about how remarkable you've been from the moment we met, and how handsome you are, and, even drained as I am, I have to admit to a remote hormonal summons. But I force myself not to respond."

"Why?"

"Because I want to be fair to you."

"You think it would be unfair to sleep with me?" he said. "I don't understand."

Of course he didn't understand. The statement was ridiculous on its face, and especially unbelievable, though Gabe couldn't know why, coming from me. Sex had always been the easiest part of my relationships with men. I couldn't figure out why I was complicating matters with Gabe. I was attracted to him, and I sensed that both of us would enjoy ourselves as lovers. But he was so starry-eyed about me, he seemed frangible; I was afraid of wounding him with my hard edges. For the first time in a long while, perhaps for the first time in my life, the idea of sex seemed inexorably linked to a mysterious pool of shivery, tender feelings—his feelings. And I was reluctant to dive in.

Gabe inhaled deeply. "Maybe that's just a diplomatic way to say you're not attracted to me," he said.

"God, no, that's not it," I said. "I promise. But you're in love with me, and . . . "

"You won't sleep with me because I love you?"

"I vowed a long time ago that I'd never let myself fall in love again, and I've kept my word."

"Just like that. You have complete control over your feelings. How's that working for you, huh?"

"I've managed all right for more than twelve years. Before that, I let myself lose control, and it was a mistake. When I was younger, I hurt some very nice men who loved me and wanted to marry me. Then it was my turn. I had my heart broken into smithereens. I figure the score is even now, no need for another tournament."

"You think you're the only one whose heart has been broken?"

"Of course not. But I feel too old to risk it again. You're probably starting to think I'm way too much trouble."

"Not really."

"What do you think?"

"I think you have a bitter wound, an old one, that won't heal, and like Lawrence with his hand on the flame you've tricked yourself into not minding. But the wound is still there. And I think I need to know about the humdinger."

"Who?"

"That's what Celeste called him that day in the hospital in Florida. The Southerner whose name she couldn't remember."

"What do you want to know?"

"What happened with him that made you give up on *bashert*. On the true love you were meant to have. And why you can't let go of the memory of him."

I turned away from Gabe and looked towards the window. The fire escape was already blanketed with several inches of snow. There was snow on the ground the day I returned from Savannah. The air felt so crisp and dry after the dampness there. It hurt to breathe.

"Miriam? Where are you? Are you with me?"

"I'm here, Gabe."

"Nothing you tell me about your past will change how I feel. Do you believe me?"

"Maybe I'm afraid of just that! I'm not in the habit of love anymore. I don't want to hurt you."

"I hear you. But love is a great, healthy habit. And I don't believe you're past the possibility of re-acquiring it."

"I'm not sure I even have the words for what you want to hear from me. I've never told anyone the whole story—not even Sarah and Beth."

"Just start. The words will come, I promise. And then maybe we'll be able to see what possibilities lie ahead for us. Tell me, who was he? What made you love him?"

I picked up my wine glass and held it for Gabe to fill. I took a deep breath, and then a sip of wine. Gabe lay down next to me on the bed. "His name was Peter," I said. "He was wildly creative, deeply romantic, and emotionally hollow. Passionate, fascinating, and dangerous. Are you sure you want to hear this?"

"Every word," Gabe said.

I began with Violet's party, then my birthday weekend in Savannah.

"Like getting struck by lightning," I said.

"If you remember, Miriam, that's what I said about meeting you."

"I do remember. In the diner, the morning I got the call about Mom. I didn't know how to respond. I have to admit, I felt something for you too at the party. I tried to push it away, make it disappear. You made me nervous."

"What scared you?"

"The way you looked at me. I felt an emotional jolt that reminded me of feelings I never wanted to feel again. Because I know where those feelings lead, eventually. To disappointment."

"Tell me about Peter."

I described my move to Savannah.

"I'm surprised. Doesn't sound like the person you are now," Gabe said. "How impulsive! I mean, leaving New York, your job, your mother . . ."

"I was on sabbatical, so I could pretend I didn't have a job to worry about. Twelve years ago, my mother was in good health and still hoping I'd finally get married. She was happy to hear I was in love, even if it meant the possibility of my leaving town. You're right, I was a different person then. I'd broken several engagements because I thought being married meant inevitable, terminal boredom. I was looking for excitement. I found it, all right." I swallowed the last gulps of wine, and I finished my story—how I came to understand that Peter could never really love me. How I felt when I returned to New York.

I was amazed that I managed to get through the whole, sordid tale without stopping, or crying. Hearing myself say what I did left me with a kind of exhilaration. I didn't feel foolish or naked. I felt relieved.

"Finally, I'm getting to know you," Gabe said.

I kissed him on the cheek and I took his face in my hands. "You're the first man I've met in a long time who's cared enough to ask so many questions about my past," I said.

"You're a beautiful, intelligent woman. For some men, that's enough. You know all the jokes about how men don't like to talk about their feelings. The Mars-Venus thing. But I'm surprised you didn't talk to a therapist. I thought New Yorkers were required to have shrinks. Especially after failed romances. I've known several."

"Several failed romances, or several shrinks?"

"Both. You didn't go to therapy at all?"

"Beth recommended someone for me. But I didn't see what I was experiencing as a problem for the couch. I was just terribly sad, and I figured that eventually I'd feel better. And I did, even if I had to harden my heart a little to protect myself."

"And now?"

"You mean, right this minute? I don't know if it's the wine, or all the talking I've done, or the coziness of being together with a storm outside—look at that snow, will you?—but for the first time in weeks I feel relaxed. And in spite of all that's going on with my mother, I feel a kind of creeping happiness."

Gabe smiled. "Creeping happiness? Is that a good thing? I'm not sure I know what it means."

I leaned forward and kissed him on the mouth, biting his lower lip. "It means, Gabe, that I want more than anything for you to make love to me."

———

THE CLOCK RADIO awakened me in the morning. A female voice was breathless with news that the city was covered with almost a foot of snow, and it was still coming down. I reached across Gabe to lower the volume. He slid his hand up between my legs.

"We never saw the end of the movie," he said, his eyes still closed.

"Is this a case of lover's remorse?" I said, lightly slapping his wrist. "You're welcome to turn the movie back on if you feel you missed something last night."

"You have the softest skin on the planet," he said, stroking my thigh. He opened his eyes. "And the most responsive body. Look at you, what gives you the right to look so gorgeous first thing in the morning?"

"Enough!" I laughed. "You'll run out of compliments by noon."

"Not possible," he said. "Every time I touch you, I'll think of something new."

"You said the right thing," I said, tracing the outline

of his lips with my index finger. "For which you will be rewarded. And then, I'll cook you breakfast."

———————

MOM HAD BEEN at Glenwilde for a month when the second stroke hit. Not a TIA, nothing mini about this one. The attack was sudden and fierce, and the doctors were blunt: no more could be done. Just a matter of time.

A week later, at three-thirty on a bitter cold Tuesday morning, the nurse's call awakened me.

"You'd better come," he said—more a solicitude than an order. "I think it's time." Forty minutes later I was at Glenwilde, being led down the bright, fluorescent-lit hallway to Mom's room. "She's waiting for you," the nurse said.

"I called a friend," I said. "She's on her way. Her name is Sarah Roth. Will they let her in at this hour?"

"I'll bring her to you when she gets here," he said, patting my hand.

Despite attempts to soften the antiseptic look of the place with oak furniture and soothing colors, it still looked like a hospital room. Mom was lying in a bed with side-rails, hooked up to an array of faintly beeping equipment with flickering monitors. IVs dispensed medication and nourishment.

Her eyes fluttered when I spoke. "It's Miriam, Mom." I pulled a chair next to the right side of her bed and reached for her hand. The entire left side of her body had been paralyzed for weeks. I gently stroked her arm, bruised up and down from a month of steady assaults by injections and IV lines.

The tape player and tapes I had brought to her weeks earlier were on the night table next to the bed. I had rounded up tapes of the kind of music she liked from the albums that played on the old phonograph in our house when I was growing up, when my father was alive. Frank Sinatra, Johnny Mathis, Broadway show tunes. The nurses had been good about seeing to it that there was music in Mom's room most of the day. They said she seemed more responsive when the music played.

I flipped open the slot on the tape player. The last tape she had listened to was the score from *My Fair Lady*. I switched it on, turning the volume low enough so patients in other rooms wouldn't be disturbed.

"Do you remember when you and Dad took me to see this show?" I said softly, as I heard Rex Harrison grumble that the English don't teach their children how to speak. "It was my first Broadway play. We had ice cream sundaes at Rumplemeyer's before the matinee and we sat in orchestra seats. Money was so tight in those days. How could you afford such a splurge? For a seven-year-old! I barely weighed enough to hold the theater seat down. My legs kept flying up and my crinolines were practically over my head. You finally had to put your coat under me to anchor the seat."

I think—no, I'm sure—that Mom tried to turn her head and open her eyes to see me. She knew I was with her. "That night when we got home you and Dad whirled around the living room, singing 'I Could Have Danced All Night.' I played the album a thousand times until I learned all the words to 'Wouldn't It Be Loverly?' complete with cockney accent. I forced you and Dad to sit on the couch and watch me perform it every night for weeks. You applauded every time as if I were Julie Andrews."

The door to the room opened. Sarah had arrived, carrying paper cups of steaming herbal tea. She handed me one of the cups and pulled a chair up next to mine.

"Beth is on her way," she whispered. "Would you like me to call your brother?"

"What time is it out there? Doesn't matter, I guess. Here, take my cell phone. His number is stored."

"Beth spoke to Gabe yesterday. He said he thought you might hesitate about calling him, especially if—if you needed him in the middle of the night, but he wanted to be with you."

"You can call him, too, but later. You and Beth will be here with me. Why wake him?"

"Because he loves you, Miriam."

"I know."

Sarah took my cell phone and went in search of an area where it would work. She was back in what seemed like seconds.

"I spoke to Neil and Kathy. They'll get on a plane today."

"Are they bringing the kids?"

"They didn't say."

"Their boys never got to know Mom, not really. She's always done what she can to be part of their lives, but it's hard to be a long-distance grandmother. Once Neil moved away, he didn't . . ."

"—Miriam, don't go down that road. Not now. Better to talk about happy times with your family. You know what I remember most clearly about your mother? The first time I met her, over Thanksgiving vacation freshman year. She was so beautiful. You look very much like her, you know. How old was she then? Not even forty yet. I spent a night at your apartment in Brooklyn, and Celeste made me feel like visiting royalty. She apologized for serving me turkey leftovers, as if everybody in America weren't having the same meal that day. And then, remember how thrilled she was when she found out that I had the same birthday as her mother? 'Kismet,' she said. She's sent me a birthday card every year since."

From the doorway of Mom's room came Beth's voice.

"Celeste sends me birthday cards, too."

"Beth! How did you get here so fast? Thank you for . . ."

"Don't you dare thank me. I love your mother. And I love you."

"She's always been crazy about both of you," I said to them.

We sat quietly, listening to faint strains of "On the Street Where You Live" against the hums and chirps of medical apparatuses surrounding Mom's bed. I continued to stroke Mom's arm and hold her hand. From time to time, Sarah or Beth would pat my shoulder or rub my back or share another recollection. I thought I saw tiny movements on the right side of Mom's face, as if she were trying to open her eyes, but her body stayed motionless, and she was unable to speak. Her breathing remained calm and steady to the end.

NEIL AND KATHY arrived in time for the funeral and stayed for the week. They brought my nephew, fifteen-year-old Matt, whom I hadn't seen in three years. Their other son, Jeffrey, was still at home, unable to miss school because it was the week of achievement tests. Matt made no secret of how bored he was, and he spent every waking hour parked in front of the TV in Mom's bedroom, complaining about the limited selection of shows on basic cable. I did my best to talk to him about the things that teenagers are usually interested in. I tried sports, movies, music, TV shows—topics that usually work even with my taciturn students—but nothing I said prompted Matt to make eye contact or respond in more than monosyllables. He was like a thousand kids I've known—not recalcitrant, but self-absorbed and hostile to adults. Unlike the kids I teach, though, my nephew has something else complicating his teenage years: affluent and over-indulgent parents. "I can't believe there's no computer in this house" was Matt's longest utterance all week.

My brother and his family stayed at Mom's apartment. I slept in my own place at night and arrived at Mom's early each morning. Aunt Sylvia, up from Boca Raton, stayed with me. Neil and Kathy were never without cell phones in hand. Grumbling about the inconvenience of having to work away from his office, Neil called the managers of each of his stores every day. These phone calls were long and loud enough so that everyone in the room could hear proof of Neil's eminence in the nationwide *tchochkes* domain.

"His gift shops are all over the country!" Mom's friends whispered approvingly.

Kathy called home three times a day to check on Jeffrey, who had been left in the care of their live-in housekeeper. "Fifty dollars max," I overheard her warn him. "If you spend more than that at the mall today, I'm taking the credit card away for a whole month. I mean it, Jeffrey."

The apartment was full of visitors paying respects, day and night, the week following the funeral. The crowd was mostly widows of my mother's generation. Mom's mah jong group—women who had been meeting for weekly games since before I was born—faithfully showed up each morning with the day's supply of what can only be described as mystery meals, purportedly healthful versions of familiar recipes they had miraculously divested of fat, cholesterol, salt, sugar, and flavor.

"What is this supposed to be?" Gabe whispered to me as he forced down a bite of a spongy, gelatinous mixture.

"If there are noodles in it, probably lasagna. If you smell cinnamon, it's apple cobbler," I whispered back.

"Tastes like drywall," he muttered, though I later

heard him rave about the dish to the woman who had created it.

Neighbors who had known my mother for most of her life came by to offer condolences and friendly gossip about other residents in the building. ("Do you remember Mrs. Stockman from apartment 3B? She won a tango contest on a cruise she went on with her new husband. He's a lot younger than she is, but I hear they're very happy.") The women pinched my cheeks as if I were still a child, made a fuss over Neil and Kathy, bragged about their own grandchildren's latest achievements, and distracted me from sadness. Aunt Sylvia, now having lost the last of her siblings, was subdued and melancholy. At the end of the week, when Gabe and I dropped her off at the airport for her flight back to Florida, she wept.

"Visit me soon," she pleaded. "Don't wait until you have to come see me in a hospital bed. Let's make happy occasions to be together."

"What do you want to do about Mom's things?" I asked Neil. "I'll have to clear out the apartment very quickly. It's still rent-controlled. The landlord can't wait to turn the place over so he can get market value for it." Neil, Kathy, Matt, Gabe and I were in a Japanese restaurant in TriBeca. It was the night before my brother was returning to Phoenix.

"What things?" Kathy wanted to know. With plastic chopsticks, she was picking at her seaweed salad. "Didn't she leave a will?"

"It's the same one she drew up after Dad died. I took her to a lawyer to update it a few years ago. I can tell you what it says. She didn't have much money, of course, but whatever is left is yours and mine to share, Neil. There are small annuities for your two boys. She made a point of leaving a few pieces of jewelry to Aunt Sylvia and the rest is mine. Most of it would be worth little to anyone except me. Her wedding ring, a charm bracelet she used to wear when we were kids, the rhinestone pin that was her mother's. The sentimental stuff. You get Dad's coin collection, but I have no idea what it's worth."

"What's annuities mean?" Matt wanted to know.

"It means money especially for you and your brother, a gift from Grandma," I said.

"How much?" Matt said, skeptical.

"I don't remember exactly. But whatever it is, you should be grateful that your grandmother thought to mention you in her will," I said pointedly. Matt shrugged, unimpressed. "I'll donate Mom's clothing to the AIDS Thrift Shop. But what about her furniture? Books? All those picture albums? Her good china and silver? Do you want any of it?"

Neil and Kathy exchanged a quick look—I could tell they had already discussed the value—or at least the price—of Mom's belongings.

"Maybe just some of the old family pictures," Neil said. "I'd like some photos of her and Dad, and you and me when we were kids. None of the furniture is worth shipping. You can have it all, but I don't know what you'll do with it. You don't have room for ánything more in that apartment of yours. Why don't you just give it all to Goodwill or something? Most of it is junk, anyway."

"It's not junk to me," I said slowly.

"I think Neil meant that none of the stuff is valuable, you know, like antiques," Kathy said. "It's only used furniture."

Talking to them was pointless. Neil and Kathy could have no appreciation for my memories of just how this furniture became "used." The mahogany desk where I practiced writing the alphabet. Dad's rocking chair, with its worn cane seat and the burn mark on the arm from his cigar ash. Mom's good china—a kitschy Victorian pattern—on which only important meals were served: Thanksgiving. Passover. Dinners with prospective sons-in-law.

"I'll figure out what to do," I said. "You're right, though, about the space issue. I don't have a spare inch in my apartment. I suppose I can put everything in storage."

"How about my place?" said Gabe. He'd been discreetly quiet the whole time, steering ribbons of pickled ginger and strips of sashimi to his mouth. In the week that had just passed, Gabe had learned the art of tactful retreat from Kaplan family symposia.

"I thought you were planning on putting in a screening room and office in that space," I reminded him.

"There's plenty of room. We'll figure it out. No reason to spend money on storing your mother's things. Besides, if they're stored, you can't enjoy them."

"See, Miriam, problem solved," Neil said, pointing his thumb towards Gabe. "He's a handy guy to have around."

―――――――――

WINTER BREAK FROM school began. I used the time off to clear out Mom's apartment, giving away her clothes and most of the stuff in the kitchen cabinets, and storing at Gabe's place the things of hers that mattered to me. We put cartons in his basement and set up one of the rooms on the second floor of his house as a kind of parlor for Mom's furniture. The room had a bay window, built-in bookshelves, and a carved mantle above what had once been a fireplace but was now a brick wall. I put some framed pictures and a pair of Georg Jensen candle-sticks (a silver anniversary present from Dad to Mom) on the mantle and filled the shelves with books and photo albums. I moved the mahogany desk against the bay window, and arranged Mom's love seat, Dad's rocking chair, and a few occasional tables around the phantom fireplace. Gabe gave me a set of keys to his house. "For whenever you want to visit Celeste's room," he said. "Or me, even."

It was mid-January before I got back to my normal schedule. School started up again the same week that Gabe was leaving for Sundance.

"Can't you play hooky and come with me?" he asked.

"If I hadn't been absent so much this year, I'd be tempted," I said. "You're on your own. Just keep your hands off the starlets."

"Yeah, right. They're all flying to Utah in hopes of meeting a balding, middle-aged guy with no money, someone who can't do a damn thing for their careers. Can I bring you anything from the wild West?"

"How about one of those balding, middle-aged guys that the starlets reject?"

———

"IN A WAY, I'm glad to have some time to myself," I told Sarah. We were at her place, examining a book auction catalog from Christie's. Sarah was hoping to nab a signed first edition of *Our Town*. So far, antique books had been her only new acquisitions since she found out that Martin's death had left her rich.

"You've had quite a time the last few months," Sarah said.

"As we all have. The last time I was here, Kevin lived with you, but the place doesn't seem much different."

"That's because almost everything in this apartment has always been mine. I still haven't heard a word from him. It's as if he's erased the five years we were together. On the basis of one night! Tell me, was I an embarrassment at the party?"

"You were a very witty drunk. But you didn't seem to pay much attention to Kevin."

"I had just found out about Brendan. I was still in shock, I think. If I hadn't been drunk, I suppose I would have waited for a private moment with Kevin to ask about his son. But I was furious, and after all that had happened that week at work, I needed to anesthetize myself."

"I don't think people truly act out of character when they drink," I said. "Especially people who seldom drink, like you and me. People like us act exactly like ourselves— just, perhaps, a different part of ourselves shows up."

"Well, a part of me showed up that Kevin didn't want to have anything to do with. You can't imagine the things we said to each other the next day! It was hard to believe we were the same people we'd always been. As if we'd each undergone sudden and complete metamorphoses and neglected to tell each other. How do people stay together, anyway? Even Beth and Jim, as much as they love each other, have been through a few ordeals."

"Speaking of which, when are we going to do brunch?" I said. "Beth refuses to divulge any more details about her day with Andrew until she can do it face to face. Have you heard any more?"

"Only that she did tell Jim that she met with Andrew, and Jim didn't take it too well. They're still reeling, but I think they'll be all right. Beth thinks so, too."

"They're planning a trip to Europe sometime in the fall," I said. "Nicole is spending fall semester in Paris. They'll stop off there to spend some time with her. I still can't quite believe you'll be living there, too."

"This is something I've wanted for as long as I can remember. You know that. I'll be back a few times a year."

"I hated it when you moved to Acedia Bay, and that was only a three-hour flight away. Besides, I worry about your being in Europe alone."

"You mean without a man? I'm finished with all of that. Listen, if I call you from there and say that I've met a man and I'm madly in love, I want you to fly right over and lock me in a closet until I start making sense again."

"Even when you say, 'But this one's different'?"

"Especially if I say that," Sarah said.

"I mean you'll be truly alone. You don't know anyone in Paris," I said.

"I know Nicole Gillian. You just said she's going to be there."

"As if she'll want to hang out with her Aunt Sarah. I meant that you won't have a job there, so you won't be meeting people that way. Aren't you afraid of being lonely?"

"I've had a bad marriage and an unsatisfying significant-other arrangement. There's nothing lonelier than coming home every day to the wrong person."

"Still, I'd love to think the right man is waiting somewhere for you. But what I'm wondering is, what will you do with your time? How will you spend your days?"

"I still have the idea that I'd like to write. I've been threatening to be a real writer for thirty years. Maybe my time has finally come. Does that make you feel better?"

"A little. When do you think you'll move?"

"By Labor Day, I imagine. I want to make sure Ellie is all set, wherever she winds up after graduation."

"We'll just have to visit very often to check up on you."

"Who's 'we'? Do you mean you and Beth? Or you and Gabe?"

"Whoever," I said, more abruptly than I intended.

"Hmm," said Sarah. "Am I missing something about Gabe? All I see is a wonderful guy who's nuts about you."

"Oh, Sarah," I said. "I do love him, really."

"Then what's holding you back?" I shrugged. "I was wondering why you didn't let me call him the night your mother died," she said.

"I had you and Beth with me. I need some breathing

room with him sometimes."

"Let me ask some questions, okay?" she said. I nodded. "First, just to satisfy my own prurience, how are things in bed?"

"Couldn't be better. He's a very sexy man—adventurous and imaginative. He makes me feel like the most desirable woman in the world. It's wonderful, starting a sexual relationship at this stage in life, when we're beyond self-consciousness. We can say anything, ask for anything, do anything. So, yes, everything in bed is fine."

"Second question, then. Are there family complications?"

"None. His son and daughter-in-law live a thousand miles away, and from what I can see, everyone gets along. Did I tell you I'm going to meet them in a few weeks? Moira is pregnant and they want to come up for a visit before she's too far along."

"Does this mean you will be the first of us to have a grandchild?"

"Not so fast. A few things have to happen before anyone starts calling me Granny."

"You mean like officially marrying Gabe and all that?" She waved her hand. "Minor details. You won't let him get away." She leaned forward, with a questioning look. "Please, tell me I'm right. You are too smart to pass this up, aren't you?"

"I know, I know. He's intelligent and sexy, and he comes complete with a grandchild-to-be and a fabulous house in the neighborhood I've lived in and loved for twenty years. He's the only person I've ever met who has seen more movies than I have. Everyone who loves me thinks he's terrific. He was an angel when my mother was sick and when she died, and, well, anyone can see how he feels about me."

"So?"

"So . . . I can't help but feel that things are lopsided."

"What do you mean?"

"He takes care of me. In every way. My mother gets sick in Florida, he hops on a plane. I need a place for Mom's furniture, he gives me a whole floor in his brownstone."

"So far I'm having trouble seeing the down side."

"It's a little suffocating. And unbalanced. I'd like to take care of him a little. But I don't know what I can give him that's comparable to what he gives me."

"Have you asked him what you can do for him?"

"You mean when we're not having sex?"

"Exactly. Communicating in bed is easy compared to everything else you have to do in a relationship. Have you told Gabe what you're telling me?"

"No. I didn't want to seem . . . ungrateful."

"He knows you appreciate what he's done for you. Here's a novel idea: why not be honest with him?"

"An interesting concept, honesty. Not everyone's first inclination. Especially when men and women talk to each other."

Sarah let out a wry laugh. "You're telling me?"

GABE RETURNED AFTER a week at the film festival, showing up at my door with an official Sundance baseball cap for me and a satchel of souvenirs for my film class. He was brimming with amusing anecdotes about parties and screenings and celebrity sightings. "You should have been with me," he said. "Next year, for sure."

One of his Film Institute students had won a prize for best original movie script. Her film was about a female college student's homicidal revenge against a professor who ruins her chances for a scholarship after she refuses to sleep with him.

"Autobiographical?" I said. "I don't mean that your student actually murdered anyone, but maybe she had the experience with a professor and then imagined how she'd get even."

"Not likely. She's a lesbian and too gentle a soul to fantasize about murder, I think."

"You'd be surprised what fantasies people harbor. And the grudges they hold on to."

"Is that a hint?" Gabe said. "Are you plotting to bump someone off?"

"I'll admit to a murderous thought or two, but not lately. How about you?"

"I was in a terrible marriage for many years. Unhappy spouses typically fantasize about getting rid of their mates, one way or another."

"Why did you stay married for as long as you did?"

I saw the muscles tighten in his jaw. "I guess I have a weakness for lost causes," he said.

"Gee, thanks," I said.

"I don't mean you. You, dear Miriam, are the . . . the antithesis of a lost cause."

"That's a compliment, right?"

"I meant it as one. When I finally got divorced, I was finished for good with rescue missions. For a long time, I stayed with Trudy because I thought I could change her. And I felt partly responsible for her alcoholism."

"I thought the current thinking is that alcoholism is a disease, something you can't cause another person to get. Like diabetes."

"Yeah, that's what I learned after about twenty thousand dollars of therapy. The operative word is enabler. As long as I took responsibility for Trudy's problems, I made it easy for her to keep drinking."

I already knew that Gabe had married Trudy when she became pregnant in their sophomore year at Tulane.

Trudy dropped out of college when their son was born and became a receptionist at a dental office so she could support them while Gabe went to school.

"We were very happy our first few years," he went on. "We didn't have a dime, but neither did anyone we knew. All of our friends were students, most were still single, and when Oliver came along, he was everyone's baby. He was healthy and beautiful and our friends would fight among themselves for the right to babysit. We loved New Orleans. It's a great city to be young in. Have you ever been?"

"Never. One year in college, Sarah and Beth and I planned to drive from Buffalo for Mardi Gras. It was an insane idea to begin with, and then a snowstorm killed our plans."

"Mardi Gras is the worst time to be there. New Orleans is pleasantly decadent most of the time, but during Mardi Gras it's just loud and vulgar. I lived in that city for nine years, right through my Ph.D., and I never got tired of the place. And then, as you know, I came back to New York to work in my family's business."

"The Dr. Drainpipe years."

"Right. The grind of that work made me crazy. Six long and tiring days a week. Trudy hated our life in New York. I was at work most of the time, and I wasn't very good company when I was at home."

"You? You're so easy to be around."

"Depends on whom you ask. Trust me, I was no fun. Emotionally detached. Eventually Trudy found other . . . diversions."

"She had an affair?"

"A series. I was too caught up in my own unhappiness even to notice. What does that say about the state of a marriage? But she had started drinking, and that I noticed. She was hanging around with some younger women she met through work. They didn't have kids so they went partying every night. Trudy would get a sitter for Oliver, who was about ten at this point, and run around with her friends. Sometimes there were drinks at lunch, too. I'd find Trudy passed out when I got home from work, or she'd smell boozy. We'd argue, she'd get defensive, and then we'd have what is commonly known as make-up sex, and we'd both swear we were going to try harder to get our marriage back on track."

"No therapy?"

"Not at first. Then Trudy lost her job. The dentist she was working for fired her when she returned from lunch one day with liquor on her breath. That was the first time I came to grips with the fact that I was living with an alcoholic."

"What did you do?"

He looked down and shook his head. "Everything. Everything! For the next eight years, I never knew how I would find her when I walked in the house. We fought. We went to AA and Al-Anon meetings. We made up. She stopped drinking; we celebrated; she started drinking again. I threatened and pleaded. She apologized and promised. We went to more AA meetings and couples counseling and family therapy. It was in a therapist's office, by the way, that I found out about Trudy's affairs. One of the Twelve Steps is that you're supposed to level with people you've been dishonest with. So she leveled. By that time, our marriage was already too battered to recover. I was having plenty of vanishing-wife fantasies, hoping I'd wake up one morning to find that Oliver and I were living alone. But Trudy and I stayed married until Oliver was out of the house. I don't think we consciously planned it that way, but once he was grown, nothing remained to keep us together."

"How has Oliver done?"

"He's been through all the children-of-alcoholics therapy, and I know he has scars, but he functions all right. He was such a bright kid, but the worst of our family dramas took place when Oliver was in high school. He lost interest in school then, and though he gave college a try to make me happy, he dropped out after a year. I'm crazy about Moira, but I wasn't thrilled that Oliver got married so young. One of my life's many ironies is that my son now works with his in-laws. I swore I'd never see my own child chained to a family business. I'm wracked with guilt about Oliver. I keep thinking that I was in absentia for so much of his childhood, working all the time, and focused on problems with Trudy when I was home. "

"It seems as if Oliver's life has turned out fine, even if it isn't the one you would have chosen for him."

"It's a complicated mix, the emotional brew, so to speak, in an alcoholic household. Anger, shame, guilt, hope, remorse—all emotions competing. At this point, I'm trying to be the best father and father-in-law I can. And I'm hoping that my grandchild will give me another chance to be a patriarch."

"I'm trying to understand why you blamed yourself for Trudy's problems."

Gabe looked away and was quiet for a few moments. Then he said, "Oliver was already a teenager when Trudy informed me that she deliberately got pregnant with him. I thought it was just one of those accidents that can happen, even when a woman is on the Pill. Turns out she had stopped taking the Pill on purpose. For all those years I had thought that I was at least half responsible for her having to drop out of school. And if we hadn't become parents so young then maybe I wouldn't have needed to work for my father."

"You must have been furious."

"You bet I was. But then I'd realize how much she

cared about Oliver and I'd think about how in love we were in the early days in New Orleans. I had dragged her to New York, which she hated. I was always working; she was always alone. I'd get enraged when she drank, especially when I saw the effect on Oliver, but then she'd be so contrite and I'd feel guilty and I'd dare to think, 'Maybe she means it this time.' She's not a bad person, and I hope she gets well, but I'm not in the business of taking care of her anymore."

"No more thoughts of violence and mayhem, then? You don't want to do her in?"

"You have to be involved, to depend on someone, in order to get that angry. Once I gave up on my marriage and my personal investment in Trudy's recovery, my evil thoughts about her disappeared. It took years, of course. Now I'm just sad for her."

"I still have trouble recognizing the Gabe I know in what you say about your life with Trudy," I said. "Even given your responsibilities at your father's business, I can't imagine you—how did you describe it?—emotionally detached."

"And I can't imagine ever feeling detached from you."

This is my chance. *Tell him it's a little too stifling, a little too much. Tell him to go slow. Tell him that we could use a little detachment here.* "Is that why you take such good care of me?" I began.

He looked puzzled. "What in the world do you mean?"

"Come on, you can't be serious. Coming to see me in Florida? Never leaving me for a moment when my mother was dying? Giving use of your house to store my mother's things?"

"I used a free plane ticket that would have expired and spent a weekend in Florida with you, Aunt Sylvia, and *Adam's Rib*. I had the privilege of getting to know Celeste. And I'm one of the lucky few in Manhattan who has a house with more space than furniture. Nothing I did was a burden to me," he said sharply.

"I'm making you angry," I said.

"No," he said, too quickly. And then, "Just a little frustrated. Look at us, Miriam, don't you see how good we are together? Everything is working here. We're so well matched. Why won't you just let things happen?"

"I just feel, sometimes, as if it's hard to breathe."

"I'm smothering you?" He sounded hurt.

"A little, yes. You've done so much for me, and I do love you, but I feel a little—off-balance. Our relationship is uneven."

"I have no idea what you mean," he said. "Uneven? Are we talking about equality?"

"You don't let me do enough for you. Take that look off your face; I'm not talking about what we do in bed."

He smiled. "I wasn't thinking about sex, though let me go on record as one very satisfied man in that regard. I was thinking about how amazing it is that the most obvious things can sometimes elude us."

"What am I missing, then?"

"I meant myself, what I was missing. All of this time, I've been certain that I'd done a good job of communicating what you mean to me, but now I see I left out the most important part."

"Which is?"

"I think it was Fitzgerald who said that there are no second acts in American lives. But I'm out to prove him wrong. I've finally got a career that means something to me, and maybe being a grandfather will give me a shot at the family life I didn't have in my First Act. In a way, that's where you come in."

"How?"

"The thing I most want is a second chance at giving Oliver good family memories, to compensate for the childhood he endured. I realize he's grown, and it may be a little late, but I still harbor a fantasy that my son and I can be more than passing acquaintances in each other's lives."

"What do I have to do with any of that?"

"I can't do it alone. I don't want to. In a way, I closed myself off emotionally when my marriage started to fall apart. Being with Trudy became nothing but work, and I was too exhausted to give anything to Oliver. Years of therapy and I learned one important thing about myself: I do better in all aspects of my life when I have a woman in it. Not just any woman—someone who's loving and honest and, especially, in light of my marriage, responsible. An adult. I need you, Miriam. I need you so I can feel my life. And I'm sorry if I pushed you away in my eagerness to hold on to you." He leaned over and kissed me on the forehead, and he whispered, "I want to spend the rest of my life with you."

I THINK OFTEN about how sad it made my mother that I hadn't married while she was alive. I hope wherever she is that she knows I've found my *bashert*. "Took you long enough," she'd probably say.

Sarah and Beth have insisted on throwing us an engagement party. They've reserved Windows on the World for a night in the late spring. Violet and Grant have promised to be here for it. Violet called the other day and mentioned that Peter had shown up at an ecology conference in Acedia Bay, and she told him I was getting married. He wished me the best, she said. Then she quickly apologized for bringing up Peter's name. "I don't mind at all," I told her. "I've moved on to the Second Act of my life."

Gabe and I are still working out the details of how and where we'll get married. I'm only half joking when I tell him that I wouldn't mind a honeymoon in the midst of a film festival somewhere. Meanwhile, I'm researching appropriate attire for a middle-aged bride. We're planning to live in Gabe's brownstone, of course. Manhattan real estate being what it is, we can sell my apartment and buy a beautiful weekend house in the country. We're looking in Connecticut, around where Beth and Jim live, for a place with a big backyard and enough bedrooms for when our grandchildren visit.

BETH:
TRUTH AND CONSEQUENCES

*"Now I'm no longer doubtful
Of what I'm living for"*
—Carole King

THE MANHATTAN APARTMENT THAT Gillian Investments bought for Jim is functional and sterile, furnished by the building's management company with more money than imagination. The color scheme is an orgy of neutrals, nothing to startle the senses. Tweedy Berber carpeting goes wall-to-wall in the living room and two bedrooms; the kitchen and bathroom floors are covered in stark white tiles. The furniture is upholstered in fabrics of unrelenting beige tones. Generic silk plants in straw baskets abound. The only items that save the place from looking like a hotel suite are family photos on a console table in the living room and Jim's NordicTrack in the spare bedroom.

Jim has met few of his neighbors; most of the apartments are corporate owned and change occupants frequently. The building has a doorman and a concierge and a staff of at least a dozen young people who will happily procure theater tickets, airport limos, nannies, and housekeepers for residents willing to ante up an arm and a leg.

The lobby leads to a parade of shops offering the kinds of products and services that suggest transient, rushed lives: a one-hour dry cleaner, a gourmet carry-out place, a Kinko's.

On the evening of the day I spent with Andrew, Jim is already at the apartment when I arrive. He's on the terrace, on the phone. His coat and suit jacket are thrown over the back of one of the dining room chairs; he's in rolled-up shirtsleeves and a loosened tie. I rap on the sliding glass door. Jim holds up his index finger, and mouths, "One minute." I put the bag of food and a bottle of champagne in the refrigerator, and I toss the shopping bag with my new sleepwear—sheer, lacy and black—on the bed.

"So, what got into you today?" Jim says on coming in from the terrace. "Not that I ever mind when you stay here with me. How long has it been?"

"Can't even remember the last time. You have a good day?"

"Nothing out of the ordinary. How come you're in town?"

"Why don't you make yourself comfortable," I say. "Then we'll talk."

Jim's eyebrows knit in worry. "Everything okay?"

"Entirely okay. I promise." He still looks tense. "Go change your clothes, and I'll get the champagne," I say.

"I recall a promise of food, too," he says. "I hope you've brought some. I'm starving."

"I've got it," I say. "You know me, Jim. I always keep my promises."

We sit on one of the beige sofas; Jim pours champagne into two flute-shaped glasses. I ask him not to interrupt, to let me tell him everything before he speaks. He agrees. I begin with Andrew's phone call before the weekend, and I'm acutely aware of how, involuntarily, I am editing what I say. I hear myself talking, and I am watching Jim's face, and I know that no matter how prudently I choose my words, they are bound to unhinge him. I say nothing about my fantasies involving Andrew, not a word about the flood of memories that surged in my brain as I dressed that morning, as I drove to a hotel to meet my first love. I position the rendezvous as if I were talking about an appointment with one of my patients— Andrew sounded desperate and depressed, et cetera. I can't find the boundaries of truth; I don't know what I should be saying, not saying. The words keep coming, and I feel like a fraud.

I can tell that it takes effort for Jim to keep his word and not speak until I am finished. He doesn't say anything, but his feelings register on his face. His jaw clenches, he squints as if he's trying to get me into focus. He sips from his glass every so often, but he never takes his eyes off me. I don't know what I was expecting, but this is agonizing.

"Is that it?" Jim says. I nod. "I guess it was inevitable," he says.

"What?"

"That sooner or later you'd figure out a way to get Andrew in your life again."

"Jim, he called *me* . . ."

"And you answered the call," he says. "I'll tell you something, Beth. I've felt for years that on some level you have always been sorry that you didn't marry Andrew." *Oh, Jim,* I thought. *I've never been sorry that I married you. I felt a longing for my youth, for the life I had before terrible things happened.*

My heart sank. "Andrew broke up with me," I say. "He didn't want to be married to me."

"That doesn't say that you were really finished with him. In your head, I mean. As long as we're being honest here—we are being honest, aren't we, Beth?—tell me, weren't there times when you would have preferred to be with Andrew? Exciting, talented, bohemian Andrew?

Instead of me, your dull, businessman husband? The life you have with me must seem so pedestrian compared to living in a palazzo and traipsing through Italy with a musician—"

"I never compared you to him," I say. "I told you about Andrew when you and I first met. I've never talked about him since. And there's nothing dull about you, or our life."

"Doesn't mean you weren't thinking about him."

"You know how much I loved being in Italy. I do think often about my life then, about Rome, and he was there. I can't change my history, any more than you can change yours."

"Andrew is no longer just historical. You were with him today."

"And I've told you, nothing happened."

"You mean you didn't sleep with him. Did you want to?"

Not exactly. I wanted him to want me; I wanted to feel young and lighthearted again. For one afternoon, I wanted a man to look at me with the kind of desire that a husband of three decades can't possibly summon. It wasn't love, it was . . .

I took too long to respond.

"Guess I've got my answer," Jim says. "And what was that little phone-sex exercise with me this afternoon? Did you think you could come here tonight and seduce me into forgetting that you spent the afternoon with the man you wish you had married?"

"I don't wish I'd married anyone but you," I say. "And I told him that today."

"So the subject came up, did it? What do you wish, Beth? You want to play same-time-next-year with your old boyfriend? You expect me to believe you're finished with him?"

"I believed you," I say slowly. "You had an affair, and I

forgave you. I took your word when you said it was over."

"Ah," he says sharply. "So now we're even."

"Hardly," I snap back. "I didn't go to bed with Andrew."

"That's not the only kind of cheating there is," he says. "You were probably more intimate with him today than I ever was with—with anyone besides you."

"Patricia. Patricia Remlin. I haven't forgotten her."

Jim puts his champagne glass on the table and he stands up. "I'm going to the office for a while. I'll be back, but don't wait up for me." He puts on his coat.

"Jim, please. Stay, let's talk."

"Dr. Gillian always thinks talking makes things better," he says in a mocking tone, throwing his cell phone into his briefcase and snapping it shut. He's speaking in code—a reference to our arguments about Adam. Jim is so furious with me that nothing is off limits.

I'm dozing in bed when I hear Jim's key in the door. I've changed into a pair of flannel pajamas I found in one of the drawers. The shopping bag with the sexy nightgown is hanging on the doorknob.

"You should have gone to sleep," he says softly as he walks into the bedroom. "Don't you have patients in the morning?"

"I slept a little," I say. "Did you eat anything?" Sleep, food, any topic except . . .

"A hot pretzel from the cart on the corner," He sits down next to me. "I have one question," he says.

"Just one?" I say with a smile.

"It's a request, actually."

"Anything," I say.

"I love you, Beth. I love the life we have. This may sound idiotic to you, but can you tell me what . . . what it means to you to be married to me? I need to hear it from you."

"Everything," I say, without hesitation. "We've grown up together. I can't imagine my life without you."

He takes my hand in his. Tears well in his eyes. "Do you remember the night, a short while after Adam died, when we argued about going to see Dr. Moros? I didn't want to continue with the sessions, and you were so angry at me."

"I thought you needed the sessions as much as I did. I was glad that I kept seeing him, and I missed having you there with me. Why did you stop going?"

"I'm sorry I dropped out. And sorry if I disappointed you. But sitting in Dr. Moros's office made me anxious."

"Anxious? I find him so comforting. Healing."

"It wasn't him. The first few sessions were all right. I actually felt better after we spoke to him. But the last time I went, when we talked about Adam's death, it made me remember—emotionally remember—how I felt when my parents died. I walked out of the session with a strange feeling."

"Strange? In what way?"

"You and I left his office together. You dropped me off at the station so I could get into the city. It was already past rush hour; I was alone on the train. And suddenly, I was gripped by a cold terror—I actually remember shivering. The sense of loss overtook me. You once told me that Dr. Moros says that many people miss the main idea of their own lives. Well, I thought as I sat on that train that I had stumbled upon the controlling, underlying theme of my life: I love people, I lose them. Nothing that means anything to me can last."

We both start to cry. "Why didn't you tell me? Why didn't you talk to Dr. Moros?" I say.

"It scared me," Jim says. "In a way, I felt that saying

the words would make it real, as if speaking about it would breathe life into my worst fears, turn my nightmare into reality. And the worst part was that with Adam, I felt like a complete failure. The whole time he was sick, I was powerless. I was his father, I loved him, and I could do nothing. I was guilty about how much time I spend at work. Great, successful businessman, who can't keep his son from ending his own life."

"You've always had your family in mind. Everything you've built, it's all for us. You've given us all a wonderful life. Adam was proud to be your son."

"In the end, though, when he needed us most, I was incompetent. During all of his treatment, when we talked to doctors and drug counselors, you were in your own milieu, you seemed to understand what was going on in a way that I couldn't. You're a shrink, at least you spoke the language."

"But not well enough to save him," I say. "Jim, Adam had his own demons. You know that. There was nothing more either of us could do for him. You're a good father. Look at Nicole—she's healthy and happy. And Adam was, too, most of his life."

Jim nods weakly. "That's what I tell myself, every day."

"Why tonight, Jim? What made you want to talk about Adam tonight?"

He takes a deep breath and gets up from the bed, his back to me. He walks a few steps, then turns to face me.

"When you told me about Andrew, the cold terror came back. I thought, 'I'll lose Beth, too.' Further confirmation that the main idea of my life is loss."

"I'm not leaving you, my love. Not ever."

He wipes his eyes with the back of his hand. "No regrets then? You're sure you're married to the right man?"

I get on my feet and walk to him, put my arms around his shoulders. I kiss him, passionately. "You'll do," I say, and he smiles.

"What's in there?" he says, pointing to the shopping bag on the doorknob.

"Just a little slinky black number I picked up today. Want to see it on me?"

"Dr. Gillian," he says. "That sounds like exactly the right kind of therapy."

DRIVING BACK TO Connecticut on almost no sleep, I call Nicole. She never takes early classes.

She can tell I'm on the cell phone.

"You're using that hands-free thing, I hope, Mom," she says.

"Of course, sweetheart. Thanks for your concern."

"Where are you?"

"On my way to work. Dad and I had a date in the city last night and I stayed in town with him."

"You two are adorable. I thought old married people didn't have dates anymore."

"You'd be surprised. Creaky bones and all, we still can manage a little romance from time to time."

"Enough, Mom. I promise not to call you old anymore if you promise not to give me anymore details of your date with Dad. What's up?"

"I've been thinking about your plan to study abroad. Is your application done?"

"Almost. I have to get some teacher recommendations and finish filling out all the forms. I guess this means I should be taking my French class a little more seriously."

"Dad and I would love to visit you in France."

"When you come over, can I stay in a nice hotel with you? I hear the dorms where they make the American students live are really crummy."

"You're not even there yet, and you're complaining

about the accommodations?"

"I spoke to some people who were in the program last year. They said about a thousand people share each bathroom, and the dorm rooms are freezing all the time."

"Yes, but you'll be in Paris. For a whole semester. A lot of girls your age would be very happy to live abroad, crowded bathrooms, cold dorms and all. You know, when I lived in Rome . . ."

"Okay, okay. Please don't start with one of your stories about the deprivations of your youth. I know how fortunate I am to have rich parents."

"I was hardly deprived. I thought I was the luckiest person on earth to be in Italy."

"Just kidding, Mom. I can't wait to go. But what will you say if I call home and announce that I have a French boyfriend?"

"I wouldn't be surprised."

"What if I say, 'Mom, I've met the man of my dreams. His name is Jacques and he wants me to travel all over Europe with him and live in his *château*?'"

I smile, thinking that there's a world of things my daughter will never know about me.

"I'd be ecstatic for you," I tell her. "Your father, however, may have a somewhat different reaction."

MADELINE FOSTER CANCELLED her last two appointments with me. Yesterday, she left a message asking me to call her at work.

I review my notes from her last session. She had talked about her husband. "When I married Bill, I thought there was nothing in the world he wouldn't do for me," she had said. "And I still feel that way. But day to day, there's nothing going on between us."

"Nothing?" I said.

"Oh, he's pleasant enough. We don't argue or anything. Of course, he's at work most of the time. At least, that's where he says he is."

"And?"

She was quiet, looking down at her hands.

"Madeline?" I said.

"I think he's having an affair. No, I know he is."

"How do you know?"

"Because he's behaving the way he did the last time it happened."

"Wait a minute," I said. "You never mentioned an affair before."

"It was a long time ago, when I was still in advertising. I was working long hours, and Bill just hated that. Well, you can understand. He'd get home and there'd be no dinner for him and the kids were with babysitters all the time. We fought non-stop. Anyway, he developed a sudden interest in golf. He'd get up before dawn every weekend morning and we wouldn't see him until late afternoon. One Saturday, I noticed he had left his wallet at home, and to be nice, I drove my car to the golf course to give it to him. I found him sitting in the bar with his arm around a very pretty young woman. Then I saw him kiss her."

"What did you do?"

"I just left. I drove home and waited for him. As soon as I saw him, I burst into tears. I cried all day, and finally he said that he'd end it. And he did, I know he did. And I promised him I'd leave my job, and take better care of him and the kids. That's when I went back to school to become a legal secretary."

"You must have felt so betrayed," I said. "How did you go about resolving things between you?"

Madeline looked confused. "Resolving things? I just told you, the day I found out, he swore he'd end things with her, and he did. We never talked about it again."

"Never? Did you talk to anyone else? A therapist? A friend?"

She shook her head. "You're the first therapist I've ever seen. And I don't really have friends I would talk to about this sort of thing."

"Why not?"

"Well, you know, I'm so busy, with work and the kids. And when I'm not at the office, Bill likes me to be at home."

"Madeline," I said, "what makes you think he's having an affair now?"

She had waited a moment, looking down at her hands again. Then she lifted her head.

"He's joined a gym," she said flatly.

I DIAL MADELINE'S number at work.

"Dr. Gillian," she says. "I'm so sorry I haven't been to see you. Um, I've been so busy and I had to . . ."

"I'm concerned about you, Madeline."

"I'm okay, I guess. But I've been thinking, you know, about what we've been doing in therapy, and I'm not sure it's right for me."

"I'm sorry to hear that. I thought you were starting to make progress."

"A little bit, yes. But, okay, let me tell you the truth. You're so nice, and I appreciate everything you've done for me, but I don't want to sit in your office for years and years."

"What makes you think it will take years and years?"

"It's just that my sister, she lives in Florida, she's been saying all along that I should just take some Prozac, and I know you don't believe in medication . . ."

"I didn't say that. Medication is fine, but you have

some things going on in your life that I think you should work out by talking about them with a therapist. It doesn't necessarily have to be me. The medication may make you feel better, but I don't think you'll actually *get* better without talking things through."

"Maybe you're right, but I went to my GP for a physical and he was willing to write me a prescription for Prozac, and I want to give it some time to work. If it does, that's all I probably need."

"If you ever change your mind, decide you want to talk with me again, just give my office a call," I say. And then I ask, "How are things with Bill?"

Madeline's voice rises, falsely bright. "Fine, just fine," she chirps.

I say nothing, and after a few moments, she continues in a whisper, "He's broken off with her. And he's promised he won't do it again. He says he's looking forward to seeing me be more upbeat, you know, when the Prozac starts working. I guess I haven't been much fun for him to be around."

———

LOVE, WORK, FRIENDSHIP. The nucleus on which therapists say human beings build healthy lives. I spend my days exploring other people's triumphs and tragedies in all three spheres. Opening minds, closing wounds. Dispensing new perspectives, fifty minutes at a time.

In spite of what I told Madeline Foster, I don't believe that psychoanalysis is the only way to resolve inner conflicts. If you do it right, just living your life will afford you all the therapy you need. My husband is proof of this. I guess I could make the case that a few visits with Dr. Moros set things in motion for Jim, but in the end, Jim's magnificent success at love, work, and friendship is his own doing.

Jim wants us to plan a big trip to France in the fall. A whole month, he says. We'll visit Nicole and Sarah and then rent a place in Provence for just the two of us. I'd love to show him Italy—we've never been there together. The Caravaggio exhibit will still be on, I tell him. "I'll pass, for now," he says. Jim is more or less at peace with what happened between Andrew and me, but for the moment he's had all he can take of ghosts from my past.

Since that night we spent in the city, our marriage feels new to me. There's a different, intimate quality in the way Jim relates to me, a kind of devotion that melts my heart. Jim has always been so strong and competent—of course, he still is—but now he has a vulnerability about him that makes me feel fundamental to his life. He calls more often, in the middle of our workdays, just to hear my voice. He wants to stay up late into the night, talking about everything and nothing. There's a poetry to our everyday routines that makes me grateful for every minute we have together.

I remember a conversation I had with Sarah a few months after Jim and I got married. "Orientation period is over," I told her. "Now we can start our marriage." Thirty years later, I feel as excited about getting to know my husband as if we were still newlyweds.

Nothing in life really begins, or ends, when we think it does.

"TAKE IT FROM the top," Miriam was saying, before I even sat down. "Don't leave out a syllable."

Miriam, Sarah, and I are at brunch for the first time in months. I picked a brasserie on the East Side where I knew we could sit for a long session. The three of us haven't been together since the *shiva* for Celeste Kaplan, where we couldn't really talk, and before that, at my fall party. So many startling changes in all of our lives during these months, changes that kept us from being able talk in person at a time when we most needed each other.

"Coffee, first," I say, trying to get the waiter's attention. "Jim and I were up very late. I'm not entirely awake yet."

The waiter rushes to our table. I order an espresso.

"Bring her a whole pot," Miriam tells him. "It's crucial that we get this woman talking." He nods and disappears.

Miriam turns to me. "I hope your fatigue is the result of a wild and passionate night," she says. "I need proof that married people actually continue to have sex."

"I hear it's been known to happen," Sarah says, "though I have no concrete evidence myself."

"Don't scare her," I say to Sarah, "or she'll never set a date."

"We're honing in," Miriam says. "Early fall, I think. They're closing the school for a week in October for some construction, so I'll be able to take off for a honeymoon."

"In Paris?" Sarah asks her. "Beth and Jim are planning their trip around the same time. We could all be there together. Just the five of us."

"Who are you kidding?" Miriam says to her. "By October, you'll have some French aristocrat crazy about you. A count, perhaps."

"Remember what I told you," Sarah says. "If you hear I'm foolish enough to fall for another man, regal title or not, you are to fly over and save me from myself. But please come for your honeymoon."

"Gabe knows a film director there who is insisting we let him be our guide. We're further along on honeymoon plans than we are on the actual wedding. Everywhere we've checked for the wedding is already booked. We call places and ask about available rooms, and they say, 'You mean *this* October?' It's impossible. We've thought about Gabe's brownstone, actually."

"When will you start saying 'our' brownstone?" Sarah says.

"I know, I know," Miriam says. "I'm still getting used to the concept."

The waiter sets a small silver pot of coffee in front of me. I pour a cup for myself.

"Drink up," Sarah says. "As my ex-boss, the eloquent Joey Selber would say, we've got some dialoguing to do."

"I have an idea," I say suddenly. "Why don't you and Gabe get married at our house? Your wedding can be our fall party this year."

Miriam shakes her head in disbelief. "You can't be serious. The fall party is yours, yours and Jim's. All your neighbors and Jim's associates . . . "

"We'll modify the guest list for this year. You can invite anyone you want," I say.

"It's perfect," says Sarah. "You two met at their house. A return to the scene of the crime."

"Of several crimes," Miriam says to her. "Fortunately, the statute of limitations has run out on a few of them." She turns from Sarah to me. "This is the most generous gift anyone has ever offered me. Let me see what Gabe thinks," she says.

"I'll take that as a yes," I say.

"Are you coherent yet?" Sarah says to me, as I reach again for the coffee pot.

"Getting there. Your turn, Sarah. Tell us, are you getting used to being rich?"

"As one of the world's great dames, Sophie Tucker, said, 'I've been rich and I've been poor; rich is better,'" Sarah says. "That about sums it up. The accountant Jim recommended has set things up for me so that I can realize one of my fondest dreams. Her office now pays all my bills. Imagine, I may never have to write a check myself again."

"Besides French real estate, what are you having her write checks for? I mean, are you spending your money on anything fun?" I ask her.

"Books and more books. I'm starting a collection of works by the Algonquin crowd—first editions, when I can find them. The most fun I've had, though, is thinking about donating lots of money."

"I remember the first time Jim and I gave away lots of money," I say. "It was to the art museum in Laurel Falls. They threw a big reception to announce our donation, and I made a speech reminding them that no one at the place had responded to me when I wrote asking for a job after college. I joked that our gift was dependent on their assurance that no poor art history major would ever be treated that way again. For the rest of the night, the folks on the board of directors were falling all over each other to apologize to me. Sweet revenge."

"And let me thank you for your gift to the Film Institute," Miriam says. "If Jim hadn't funded that and given Gabe his job, I might never have met him."

"So, what are you planning to do with your money?" I ask Sarah.

"I want my first big donation to have special meaning," she says. "I think it's going to be the Ms. Foundation. I'm researching exactly how I want to earmark the money. Probably a scholarship."

"Fantastic," I say. "One of us may finally get to meet Gloria Steinem."

"Could happen soon," Sarah says. She leans forwards and drops her voice. "My people are talking to her people."

Miriam and I scream with laughter.

"You have people?" Miriam says. "My God, Beth, Sarah has people. Do you and Jim have people?"

"Of course we do. Doesn't everyone?"

"Life is so unfair," Miriam says. "I want to have people,

too."

"You've got something more important," Sarah says. "You managed to nab the last decent middle-aged man on Earth."

In the center of our table, the waiter sets out a *dégustation* for us to share. Tuna tartare, celery rémoulade, three kinds of pâté. We fill our plates and I tell Sarah and Miriam about my day with Andrew, and my night with Jim.

"Who knows if Andrew and I would have been happy if we had stayed together," I say. "Anyway, after all this time it's hard to imagine being married to anyone but Jim."

"Were you still attracted to Andrew?" Sarah asks. "You said he looked great."

I shake my head. "Oh, he's still something, all right. But what I was attracted to was my memory of Andrew, of how we were when we were young. He's handsome and seductive as ever. What I felt, though, was sort of an attraction once-removed. Like I was reading a book or watching a movie. My own coming-of-age story."

"And how is Jim about everything?" Sarah asks.

"In spite of the way I told him about my day with Andrew—trying to make it seem as if I went to Andrew's hotel to conduct a therapy session—Jim knew what kinds of feelings were awakened in me. But he loves me. In the end, our shared history and our future are what matter to us—more than what happened before we met."

The check arrives. Sarah reaches for the leather folder. "Mine!" she says triumphantly.

"Hey, you know we always split the check," Miriam says.

"Not today," Sarah says. "I haven't properly celebrated the start of my new life yet. I was waiting for the three of us to be together. My treat."

"In our own ways, each of us is beginning something new," Miriam says. "And we're still together. Who could have predicted the lives we have today?"

I reach across the table for their hands. "No one could have known how good we would be for each other," I say to my best friends. "I love you both."

EPILOGUE

To: BethJG@cyber.com,
        MiriamKap@McCSchool.edu
From: SarahR@ParisTel.com
Re: Movable feast

18 September 2001

Hi, you two:

At last, my email is up and running. As I told you when
we talked over the weekend, I had no end of problems
with the first laptop I bought. Consumer rights appears
to be an American concept not well understood here on
the Continent. The people at the computer store nearly
wore out their shoulders with Gallic shrugs, completely
mystified as to why this crazy American woman kept
insisting on a new computer simply because the one
they sold her didn't work. Obviously I prevailed, but
not without giving my subjunctive a good workout.

Like everyone else, I'm glued to the TV a good part of
every day, hungry for images of Manhattan in the aftermath of the 11th. I keep thinking of your engagement
party at Windows on the World, Miriam, and my long,
happy conversation that night with your friends Wayne
and Thomas. Wayne mentioned his fear of heights—
said Miriam was one of the few people for whom
he'd ride up a hundred and ten stories in an elevator.
Thomas told funny stories about being a firefighter—
he made me laugh with a slightly off-color joke that
had to do with climbing up ladders and sliding down
poles. Now that he's buried beneath rubble in downtown Manhattan, I wish I could remember the damn
joke. Can you tell me where to send a donation in his

memory? And is there anything I can do for Wayne?

Beth: I speak to Nicole every day. I was glad she could stay with me when they closed her school. They were wise to cancel classes for a couple of days. Everything even remotely connected to Americans who live here was shut down last week. Nicole is happy to be back in the dorm, dilapidated though it is. They've now got a security guard at the front door. Nicole seems fine, though she was beside herself at the thought that Jim might easily have been in the World Trade Center when the towers went down.

Ellie's classes at NYU resume this week, though they've been displaced to a midtown location. She'll always remember her first month of law school. Doug's classes were never cancelled at Columbia—far enough uptown, I guess, to let business go on more or less as usual. Today is Ellie's birthday—I FedExed her a Chanel bag. Probably not different from anything she can find in New York, but I somehow feel Chanel you buy in Paris is different. Miriam, next time you talk to Ellie, will you try to get a line on how quickly she and Doug are moving towards the altar? Trans-continental prying is so inconvenient. Anyway, she's more likely to confide in you.

My friend Lawrence Zimmerman forwarded an article that ran in an online magazine over the weekend. It's about businesses that have already figured out that there's profit to be made from 9-11. The article was called "Notes from the 'Greed is Good' Underground," and it offered a top-ten list of companies that were acting in unethical—not to mention heartless—ways since last Tuesday. Number 4 on the list, was . . . Tri-Tech. It seems that the company's president, one Joey Selber, posted a note on his company's website saying, "We want to remind our clients that they don't have to travel to benefit from our expertise. We can put state-of-the-art video conferencing to work for you!" Joey's bio and picture appear underneath. Some patriot, huh? To hell with trying to get people back on planes. Vive le Tri-Tech!

Myself, I'm jittery about flying, but nothing will keep me away from your wedding, Miriam. Nicole and I will travel back to New York together, and then all of you can fly back over with us. Beth, I insist that you and Jim stay with me while you're over here. Miriam, I've made your honeymoon reservations at L'Hôtel, just down the street from my apartment. The place is quite small, about twenty rooms. Oscar Wilde died there. I told them to give you the grandest room (not necessarily poor Oscar's)—my wedding gift to you. I figure you and Gabe already have all the toaster ovens you need.

Galeries Lafayette Maison delivered my new sofa one night last week. The guys made so much noise steering the thing through the narrow hallway that they woke my very attractive neighbor, Dr. François Dubreuilh, who came to the door in his not very attractive pajamas. He introduced himself; I apologized for the racket. Before long we were sipping brandy (he ditched the pj's for jeans and a sweater), and he was telling me how sad he was about the WTC and how he loves New York. Essential info: Doctors Without Borders cardiologist, heterosexual, divorced ten years ago, has a grown son in London. Speaks charming English, if you go for that Louis Jordain/ Maurice Chevalier thing. I'm having dinner with him tonight. Full report to follow. Okay, I'll allow you just one I-told-you-so. What can I say? Hope springs eternal.

I've promised myself I will write every day. I shipped over some boxes of old files, blew off the cobwebs, and found notes I'd made years ago for short stories. They still look pretty good to me. I've got a few things on my side that I didn't have back then to support my writing habit: menopausal zest and a fair amount of money. What is it they say in murder mysteries? Doing the deed requires means, motive, and opportunity. I've got all three now, but I'm not much for homicide. Guess I'll try literature.

Love, Sarah

ACKNOWLEDGEMENTS

Writing is a solitary business, but producing a novel takes a village. My little hamlet is full of bright, patient, generous, tenacious, and loyal denizens to whom I am thoroughly grateful.

Many thanks to the dream team of talented pros at Amberjack Publishing. Dayna Anderson and Kayla Church embraced this book (and me) with warmth and enthusiasm from the start. Gaby Thompson was an early and persuasive fan. Jenny Miller, my astute, lightning-quick, and *bravissima* editor, nurtured every page. Cami Wasden kept all the moving parts moving in the right direction.

Erica Stellar, Janet Burnham, Esther Marvet, Riva Naiman, Chani Steinmetz, the evanescent Michael Thomas, and the late, great MaryJo Milone (along with her Wallingford book group) read the early work in progress and provided invaluable, unflinching critiques.

The good folks at the Authors Guild dispensed sensible advice in record time.

This book is about female friendships. These women taught me what I know on the subject: Andrea Appelman, Glenda Greiff Kaufman, Pam Buchanan, Marilena Sanò, Elaine Rosenthal, Sylvia Handler, Eva Askew-Houser, Barbara Robertson, Donna Brown, Janet Burnham, Witty Muehlbauer, Angie Michael, Abby Moline, Carol Patton, Shelley Banner, Maureen Feduniak.

I've also learned plenty from my friendships with Bruce Newman and Jonathan Weisgall, remarkable men who get it about women and always have.

Loved ones and mentors live on in memory and inspire me to keep writing: My mother Stella, who provided Nancy Drew books, Broadway tunes, and a role model for *chutzpah*. My grandmother Sadie, whose default emotion was unconditional love. Mildred Lewis, my fifth-grade teacher at P.S. 186, who invited me to help her write the class play. Richard Dorfman, my English teacher at Great Neck South, who demanded a gazillion revisions of my paper on *Look Homeward, Angel*. Leslie Fiedler, my professor at the University at Buffalo, who gave me permission to disparage *The Last of the Mohicans*.

Count Tolstoy contended that happy families are all alike, but I believe that my happy family stands apart. I am fortunate to have relatives who are loving by nature and literate by design and whom I would have chosen under any circumstances: My brother Steve, whose brilliant life is even more of a success than he realizes. My daughter Erica, son-in-law Dan, and grandson Eli, who are everything to me and a gift to the world.

My deepest gratitude and love belong to the family member I did get to choose, the one I'd gamble on any time: my husband Ken. *De tout mon cœur pour toute ma vie.*

ABOUT THE AUTHOR

Teri Emory is living proof that liberal arts majors are not necessarily unemployable. As evidence: She has taught writing and literature at the University of North Florida, Hunter College, Yeshiva University, and Fordham University. She lived in Rome, where she taught English to Soviet immigrants awaiting visas to the U.S. She survived an extended tour of duty as a corporate writer. Her articles and poems have appeared in print and online publications. She has edited essays and book-length manuscripts on absurdly esoteric topics.

Teri was born in the Bronx and grew up in and around New York City. She is proud to have been educated entirely in public schools, from kindergarten at P.S. 77 through grad school at U.C. Berkeley. She has lived and worked in several cities, some more fun than others, and has traveled widely. A devoted mother and besotted grandmother, she now resides in Las Vegas, married to a man whom she re-met, after almost forty years, at their high school reunion.

Visit her website at www.teriemory.com.

DISCUSSION QUESTIONS

1) How does the structure of the novel—with three narrators—add to the reader's understanding of each character? Are they all reliable narrators?

2) Every chapter begins with a lyric from music written in the 1960s, and additional lyrics are scattered through the book. Why did the author include these? What role did music play in Sarah, Miriam, and Beth's generation?

3) Each of the main characters experiences the loss of someone close to her. How do these losses affect them? What do they learn about forgiveness, and about themselves, as a result?

4) How does the era in which Sarah, Miriam, and Beth first meet—the late 1960s—color their friendship? Which elements of the friendship remain the same over time? Which change?

5) Sarah faces sexist attitudes at work, from her boss and even from a female co-worker. Could Sarah have done more to combat sexism at her office at that time (the end of the twentieth century)? Have things changed for women at work since then?

6) Miriam relates many of her experiences to movies she loves. Has her appetite for on-screen romance given her unrealistic expectations about life? What role does her keenness for movies play in her relationship with Peter? With Gabe?

7) Beth notes that she, like one of her patients, is part of the "first generation of women to feel entitled to interesting lives." Beth also says that, "…we speculate from time to time about what life might have held in store had we married different men, or not had children, or not married at all." What does Beth mean by these observations? Are they contradictory? What do they reveal about Beth's marriage to Jim?

8) Though the three main characters are New Yorkers, they spend time in, and have emotional connections to, other locations as well: Acedia Bay, Savannah, Rome, Paris. Are these places "characters" in the book? How so?

9) What do Sarah, Miriam, and Beth think about marriage? Are they optimistic about it? Resigned? Cynical?
10) Sarah raises her daughter mostly alone; Beth loses a son; Miriam has no children. What does the novel have to say about motherhood?

11) How did trust between Sarah and Kevin erode? In what ways is Kevin's behavior like that of Martin, Sarah's first husband? Were there signs that Kevin was distancing himself? If so, why did Sarah ignore them?

12) Each of the women is forced to compromise on something important to her. What do these compromises entail? How do the three differ in the ways they handle setbacks or disappointment?

13) In assessing her long marriage to Jim, Beth says, "Nothing in life really begins, or ends, when we think it does." In what ways is this statement true for each of the three women? How is this idea likely to affect their "second acts?"